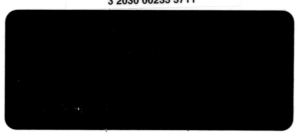

DANCING FOR THE HANGMAN

DANCING FOR THE HANGMAN

MARTIN EDWARDS

FIVE STAR
A part of Gale, Cengage Learning

GALE
CENGAGE Learning™

Set in 11 pt. Plantin.
Printed on permanent paper.

LIBRARY OF CONGRESS CATALOGING-IN-PUBLICATION DATA

Edwards, Martin, 1955–.
   Dancing for the hangman / Martin Edwards.
     p. cm.
   ISBN-13: 978-1-59414-848-4 (alk. paper)
   ISBN-10: 1-59414-848-1 (alk. paper)
   1. Crippen, Hawley Harvey 1862–1910—Fiction. 2. Physicians—Great Britain—Fiction. 3. Spouses—Crimes against—Fiction. 4. Murder—Great Britain—Fiction. 5. Trials (Murder)—Great Britain—Fiction. 6. Pentonville Prison—Fiction. I. Title.
PR6055.D894D36 2009
823'.914—dc22   2009032188

First Edition. First Printing: December 2009.
Published in 2009 in conjunction with Tekno Books and Ed Gorman.

Printed in the United States of America
1 2 3 4 5 6 7 13 12 11 10 09

For Mandy Little

PROLOGUE

Note, marked "Declan—for your eyes only," from Chief Government Archivist to the Director of Media Relations, 1 May 2008

A dead man talking.

The sheets of foolscap are yellow and smell of damp, but when I read Crippen's words, I hear his voice. Soft, plaintive, oblivious to irony.

These papers—a memoir in manuscript, scraps from a secret diary, jagged clippings—were meant to make a man's fortune. Instead, they have lain hidden for close on a hundred years. Even now they could embarrass us. They speak of a murder that no one knew or dreamed of.

Crippen didn't have a clue what was going on, but he wasn't alone. Everyone focused on the wrong crime. And so a determined murderer and his friends escaped scot-free. Read between the lines, and you will discover a plot that stains English justice.

No wonder our people kept quiet once they satisfied themselves that the story was authentic. Nothing Crippen says, however bizarre, contradicts the established facts. All he does is fill in the gaps, without seeing the picture he's painted. The file has been classified since 1930, twenty years after his death. The Metropolitan Police recovered the papers from a house in Chelsea in October of that year.

The house belonged to an elderly private investigator. He had died from natural causes and a junior officer attended the scene. He found the papers in a locked trunk. The dead man had a history of money-grubbing on the windy side of the law, but he never dared to publish. He once served a three-year term of imprisonment, but he was no fool. He was determined that no one should ever learn of this most outrageous crime.

Wednesday, 19 October 1910

The slice of flesh bears a pale mark, curving like a horseshoe. Bending over the dock rail, I screw up my eyes to study the specimen. I dare not picture the person of whom it once formed part. Did I stroke that same strip of skin? That blemish: is it a scar, or merely a fold? The answers might hang me.

Fringed by short dark hairs, the flesh squats in a jar of formalin. The reek of disinfectant corrupts the courtroom air, its bitter taste is on my tongue. I want to retch, but everyone's eyes are boring into me, searching for a clue to guilt. Grinding my teeth, I stretch my features into a mask of unconcern. I must betray no hint of horror— far less a gasp of recognition.

With a conjuror's flourish, the pathologist takes a pair of forceps and plucks his trophy from the formalin. The flesh is hardened and horny, the texture of leather. My finger ends tingle as I imagine how it would feel to the touch. The doctor squints through gold pince-nez, an illusionist play-acting, as though he can discern a sign invisible to all but himself, the Great Doctor Pepper. Doctor Augustus John Pepper, to be precise, "in active practice as a surgeon for thirty-five years," Fellow of the Royal College, witness for the prosecution, practitioner of forensic hocus-pocus. If his moustache were any longer, no doubt he would twirl it. His audience is in the palm of his hand. Not even the Lord Chief Justice, so awesome in his scarlet robes, lets out a breath as the sorcerer places the flesh upon a gleaming soup plate.

The fat gills of the wrinkled vaudevillians in the gallery have turned a bilious green. The Old Bailey has become the Old Marylebone Music Hall, lacking only plush curtains and a trained dog act; earlier, the judge even permitted the pretty little Belle of Mayfair to share his bench.

I glance at my lawyers, yearning for a nod of reassurance. Mr. Tobin, my attorney, has a face of stone, but thank God for the elegantly attired man who leans forward to whisper in his ear. Your good self, the renowned Mr. Arthur Newton, solicitor instructing learned counsel, and the man to whom I have entrusted my fate.

When the attorney answers through gritted teeth, you shrug off the reply, much as you might brush a speck of grime from your elegant morning coat. As you settle back in his place, you catch my eye and bestow upon me a wonderful smile. I relax my shoulders, glad to be in safe hands.

A flat-footed usher marches up to collect the exhibit, sombre frown mocked by the squeaking of his shoes. He alone lacks any sense of theatre. Mournful as a waiter serving a dish of suet, he presents the soup plate to the foreman of the jury. My sphincter tightens, but I dig sharp nails into my palms and keep control.

How can anyone prove that *this* was Cora? Cora, of the wobbling soprano and scarlet ostrich feathers, Cora, who would (so to speak) have thought herself in Heaven had ever she sung for such a rapt crowd? The foreman passes the soup plate to his neighbour as though it is scalding his fingers.

While the trophy moves along the jury box, Pepper recites a list of finds from the cellar. "Viscera of chest and abdomen, heart and lungs, lower windpipe, gullet, liver, kidneys, spleen, stomach, and pancreas." But his very confidence is a sleight, for the evidence is scarcely damning. They found no head, no limbs, not a single bone or organ of sex. The deceased might be man or woman, old or young. The remains were packed in clay and lime and the tissues transformed into a soapy mass of adipocere.

The Lord Chief Justice clears his throat. "What would be the distance between the navel and the pubic bone?"

Details, details, always squalid little details. Why does the light of the law not shine on the larger truths, instead of petty, tiresome facts? I square my shoulders, straighten my back, visualising Ethel's pale cheeks and parted lips. Yes, she loves me as few women love men. If we have yielded to dictates of the heart, that is no crime. Trusting in God, I shall submit to justice. I murdered no one; I shall never dance for the hangman.

From St. Pancras Chronicle, 15 July 1910

CAMDEN TOWN CRIME

ACTRESS MURDERED
MUTILATED BODY FOUND IN A COAL CELLAR

The discovery, on Wednesday evening, of a terrible crime enacted at 39, Hilldrop-crescent, Camden Town, created a sensation throughout the district. The body of a woman was found buried beneath the flagstones in the coal cellar.

Later in the afternoon, Sir Melville Macnaughten, Assistant Commissioner of police, and Superintendent Froest, paid a visit to the premises. Digging operations were commenced in the garden, but the arduous efforts of the officers were not rewarded. Attention was then turned to the house. The removal of some flagstones in the coal cellar, which is beneath the front door steps, revealed a ghastly spectacle. There were found the mutilated remains of the unfortunate victim, the body having been cut up, and large pieces of flesh were lying about in various directions.

The sight, to quote the words of one of the excavators, was absolutely sickening and enough to knock over the strongest of men.

The strictest possible vigilance is being kept at the premises by the police, and the authorities are busily engaged in scouring the country to ascertain the whereabouts of the woman's husband.

"Each of you is responsible for his verdict to his conscience and to God."

The words of Mr. Tobin echo in my ears as I wait for the jury to decide. His closing speech lifted my heart. You will understand that, Mr. Newton—or, given that we have been through so much together, may I call you Arthur? Each night during the course of the trial, I overheard the warders deriding the barrister you engaged to defend me. *Plodder* was a recurrent description, and *No match for Mr. Muir* a morale-sapping critique of his adversarial skills. To a casual listener, the relentless logic of the prosecutor may seem unanswerable. Yet to me, Mr. Tobin's pleas for understanding rang true.

"Strange things are recorded in our legal history where a man has been convicted of murder, where he has been hanged, and where, afterwards, the supposed victim had appeared alive again."

A desperate last throw? Far from it. Surely a cogent point that no honest juryman could properly dismiss. My disappearance, my lies, my flight, reared mountains of prejudice against me, as counsel said. Yet no one could be sure that the flesh passed around in court belonged to Cora.

So my bowels churn when you say with a wily grin, "At least we gave them a good run for their money, eh?"

Your phrase rattles around in my brain, leaving me dizzy as I detect anticipation of defeat. Giving up in the face of insuperable odds is foreign to me. Remember Mr. Tobin saying that, to commit the crime of which I was charged, *there was needed the fiend incarnate?* But I am no fiend, just a man misunderstood. *I do not plead for mercy,*

14

Mr. Tobin insisted (although frankly I would have settled for that), but rather that the twelve good men and true should not forget the great principle of the benefit of the doubt. His confidence stiffened my sinews. Any English jury properly charged would acquit.

When you ask if I am ready to unburden myself at last, the question knocks the breath out of me. Of course, the evidence for the Crown was piled as high as the Matterhorn. I suppose Mr. Muir's ruthless arguments are tweaking your nerves. And then, as I am urging you to keep faith, suddenly the call comes. After twenty-seven minutes—you check your watch in disbelief—the jury is back.

Twenty-seven minutes—and in a capital case!

Have they decided that the case for the Crown was so speculative, so circumstantial, that it could not possibly succeed? How could a jury sentence a man to death on the strength of twenty-seven minutes' deliberation? For the first time, the colour leaves your cheeks and you mutter that they should have had the decency to make a show of considering our case. My mouth and throat dry, yet I cannot conceive that they had decided to destroy me. Holding my head high, breathing hard, I follow the warder back into the courtroom, to learn my fate.

Guilty of wilful murder. The foreman averts his gaze like an embarrassed boy as he answers the clerk of the court. When asked if I have anything to say why the court should not give me judgment of death, my response is implacable.

"I am innocent."

The clerk asks again, as if expecting me to change my tune, but I do not waver.

"I still protest my innocence."

Yet when the usher calls for silence, the judge places the square of black upon his head.

You speak of my coolness under fire, and wonder what lies beneath the calm exterior you perceive. I cannot help but be flattered. I like to think that we have become friends, Arthur. You shall learn what I could not say in my defence.

Here is my confession:

I am no murderer.

Do not shake your head, I implore you. Do not click your tongue in impatience at my stubbornness. Bear with me and all will become clear. Justice has been betrayed. Oh, yes, you will have your manuscript, and it will be much weightier than the dozen pages I dictated to your clerk at Brixton. Incidents flicker and glow in my mind, like scenes on lantern slides. Yet remember this. I am accustomed to keeping my own counsel. Candour does not come naturally to me. In that, if nothing else, my enemies are right. If I am to tell the truth, it must be in my own way.

Harness the might of the Press! You insist there is no choice if I am to be saved. I must hold nothing back. No jot or tittle, however intimate or discreditable. We must give to trusted journalists everything they demand. Yet I pray that you will exercise your professional discretion in editing my recollections, in determining how to convey the core of the truth. There is so much that, if only for reasons of decency, *is not for publication.* Even my most ardent supporters might turn against me if certain matters were made public. I rely upon you to pass on to the waiting world the minimum details necessary to explain Cora's fate.

It is a solemn task. You, Arthur, are the only man alive who can save me from the gallows.

Confession?

Confession began for me at Coldwater, in the state of Michigan. How I flinched each time the oak door crashed shut behind me, trapping me in the tiny chapel. Even in spring or summer, the place seemed as dank as a tomb in the graveyard.

I would trot up the aisle behind my grandfather and my parents, stiff and creaking in Sunday best. As the adults nodded to right and left, the townsfolk bowed, treating me to pleasant smiles while my mother interlaced her warm fingers with mine. Pride never spurted through me; all I remember is the hot flush of embarrassment. Having to live up to the family's formidable standards daunted me. Our very names bespoke distinction: Philo, Myron Augustus, Andresse, and Hawley Harvey.

We sat in the front pew, a place of honour. The hardness of the wood against my bony buttocks, rough flagstones grazing my knees when I knelt to say my prayers. Surreptitiously, I touched where the skin was broken and smudged with blood, then wiped my fingers on the soles of my shoes.

The minister's voice echoed from the rafters. His jabbing forefinger accused me of unnamed crimes. Wind rustled through cracks in the chapel door. Oh, the moistness of my palms, the chill on my spine, the urge to shiver even at the height of summer. Grown-ups chanted the Confession with the fervour of natives, hoping to ward off evil spirits.

Almighty and most merciful Father; we have erred and strayed

17

from thy ways like lost sheep. We have followed too much the devices and desires of our own hearts.

Devices and desires? I had not knowingly committed a single act of delinquency. Frankly, I was too scared of the prospect of savage retribution. And yet I was a sinner. The reek of candle wax made my gorge rise. In half-remembered nightmares, I vomited instead of responding to the Litany. My skin prickled and all I could manage was a frog-like sound. I saved face by pretending to have a coughing fit.

From all evil and mischief; from sin, from the crafts and assaults of the devil; from thy wrath, and from everlasting damnation.

"Good Lord, deliver us."

From all blindness of heart; from pride, vainglory, and hypocrisy; from envy, hatred, and malice, and all uncharitableness.

"Good Lord, deliver us."

From fornication and all other deadly sin; and from all the deceits of the world, the flesh, and the devil.

"Good Lord, deliver us."

From lightning and tempest; from plague, pestilence, and famine; from battle and murder, and from sudden death.

"Good Lord, deliver us."

My heart thudded inside my scrawny frame, like a prisoner desperate to escape. The noise was so loud that surely the towns-folk must hear. Would God rescue me before I sank into Satan's clutch?

My father owned a dry goods emporium. The store was founded by grandfather Philo, when the town was a huddle of log cabins at the intersection of the Coldwater River and the Chicago Turnpike. Hours were long, but trade was good. By the time I came along, Coldwater was flourishing and the Crippen house on the corner of Grand and Monroe was the most palatial in town. Crippen menfolk were renowned for working hard and fearing God.

On Sunday evenings, we gathered in the best room for readings from the prophets. My grandfather's declamatory tone would have suited a hellfire preacher. My parents and I were his congregation. When I was very young, only the warmth of Mother's body next to mine made the listening bearable. I told myself that I loved my grandfather, but something about his erect carriage, his unrelenting honesty, made me flinch. So did the speculative look that came into his eye when he studied me. Far more than any minister, I was sure that he could see inside my heart and recognise that I was an unworthy heir.

Isaiah was his favourite book, and my father's. In turn, as I matured, I came to share their taste in the prophets, one more miserable offender overwhelmed by the roaring condemnation. *"Moreover, the Lord saith, Because the daughters of Zion are haughty, and walk with stretched forth necks and wanton eyes, walking and mincing as they go, and making a tinkling with their feet."* A pause, a clearing of the throat for emphasis. *"Therefore the Lord will smite with a scab the crown of the head of the daughters of Zion, and the Lord will discover their secret parts."*

The final phrase took board and lodging in the attics of my mind. Sitting cross-legged on the floor, I let my thoughts slide to the daughters of Zion, my curiosity about those secret parts stirring with the incompetent prurience of youth. I was trying to piece together an anatomical understanding, aided by covert study of Uncle Bradley's medical texts.

A belief in God and divine justice sufficed for my grandfather. I shared that faith: from a tender age, it seemed nonsensical to credit that our earth, with all its intricacies, had been created by chance. There must be some divine guiding hand behind the world we can see. To this day, I hold to that belief with the fervour of a falling man who clings to the rock face by his fingertips.

Yet for all the promise of Heaven, I concluded that life must have more to offer than the straightforward existence of Coldwater folk. There must be Something Else. I began to speculate about whether unravelling the secrets of womankind might release the obscure emotions burning within me. I would moon after pretty young women who, thank God, were blissfully unaware of my covert admiration. But each veiled hint of promise was matched by words of warning. Menacing lines from Proverbs rolled from my grandfather's tongue.

"For the lips of a strange woman drop as an honeycomb, and her mouth is smoother than oil: But her end is as bitter as wormwood, sharp as a two-edged sword."

When did I first yearn for the world beyond Coldwater? No single event fuelled my dissatisfaction. According to my grandfather, I enjoyed great good fortune and owed it to myself as well as my family not to fritter my life away in idle games and daydreams.

"Discipline," the old gentleman insisted, "you need discipline, Hawley. A man is nothing without discipline."

I wanted to say that I was a boy, not a man, but of course I did not dare. An only child is blessed, but also cursed. I occupied the centre of my parents' lives and my delight in their attention was matched by dread of their disapproval. I acquired the habit of eavesdropping on the adults, becoming fascinated by their sophisticated talk when they believed that I was out of earshot. From slivers of overheard conversation, I learned that my mother's pregnancy had been difficult. She had lost an infant daughter in the year before my birth and could never have another child. I rejoiced, for I had no wish to share my little world with a dribbling rival. Yet as the years passed, I felt crushed by the burden of unvoiced expectation.

One afternoon in summer, as I skulked in my room, reading rather than helping in the store, I overheard my grandfather telling my mother that I was a spoiled brat. Usually she responded to the old fellow's remonstrations with a gentle smile, but this time she answered back in a rare flash of indignation.

"The boy is sensitive, that is all."

"Sensitive!"

"Don't you see?" she demanded. "Hawley simply longs to be loved."

My grandfather grunted, but what instinct is more deeply rooted in the human soul than the urge to love and be loved? In me, my mother saw the Crippens' practical turn of mind melding with her family's rich gift of imagination. The very name Andresse, testified to the Skinners' romantic streak and the fairy stories she read me as an infant, stuck in my mind as vividly as grandfather's stern parables. She was a dutiful housewife, but when she became a storyteller, her face lit up, as the fables transported her to faraway times and lands.

We lived cheek by jowl with vast, open skies and heart-stopping ochre sunsets, the rush and gurgle of innumerable streams, and cool, shimmering lakes with unknowable depths. In springtime Mother taught me to watch out for the daffodils and the blue and white splashes made by the hyacinths. The world awakening after winter, she said, and everywhere I could smell fresh earth and rain and pine trees. The moral I drew was not what she intended. I told myself that, when I was up-grown and free of the confines of childhood, my life too would blossom. Oh yes, I had much to be thankful for, and yet it was never quite enough. There *must* be Something Else—and I concluded that I would find it Somewhere Else.

Of course I never revealed this to her. I learned—not to dissemble, but to keep my thoughts to myself. I wanted neither to hurt nor be hurt by lack of understanding. The very name of our town seemed to pour cold water over those with longings for excitement.

The Crippen store owed much to passing trade. From the early days, fur trappers and loggers, on their way through town as they headed for the woods in the far north of the state, provided our main source of income. The travellers reeked of tobacco and ale and some relished the chance to talk to an impressionable lad. Not until I was older did I realise how many of their anecdotes about past encounters with the Sioux and Cheyenne owed more to imaginative reworking of old campfire tales than to fact. Some portrayed themselves as latter-day Natty Bumppos, others were battle-hardened veterans who had fought on both sides of the Civil War, serving under Hooker or Robert E. Lee. One amiable fellow with a piratical patch over his left eye entranced me for half an hour with his memories of fighting alongside Stonewall Jackson at Bull Run. After he had journeyed on, my father discovered that the man had paid for his purchases with dud notes and no doubt his stories of valour were equally counterfeit. No matter. Even if the travellers were not the heroes they claimed to be, at least they had confronted the world and all its dangers—and survived.

They talked about lynch law and of the rough justice in the wilderness. One old fellow yarned so vividly that I imagined I was lurking in the grove of ancient beeches that he described, under a pale moon, with the plaintive cry of the whippoorwill in the distance. I pictured the knot of men, digging a pit beside the rutted wagon track, the tree thrusting out an arm, and two men beneath it, astride their horses. Their elbows were strapped to their bodies, their mouths gagged with saddlecloth. Behind them, a man worked with a colt halter, unravelling the twine that bound the headpiece, so as to gain a greater length of rope.

Were the men about to die cattle rustlers or simply in the wrong place at the wrong time? The storyteller smiled and said that life was hard in the old days, out in West Virginia.

The travellers talked of labouring on half-finished railroads, of rafting down the Columbia River, and of vast yawning canyons, where one false step meant instant death. They spoke contemptuously of the quitters who turned back at Fort Laramie, and in hushed admiration of the Pawnee tribesmen who could steal a horse from under its rider. But I could never have been a pioneer. What entranced me most were images of metropolitan wealth and splendour. I loved to visualise the manor houses of old Dutch and English river families that speckled the hillside above the Hudson, and dreaming that one day I would sit in a cab scything along Broadway and Fifth Avenue. Nor was my fascination with sophisticated urban life confined to New York. Philadelphia, Chicago, and San Francisco were names that rolled so easily off the travellers' tongues, and for me they had a magical sound. In those cities anything was possible. The secret was to rely upon brain rather than brawn or bravery. A clever man could make his fortune without a risk of physical harm. One day, I promised myself, I would make my name, but throughout the years of adolescence I had to content myself by finding excitement at second hand.

Lacking the physique to relish the rougher games that other boys played in the street, I obeyed my mother's injunctions to stay inside and avoid catching a chill. Not for me the outdoor life of hunting geese and ducks, sailing by canoe or kayak on Coldwater, or fishing for salmon and trout in Lake Michigan. In truth, my fellow feeling was not with sportsmen but with their prey.

I had friends among my classmates, but no one close. Most of them loved diving and bathing in the streams outside town, but I was a poor swimmer and dreaded the chill water flooding the narrow passages of my nose. Older boys were apt to jeer at me whenever I trotted along the sidewalk on my own. For them I was an easy target, a weakling, a sissy. I laboured doggedly at school, without laying claim to academic brilliance. Too often I ruined a competent piece of work with careless errors. The masters liked me, since I never caused a moment's trouble, but my peers were less impressed. I suffered from being short of build and sight, and many times the bullies reduced me to tears. In the end I taught myself not to care so much. After all, my father said that our forebears had come to this land on the *Mayflower*, forging a new life in the face of indescribable privations on their westward journey. What was it, in comparison, to bear a little mockery from other boys?

Girls were a different matter. Aged ten, inspired by my uncle's example, I played the physician in hospital games, with school fellows of both sexes taking the part of nurses and patients. My ministrations were guileless, even though once or twice I became aware of strange excitement when seeking to diagnose the cause of the girls' supposed ills. All too soon, I became tongue-tied in female company, while my private thoughts raced far beyond the borders of propriety.

For all my assiduous efforts to keep in the warm, I caught more than my fair share of chills. Whenever I coughed and spluttered, I found myself longing for a potion that would make me fit and strong and pestered Uncle Bradley for a mixture that would put me right. I came to regard him as more than a doctor. I believed he could cure anything, and he did not trouble to dissuade me. For me, he was a fulfiller of dreams, a shaman, a wizard. The gift of healing seemed to me even more precious than the gems in the museum.

In sickness and in health, I read voraciously. I loved dime novels and their tales of derring-do. Never mind attempting deeds of valour: it was so much pleasanter to stay safe and sound in my room and experience dangerous excitements at second hand. So I thrilled to the exploits of Deadwood Dick, the frontier scout; of California Joe, the mysterious plainsman; of Old Sleuth, the Detective (in truth a young man with an entrancing talent for disguise). But my favourites were Poe's chilling tales, which I devoured on winter nights when a gale howled down Grand Street.

When I slept, the horrors of the House of Usher and the Masque of the Red Death haunted my dreams. Many times I awoke drenched in sweat after a nightmare peopled by the corrupted scions of Usher or the damned partygoers at Prince Prospero's masquerade, encountering the gaunt figure whose mask was the countenance of a stiffened corpse.

One story fastened itself in my mind like a limpet. A tale about a telltale heart. I read it over and over again, memorising the lines until I was word perfect. I can recite them still without recourse to the original text.

If still you think me mad you will think so no longer when I describe the wise precautions I took for the concealment of the body. The night waned, and I worked hastily, but in silence. First of all I dismembered the corpse. I cut off the head and the arms and the legs.

I then took up three planks from the flooring of the chamber, and deposited all between the scantlings. I then replaced the boards so cleverly, so cunningly, that no human eye—not even his—*could have detected any thing wrong. There was nothing to wash out—no stain of any kind—no blood spot whatever. I had been too wary for that.*

No clocks chime in a prison cell. Nothing but the thud of one's heartbeat marks the seconds of one's life. Ticking away, ticking away, ticking away.

So, the date for my execution is set. *Tuesday 8 November.* I have sixteen days remaining. In the small hours I woke in a cold sweat, desperate to count the hours, and then the minutes and then the seconds, so that I would know precisely how much sweet life was left to me. My nightshirt was wet and my stomach felt as though weighted down by pebbles. And then I recalled our last conversation and, even in the lonely darkness, I breathed more evenly.

You are right, Arthur; we must not lose heart. The first step is to appeal, so that the execution *must* be deferred. And there are crumbs of good news. Old friends and new are coming to my aid. Professor Munyon of Philadelphia has cabled that he will spend £12,000, if it will set me free. He is asking the State Department to use their good offices with the British Government to urge the police to examine reports that a woman answering Cora's description has been spotted in Chicago. A red herring, no doubt, but I am sure Munyon's concern does not arise solely because he fears bad publicity from having employed a suspected wife-murderer. He would never stoop so low. Meanwhile, my old backer, Eddie Marr, has already contributed to your fees.

As for Mr. Horatio Bottomley, parliamentarian and proprietor of *John Bull,* please convey my most sincere thanks for the funds he has donated to my appeal. The knowledge that an eminent Member of Parliament stands in my corner does wonders for my morale.

I am aware that Mr. Bottomley is a noted patriot, devoted to the twin foundations of English society—justice and fair play. Like me, he has had to contend with hurtful criticism and scorn, both within Westminster and without. He is envied by lesser men, those who fail to understand that in matters of business, the cutting of corners is sometimes a regrettable necessity. As you say, Mr. Bottomley is a man after my own heart. Truly, *John Bull* speaks not just for him but for all ordinary people. If all he seeks in return is the exclusive right to publish my account of the events that have led me to the brink of the gallows, it is the smallest price to pay.

So I am not on my own, even though for a time following my arrest, I was the most hated man in England. No—the most hated man in Christendom. Let me tell you this, Arthur. Nothing, not even the elaborate precautions taken by Chief Inspector Dew, could insulate me from the rancid loathing of the mob.

As the *Megantic* entered the River Mersey at the end of our long ocean crossing, gun fire from the fort at New Brighton marked the hour of one. Not until the rest of the passengers disembarked did the Chief Inspector and his men guide Ethel and me down a second, inconspicuous gangway linking a steel door in the side of the vessel with the landing stage. As I stepped out into the cold English air, my footsteps clattered like the gun we had heard, but that was not why we were noticed. My head and face were muffled to the point of suffocation, and the brim of my hat was pulled down over my nose. Our very disguises made us look conspicuous; small wonder that people on the shore were not deceived. I heard a cry of fury and through the slit in my makeshift mask I saw a tall young man with an uplifted cane rushing toward me, followed by a mass of baying accomplices. For a few seconds I knew what it is to be a small fox, when the hounds are in full cry. They would have ripped me to pieces without a second thought.

Mercifully, the police officers were ready for them and repulsed the onslaught, striking out with fists and truncheons and shouting at my enemies to disperse. A way was cleared for our little parade, and I was bustled along to the railway station to begin my final journey to

London, my adopted home.

As we marched along the platform at Euston, I witnessed a terrifying spectacle. Beyond barriers patrolled by burly policemen, a thousand souls pointed at me and screamed with one voice. They howled my name as if it were a curse. Mr. Dew had warned me of a hostile reception, but nothing could have prepared me for such a tidal wave of scorn and disgust. I was vile. I was the man who sought to get away with murder and mutilation. I was not—I could not be— human.

Evidence in chief of the accused, R v Crippen, 3ʳᵈ day, 20 October 1910

"I have been in the habit of purchasing drugs. I always made up their prescriptions for them when I was in America . . . I have for years been familiar with the drug hyoscine. I first heard of it when I came over to England in 1885."

Yes, there is a magic about medicine. To take a sick person and make him well, that is a trick of which any prestidigitator would be proud. Uncle Bradley was Coldwater's sole physician. People held him in awe. When, after sober deliberation, he recommended the mildest placebo, they would wring his hand in gratitude for his expertise. Not every spell he cast succeeded. For the seriously ill, miracles will always be in short supply. But he looked after his patients well enough to earn legacies aplenty when they died.

As a child, I revered my uncle. I dreamed that one day, people would credit me with the same power to make the difference between life and death. I set my heart on becoming a physician. The path was smoothed because my parents were keen to see me following a medical career. Later, I realised that everything in the family was not quite as it had seemed. When the old man died and the opportunity came to move far away from Coldwater, my father seized it. He too believed that there was more to life than running a dry goods store.

From the time I first read about homeopathy, I became fascinated by its brilliant simplicity. *Like curing like.* Disease throws a body out of kilter. To restore health, one must first restore the natural equilibrium. To treat a patient's malady with a small dose of the substance that causes similar symptoms in a healthy volunteer seems foolhardy to the uninitiated, maybe even dangerous. Yet what could be more logical? The remedy mimics the effects of the illness and makes it easier to regain strength and vitality.

I decided that travel would broaden my mind. What better than to leaven the drudgeries of academic study with an exploration of the world? From boyhood, Europe intrigued me. I read Dickens and *A Tale of Two Cities* was a particular favourite. Sydney Carton I much admired. *It is a far, far better thing that I do now than I have ever done before.*

I discovered that I could take a course in homeopathic medicine in London. London, city of pomp and pagaentry, hub of the greatest empire the world has seen. I booked my passage before breaking the news to my parents. There was a life to be led outside Michigan.

Bedlam, Bedlam, Bedlam. As a young fellow, I spent three months in a madhouse. Cora used to tease me that it turned my mind. Not quite, not even in Bedlam—the Royal Bethlem Hospital for the Insane, known far and wide by its corrupted name, a name to strike fear into innocent hearts. But I was no inmate; I was there to study, and each night I pored over my notes of the day's lecture.

Hyoscine: an alkaloid found in henbane, a member of the nightshade family. In its natural state, impossible to handle: too gummy, syrupy. Used in a salt: hydrobromide of hyoscine. Given internally in the main in tabloid form and by hypodermic syringe to inject the solution under skin. Rare alternative is oral ingestion, e.g., in cases of nervous debility, but the taste is salt and bitter. Powerful sedative for all causes of mania and delirium. Also suitable in cases of meningitis. Possible hypnotic for insomnia. Nota bene—depressant effects. Care needed with dosage. Injection—one-hundredth to one two-hundredth of a grain. By mouth—infinitesimal.

Fellow students, invisible to me behind a tower of books, joked *sotto voce* while I worked at my desk. One conversation embedded itself in my mind, even though I never met the young men who were talking.

"Missing her already, old fellow?"

"Don't worry, my dear chap, there are plenty of alternatives. They say that if you creep around the place at night, the puffing and groaning you hear won't all be from the lunatics."

"What do you mean?"

"You can't see much in the dark, but you can listen to the night attendant, taking his pleasure as he finds it, if secondhand excitement has any appeal."

"I think not! Heigh-ho, there's always the gin palaces of Saint George's Fields."

"No, thanks. You're lucky if you get away with just your pockets picked. I've seen enough demented syphilitics to last a lifetime. Bedlam's bad enough for us. I don't want to finish up as an inmate, clawing the bars by day, and being fucked each night by some drunken night man."

"Hard to please, aren't you? Well, then, it's a dose of hyoscine for you."

"Do I look like I have the DTs?"

"Listen, you don't know the half of it. The lecturers never tell us everything, do they? They aren't allowed to deviate from their script. Just a touch of the stuff, that's all you need. To save

31

you from becoming a lovelorn maniac, there's nothing better. It'll calm you down a treat and then you won't have any problems, preserving your innocence till you see your sweetheart again."

I lodged a stone's throw from the hospital. For reading matter, I often turned to an old copy of *The Newgate Calendar,* which I had picked up at a nearby bookshop. The melodramatic accounts of how executioners had turned off malefactors over the centuries gave me a *frisson*—much like the fiction in a penny dreadful. The gruesome woodcut illustrations lent piquancy to the tales. But overindulgence in stories of the scaffold was unwise as consuming a surfeit of oysters. My imagination became too heated. At dead of night, I fancied I could hear the wailing of men and women incarcerated in the padded cells of Bedlam. The vision of a depraved attendant imposing himself upon the poor raving creatures kept stealing into my mind.

Other students said that London was a modern Babylon, a pit of sexual degeneracy. They talked freely and unashamed about the young dollymops strutting down Haymarket and Regent Street. "Never to admit to being a med," the wiseacres reckoned, for doctors in training had a reputation as larky young blokes with little cash to spare. If you pretended to be a lawyer, you might get somewhere with the better class of courtesan, rustling in satin and silk.

My heart lurched at the thought of what might happen. At twenty-one, my romantic encounters had been confined to a few chaste kisses and a couple of brief twilit fumbles with the inordinate complications of young women's clothing. I itched to experience the emotions of which I had read, to feel hot-blooded passion coursing through my veins, but I feared that I was destined for celibacy.

In London, money mattered. A stone's throw from handsome

Georgian mansions with carefully tended laurel bushes, one would find tenements and cellars that stank of bodily waste and where the scurrying rats seemed more alive than the human inhabitants. In the streets, blind cripples sold matches and patterers recited rhymes about wicked deeds and murder most foul in return for pennies from passers-by. London was one place in the light, quite another when darkness fell.

One evening curiosity overcame me and I started prowling the narrow streets of St. George's Fields, but when I passed a beer-house as shadows lengthened and smelled the stench of alcohol and heard fragments of coarse conversations from within, I doubled my pace and headed for home.

My path took me past a certain shop. I'd heard mention of it in the library when the discussion turned to forbidden books. At the door, I hesitated, then shuffled inside. The pot-bellied man behind the count yielded no hint of judgment, far less hilarity or, even worse, pity, in his expression. All he wanted to make sure of was that I was no agent of the police. It proved easy to satisfy him on that score and I scuttled back to my room, to unwrap and study my purchases—*Miss Bellasis Birched for Thieving* and *Juliette*—in shameful privacy.

My first tour of the ward for the chronic incurables. Spiteful, contorted faces mocking anyone who passed, claw-like hands pointing and reaching out. The air was fetid with foul breath and the stink of urine. A wave of nausea lapped over me. At one time the lunatics had been exhibited to anyone who could muster four shillings. Who in God's name, I wondered, would want to witness such a display?

"The principal drugs we employ are sedatives," my guide explained. "Laudanum, camphor, chloral hydrate. It is the modern way, so much more civilised than harnesses and straight jackets, let alone the chains and fastenings of the bad old days."

"And hyoscine?" I asked. "We were told about hyoscine."

The man, rotund and smiling, gave me a nod. "In moderation."

Alas, Bedlam was not a place for moderation. There was never a moment of complete silence. Always, in the distance I could hear some form of commotion—or the tolling of the bell.

I knew my Hogarth, had seen his depiction of the old Bedlam in *The Rake's Progress*. I had read of Dadd, who murdered his father and was incarcerated in the hospital for years before his transfer to Broadmoor. He spent his time painting fairies, poor devil. Bedlam had changed with the times. Gone were the days when Londoners took pleasure at weekends by coming to gape at the lunatics. No longer did the powers-that-be deceive themselves into believing that madness could be cured like a child's ailment. The best that one could do for many of the poor inmates was to offer a domicile, permanent and secure.

"The daily routine is strictly regulated," the man told me, chest puffing out with pride. "The divisions are marked, as you hear, by the ringing of the bell. All of us must adhere precisely to 'the hours to be observed.' "

"There seem to be many more women than men."

"The fair sex succumbs more easily to melancholia."

"And the restraints?"

"The minimum necessary to preserve decorum and good order."

I nodded sagely, and as soon as I made good my escape I hastened back home and sat for twenty minutes in the bath, trying furiously to scrub myself clean.

Damp and dripping yellow fog. Nothing in *Bleak House* had prepared me for the sheer *opacity* of it. The evening ahead was long and lonely. I had sated my appetite for stories from *The Newgate Calendar* after reading about John Muskett, the soldier executed for the murder of his wife, with whom he quarrelled because he had no potatoes for dinner. Despite the inclement conditions, I decided to venture out. I had a fancy for exploring without being seen and if London was invisible, then so was I.

Even in my thickest coat, I felt the cold seeping through to my bones. Mist smothered the street lamps. Straining my ears, I could hear a cart grinding on the cobbles and a cab whistle every now and then. Within minutes I was lost. I stretched out a hand and found myself touching a broad bow window of diamond panes. Further on was a brick wall and I used it to feel my way along the path. Presently I heard a guffaw from a doorway. I was outside a gin palace. Someone approached me, but the footfalls were uneven. I stepped aside to let the person pass and felt an arm brush mine.

"Excuse me," I said automatically.

"That's all right, dear." A woman's voice, uneducated. "I didn't mean to knock you."

I hesitated and reached out tentatively for the rough surface of the wall. But I miscalculated, and this time it was my arm that struck the stranger, clipping her on the side. Through the cheap fabric she wore, I felt a bony hip.

"You're a forward young feller-me-lad," she said. "Touching a lady up without so much as a by-your-leave. What's your name?"

I did not know where I was and I could scarcely make out the woman, but I saw enough to be aware that this was no lady. Her scanty clothing was wholly unsuited to the weather. Timidly, I averted my eyes. The wall had disappeared. As I inched around on the paving stones in the hope of touching it, I had the giddy feeling that I was on a narrow window ledge, far above ground. She was wearing a horrid scent and I knew I was in danger. By rights I should have been seized by panic. Yet flames of excitement were licking my bowels.

"Peter."

The name came from nowhere. I had no friend called Peter, no family connection with that name. It was a good name, short yet solid and suitably English. Dependable, I thought, perfect for the concealment of my identity.

"Well, hello, Peter. Pleased to meet you, I'm sure."

I gulped in foggy air, tasted its cold moisture. "What's your name?"

"You're a Yank, ain't you?"

I cursed inwardly. How easily one gives oneself away. To cover my anxiety, I gave a noncommittal cough. She took it as encouragement.

"Lovely blokes, Yanks. Always keen to have a good time, eh?"

When I failed to reply, calloused fingers curled around mine. "My, dearie, but you're freezing. We'll have to think of some way of warming you up. You'd like that, wouldn't you?"

"Yes," I mumbled. God forgive me, I could not help myself.

"Easy," she said, starting to fiddle with her clothing. "Easy."

She guided my hand to the secret parts of which the prophet had spoken. It was the moment of which I had for so long dreamed. But not in the fog; not with a whore.

"Oh," I said, gasping with the shock of her attentions.

As suddenly as she had taken hold of me, she released her grip. It was what I wanted, and yet it was not. I was as confused and helpless as a toper awaking in the gutter. Yet I had not swallowed alcohol more than twice in my life, and on those two occasions it had made me sick in the stomach.

"You will be generous to me, Peter, won't you?" she said with an artful coyness that I found detestable. Yet I could not articulate my repugnance. I did not wish to be unkind. Besides, I was still very much afraid.

"I . . ."

I realised that I had to escape her. It was the right thing to do and the safe thing to do. Yet I did not want to offend her. For all I knew, she had ruffian friends within earshot, ready to rob and beat me and leave me for dead.

"You're an educated gent, I could tell in a trice. You wouldn't happen to be a medical man, would you? One of the Bedlam boys, by any chance?"

A terror seized me. She had guessed! I had a fleeting vision of ignominious expulsion and public disgrace. Thrown out of Bedlam! The shame would be more than my dear mother could bear.

I stepped backwards and lost my footing. As I tumbled to the ground, she said, "Careful, dear. There's no need to take on so. No need to worry about little me."

My head hit the cobbles and tears filled my eyes. The rounded shape of the harlot bent over me, in a caricature of solicitude. Speechless with horror, I slithered out of her reach and scrambled to my feet. My scalp was stinging and my heart was about to burst, but I began to run. I could not see where I was going, but my feet hammered along the pavement as I heard her angry squawk behind me.

"Skinflint bastard! You young meds are all the same! Tiny cocks and no money!"

Hyoscine helped me to survive. For days after my encounter with the whore, I was consumed by self-loathing. In the end, a dab of hyoscine did the trick. A minute dose was enough to calm my nerves, as well as my less savoury appetites.

I repented of my sinful curiosity about the fair sex. One evening, I ripped *Miss Bellasis Birched for Thieving* and *Juliette* into tiny shreds, which I stuffed into a bag. It was another foggy night, but I had learned my lesson. Unseen, I threw the bag into the river, and on the way back my heart leapt. I felt cleansed at last.

Wonderful news! Ethel has been saved!

Arthur, I am seized by the urge to hug you the moment you disclose the good tidings. For a few precious seconds, I hear bird-song and smell the dampness of the autumn leaves in the world outside these walls. Ethel and I have placed our trust in God, and at last our faith has reaped its reward. Through the past terrible months, my sole concern has been that my darling should not pay the ultimate price for loving me. As soon as I could collect my thoughts upon my arrest, I told the Chief Inspector that it was "only fair to say that she knows nothing about it." All I wanted was to save her and yet the Lord Chief Justice seized on the phrase as evidence of guilt, rather than as a token of love. No wonder the jury made such a terrible mistake. Despite your words of warning, Arthur, I have always been determined to conduct my defence so as to exculpate her. She was, and is, everything to me.

Even though I have never let fall the smallest tidbit that might incriminate her, the authorities persisted in prosecuting the poor creature as an accessory after the fact. Their spite was revenge for the humiliation of our disappearance. I feared that, by appointing lawyers other than yourself and Mr. Tobin, men so deeply versed in the minutiae of the case, she was risking her life. Do you know that her family was responsible for terminating your services? They argued with her that your part in the Cleveland Street scandal rendered you unfit to represent her in a capital case. How unfair and how naïve! The Cleveland Street business was regrettable; as a man of honour you would be the first to admit it. But the reason you helped the witness to flee to the Continent was to protect your client from his testimony. Six weeks in prison is a heavy price to pay for devotion to a client's cause. Some may call it obstructing justice. To my mind, it is loyalty.

I prefer to recall your triumph in the Camden Town murder trial. Had it not been for your tireless efforts on his behalf, that young fellow Wood might have swung for the murder of the prostitute. That the police failed to find the true culprit is hardly your fault.

Sometimes I have suspected Ethel of nurturing a prejudice against you merely on account of the grey kid gloves you always wear. Thank the Lord, her wilfulness has not betrayed her. Her jury acquitted her in even less time than mine took to settle upon its cruel verdict.

Our battle is half won. I have absolute faith in you, Arthur, to make sure that I survive this ordeal. Once free, I can take my place again in the world outside, together with the woman who means everything to me. On with the appeal!

From The Daily Mail, *16 July 1910*

CRIPPEN'S FIRST WIFE

The Press Association is informed on good authority that the circumstances of the death of the first Mrs. Crippen are now being made the subject of inquiry.

Unfortunately, the formalities necessary have prevented the foreign police from being instantly notified and put on the alert. Astonishing as it may seem, the Paris Criminal Investigation Department yesterday had not been notified that Dr. Crippen and Miss Le Neve were "wanted." The notice has to go first to the Foreign Office, whence it is transmitted to the British Embassy in Paris, when again it is communicated to the French Government, and by them it is forwarded to the French police. This elaborate process gives the offender every chance.

Poor Charlotte. Perhaps I should be furious that the general public, that vast anonymous swarm, should be duped into believing that I killed her, together with my unborn child. I prefer to treat it as a source of bitter amusement. I have become a source of profit to newspapermen, a catalyst to let their imaginations rip. No crime is so abominable that it cannot be laid at my door.

Mr. Dew never had any truck with these absurdities. The two of us only ever spoke of Charlotte in passing. He is a true English bulldog who would never succumb to a flight of fancy. I found my conversations with him oddly comforting. How ironic that my nemesis treated me not as a monster, but as a fellow man.

Memories of Charlotte are misty. How imperfect is my recollection of the years with her was brought home to me only when I stood in the dock. Counsel for the prosecution read out the statement I made to the good chief inspector, on that first fateful day when he and I met.

"I was married to a lady named Charlotte Bell of New York, and she accompanied me to San Diego. We then came to New York. I have had only one child by my first wife. He was born at San Diego, about 1887 or 1888, and his name is Otto Hawley Crippen. He is now married and lives at Los Angeles. My first wife died, so far as I can remember, in 1890 or 1891. We were living at Salt Lake City, where I was practising as an eye and ear specialist. She was buried at

41

Salt Lake City in my name."

My purpose was to assist Mr. Dew by providing an explanation as to my background. If he knew the history of my life, he would understand the man that I am. But the bleak faces of the jurymen told me I had made a bad mistake. Dates have never been my strong point, but vagueness as to the precise years in which my son was born, and when my wife died, was viewed askance by those who did not know me. Too late, I realised that my words suggested that I had not cared.

My wedding night—in whatever year it was. The longed-for end to my virginity, the chance to make a new beginning with my Irish bride. A student nurse, quiet and earnest, with an enticing brogue. Inches taller than me, but what did that matter? Charlotte, Charlotte, how I had ached for her.

Surveying her tense frame, clad in a nightdress made of muslin with frilled collar and sleeves. Arranging her beneath me in the bed. Lifting her arms so that I could slip off the nightdress. Marvelling at the lily-whiteness of her skin, the darkness of the nipples I had envisioned so often in my bachelor dreams. Gazing down into her luminous face, wishing that she would not avert those long-lashed eyes, but understanding that this was a precious and terrible moment for her, when there was no possibility of resistance, when at last she must yield to my will.

My infinite care as I traced with my fingertips around her the mole beneath her breast, skin brushing against skin. Her flesh icy to the touch, her whole body taut, as if she hardly dared to breathe.

I was so hungry for her that the urge for conquest became a grinding pain. Tonight she would experience a passion for which the convent in Dublin had never prepared her. I desired nothing more than to honour her with my body and to share with her a perfect love. Nuzzling her thighs, praying that her involuntary twitch when the sweat of my brow touched her belly was a token of subtle pleasure rather than a shudder of distaste. I stifled a pang of alarm, told myself her reticence was only natural. When I could contain myself no longer, I took her swiftly. My mind emptied, and for a few moments I became an elemental beast. Once I was done, I heaved myself up with a grunt of triumph and surveyed my wife. Her eyes were closed, but her lips moved as though in silent supplication. She might have been a mourner at a funeral, remembering the dead.

How many times had I rehearsed the scene in my head. The thrill of possession, the totality of her surrender. Nothing had prepared me for this. Seeing shadows of the window bars on the white painted wall above our bed, as if our room had become a prison cell. Struggling for breath, suffocating with the knowledge that we were bound together for the rest of our lives. The Arctic stillness of her body. The throbbing in my temples. The panic bubbling up inside me.

I could not melt her.

From the first I was intrigued by Miss Charlotte Bell. She was a quiet woman, no longer in the first flush of youth. Gradually my awareness of her occasional covert glances caused me to respond in kind. Before long I plucked up the nerve to talk to her. When she answered shyly in that charming Irish tone, my heart leapt. Soon I had convinced myself that ours was a match made in Heaven. As if to test my resolve, she insisted that I obtain a special dispensation to marry her, because she was a Catholic and I was not. I agreed without a second thought. Anything to make her mine.

Within weeks of our wedding, I realised I was a mouse caught in a baited trap. Charlotte had found what she wanted—bluntly, I had taken her off the shelf—and she was more than willing to offer fidelity in return. At least, I sought to console myself, I should never become that most desperate of men, a cuckold. Charlotte was an accomplished homemaker, at least the equal of my mother in that regard, and an even better cook. Even when money was short, she could always be relied upon to make a wonderful mutton broth.

Alas, she was a creature of moods. The slightest disharmony made her sullen for days on end, and I found myself thinking wistfully of the freedom I had enjoyed in my bachelorhood. More than ever before, I needed Something Else, and now I could put a name to it.

Passion, that was what I sought.

I prayed that Otto's birth might save us from drowning in the tepid shallows of mutual indifference. Charlotte was made for maternity. Having a husband was the fee to be paid for the prize of bearing a child. She relished pregnancy, delighted in the filling out of her already solid form. After the child was born, she found it difficult to shed the extra pounds, and when I listened to her rumbling snores in our marriage bed, I struggled to recall the young woman I had sought out as my bride. More than once, as she turned her back in response to the most timid of overtures, tears of disappointment dampened my cheeks in the darkness.

No matter: I took my sacred vows solemnly. *For better, for worse.* Or, perhaps: "What cannot be cured, must be endured." I threw myself into my work. Much as I admired my uncle, I had resolved not to follow his course and practise in a backwater. Yet I found it more testing than anticipated to establish myself in an urban setting. We moved around as I sought a niche as a specialist in maladies of the eye and ear. After leaving Detroit for a second time, I found openings first in San Diego and then in New York, but they flattered to deceive.

I applied my brain to the problem. In those days, children often went about with ears clumsily plugged by wads of cotton wool, jaws and crown bandaged with red flannel, or one eye masked by a crude patch or shield. Given the Mormon attitude toward matrimony, Salt Lake City would have no shortage of children. I explained to Charlotte what I proposed and she fell in with the plan. Within weeks I had secured a position that promised much.

Before long, Charlotte told me that another little one was on the way. At least my virility was beyond question: my wife fell pregnant after submitting to me for the very first time since Otto's christening. I suppressed the unworthy thought that it might have suited me better if difficulty in conceiving had compelled her to grant my conjugal rights routinely. But I counselled myself not to take refuge in the easy shelter of selfishness. Our family was taking shape and, if I felt a void within my heart, yet I struggled to keep in mind my grandfather's injunctions and pause to count my blessings.

Salt Lake City

January 27, 1892

Dear Mother and Father,

First and foremost, let me thank you from the bottom of my heart for the kindness of your response to my garbled wire. I must apologise for my lack of coherence, but you will understand that my shock and desolation is compounded by the double tragedy. To have snatched from me only my beloved Charlotte was a dreadful blow, but also to lose our unborn child is more than a man should be asked to bear.

Thank you so much for your invitation to join you in San Jose. Of course, I accept. Somehow I cannot face up to the prospect of continuing here in Utah any more. We never settled and Charlotte herself suggested only a month ago that, once the baby was born, we should return to New York. It is the most suitable place in which to practise as a homeopathic physician. With a small child to look after and lacking wifely support, however, my planned return to Manhattan takes on the character of an idle dream.

I have determined to survive. I owe it to the memory of your daughter-in-law, my wife, as well as to my son. With your willing assistance, and comforted by the belief that somehow I am fulfilling God's inscrutable purpose, I shall start my life again.

Your affectionate son,
Hawley

Brooklyn
26 June 1892
My Dear Mother and Father,
I am delighted to hear of Otto's progress, however unsteady it may at present be. He is in the best of hands and I trust that his presence in your home will continue to prove a source of comfort at a difficult time.

I am glad to report that my gamble in coming back to New York has paid off. I have secured a post as assistant to a highly regarded doctor for whom my expertise in afflictions of the eye and ear is a considerable boon. Dr. Jeffery and his wife have offered me the chance to lodge with them until I find a place of my own. My plan is to make myself indispensable. My aim is to repay the faith you have placed in me, as well as your kindness in caring for my boy in the way you once cared for me.

Yours ever,
Hawley

Letters from a distant town. The recipients will pore over the text, alert to every nuance. All the more important, therefore, to devote care and attention to the message conveyed as well as to elegance of calligraphy. With pen in hand, I enjoy rising to the challenge of choosing my words subtly and with sensitivity. Ensuring that what I say accords with the actual truth is a discipline, a challenge that I strive to meet. Pulling together the threads of a made-up story has always come more naturally to me.

Never had gratitude been more sincere. Left alone with Otto, I might have found myself imprisoned by the obligations of paternity. Instead, my mother's longing once again to enjoy the companionship of a little boy, to recapture the pleasurable emotions of a quarter-century earlier, had set me free.

Charlotte's death was as sudden as it was shocking. One day a young and healthy woman, about to bear her second child, the next a corpse on the mortician's slab. At first I was numb, unable to take in the catastrophe that had befallen our little family. Instead of four of us, there were only two.

Little by little, the jumble in my brain began to clear. For a time, I reproached myself bitterly for hankering after my premarital liberty. In superstitious mood, I felt as if somehow I had wished death upon my wife and Fate, in punishment, had taken my second child as well. But I was not responsible. God was moving in His mysterious way.

With my parents' aid, I came through. As for Charlotte, I felt sorrow tempered with realism. Matrimony had become a gaol. Had I known her true nature, I never would have proposed to her at all. Never again would I be so misled. If I were ever to share my life again, I must experience the passion that Charlotte lacked.

At the risk of straying far beyond the boundaries of decent taste, I have nothing now left to lose by confessing the shameful truth. Charlotte's apoplexy was, for me, a stroke of fortune.

Ethel has written to me, and at once I am in Paradise. I rush to take up the pen myself, so that I can let her know how much her letter means. I have longed so passionately to have again before me her looping, careful script. My heart has been bursting and throbbing with the pain of longing for her, and for even a handful of written words.

Reading between the lines, I shiver at her despair. She is saved, but she fears for me; I think she truly believes that my fate is sealed. Hastily, I reassure her about the offers of support that are flooding in. As you predicted, Mr. Horatio Bottomley has thundered in the pages of *John Bull* that I was denied a fair trial. Thank Heaven that, in addition to yourself and Mr. Tobin, I have such a formidable advocate on my side.

And now—the Governor, that kindly man, tells me that she is here to see me!

Arthur, you will understand if I decline to disclose what passed between the two of us. Our conversation was entirely private—or as private as it could be, in the circumstances. I came close to breaking down, but struggled for composure, so as not to upset her. If only I had been allowed to touch her hand! So all my good things have come at once today. A letter and a visit!

Ethel spoke at length about money. She worries about our finances and so do I. My life depends on the appeal, and yet my thoughts are as occupied by the prospect of poverty. On the day that my trial opened, the Charing Cross Bank collapsed. How could crooked land deals in Canada destroy such a respected British institution? It is a

48

cruel blow, and yet of one thing you can be sure. I am not cut from the same poor cloth as that wretched engineer in Yorkshire who swallowed ammonia because his life savings were with the Charing Cross and he could not contemplate the humiliation of the workhouse. Even here, sitting on a hard bench in the condemned cell, I refuse to surrender so irrevocably to despair.

My prayer is that, when all is settled, a dividend will be paid to creditors. In the interim, Arthur, may I ask you to allow thirty shillings a week to Ethel as an allowance for keeping the wolf from the door? Treat it as an advance against the dividend. Failing that, speak to Eddie Marr. I am sure he will be glad to help.

As for this notion of Ethel appearing in a vaudeville sketch—no, no, no!

I refuse to have the love of my life embarrassed upon the stage, even in consideration of two hundred pounds. There are other ways of making money, and not merely from the writing of memoirs. I gather that the five hundred from the *New York American* has already been swallowed by your fees.

What I have in mind is the prescription for *Sans Peine*. The phial and powder that Mr. Dew took from me at the time of my arrest are neither here nor there. It is the means of combining those ingredients to best effect that Ethel needs. Please ensure that the prescription is forwarded to her without delay. I have been in business long enough to recognise a sure-fire winner. Patent pain-killers are all the rage. When the present unpleasantness is over and done, *Sans Peine* holds promise for our future. Who knows, who knows? We may yet make our fortune.

R v Crippen, evidence of the accused, 4th day, 21 October 1910

The Lord Chief Justice: *"Now, Dr. Crippen, listen to me. We have heard a description of your wife and her habits by these witnesses as to her vivacious manner and bright spirits and all that. Apart from the quarrels with you . . . you agree in that description, I understand?"*

"Yes."

Walking into the waiting area outside Jeffery's private consulting room. Pausing in surprise at the whiff of musk in the air. A young woman perched on the wicker chair, scrutinising a dainty silver ring on her little finger with as much care as if she were valuing it for insurance. I drank in the sight of her. Full lips, dark hair, and big, brown eyes. Good cheekbones, a charming, turned-up nose.

She glanced up as I sauntered toward her and our eyes met. She might be no more than nineteen years old—barely more than a child—but the self-assured gaze belonged to a woman of experience. Her jaw was strong. Her perfume made my head swim, as if I had consumed too much wine. She smiled and, in an instant, I understood what Herr Mesmer meant long ago when he talked of "animal magnetism."

"Good morning, Doctor." She had an easy drawl, but I felt as if she were seeking to invest those three commonplace words with a special meaning.

I lifted my chin. "Good morning."

"You're Dr. Jeffery's partner, I guess."

Not the exact truth, but near enough. I nodded, wanting to tarry. With elaborate unconcern, I glanced at the plants growing in the Waudian case that Jeffery kept on the table by the door. I am no botanist; one mass of tight green fronds looks much like another to me. Yet I might have been a modern Linnaeus, given the attention I devoted to those ferns during the next minute or so. My legs were shaking, but somehow, I kept my eyes off her, inhaling that devilish fragrance all the time.

"I see . . ." she began, but then Jeffery's door opened and his bullet-shaped head appeared.

"Miss Turner?"

Rising to her feet, she bestowed upon me another smile, one part apology to three parts amusement. In a moment she was gone.

"Your last patient of the morning," I said to Jeffery as I helped him to lock up that night. Careful to make sure that my tone was casual, offhand. "A Miss Turner?"

His eyebrows were fat caterpillars of greying hair. They lifted in enquiry. "Yes?"

"I wonder . . ." I began.

He interrupted me with a cough. Discreet, yet knowing. "From what she said to me, you seem to have made an impression upon her."

My heart jumped. "Really?"

"Really."

"She is a patient of long-standing?" I hazarded a guess that she was the daughter of a wealthy businessman. Jeffery's services did not come cheaply.

Jeffery pursed his lips. I guessed that he was wondering how much he should tell of whatever he knew. Or perhaps—he was not above this—he was simply relishing the opportunity to prolong the agonies of suspense.

"She was introduced to my practice by C.C. Lincoln, of Water Street. The stove manufacturer, you know."

"Oh, yes?" My knowledge of the city's stove manufacturers was skimpy in the extreme.

"Miss Turner is, shall we say, living under his protection." Jeffery paused. He always chose his words with care. "She has an apartment two blocks from here. Lincoln pays the bills, just as he has underwritten her treatment from myself."

"Ah." I swallowed hard. "I see."

"Perhaps you do, but perhaps you don't. There is a Mrs. Lincoln, by the way."

"Really?"

"I met the woman once. *Long-suffering* is the phrase that springs to mind. That, and *plain*. Lincoln will never leave her, of course. All the same, he pays for Miss Turner's singing lessons. Grand opera, no less."

"She is a performer?"

"Hmmm—aspiring. What she may lack in terms of perfect pitch, she more than compensates for with ambition. You may also care to know that she was evidently interested in learning more about my junior *partner.*"

My cheeks burned at the emphasis he laid upon the final word. "I think there may have been a misunder—"

"Evidently," Jeffery interrupted. He was, all things considered, a decent man, but I found him wearisome when in a sardonic mood.

This was not the time to shilly-shally. "May I ask what she said . . . I mean, with regard to myself?"

Jeffery shrugged. "She asked questions, rather than scattering compliments, but do not let that disappoint you. I took the liberty of mentioning that you were recently widowed in tragic circumstances and that your parents have agreed to take charge of your boy for an indefinite period. I trust you do not regard that as abominably indiscreet."

"Of course not," I said warmly.

"And for your information, may I mention that her next appointment is listed in the book for four o'clock on Tuesday afternoon?"

A summer evening in Central Park. A light breeze whistling through the trees, the clatter of hooves in the distance. The two of us shaded our eyes from the dipping sun as we dallied on a bench facing the granite obelisk. I told Cora that I had seen the monument's twin, on the banks of the Thames, and she listened wide-eyed to my tales of visiting London. Naturally I said nothing about Bedlam or women of the night.

This was our fifth meeting. I counted each one, committing every detail to memory, and whenever her soft palm brushed mine, my heart sang. Her zest for life was infectious. I loved her confidence that anything was possible. Thanks to her stepfather's teaching, she spoke good German, but she was no reader. Cora lived life to the fullest, rather than absorbing it at one remove.

We talked incessantly. When I described the virtues of homeopathy, she listened with flattering attention, asking just the right number of questions to encourage me to share my opinions on the future of the discipline. For her part, she described without self-pity the travails of growing up in Brooklyn, dispossessed and sharing her mother and stepfather with five half-brothers and half-sisters. Her great love was music. She sang soprano solos with the parish church choir and Herr Mersinger, who had married her mother when Cora was two, had taught her how to play the zither. In later years, she and he would sit together in the peanut gallery of the Metropolitan Opera House, gazing on the wives of rich men in the boxes of the Golden Horseshoe, flaunting their rubies and their diamonds. Jewellery she loved with a passion so intense that it could never be requited. Lincoln had sought to buy her affection with rings and bracelets. Who could blame a girl as young and innocent as Cora for being swayed? But Lincoln failed to understand her. Her artistic sensibility meant nothing to him and, in consequence, he could not hope to fulfil her most fervent wishes. What mattered most to Cora was that dream of a rapturous audience. Whenever she went to see a play or opera, a solitary thought coursed through her mind.

That could be me. I could be out there on the stage, taking the curtain calls, bowing to the applauding audience, basking in the heat of their admiration.

Sometimes she spoke about her life with Lincoln, and her discreet yet telling hints of his brutal lust swamped me with misery. From the age of sixteen, she had been a helpless recipient of the vilest attentions. He regarded her as his chattel.

I had come to suppose that we shared a special intimacy, but I had not dared to venture beyond a peck on the cheek the previous night, when I wished her goodnight outside her home. Her very presence by my side, the way her silk-clad leg grazed mine, made me giddy with delight and disbelief. I was possessed by an overwhelming devotion toward her, such as I had never known before. Slipping my hand in hers, I felt the return of pressure as she closed her fingers around mine.

A wistful sigh. "Oh, Hawley. If only this could go on forever."

"It can go on." A pause, designed to be meaningful. Masterful, even. "It will go on."

We approached a bench. The scent of mown grass lingered in the air. We sat side by side and I wished that the sweat had not plastered the thinning strands of my hair to my brow, but she did not seem to notice. Emboldened, I took her hands in mine. She bowed her head, the soft black curls tumbling against my nose.

"I'm sorry, Hawley. But it can't go on."

If a horse had bolted from its carriage and kicked me on the head, it would not have administered such a ferocious blow. I gaped at her in shocked dismay, unable to take in what she was saying.

"It . . . it can't be . . . surely . . ."

"I guess this time he really does mean it. He's making arrangements."

"Arrangements?" I squeezed her hands hard, as if to stop her escaping from me. She gave a little yelp of pain.

"Please, Hawley, you must listen. He means to leave New York and take me with him."

"Dearest, he is married."

She pulled her hands away. "He says he cannot stand his wife. She is a leech, sucking out his wealth. He wants to leave her. He says he only cares for me."

"He doesn't care a jot for you! You say he's only interested in you for one thing." Terror gave me a voice that I scarcely recognised as my own. "The singing lessons are just a way of getting what he wants. He's selfish to the core. He doesn't truly believe you will become a star upon the stage. When you were carrying his child, he insisted that you have an abortion."

A low blow, but I was desperate. Cora, to her credit, was barely shaken. Nothing ever seemed to knock her off her stride.

"He wouldn't have forced me to, Hawley, he couldn't have. He knew how much I love little ones, how much I always wanted a baby of my own. If I hadn't had that miscarriage . . ."

"But he asked you to destroy your unborn child! For God's sake, what kind of a lover is that? How can you possibly contemplate . . ."

"Hush, hush! You are raising your voice, Hawley. People will stare."

"I'm sorry, my darling. But I can't bear any of this. The thought of losing you . . ."

"You called me darling." It was as though for a moment she had lapsed into a reverie. "You have been so restrained until now—I have not known what you truly thought of me."

"How could you doubt my devotion?"

"Well . . ." She gave me a sidelong look, coquettish and wholly charming.

I filled my lungs with air. "I love you, Cora."

Her eyes locked with mine. "I love you too, Hawley."

I could not believe it. This delightful young creature, a dozen years my junior—she loved *me!* Half-forgotten lines from Shakespeare echoed in my brain. *There is a tide in the affairs of men.* Now was the time to take it at the flood.

"Then say you will not go," I implored her.

"What else can I do? I have no money, and my family has none. Until we reclaim our old estates, we are penniless. It takes more than guts to make a career in the opera. And Hawley, you know how much that means to me."

She looked at me beseechingly. I gathered up her hands again and said breathlessly, "You can marry me."

"What?"

At once she was very still, examining my expression minutely.

"I mean it, Cora. We can be happy together. I can make you happy." I was acutely aware of the face that stared back at me from the mirror each morning: the slight bulging of the eyes, the scrawniness of the neck. If only she could see beneath the surface! "Oh, I realise I'm not much to look at . . ."

"Say there, don't be so modest," she whispered. "You're gentle and you're kind."

Her words fired me. "You needn't worry about the cash. I don't have a fortune, but we'll get by. I'll make sure there isn't a soprano in New York who's better loved than Cora Turner—if you'll only say yes to me. So, let me put the question to you fair and square and in the proper manner."

I slid off the bench so that I could kneel in front of her. I banged my knees and felt ungainly, but that did not matter at all.

"Cora, darling, will you marry me?"

With a smile of delight, she nodded and squeezed my hand.

Once more I escorted Cora to the block where she lived; once more I moved to kiss her on the cheek as we reached the front door. This time she stopped me with a playful smile.

"Say, would you care to accompany me to the second floor, my dear Dr. Crippen?"

I returned her smile eagerly. "With pleasure, my dear Miss Turner."

Inside, the air smelled of cabbage. The lights on the staircase were dim and I stumbled the uneven steps as I followed her. My pulse raced. With this woman, I never knew what to expect.

We reached the door to her apartment. "You will come inside, won't you, Hawley?"

An eternity passed as she rummaged in her bag for the key and then at last we were inside, gliding wordlessly through the vestibule to her room, sinking down on the bed, our arms wrapped around each other as though we meant never to let go.

My head kept spinning as I struggled with the buttons of my shirt. I was scarcely able to take in my surroundings. Everything seemed hazy, a blur of pink. Pink underclothes, pink blankets, pink piping on the pillowcases. I saw a chipped candlestand, battered wardrobe, and chest of overflowing drawers. Cobwebs on the ceiling, grubby sheets, folios of music with corners curled. Knickknacks scattered everywhere, many of them with a dusty patina. A whiff of rotting wood not quite concealed by Cora's heady fragrance.

The seedy ambience enriched my triumph. Lincoln, the hated Lincoln, had not provided for my love as well as I had in my misery supposed, or as she had in her innocence led me to believe. The sweet girl had shown the utmost loyalty to her protector, but he had done nothing to deserve it. At all events, it did not matter now. She was mine and I was hers.

"Your mitts are shaking. Don't tell me you're nervous!"

"Cora, I'm . . ."

But words failed me.

"My, my. A medical man, too." She bent over, attacked by the giggles. "You've seen it all before, I guess, and yet for me you're all of a twitter."

My eyes feasted as she peeled off her clothes. I was so hungry for her. Her response was bold, daring me with her smile to keep my gaze upon her as she sat on the side of the bed and unlaced her corset. Her aureoles and nipples were a delicate rosy shade, uncannily matching the décor. I made as if to help when she took off first her gartered black stockings and then her underskirt, but she wriggled from my grasp, laughing at my clumsy zest for her.

"Not so shy now, are you, Hawley? Getting quite an eyeful there, aren't you? Come on, at least take those glasses off. Or do you want to make a *spectacle* of yourself?"

I strove to match her bantering tone. "I want to be able to see you perfectly."

An uproarious laugh. "Hawley, you say the nicest things! You're such a gentleman. Not like some I could mention."

I reached out and put my hand on her bare shoulder, felt plump flesh yielding to my touch. She was so *hot* compared to Charlotte, the only lover I had taken until now.

"Don't speak of him," I urged her. Lincoln, like Charlotte, had no place in our lives. "He means nothing to you now you are mine. You must leave this tawdry place."

She prodded my chest with her thumb. "Hey you, not so much of the *"tawdry"!* It ain't the Ritz, but I designed the colour scheme myself. Go on, guess my favourite colour! I do love pink, don't you?"

Smiling, she slipped the lacy knickers down her short and curving legs. My breath was coming in short and jerky gasps. I wanted her so much that I feared my heart would burst.

"Come here," she said, crooking her little finger. She had a habit of command and I could not help but obey. I *wanted* to obey. She whipped off my spectacles and tossed them onto the floor. When I winced, she put her mouth to mine and within a moment I did not care if the glass smashed into a thousand pieces. Charlotte had never once kissed me like this, but now I was making love to a woman of whom any man would be proud.

She put one hand behind my head and guided my mouth to the breasts of which I had dreamed the night before. Her directness electrified me. I had doubted whether a respectable woman could respond so fiercely to a man's desires, let alone express unambiguously carnal longings of her own. Cora was young, yet she was teaching me so much so soon. The coarse words she used struck me like a slap across the cheek—but a slap that excited me. I responded in kind, in a hoarse voice I scarcely recognised as my own. For reply, she wriggled over onto her stomach and hissed an instruction that shocked and enthralled me in equal measure. When I complied, she shuddered with ecstasy, her whole body writhing against mine.

I wanted to shout with exultation. At last I could forget my juvenile fantasies about the secret places and the mocking words of the whore of Bedlam. I had found passion. And perfect happiness.

Wonders never cease—the food here is excellent! Last night I feasted on roast mutton, soup, vegetables—all served piping hot—followed by a pudding made of bananas. Before long I was belching with satisfaction, much to the amusement of my guards. The people here are civilised and kind—true Englishmen! The warders do their duty with amiable efficiency and I take care not to cause them the slightest bother. What is more, I have made quite a friend of Major Mytton-Davies. As one would expect of a retired army officer, he is the soul of discretion, but his sympathy and willingness to chat are such that, plainly, he believes I am innocent. Of course, he is in an invidious position, but if the governor of Pentonville refuses to accept my guilt, surely the judges on appeal will be persuaded to right a dreadful wrong?

The major keeps asking whether there is anything more I wish to tell the police. It is as if he suspects that I am withholding the identity of the true culprit or an unknown "confederate." Naturally, Arthur, I am fervent in my denials. This speculation is *dangerous*—and yet the major hints that Mr. Horatio Bottomley has suggested there is much more to this case than meets the eye. I beg you to ask your friend to have a care. We must do nothing to encourage such wild talk, even if from the purest of motives. One miscarriage of justice is surely enough.

R v Crippen, first day, 18 October 1910, evidence of Dr. John Herbert Burroughs

Mr. Muir K.C. *"What kind of woman was Mrs. Crippen?"*

Dr. Burroughs: *"She was a vivacious woman . . . bright and cheerful . . . she was very fond of dress and dressed very well indeed. At times she wore a quantity of jewellery."*

Names, names, names. They define us and describe us. Ethel, so sensitive to nuances, understands this perfectly. That is why, before we ever met, she took an identity that separated her from the father whom she loathed.

The Crippens had a tradition of sonorous nomenclature. Cora always said that Hawley Harvey was a handle that made her cringe and I could not help but sympathise. When I sought to fashion a life far from Coldwater, I realised that names can offer a wonderful disguise. *Peter* rolled more easily off the tongue; that I discovered early on in London. Eminently Anglo-Saxon, neither prissy nor pompous.

The surname was little better than my Christian names. *Cripple,* the bullies of my childhood called me, even though I was healthy enough. I simply lacked their athletic physique. Small wonder that in the later years, for business reasons, I opted for a change. Franckel, I called myself sometimes: hardly a common name, it seemed to me to have a continental flavour, a hint of mystery that appealed. But no one could hold a candle to Cora when it came to changing names. Early in our married life she broke the news to me that she had been born Kunigunde Mackamotzi, daughter of a Polish nobleman, whose lands had been stolen from him. This came as a complete shock. For the first time I wondered how well I really knew her.

For Cora, names flitted in and out of fashion, as though they were hats or shoes. Cryptic clues, not so much to her identity, but to her current frame of mind. Briefly, she had a liking for Cunigunda; later, she favoured Corrinne. In the end, she settled for Belle Elmore.

"Why did you lie to me?" I asked. My voice was low and my hands could not stop shaking. After a long day devoted to polite and inane conversation as I did my duty in getting to know my in-laws, all the bones in my body ached, the pain compounded by disappointment and a sickening sense of betrayal.

"I didn't lie!"

Frowning, I put a finger to my lips. "Keep your voice down, will you? Your sister's room is next door, don't forget. We don't want her overhearing."

"I don't care. Tessie's a great kid. She's always looked up to me. Not like some I could mention."

I was sitting on the end of the bed in the dusty attic at the top of her stepfather's Brooklyn home. There was barely enough space to stretch out my legs. She was standing in front of me in her new linen nightdress—of course, the ribbon ties were pink—and trying to stare me out.

"I don't like being taken for a fool, that's all. You said your father was a baron."

"Was that why you married me?" she demanded, hands on hips.

"Of course not, Cora. You ought to know me better than to suggest it. I just wish you'd told me the truth."

"Things got confused way back in Poland. Mother always said that he owned vast estates in the country. They were taken from him somehow, by the authorities, I guess."

"Your father was a grocer! He kept a fruit stand—good ole Joe Mackamotzi of Brooklyn!"

"Want to make something of it?" Her back-street twang always became more pronounced in the course of an argument. "Trying to say I'm not good enough for you, is that it? Or maybe my pa wasn't?"

"No, no, it's just—well, he was hardly a member of the landed gentry, was he?"

She came up and pushed herself onto the bed beside me. The yoke neck of her gown was cut low and her breasts nuzzled my chest. When she spoke again, her tone had softened. "I told you. The family fell on hard times. I was only two when he died. Maybe Mom got things a little mixed up, but I'm not ashamed of who I am."

"You didn't tell me the truth."

"Hey." She nibbled at my ear. "Don't be so prim and proper, huh? Not everything a person says has always got to be one hundred percent accurate, you understand? You should know. You spin yarns more than most."

Stung, I retorted, "I never misled you."

She bit my ear and laughed when I cried out. "Serves you right. Now, what was that again?"

Struggling for dignity, I said, "I didn't lie to you."

Her mood had swung; she loved amusing herself at my expense and it was clear that she had spotted a way of doing so.

"Oh no, Mister *Junior Partner?*"

After thinking this out, I said, "You knew all the time, didn't you, that I was just Jeffery's assistant?"

She giggled. "Let's say I had my suspicions right from the off. But it didn't bother me. Right from the time we met, I would have bet my last cent that you and I were made for each other. We're different in a lot of ways, but I reckon we're two of a kind."

"How do you make that out, Cora?"

She started to unfasten the ties of her nightdress. Her breasts swayed in a slow, hypnotic rhythm. "Come on, we understand each other, don't we? We know what we each want, in bed and out of it. Everyday things aren't good enough for you and me. We always have to make them a little better. Improve upon reality, huh?"

And then she started improving on reality with me.

As an only child, I found Cora's large and complicated family overwhelming. When we stayed with them, there was no chance of solitude until bedtime, no prospect of escaping from their company to enjoy a few moments of tenderness as man and wife. Whenever we crept into some remote nook and cranny in quest of an intimate embrace, a relative of Cora's was bound to show up and engage her in voluble discourse.

In the midst of a crowd, Cora flourished; her eyes sparkled and her raucous laughter echoed around the room. Yet for me, the house was claustrophobic. The reek of herrings hung in the air long after breakfast was over, and the girls' babble caused me constant headaches.

Of course, there were consolations. Cora was not the only pretty girl in the house. Teresa—Tessie, as she was known—was younger, and it seemed to me that she truly possessed the naiveté that her sister affected. Certainly, on an occasion when the two of us were alone and I essayed a mildly *risqué* joke, of the sort that my wife would have discounted as "tame," Tessie's face crumpled and I had to move the conversation swiftly on to safer ground.

Cora's half-sister, Louise, was courting a fellow called Robert Mills. A pretty girl, Louise, and I gained the impression that, notwithstanding her impending marriage, she had taken a fancy to me. Cora even teased me about it. Perhaps it was merely that, anything Cora had, Louise wanted.

One Sunday morning found us sitting alone together in the parlour of the house on Green Street. The rest of the family had left for church, but Louise excused herself on the ground of a headache. We chatted companionably about Cora's musical accomplishments, and Louise expressed the opinion that I must regard her as dull indeed in comparison to her sister. When I denied this hotly, I found somehow that our fingers had become intertwined. She did not seem to consider this objectionable. Yet when, encouraged into uncharacteristic boldness, I ventured the mildest peck upon her powdered cheek—a gesture of brotherly affection, nothing more—she let out a little cry of horror. I was shocked by her change of tack; all at once, it was as if she had been attacked by a kraken from the deep. As she pushed me away, I began to apologise, confusion and mortification making the words that tumbled from me sound desperate and absurd.

"I never meant . . ."

"I think I know precisely what you meant, Dr. Crippen." Already she had recovered her composure.

"Louise . . ."

"Please. Let us speak no more of it." She rose. "Now, if you will excuse me, I am still fatigued."

She retired to her bedroom and, needless to say, I did not dream of following her. Instead, I cursed myself bitterly for having been led—I might almost say seduced—into that tiny scrap of a kiss. Although I had been twice married, there was still much about the opposite sex that I failed altogether to understand.

Louise said nothing, at least not at the time. Yet some six weeks later I learned that she had indeed confided in her sisters. Cora and I were squashed up against each other in the tiny bed. My eyes were closing and I was ready for sleep. Unlike my wife.

"Say, Hawley, what do you think about when I cover your eyes?"

"What else can I think of but you?" I murmured drowsily. Cora's eagerness to discuss the most intimate matters in vivid and astonishing detail excited me more than I can describe. Nevertheless, I preferred our "dirty talk," as she termed it, to take the form of a preamble to love-making rather than an inquest upon it.

Her chubby legs intertwined with mine. "Are you sure?" she whispered in my ear. "There's no-one else to fill your dreams, is there?"

"Who else could there be, my darling?"

"You've taken a shine to Louise, I hear, you naughty boy."

I swear that my heart stopped for a moment. When I recovered, I simply repeated in a stupid voice, "Louise?"

"Oh yes, she's told me about what you did that Sunday we went to church and left you two here."

"What?" I was aghast.

Cora's hips pushed against mine. "By her account, it was practically a rape."

I sat bolt upright in the bed. "Cora, what in God's name has she said? Tell me!"

"Hush, Hawley! No need to squawk. You've been a silly boy, that's all."

"Cora, I swear, there was nothing . . ."

"Nothing?" she asked mischievously. "My dear, I know Louise of old. She needs a morsel of straw in order to make her bricks."

I tried to explain, but after a few moments she put her hand over my mouth to cut my protestations short.

"Hawley, that's enough. You just need to be more careful, that's all. She's always envied me and my men, always told tales to help her score points against me. All the while pretending to be my bosom friend. But remember which sister you married from now on, huh?"

Her calm understanding transfixed me. Baffled and relieved, I showered kisses of gratitude upon her face and neck and body until she gave me the chance to demonstrate the extent of my devotion to her.

When we were finished, she put a finger to my lips and said with a wicked grin, "Now then, wasn't that a thousand times nicer than ever it could be with that skinny little half-sister of mine?"

"Don't cry, Cora. Please."

After her bath, I used to dry her as a treat, massaging her back and shoulders with the towel. My ministrations were done, but her cheeks remained wet. I rubbed them with my handkerchief.

"Thanks," she said. "Sorry, Hawley. I don't know why I came over all funny. I never meant to weep."

"It doesn't matter, I promise."

She covered her lower half with the towel. Cora was never one for modesty, but since the operation, she seemed less in love with her body than before. Nor was she taking proper care of it. Lately I had noticed a roll of fat around her middle, evidence that, since our arrival in St Louis, she had put on more than a stone in weight.

"I hate that scar. Oh, how I hate it! Oh, God, the day Tessie caught a glimpse of it, I thought she was going to drop down in a faint."

"She's young, my dear. Believe me, the scar is not so unsightly."

"How can you say that, for Heaven's sake? It's awful. Disgusting."

"Dearest, I never notice it."

I did not scruple at such a lie, although the puckered flesh just above her pubic hair caused me to flinch each time I saw it. Her profound distress was all the more shocking because normally she allowed nothing to interfere with her robust enjoyment of life. The ovariectomy affronted her womanhood.

"It's what the scar means to me, you know that." Her cheeks were ghostly. "I so much wanted a baby of my own. Wanted it more desperately than I can say. You know that, don't you?"

I put my arm around her shoulder, inhaling the scent of her lemon soap. "We have each other."

"But I don't have ovaries!" she wailed. "And I need ovaries, to start a family. You're a doctor. Tell me, am I wrong? Can you work some kind of miracle cure for me?"

"Cora, if I could have anything in the world, then I'd want us to have a child together, but . . ."

"You don't mean that," she interrupted with a sniffle. "You had a kid of your own, little Otto. So what happened? You left him with your ma and pa."

"Would you rather," I asked pointedly, "that I ask them to send him back to live with us?"

"You know that isn't what I meant at all!"

And it wasn't. She'd only met the boy once, when we travelled to California after our marriage. He had coughed up his dinner all over her. Her very best gown was ruined. Worse, Cora's efforts to impress my parents with talk of her future in the music hall had made my toes curl with embarrassment. My parents were studious to avoid the faintest hint of disapproval. Their quietness in her presence, however, spoke louder than any words. I guessed that they regarded her as a deplorably blowsy replacement for the taciturn, respectable nurse who had been their first daughter-in-law.

"What, then?"

"It's just that—oh, I suppose I'm used to family life. You don't realise what it's like. You were an only child." Leaning toward me, she let the towel slip; I kept my gaze averted from the scar. This was her way, to counterattack, to compensate for her sadness by engaging in spiky retaliation. "I just wish you were making some money so I could have those singing lessons you promised me."

"It's a bad time. People aren't paying my bills."

"Hirsch is paying you in buttons. It's like we're locked up in jail."

"The tide will turn," I said, with more confidence than I felt. "Hirsch is the best optician in town, and human beings will always have eyes and ears! We just need to wait until I can build my own practice."

She reached for her nightgown. "Well, I'll tell you this, I never found waiting easy. Haven't I waited long enough for you to start making a few bucks?"

"We're not queuing in the breadline, Cora."

"But what happens in six months' time? Can't you see? People don't have the money to afford fancy doctors." She took a breath. "Maybe it's time for you to bury your pride. We'd better head back for New York."

My heart sank. One thing about Cora: she would not be denied. I was familiar with the jut of her jaw. She would brook no defiance.

In weary resignation, I said, "Munyon?"

She bowed. "Munyon."

So, it had come to this. Our hope of financial salvation lay in Munyon. Professor James Munroe Munyon, LLB, to be exact. He insisted upon the title, and acknowledgment of his degree; not, he said, out of personal pride, but because it was essential to observe the proprieties. His face was familiar to the masses because it gazed out from a thousand full-page advertisements in the popular press. Severe in his frock coat, arm aloft, pointing to Heaven as if to say *mine is the glory, the power, and the kingdom.* He possessed the answer to everything.

"Heed the Sign of the Cross!" he proclaimed—and his terrible righteousness reminded me of the preacher at Coldwater's little chapel. Except that Professor Munyon boasted an international congregation. Munyon's Homeopathic Home Remedies were renowned at home and overseas for their restorative powers, whatever the ailment. Cures for colds, catarrh, headaches—*There is Hope* was his enticing promise. That upraised index finger combining with an undertaking to treat "Piles, blind or bleeding, protruding or internal," to heal "fissures, ulcerations, cracks . . ." meant that Munyon's Pile Ointment provoked much coarse amusement. But the professor had the last laugh, as usual. Sufferers bought tubes of his Pile Ointment by the thousand.

This was not what I had trained for. I saw myself as a healer first, a man of business second. But needs must. So few people had the money in their pockets to pay for doctors' fees. Instead, they invested in self-medication; the market in patent remedies was booming. Cora was right, it would be absurd to stand aloof from a profitable occupation because of nagging moral qualms. After all, Munyon stood aloof from the retailing of lethal concoctions of opiates such as Mother's Treasure and Kopp's Baby Friend. Less scrupulous competitors had deaths on their conscience, but as Munyon pointed out, he was merely developing the ideas of Hippocrates and Hahnemann along commercial lines to satisfy a populace seduced by the lure of coupons offering money off.

Although his headquarters were in the City of Brotherly Love, the professor interviewed me at the premises he had recently opened on East 14th Street, close to Sixth Avenue. On the wall behind his head, a framed advertisement for Munyon's Paw-Paw Pills promised salvation from constipation, dyspepsia, and ailments of the digestive tract.

"I like a man with diverse entries on his *curriculum vitae*. Take my own case. D' you know, I've been a bobbin boy in a fabric mill and I've enjoyed no little success with the songs that I've composed? Crippen, I've seen the world and I know this. Understanding our fellow man and his fear of sickness, that's the key to our prosperity. Fathoming human nature is our stock-in-trade."

Encouraged by his confidential manner, I beamed. "I could not agree more."

"I'll be frank with you, Crippen. That's my way. There are those—two-a-penny newspapermen, jealous competitors—who describe me as a huckster."

"How unfair . . ."

"I believe in giving people what they hanker after," he interrupted. "Do you know what that is? It's hope. When I explain about the pills being formulated from roots and herbs I discovered long ago, in Connecticut, their eyes light up. In certain instances, that is—let's say, a metaphor. But technical details count for little. My patients have faith, you see, and that in itself guides them along the road to recovery."

"I understand, Professor."

The cure of ailments is a mysterious science. Hahnemann himself was excoriated when Prince Schwartzenbeck died while

71

in his care, but such a misfortune can happen to any physician. Munyon was smart, and when he made me an offer, I accepted without demur. The remuneration was modest, but I succeeded in persuading him to appoint Cora as cashier and to allow us to sleep in a room above the office.

Saturday midnight in our airless bedroom on East 14th. Cora's voice, soft and persuasive in my ear.

"This won't hurt."

"It hurt last time," I said.

She ran a sharp fingernail along my spine. "I tied the knots too tight, that's all. It's an easy mistake to make."

"My circulation was cut off. There could have been serious consequences, Cora. Remember, I'm a medical man, I'm familiar with these things."

"And I'm familiar with what you secretly long for," she cooed in my ear. "Never mind those silly old serious consequences. Don't be so solemn. You like what I like. Truly you do."

It was futile to argue and in truth, she was right. I loved our games with blindfolds and neckties. Mostly Cora liked to be in control, but from time to time she begged me to tie her up and then let my imagination roam. She told me that she liked to have her hair pulled at moments of intimacy, that pain and pleasure were two sides of the same coin.

Images of her with the debauched stove manufacturer kept springing into my mind: I could not help it. In bad dreams, I saw Lincoln's fat white body lying like a beached whale on top of her. Often I woke from such dreadful moments in the small hours, to find myself drenched with sweat while she slept beside me. Fighting to suppress my fear and jealousy, I used to run my hands over her flanks—flabbier now than during our court-ship—and tell myself that she was mine alone. Cora would never belong to anyone else again.

"Professor Munyon, we meet at last! What a pleasure this is to be sure!"

Cora essayed an elaborate curtsey. I was always proud to introduce her to other men. She was so fetching. For this special occasion she had taken care to look her most attractive, in a pink dress brocaded with violets. A cluster of gems glistened about her throat, falling into the wide vee of her bodice, so as to nestle in her splendid bosom. Often, I could read people's minds. They were startled that such a small, insignificant fellow had managed to capture such a prize. I used to hug myself at the thought of the reluctant admiration that meeting my new wife would prompt. But the professor was not easily impressed.

He subjected Cora to a curious scrutiny, as if surveying a rare creature through the railings of a zoological garden. "Mrs. Crippen, I am glad to meet you. Allow me to introduce my son, Duke. He is accompanying me to learn about the business."

"How charming, how delightful! And what a handsome young man, too! A chip off the old block, I dare say!"

Cheeks reddening, Duke Munyon responded with a stiff little bow and a nervous shuffling of the feet. He was much the same age as Cora, but an unsophisticated child in comparison. I felt a pin-prick of sympathy for him; the position of son and heir to a man such as the professor would be no sinecure. I asked about the Permanent Asthma Cure, but Cora found discussions about commerce wearisome.

"Of course, I ain't got much experience in office work. My father, you know—not my dear step-father, who married my mother when I was a baby orphan—he was a Polish nobleman. What that wretched government did to his estates . . ."

"Ah yes, governments are the same the world over," the professor interrupted briskly. "Now, Crippen, the manager in charge of the Philadelphia office is leaving my employ. Duke here is a fine boy, but he is too young to fill the vacancy. I need a right-hand man who is capable and experienced. Are you interested, or should I look elsewhere?"

The proposition was so unexpected that, as Cora squealed in delight, I found myself stammering: "You . . . you wish me to run the head office?"

"You will be advisory physician, with charge of the chemical laboratory, reporting directly to myself. If the prospect of a move does not trouble you . . ."

"Not at all."

"Mrs. Crippen, what do you say? Are you prepared to move to Philadelphia?"

"I can hardly stay here without my husband," she said, with a twinkle in her eye. "It is unwise for a couple to separate, in my opinion. You never know what *either* party will get up to in the absence of the other, do you?"

Professor Munyon raised his eyebrows, but simply said, "So it is agreed. Now, Crippen. Let us discuss terms."

My promotion and the transfer to Philadelphia enabled me to provide more lavishly for Cora than I had previously found possible. I engaged on her behalf the services of the most highly recommended teachers of *bel canto* in the city. Once the American public was at her feet, she would move on to Europe and make fresh conquests.

Lust for money may be the root of all evil, but the two of us had learned that poverty offers no pleasure. I had no qualms about buying trinkets for Cora and, when finances permitted, more extravagant items that complemented her looks. Before leaving New York, we patronised Tiffany's emporium in Union Square. Gemstones were rare luxuries, but I was happy to grant my wife her heart's desire. No matter what the prophet Isaiah might have said, my heart almost burst with pride at the sight of her wearing her rings and bracelets, her necklaces and tiaras.

The most special moments came in the sanctuary of our bedroom. She loved to adorn herself, and her flair for self-decoration knew no boundaries of convention. Often when she called me to her, I would discover a garnet gleaming from the dark quilt between her legs or sapphires clustered within the cleavage of her breasts. Not even Cleopatra with all her baubles could have seemed to me so splendid as Cora, my bare, bejewelled wife.

Diamonds fascinated her most of all. Soon I developed an equal passion for those most lovely stones, not merely because of the intimate settings that she found for them. In their iridescence, coupled with their ability to conceal their true nature and identity, lay the secret of their appeal. The subtle changes in their appearance struck me as hazy and mysterious, like life itself. Once I tried to say something of this to Cora, but she did not understand. The appeal to her of diamonds lay in how their brilliance complemented hers.

Our every spare cent went on purchasing fresh trophies. Yet material wealth brings its own anxieties and Cora became nervous about the possibility of our being burgled. To placate her, I bought a six-chamber revolver. My fingers twitched as I examined the weapon. Even though I had never used a firearm in anger, I trusted that the mere sight of it in my hand would terrify any nocturnal thief.

Cora stroked and caressed her gems as tenderly as any lover. More than that, she *talked* to them. I often came across her in the parlour, whispering endearments and sharing little jokes with her rings and brooches. In treating the stones as intimate acquaintances, she was far from unique among her circle of friends. It was a fashion for women to converse with their jewellery, much as a man might talk to his Labrador.

I never sneered at this strange habit. Gems were substituted for the children that she had been denied. Many times, I watched with a tolerant smile as she lifted her favourite gems to her lips and gave them each a kiss. At least, I thought with private satisfaction, when watching her fingers running delicately over the smooth shining surfaces, I need not fear that diamonds would steal her from me.

When first I learned that Lady Isabel Somerset was taking an interest in my case, my skin was all goose-flesh. A titled supporter! A philanthropic crusader with money to burn! But this saviour had feet of clay. When Ethel was at her lowest ebb, Lady Somerset wormed into her confidence. Ethel spoke frankly of the time when she had lived with me—and how was she repaid? By the offer of accommodation in her ladyship's hostel for "soiled doves"!

After that slur, mention of the woman's name is enough to make me shudder. That is why, Arthur, I welcome your advice that under no circumstances should I meet her, or lend credence to her busy-bodying. I am not a character in a freak show, a bearded woman or a two-headed midget. Nor is Ethel tainted by her devotion to me, far less a proper subject for a campaign on behalf of "fallen women." I am glad to learn that she, too, has accepted a goodly sum to explain the truth about our friendship and flight. My only regret is that she did not retain you to conduct the negotiations on her behalf.

You are wise, Arthur, to warn me of the traps that abound for the unwary in a *cause celebre*. It is an odd boast, but my case has captured the imagination of the world. Every Tom, Dick, and Harry wants to have his say, and many have spotted an opportunity to exploit my sad circumstances for their own profit. Now I see the truth in what you said when first we met—there is money in a murder case.

How lucky I am to benefit from your expert counsel. Not every lawyer has such a flair for business, let alone such influential associates. You said yourself that you prize commercial acumen ahead of mastering dull legal technicalities. It was a happy day for me when you agreed with Eddie Marr to act on my behalf. In captivity in Quebec, I received your cablegram with the profoundest gratitude. Of course, I was glad to obey your initial instruction: to keep absolute silence and not to resist extradition.

I realise that the discussions that you and Mr. Horatio Bottomley are conducting in relation to the sale of my memoirs are cloaked in the utmost confidentiality. The story is a valuable property; to my great good fortune, you are drawing upon the might of the popular press in our campaign. Let the stentorian voice of *John Bull* be heard!

I seek to repay you by striving to recapture in my memoirs each step along the way that brought me here—I promise to omit nothing. Of course, I do not pretend that in every respect my behaviour has been wise. Upon occasion I may have made an embarrassing mistake. But what a price to pay!

You have been as assiduous in identifying entrepreneurial opportunities as in preparing my case for appeal. Now, let us speak about this interesting proposal you have received that, following my release, I should establish myself in business in America.

Soon the professor offered me a fresh assignment. Munyon's Homeopathic Remedies were to establish a branch in Canada, and he wished me to superintend the operation in Toronto until such time as the business could safely be left in less experienced hands. Cora agreed that I could hardly say no to such a pressing invitation. To my surprise, however, she elected to stay on in Philadelphia.

"I'm settled here, Hawley. The singing lessons are going wonderfully well. I'd just hate to give it all up when I've waited so long to get this far."

"It will only be for a few months, my love."

"Then we shall not be parted for long, will we?" Seeing my face fall, she spoke more gently. "Of course you must go, Hawley, and I'll join you in a while. Meantime, you can spend your evenings imagining the fun and games when we celebrate your return."

Toronto I found fascinating, a handsome city of infinite commercial possibilities. I rented an airy apartment near the waterfront and within a short time I was on good terms with prominent local businessmen. The new branch of Munyon's saw a steady rise in turnover and profit. Even so, I counted the days until Cora was with me again.

To my disappointment and surprise, when we were reunited, her mood was disagreeable. Hour after hour she spent in an apparent sulk up in our bedroom, with the door firmly closed. I talked to her tenderly, asking what was the matter, but never received a satisfactory answer. A few weeks later, the professor agreed that I could hand over the reins to my assistant, and Cora and I travelled back to Philadelphia. Alas, her mood worsened and she showed little appetite for my company. Within a fortnight of our return, she told me she had taken her lessons as far as they could go in Philadelphia. For her voice to be trained sufficiently to enable her to make a career as an opera singer, there was no choice but for her to return to New York. I had to stay at head office, but the idea of living in Manhattan again had plainly been brewing in her mind. Her attachment to Philadelphia was a fast-fading memory and nothing I could say could deflect her from her plan.

"Hawley, don't take on so. You're always at the professor's beck and call. I'm ready to see what I can do for my own career." She clutched my hand. "Just imagine it—little me starring at the Metropolitan Opera House! Besides, you've spent all that money on my singing lessons. Surely you want a return on your investment? Don't you see? My very first contract will repay you everything you've spent and more!"

Later that same night, she was looking down on me, her face wreathed in smiles. For the first time in an eternity, she was paying me attention as a man, as her husband. From the moment she had beckoned me upstairs, I had made plain that her wish was my command. Now I was at her mercy, stretched out on the bed with my wrists and ankles tied to the posts. The cords bit into my flesh but the pain was not severe enough to be other than exquisite. Not for one moment did I feel humiliated by the extent of my subjugation. Rather, I relished being at her disposal. I relished it more than I can properly describe.

She was rocking up and down in a relentless rhythm. The two of us were a perfect match. She loved to be in charge of me just as much as I yearned to be possessed by her. The smell of the sweat that glistened on her brow, the movement of her blue-veined breasts against my chest when she bent toward me, the moistness of her tongue when my lips felt its tantalising touch. How blissful to know that such a woman belonged to me. My throat was parched with excitement as well as a secret fear that she might do something to me that we had not discussed before, something that might hurt even more than I could bear.

"Darling," she panted. "You will let me go to New York, won't you?"

"That is what you want?"

She lowered the head and I strained so as to lift mine to meet her. The thick dark curls brushed against my cheeks. I closed my eyes and felt her teeth grazing my ear.

"Anything," I whispered. "Anything."

As soon as my commitments allowed, we met in Brooklyn, at her stepfather's home.

"Hawley, there's something I want to tell you," she said as soon as we were on our own in the familiar little attic room.

I took her hand in mine. "What is it, my sweet? You have missed me, haven't you?"

"Of course," she said quickly. "Now, Hawley, pin back your ears and listen to my news. I've come to my senses and realised the mistake I've made. I was wrong about opera. It's not the right place for a singer like me to start. Vaudeville, that's the thing. As a vaudevillian, that's how I'm gonna make my name."

I swear that my mouth must have dropped open. *"Vaudeville?"* I repeated in bewilderment. "Cora, what are you saying?"

"Gee, don't take on so! Yes, vaudeville, I said. You know it's all the rage. My teacher was grumbling at me as usual and it came to me like a flash of light. You're always saying what a lively personality I've got . . ."

"That's true," I said, "but I never meant . . ."

"You're not the only one who believes my talents have been wasted. It's a matter of making the most of what I've got. Since I arrived here, I've been talking to people in the know. I've made a lot of good friends. Influential types who can help me reach the heights."

"And they've advised you to try your hand at vaudeville?" I could not keep the hurt and shock out of my voice. "What sorts of friends are these, Cora? How can you possibly believe they have your best interests at heart?"

She pursed her lips. "Now, Hawley, you ain't been here more than five minutes and already you're spoiling for a fight."

"Cora, I am not! It's just that . . ."

"Listen up, will you? Opera's fine, but these days you need to cater to the masses. I've met this scout. He's real smart, and he tells me sketches are the best way to showcase my talent."

"*Sketches?* Are you seriously contemplating performance in the music hall when I have incurred such heavy expenditure on your operatic training?"

Her face hardened. The contours of her cheeks became flat instead of round; those full, red lips were suddenly tight.

"Don't look down your nose at vaudeville, Hawley. Not you, of all people—a huckster's salesman."

"May I remind you that Professor Munyon . . ."

" '*Professor,*' " she scoffed. "Oh, yeah? He's no more a professor than that wet fish of a son of his is a duke."

"Professor Munyon," I repeated, with as much quiet dignity as I could muster, "pays my salary. The same salary, may I remind you, that pays for your board and lodging and all your finery."

"Don't quarrel with me, Hawley Crippen, or it'll be the worst for you!" she shouted. "And there was I, thinking you were still in love with me. What a fool I've been!"

She threw herself down on the bed and began to weep. The sight of her crying always made my legs turn to mashed potato. Soon I could bear no more. Softly, I approached her, and laid my hand upon her bare arm. She recoiled, as if from a leper's touch.

"Darling Cora, we must talk about this. I'm sure we can work something out. Don't take on so after we've only been together again for a few minutes. You haven't even seen the present I bought you."

By and by, the sobs subsided. She hauled herself up, eyes puffy, face red and blotchy with distress.

"What present?" she asked in a muffled voice.

I opened my case and handed her the diadem that I had taken such pains to wrap in pretty paper. The cost had swallowed three months' savings. When she ripped the wrappings off, she gave a squeak of delight.

"It's lovely!"

I presented my cheek and her wet lips graced it with a kiss. "My pleasure," I said.

"Thanks, Hawley. I guess you didn't realise how much the stage means to me."

Her hand strayed on to my knee and within a minute I was undressing her. Tearing off her undergarments, drinking in the familiar heady fragrance. As she pulled me down on to her, she whispered in my ear.

"So you don't mind about the vaudeville?"

"Ten thousand dollars per annum," Munyon said.

"Ten thousand *per annum?*" I repeated foolishly.

"I am not expecting a refusal," my employer said, forthright as a feudal lord.

"England is a fine country," I mused. "It will be good to go back."

Suddenly, a shameful image sprang into my head. A forbidden but enticing shape, looming out from the fog. Hastily, I banished the memory.

"Excellent, Doctor. I propose that you remain in England for the long term. The market is second only to that in the United States. I need a permanent representative there whom I can trust implicitly."

"You need look no further, sir."

"Very well, then, it is settled. Perhaps you would be ready to sail at the beginning of April?"

No sooner had I assented than the question leapt to my lips: *What about Cora?* I kept my counsel. I had no desire to allow the professor to become aware of my personal anxieties.

In truth, I did not much care for the company Cora had been keeping. Fly-by-night fellows whose taste for alcohol was matched only by their lack of taste in clothes. Why she relished their boastfulness and raucous laughter defeated me. When I asked, she simply said that they were "fun."

To my good fortune, the secret fears I had nurtured proved unjustified. Cora shared my pleasure in the promotion—and in the scale of my remuneration.

"Ten thousand dollars," she said dreamily. "What is that in pounds sterling?"

"As I explained, the transfer is permanent. I shall be the face of Munyon's in Great Britain. No, more than that—in the Old World. I shall send for you at the earliest opportunity."

"Once July is over," she said. "I do so like the summer in New York, Hawley."

An acceptable compromise. Although I was sorry that she had not wanted to join me even earlier, a short separation was a small price to pay when a new and affluent life together was at last within our reach.

★ ★ ★ ★ ★

Munyon's first European office was located in Shaftesbury Avenue, a prestigious situation opposite the Palace Theatre. The resources that the Professor had made available allowed me to furnish the rooms to the highest standard. I even purchased a glass case that contained a stuffed parrot. When it came to selecting a colour scheme, I seized the opportunity of a small gesture of independence, and indulged my own taste. So, green drapes, green carpets your feet sank into, green upholstery on the armchairs; it seems more like a manor house than business premises. Never mind that green was Cora's hoodoo colour; she would have ample opportunity to surround herself with pink when at last we were together.

I dined from time to time at Blanchard's on Beak Street or the Holborn Restaurant, and I took in shows from burlesques to operettas. How far I had risen in the world since those penurious days as a student at Bedlam! I was able to increase the allowance that I sent to my parents for the care of my son. Otto was growing into a fine lad, they told me, and he and I wrote fortnightly to each other. Otherwise, I devoted my funds to the acquisition of more precious stones, for Cora's delight as well as my own, and continued my researches into the diamond cutter's craft.

I resided at Queen's Road in St. John's Wood. Elegant women carrying parasols to shade their fair complexions from the sun, little boys in sailor suits and pinafored girls walking sedately with their nursemaids all thronged the streets on weekends. In the evenings, when I liked to take the air, the area was quiet and, frankly, dull. As the weeks passed, my perambulations lengthened to take in districts that displayed the capital's rich variety. On fine July days, I ventured south of the river, where there came wafting through the streets the rich aromas of food and drink that the peddlers offered for sale: meat pies and eels, strawberry sherbets and peppermint water. I hummed to the tunes of the hurdy-gurdy players, nodded at the rag-and-bone men, and exchanged banter with the pretty lasses who sold scarlet geraniums. Sometimes I would buy the girls' wares and be rewarded by an artful wink or the blowing of a kiss.

Once or twice, I was tempted to extend our acquaintance, but I soon found a cure for any stray thoughts of impropriety brought on by abstinence and my unrequited longing for Cora. I recalled how I had followed the advice of my fellow student and purchased from a chemist in Lambeth half a dozen grains of hyoscine. A minute dose would soon do the trick; to take in excess of a quarter of a grain was to risk one's life.

I devoted long hours to establishing the new business, but when at last I went home at night, my heart still ached for my absent wife. Hyoscine could not compensate me for the lack of her company, and I prayed that she was missing me in equal measure. I counted the days until the end of August, when we would be as one again and scoured around for a suitable place for us to live together, settling upon a flat at South Crescent, off Tottenham Court Road.

I could not help wondering what Cora was up to in New York. The undesirable young fellows she mixed with were not to be trusted. I told myself that I should rely upon her fidelity and common sense. No woman who gave herself as completely Cora gave herself to me could fail to be besotted. In moments of melancholy solitude, I consoled myself by recalling the giddy heights of passion we had touched together.

"What do you think?" Cora demanded, on the night of her arrival in England.

I laid the manuscript to one side. Prudence dictated that I should avoid her gaze. "Very promising, my dear."

"Is that all?"

I scratched around for the right words and remembered a phrase from a newspaper review. Weighing my words with the care of a judge, I said, "You write with a pleasing lightness of touch."

She preened. "Why, thank you, Hawley. Anything else?"

"Um . . . I look forward to reading the final version the moment that you've completed it."

A scowl disfigured her pretty face. "*That* is the final version."

I cursed myself for saying too much. Hurriedly, I sought to retrieve lost ground. "Oh well, yes. I see it now. Very good, very good."

She thrust out her lower lip. "You're only saying that. You don't really care for my writing."

I went over and knelt by her side. "My dear, I worship you and everything you do. You of all people should know that. I can't describe how much I've missed you since I arrived in England. These . . ."

"You needn't soft soap me," she interrupted. "I'm going to bed!"

Within hours of our first kiss of greeting, I had become aware of a change in her. Since our first encounter in Jeffery's waiting room, she had never lacked confidence, but I had always been sure that, in her way, she needed me as much as I needed her. Now, however, her manner seemed casual, almost offhand. It was as if she wanted my opinion of her manuscript not so much because I was her husband, but rather because of my ability to spot a good business proposition.

I watched in dismay as she flounced out of the room. Cora was so easily dissatisfied. I put it down to having to leave her roots in New York, although she had enjoyed the voyage across the Atlantic. Men of good position travelling on the boat had made a fuss of her, she said. I experienced a glow of pride, rather than jealousy. How those wealthy businessmen must have envied the doctor to whom their vivacious shipboard companion was returning.

I picked up her manuscript again. *The Unknown Quantity* bore on the title page the name of Belle Elmore, a pseudonym my wife had coined. The work purported to be a one-act operetta. Cora's plan was to take the West End by storm. To help her to secure top billing, she had decided to write her own material. "That way," she explained, "I'm not beholden to anyone else." The theory struck me as sound, although she had never before shown an interest in writing for the theatre.

I undressed slowly, wondering how to make amends when I joined her in bed. Despite the season, she might be suffering from the after-effects of a chill. The health benefits of sea air are commonly overestimated. I suggested that she might like to take a tonic, but her response was sharp and sarcastic.

"No, thanks. Next thing I know, you'll be prescribing some of Munyon's sugar pills."

I said I had been thinking about how she could make best use of her manuscript. She had hidden under the covers, and at first she made no response. This was, however, a ploy that had become familiar, and I warmed to my theme.

"You're wise to insist on retaining control of the text. One cannot afford to cede the rights to a valuable property. The question is whether you would gain from having an experienced local writer cast an eye over it. The English are by nature suspicious of anything foreign. If your sketch enjoys the benefit of editorial assistance . . ."

"It ain't a sketch," she muttered.

"Operetta," I corrected myself. "Yes, with a little work on—on *Anglicising* the text, perhaps extending it, why, there's every chance that in no time at all you'll be filling the Empire in Leicester Square."

A movement under the bedclothes. Her tousled head appeared. "The Empire?"

How well I knew my wife, her little foibles, and how to win her round. "You know of the Empire?"

She sat up in bed. "Do I know the Empire? What do you think I've been doing since I arrived here but working out the best places to perform?"

"Well, then." I feasted greedily on the sight of her. The nightdress was new. She must have bought it following my departure from New York, no doubt as a treat for me upon our reunion. "Shall we find a writer who might be willing to assist?"

"Good idea." Her tone was grudging. "The English are funny. You never quite know what's going on inside their heads."

I smiled and moved toward the bed. When I put my arm around her shoulder, she wriggled a little and then eased the nightdress up and over her head. My wife could never be mistaken for an Englishwoman, I thought, as I devoted myself to her. It was not simply a matter of accent or her exotic taste in clothes. I could always tell what was going on inside her head.

Locked inside a cold condemned cell, I encounter a delicious paradox: so many doors are opening up before me. Lecturing, touring, writing for the newspapers. Arthur, I am lost in admiration for the industry with which you seek to carve out business opportunities for me. Even though the prospect of any dividend from the Charing Cross Bank appears remote, there is every chance that I could quickly recoup my losses. But first I must regain my freedom.

Ah, freedom. Freedom to undertake mundane daily tasks as well as to dream up grand schemes. Freedom to walk the glistening pavements on a rainy day, to scythe the lawn at home, to cut a begonia to display in a vase. How I yearn to stroll down the corridor at Albion House again, and nod in greeting to Rylance, Long, and the office girls.

So, the appeal is scheduled for Thursday? Let us hope that justice will this time be done!

Music Hall Programme—front page

VIO & MOTZKI'S

AMERICAN

Bright Lights Company
From the Principal American Theatres

FUN, MUSIC & VARIETY

Acting Manager .... H.H. CRIPPEN

"Mrs. Harrison?" I extended my hand. "Welcome to my offices and may I say what a pleasure it is to meet you at last."

"Dr. Crippen, I am charmed to make your acquaintance." Adeline Harrison was a noted writer of song lyrics and sketches. I wanted her to look over Cora's work with a view to editing it into a shape that a London audience might appreciate. With rosy, dimpled cheeks, expansive figure, and rustic vowels, she might have passed for a farmer's wife, had she not been so expensively attired, in a satin fabric dress of Venetian red with cream shoulders. "Well, I have seldom seen professional surroundings of comparable luxury!"

91

"Munyon's Homeopathic Remedies is an international concern. My principal insists on nothing but the best." I never missed a chance to advertise. People of influence such as Adeline Harrison were the perfect customers for our products. "Thank you for coming here to speak to my wife. I trust that your conversation has been fruitful?"

I cast an eye toward Cora, hoping that my talkativeness concealed the anxiety that I felt. She was wearing her showiest dress, but in the company of Adeline Harrison, it seemed positively vulgar. Much as I loved her, no one could have mistaken Cora for an English lady. Her smile was uncharacteristically brittle, and I deduced that Mrs. Harrison had failed to rhapsodise over the operetta.

"The two of us had a very frank chat, darling." Cora's voice quavered with unusual diffidence. "Mrs. Harrison has been most encouraging. She's going to help me work on the sketch."

Better news than I had feared. "Capital! I'm sure you won't regret it, Mrs. Harrison."

"And I am equally confident," she returned. "The moment I set eyes on your wife, Dr. Crippen, I was quite bowled over. Such *joie de vivre*, such personality! Twinkling eyes and a dazzling smile, all set off by flattering clothes and exquisite jewellery! Someone so delightful is exactly what the English music hall has been waiting for."

"Adeline here tells me that American artistes are all the rage now in London," Cora said, brightening at the generosity of her new friend's words.

"Absolutely, my dear. As for the sketch itself, Doctor, I told your wife bluntly it is not simply a question of adding length. No, there must be plot. Audiences today demand form and structure. Never mind. Nothing is impossible!"

So she was taken with Cora after all! Happily, I exclaimed,

"The Empire awaits!"

The music hall at Marylebone was scarcely the Empire, but the audiences were said to be more discerning, less rowdy and drunken, than those at many palaces of variety. Rotten vegetables were seldom thrown—not, Adeline Harrison hastened to reassure us, that there was any danger of such a reaction to Cora. Even Marie Lloyd began her career at The Grecian, and was not paid a penny for her performance. Adeline knew the Queen of Music Hall and was sure that Marie and Cora would hit it off. In her opinion, they were twin souls.

For days leading up to Cora's stage debut, we had brimmed with excitement. The manager at the Marylebone had offered a contract of one week's duration only, although he hinted at an extension if takings were good. My investment in Cora's career was still heavily in the red, although I trusted that we would soon reap the dividends. For her part, Cora manifested a true artistic temperament with little outbursts of nervous temper. Her recurrent complaint concerned the billing I had chosen, "Cora Motzki"—I had coined the second name as a neat contraction of Mackamotzi—struck me as a tempting blend of glamour and exoticism, but she favoured "Belle Elmore." I insisted that it was a mistake to put her faith in a stage name so commonplace.

Cora's male counterpart was an Italian—at least, he was supposed to be Italian, although I nurtured secret doubts—by the name of Sandro Vio. He was tall and handsome and had as much personality as a wooden leg. With Adeline's help, Cora had contrived a dramatic finale to the playlet. As she reached for the highest note, she would fling at her lover's feet a sheaf of banknotes. In the quest for verisimilitude, she had insisted that counterfeit money would not suffice.

"Real cash," she said. "It's a must, Hawley. Please don't be mean. Gee, can't you imagine their faces as they see all that money floating in the air? It will knock 'em dead."

Watching from my draughty vantage point behind the back benches, I wondered if the first night audience was already deceased. The silence subsequent to the polite applause at the raising of the curtain made me shiver on my wife's behalf. Alone on the harshly lit stage, she cut a small and oddly nervous figure in her embroidered gypsy gown. I was mortified to realise that glimpses of her bosom occupied the clerks and shopmen in the crowd more than her songs. Poor Cora! The harder she strained for the upper register, the more her voice trembled. I had to suppress the urge to run up to the stage and beg her to keep calm.

The building smelled of stale cigars and orange peel. I prayed for the end to come so that we could flee and never return. As the performance reached its climax, I could hear bored conversation all around me. Cora's plump cheeks were pink, although whether with exertion or embarrassment I could not tell. She was decked out in her extravagant new pink frock, with rings gleaming from her fingers and a diamond pendant decorating her bosom. At long last she had fulfilled her ambition, only to meet with a fate worse than vegetable-throwing—indifference.

The final scene could not come quickly enough. Amidst audible dissatisfaction, Cora grasped the wad of money in her hand. As she strove for high C, she hurled the sheaf of five-pound notes into the air. As though by magic, the susurration of discontent was stilled.

Someone bellowed in the darkness. "They look real!"

Pandemonium broke out. As the banknotes fluttered before landing, people cheered and hooted and stood on the benches to get a better view of where the windfalls might land. I caught a glimpse of a couple of men rushing forward toward the stage. I raced to the front, but found my path blocked by spectators scrabbling like common thieves to collect the banknotes from the ground. If anyone was to be knocked dead tonight, it would be me if I was pushed over and trampled by people fleeing with their ill-gotten gains.

I picked up as many notes as I could and asked a couple of fellows who had seized trophies to surrender them. "I am Miss Motzki's husband," I insisted. "The money is mine."

"And I'm the Prince of Wales," one of the men retorted, disappearing into the gloom.

I glanced up at the stage. Cora and Sandro Vio were waiting to take the applause. Her eyes and mouth were crushed; even the tenor's face betrayed a flicker of embarrassment. When Cora caught my eye, I waved at her, meaning that she should get off the stage. I did not wish her to face further public misery, but the hard look in her eyes as the curtain belatedly began its descent suggested that she had misinterpreted my gesture and thought that I felt humiliated by her, rather than on her behalf.

"Guess what?" Cora demanded one night. "I've been offered another engagement. Middle of the bill!"

"Marvellous," I cried, squeezing her hand. "Not the Holborn again?"

Cora shook her head. "The Grand in Clapham. Not bad, eh?"

"Congratulations, my dear. Has the fee been negotiated?"

"It's always money with you." She wrinkled her nose, as if in distaste at the smell of capitalism. "Well, it ain't a fortune, that's for sure. But what can you expect? I'm just glad I'm back on my feet. There's many an artiste would have been pole-axed by what happened at Marylebone."

"That was your first time," I said soothingly. "Plenty of water under the bridge since then."

"Booed off the stage the second night!" she said, with a tremble in her voice. "The indignity of it! I wasn't so bad!"

"Of course you weren't," I agreed, although that dreadful evening has showed the management's wisdom in covering the orchestra pit with netting to avoid the musicians being struck by fruit hurled by the rabble: those who frequented the Marylebone were less sophisticated than Adeline had claimed. "I told you, it is uncommon for an entertainer to have her very first engagement extended. You mustn't reproach yourself."

"Oh, I don't, don't worry!" Cora gave me a dark look. "I know who to reproach, all right."

"My dear," I protested. "Surely you don't still hold it against me that I wanted you to keep your Christian name?"

"You don't understand." She uttered a deep sigh. "Though why should you? After all, you're a pill salesman, not an artiste."

"Cora!" Her sting inflicted more pain than that of any wasp, all the more so when she was not even trying to hurt.

She cradled her head in her hands, heedless of my dismay. "Well, I suppose I can't expect you to understand or care what happens to little old me."

The best course with Cora was always to turn the other cheek. Even so, I could not permit such sheer unfairness to pass.

"My darling, that is hardly just. Think of the gowns I have paid for. Those photographs by that mountebank Hana scarcely came cheap. I have acted as your business manager. I have sought to provide everything that you have asked for. Even the . . ."

"I know, I know," she said wearily. "You do your utmost for me. That's what you always claim. Adeline says you're a likeable cove, and I don't tell her anything different. I'm a loyal wife, even when everything I care for is reduced to pounds, shillings, and pence. Even when your selfishness torments me beyond endurance."

"Selfishness?" I felt the colour rising in my cheeks. "Beyond endurance?"

She shrugged, a gesture that was acquiring the status of a habit. "You heard what I said. Why must you always repeat everything, like some sort of echo?"

I took a step toward her. "Shall I tell you about being tormented beyond endurance, Cora? Must I explain the bitterness that a man feels when his wife encourages gentlemen to call upon her in the middle of the day, when she entertains them as though she were a single woman?"

"What are you saying?" she jeered. "You're jealous, aren't you? That's what it is."

"I have never been jealous, Cora," I retorted. "It is simply a matter of propriety. You seem to forget you are married."

"And what do you think I got up to at South Crescent when you were out at work?" she demanded. "What are you accusing me of? Just because I made friends with one or two people I met on the voyage over here! I gave up everything I had in the States, left my ma and pa, my wonderful sisters. Left them all— and for what? For you!"

Later that night, when we were in bed together, I tried wrapping my arms around her, but she shrugged off my attentions. Of course, I did not attempt to insist upon my conjugal rights. I told myself that I wanted her to give herself willingly or not all.

"How long?" she demanded.

"The professor cannot say. At least three months, perhaps longer."

"And when the Philadelphia branch is ship-shape again, what then?"

"He wishes me to return to Shaftesbury Avenue."

She brightened instantly. "That's all fine and dandy, then. You go back to the States till you've sorted things out and I'll stay here."

"Very well, my dear."

I watched her poring over a script that Adeline Harrison had edited. Head bowed, lips moving, concentration absolute. Surely it would be safe to leave her in England for a while? Perhaps once I was able to settle permanently, we would take up the threads of our earliest days together. She was *my* wife. She loved *me*. No one else.

One of Professor Munyon's gifts was a mastery of disdain. As he studied the theatre handbill, his eyebrows arched and his mouth tightened. He might have been Isaiah, perusing a blasphemy.

"*Vio and Motzki's Bright Lights Company, Fresh from its Broadway Triumph.*" His voice was clear yet quiet, betraying the merest hint of incredulity. "Well, Crippen, you have been busy. I see you are named as the manager of this—ahem—unlikely theatrical enterprise."

As he put the handbill down on his lap, anger welled up inside me. "May I ask, Professor, from where you obtained the handbill?"

He shrugged. "I had heard rumours that your wife was pursuing her ambitions in vaudeville. Naturally, I made one or two enquiries through my connections in England. We must be particular about the company we keep, Crippen. I am sure you understand that. Munyon's success is dependent upon its maintaining its good name."

"I hardly think that my wife's career on the stage is apt to damage that good name," I said stiffly.

"If I may say so, Crippen, that is not a view likely to be shared by the world at large." He leaned back in his chair. "Do I have your assurance that there will be no repetition of this kind of unsavoury publicity?"

"No, sir, you do not!"

I surprised myself by jumping to my feet. Standing over my employer, I did something that otherwise I would never have dared. I wagged a finger and embarked upon a lecture.

"My wife's stage career is her own affair, sir. As for myself, I am proud to support her. She adds lustre to any performance in which she participates. She . . ."

"Crippen, Crippen, Crippen." Munyon shook his head. "Please do not fight a battle that has never been joined. I am anxious to preserve the integrity of my business, that is all. May I have your word as a gentleman that you will cease to lend your name to such tawdry entertainments?"

I took a deep breath. Never in my long acquaintance with my employer had I been so bold as to contradict him, but I was not a serf without a mind or life of my own.

"I am sorry, Professor. My first obligation is to the woman I married, to stand by her side come what may."

Munyon thrust out his jaw. "Crippen, you are not irreplaceable. I cannot allow my employees to behave in a manner that is inconsistent with the highest standards of decorum. Vaudeville is no career for the wife of a professional man. Or for any respectable woman. Have a care, Crippen. You cannot afford to become embroiled in scandal. Perish the thought that your wife might be mistaken for Miss Marie Lloyd."

He uttered the name as though it were a profanity, yet Adeline Harrison had promised to introduce us to the Queen of the Music Halls, once she returned from her latest overseas tour. If her repartee was thought saucy, was that not as much the responsibility of those who chose to interpret it in a particular fashion? I stood up very straight.

"There is nothing indecorous about my wife's theatrical

performances, Professor. You talk about the company's reputation, but I am even more concerned about hers. I fear I cannot remain in the service of someone who casts doubt upon her integrity. In these circumstances, sir, I must tender my resignation with immediate effect."

"How dare he!"

"Of course, I made my position crystal clear," I said on my first evening back in England. "The salary was not in issue. My only concern was your good name."

"He always was a charlatan," Cora muttered.

We were in the bedroom and she was unlacing her corset. During the weeks apart, I had yearned for this moment, but her uncertain mood troubled me. She was brooding over Munyon's distaste for her career on the stage, but she seemed not to recognise the scale of the sacrifice that I had made on her behalf.

"I told him he must keep his ten thousand dollars a year." I wanted to touch her, but deemed it prudent to await the right moment. "Your reputation was beyond price."

"That was nice of you, dear." It was the closest to thanks that she had offered.

I ventured to lay my arm upon her bare shoulder, gathering a fold of flesh between finger and thumb. "I have missed you so much, my darling."

"And I have missed you," she replied.

I tightened my grip. Was it my imagination, or did her words lack the fervour that I had fondly anticipated?

"Have you really?" I asked, in my most persuasive tone.

"Uh-huh."

She closed her eyes and I told myself that I could guess the thoughts that were swirling in her mind. I allowed my hand to wander to her bosom and at once her body stiffened. For a few seconds I myself froze, until she expelled a breath and, without a word, lay back upon the bed. Thank God, I thought. I might have lost my employment, but I still possessed Cora.

Hard though I strive to be cheerful, at times my vertebrae tighten with despair. What if the appeal were to fail? For all your breezy optimism, Arthur, I recognise that we cannot exclude the possibility. A phrase returns to me from a volume of *The Newgate Calendar* that I devoured long ago. A story of an unhappy murderer—I forget his name—who prayed with the ordinary before making his way to the fatal platform, a story of how *"the executioner then proceeded to his office, and in a moment, terminated the fellow's mortal existence."*

He *proceeded to his office.* So quick, so final. But it is not always quick, not even today after so many advances in the technology of execution. I am too well read in hanging lore for my own peace of mind. When Calcraft was Lord of the Gallows, he often choked his murderous clients by mistake. Slow strangulation is the most horrid of deaths. I might almost say: "Thank God for the Long Drop." But I tremble to think of what the Long Drop means.

R v Crippen: evidence for the prosecution, first day, 18 October 1910. Testimony of Bruce Miller.

"I did not exactly love her; I thought a great deal of her as far as friendship was concerned. She was a married lady, and we will let it end at that. It was a platonic friendship."

Bruce Miller, Bruce Miller, Bruce Miller.

Whenever I used to wake in the small hours, the words echoed in my brain like the foulest oath from Hell. *Bruce Miller.* Now I no longer fear the name, feeling only a cold contempt for what it represents. It is a name for spitting out, like a mouthful of rotten fruit. I never even met the man, did not so much as spy him through a misted window or a crowded room, yet for years he haunted my life. Over time, he ceased to be a creature of God's earth, a mortal made of flesh and blood. Rather, he became a poltergeist, a malign spirit, a bringer of discord and dread imaginings.

In our failure to cross paths, far less swords, one might detect an irony. During those torrid early days of our nonacquaintance, that we were never in precisely the same place at precisely the same moment may have been due to sheer chance. Later, both of us had reasons not to seek an encounter, eyeball to chilly eyeball.

His face was sickeningly familiar to me, from the brass-framed photograph standing proud upon the piano, as well as from those she kept in our parlour. The very first time I saw him in the flesh was in the bear pit of the Central Criminal Court. I stood up straight in the dock as he was called, watched him stride toward the witness box. I had feared my bowels might turn to water at the sight of my old adversary, but—thank God!—I held firm and I flatter myself that no trace of my tormented emotions disfigured my features. Neither then nor at any point during his testimony did he cast a glance in my direction. Even as he squirmed under Mr. Tobin's pitiless cross-examination, he turned his face to the judge, to the jury, to the hyenas in the gallery, but never once to the dock.

With prosperity, his jowls had become flabbier than in the photograph. I cannot deny the pleasure with which I spotted that his stomach had begun to spread. Yet an expensive Chicago tailor had lavished care upon the cut of his suit, and only the keenest observer would spot that here was a man who would soon be past his prime. At one time he had been a prize-fighter. Even before his shadow darkened my life, I had held no brief for pugilism. Violence remains abhorrent to me.

His face had caught the sun. I scanned his features in the hope of observing signs of damage that he might have concealed from the studio photographer's camera, and felt a punch of disappointment when I saw not so much as a blemish on his cheeks, far less any hint of a cauliflower ear. Miller was, I surmised, too vain to allow his rugged looks to be compromised by fighting anyone who might do him real harm. A coward whose victories came at the expense of those weaker than himself.

Within weeks of my return from Philadelphia, Cora had developed a tedious habit of dropping his name into conversation, no doubt, to irk me when we quarrelled. I was so foolish as to play her game by failing to conceal my anxiety about what he might mean to her.

I chanced upon her in the front room one evening. She was curled up in her favourite armchair, studying a letter as closely as if it were a personal message from the King. On the occasional table by her side was an envelope with her name emblazoned upon it in a bold, florid script. The oblong postage stamp bore a design unfamiliar to me, together with the legend *Republique Francaise.*

"You have received correspondence from France?" I asked. "I was not aware you knew anyone there."

With a tinkling laugh, she folded the letter. "This is from Bruce. He is in Paris, you know, concluding important business with regard to the Exposition."

"Bruce?"

"Mr. Miller, the businessman. I told you, he came to say hello when my teacher invited me for dinner after my singing lesson at Torrington Square. Don't you ever listen when I tell you about my friends?"

In truth, I often lost track. Cora enjoyed a busy social life in London and invariably peppered her chit-chat with anecdotes about people whom I had never met. According to her, they were always such fun and so gifted. If ever I got to meet them, my impressions were less charitable.

"Mmmmm."

"Well, Bruce's apartment was next door and when he looked in that evening, of course, we were introduced. We got on famously—two Americans far from home, you know. Bruce was on his way to Paris. He was in partnership with a man who was furnishing the money for the attractions. Back in Chicago he won plenty of prize fights, but he's sensitive too, a very skilled musician. He can play all sorts of instruments. That's how he comes to be so friendly with a music teacher."

Another paragon. How much I would have preferred her to devote time spent in the company of her music teacher to improving her own skills rather than to providing a willing audience for the boasts of his male neighbours. Throughout my time in Philadelphia, I had wired money to Cora at fortnightly intervals, but the expensive—and evidently intensive, to judge from the invoices—tuition she had received did not seem to have had any conspicuous benefit.

"So Miller is still in Paris?"

"For a month or so he came back to London, but there was more for him to do in France. The last time I saw him, he said he was thinking of trying his hand at show business. Getting up an automatic orchestra, that's his idea. He says they are all the rage these days."

"I thought you only met him the once, at Torrington Square."

She had the letter in her hands, as if it were a talisman to ward off evil. "He called upon me when he returned. Of course, while you were away I was so lonely."

"You have plenty of friends," I said sharply. "You're saying that this Miller has been here? In this house?"

She gave me an implacable smile, as if daring me to find fault with her behaviour. "Why yes, Hawley, that is what I am saying. I'm fortunate to count Bruce as a good friend. When we met, he promised to keep in touch and he's a man of his word."

Gazing into her dark, determined eyes, I realised that I must make a choice: object to her behaviour and seek to forbid any repetition, or turn the other cheek. A precedent had been set. My mistake was to raise no specific objection to Cora's inviting men whom she had met onboard ship to the house following her arrival in England. Now it was too late to apply a different rule.

"I see, I see. Well, it is nice that you have met someone so interesting."

Her forefinger caressed the letter from the retired pugilist. "That's right, dearest. I just knew you'd understand."

For a wild moment, I contemplated asking her if I could see the letter, but it was an absurd notion and I dismissed it instantly. If she refused, I could not insist without provoking a tirade of abuse. No doubt what Miller had written was entirely innocuous. It should, I said to myself, be perfectly possible to turn this episode to my advantage.

"Of course, my darling. No one understands what you like better than I. And this evening I have in mind a special treat for you."

Her eyes opened wide, as if it were Christmas and she were seven years old. "You have?"

"Only this afternoon I called in at a shop off Regent Street and made a purchase. A strip of black silk, delicate to touch, yet quite opaque. Perfect, I thought, to make a blindfold."

She laughed out loud and clapped her hands. "Show me! Show me!"

Success! I had negotiated a passage through tricky waters and now I had nearly reached my destination. Soon all thoughts of this Bruce Miller would be driven from her mind. Quickly, I led her up to the bedroom so that I could submit to her bidding before she had any reason to change her mind.

Pacing around my tiny cabin on the voyage back to England, I determined to teach the professor a lesson in commerce. I had learned a good deal about the advertising and sale of cures by post. My revenge for his scorn of Cora would be to take a position with a direct competitor of Munyon's Homeopathic Remedies. Then the professor would see what Hawley Harvey Crippen, M.D., could do!

Directly upon my return, I entered into correspondence with

the principal of the Sovereign Remedy Company. He had taken premises in Newman Street and was seeking to challenge Munyon's pre-eminence. Without wishing to be immodest, I should say that I made an excellent fist of the interview: the post of manager was offered to me that very afternoon. Sadly, the firm was never adequately capitalised. Within eight months, Sovereign failed.

I saw the writing on the wall in the weeks preceding the final collapse, and thus was able to plan ahead. The attraction of making money for others had palled: why not indulge in a little private enterprise on my own behalf? Crippens were not natural servants, I told myself, remembering how my grandfather had laboured to establish the store in Coldwater. We were better suited to taking charge of affairs. Cora gave me every encouragement; the prospect of the status and resources accompanying marriage to a well-to-do man of business entranced her. Having formulated a recipe for a nerve tonic, which, at my wife's charming suggestion, I named Amorette, I was ready to take the plunge.

At this point I made a mistake. During my time at Munyon's, I had become friendly with a man called Eddie Marr. He was a fellow countryman who dabbled in a variety of enterprises, including the sale of patent medicines. Marr was an affable, quick-witted fellow, and although most of his business ventures seemed not to last long, he made a penny or two from them. In several cases, I gathered that the profits had come at the expense of unsatisfied creditors, and he was rather fonder of an alias— Professor Keith-Harvey or Elmer Shirley were contrasting favourites—than most conventional entrepreneurs. At Marr's suggestion, the two of us had engaged in a number of small transactions, which I needed to keep separate from my work for Munyon's. To guarantee privacy, I needed to coin a name under which I might conduct these dealings. I called myself Franckel, a name combining a hint of candour with a certain exoticism. For a first name, I chose Peter.

Marr suggested that we go into partnership. He would provide the financial backing and I the technical expertise. I demurred, explaining that I had long nourished a burning ambition to make a go of a business unaided. He took my rejection in good part, but warned me humorously that I would be sorry.

My conviction that tenacity, organisational flair, and a dash of imagination would prove unbeatable was soon tested. I encountered the age-old problem that has caused so many promising companies to sink within months of flotation. It takes time for a new brand to establish itself in the market, and time is a luxury that only money can buy. Alas, I lacked deep pockets. Not only had I forfeited the handsome salary that Munyon's paid, I had no savings to fall back upon. Cora and I always lived up to our income, thanks to the cost of stage outfits, as well as hospitality for her innumerable friends and the endless singing lessons.

Faced with a crisis of finance, I instituted a regime of strict domestic economies. The days of investing in diamonds were gone, and more than once I found it necessary to stifle my pride and pawn items of my wife's jewellery in order to meet a pressing expense. When I bought a "gem" for Cora's birthday present that year, it was made of paste. She started to make her own dresses, and we moved from Guildford Street to less expensive accommodation near the museum. When these savings did not suffice, I devised another commercial sideline, engaging local women to paint miniatures, which Cora, making the most of her charm and repartee, could sell from our home.

The sign I put up outside our door bore the name she had coveted since her arrival in England. In all conscience, I was bound to admit that "Cora Motzki" was no draw. Her persistence wore down my reservations and I allowed myself to be persuaded that the time had come for her to adopt her favoured sobriquet.

"Miss Belle Elmore," she said delightedly, rolling the words off her tongue. "Things will start looking up for me right away, just you wait and see."

As luck would have it, she obtained a growing number of engagements in suburban music halls and, even though the miniatures failed to sell in the quantities I had anticipated, we managed to keep our heads above water.

"Told you so," she crowed one evening. "A good name makes all the difference. There's just one other thing."

"What's that, my dear?" It was late in the evening, and I was eager for us to go to bed before I became too tired following the efforts of a long day at work.

"Hawley Harvey is such a mouthful, don't you think? That other name you use sometimes is so much easier. Peter. Short and sweet. Yes, why don't you become Peter Crippen?"

My knees trembled as I remember the night when I had first adopted the alias, but I managed to smile. "Dr. H.H. Crippen has a certain ring to it, my dear."

"Sure, but how about you being Peter when we're together?"

It was not a moment to deny her. "Very well," I said.

She beamed. "One last question, then."

"Go on."

"Are you ready to take me upstairs yet, Peter?"

That night, in the throes of ecstasy, she shut her eyes and called out my name.

"Peter! Peter!"

Hearing her warmed my heart. It never occurred to me that the pseudonym made it easier to imagine that the man in her bed was not her husband.

"Clothes maketh the man." It is true, thanks be to God. One

can do little or nothing to change the physique one is born with. I have always been short of stature and, given my distaste for the outdoor life and most forms of exercise, it is unsurprising that I am not heavily muscled. No matter. One can always take pride in one's clothes and, from the time I first worked in New York, I developed a taste for fashionable attire. While earning a fat salary from Munyon's, I was able to indulge myself, and Cora encouraged me to do so. When I attended at the tailor's, she would take charge of the discussions, debating with the man the most suitable colour for my trousers.

A frock coat became a man in my position, but she convinced me that there was no reason why I should not indulge in bold contrast. I settled for a butterfly tie and shirts of mauve, yellow, and green, the whole set off with a pin or small diamond from the jewellery box. Exotic, perhaps, but pleasurable too.

The sight of Cora dressed up afforded me even greater enjoyment. Adeline spoke in affectionate jest of my wife's "brilliant plumage." In her prime, my wife was dazzling, a fabulous bird that had landed in England after a long flight from a faraway country.

Cora was a capable seamstress, a skill that proved invaluable when circumstances compelled financial stringency. I took a simple pleasure in watching her, bent over her work in the front room. She possessed the ability to maintain concentration even while keeping up a stream of anecdotes about acquaintances from the music halls—a motley assortment of trapeze artists, sword swallowers, and supposedly Parisian dancing girls, most of whom hailed from Bermondsey rather than the Moulin Rouge. I sat quietly, content to allow the stories to wash over me. Merely to see her there and know that she belonged to me, and me alone, gave a rich pleasure, tainted only if she happened to mention the name that I had come to dread.

Bruce Miller had returned to England and, evidently with

Cora's encouragement, was pursuing a career upon the stage. His speciality was to play the harmonica, the banjo, and the drum at one and the same time. Evidently this was a man given to excess. While Cora marvelled at his versatility, I cringed in the shadow darkening our marriage.

"So you think I look nice in this?" Cora asked one evening, peering at me over her shoulder as she smoothed down a new blush-pink gown with a plunging neckline.

"Wonderful," I said fervently. Unfortunately, the cut struck me as somewhat lacking in generosity, an impression confirmed when she spun round to face me and I heard a ripping sound that prompted her to utter a profanity.

Cora had a natural tendency to *embonpoint* and her figure had filled out during our time in London. We might be short of money, but we did not starve, and Cora enjoyed her food. I found that I liked her plumpness more than I might have imagined. Her flesh was no longer taut and lean, but at least it was soft and melted at a touch.

"Fetch me a couple of pins, Peter," she said ruefully as she contemplated the damage. "Maybe I should have made it a size bigger."

"It is lovely," I said. Gallantry, in my experience, was always the best course with Cora. She adored flattery, a failing that no doubt that odious phantasm Bruce Miller was quick to exploit.

"Promise that you like it?" she pleaded coyly.

"I swear it to you."

The dark eyes glinted, a sure sign that a wicked thought had occurred to her. "You know, Peter, I truly believe that you like my clothes as much as I do."

"Certainly," I assured her.

"Maybe you'd look well in them yourself," she said with a sly wink.

The suggestion took me aback. I supposed that she was joking and responded with some light-hearted quip.

"No, no, I'm serious! What's the matter, Peter, are you scared?"

Baffled, I said, "Of course I'm not scared. But . . ."

"No buts! This dress would suit you a treat. You may be a touch taller than I am, but so what? You're skin and bone compared to me. It'll make a perfect fit."

So it began. A fiction that we indulged for all it was worth. After I had overcome my initial uncertainties, I found myself participating with an unexpected zest in our brand new game. For me, the rewards warranted any abandonment of dignity. I wore French knickers and when the charade was over, Cora would strip them from me with a determination that I found exhilarating.

Bruce Miller could not do this, I thought. That burly prize-fighter could never masquerade as a member of the fair sex, could never subjugate himself to the whim of a woman, however enticing. By allowing Cora to dress me as a woman and then undress me with loving care, I was stealing a march on my rival, and in a strange and unorthodox manner reinforcing the sacred bond between man and wife.

As I grew in confidence, I intensified my quest for verisimilitude at our play-time. My moustache presented the greatest challenge. Cora suggested that I shave my upper lip, but I stood firm. Some sacrifices I was not prepared to make. It delighted me to inhabit the garb of a woman when the dividends from my performance were so munificent, but the reality was not in doubt. However ladylike my appearance, under the pretty clothing I remained a man from head to toe. Eventually I hit upon the notion of covering my moustache with wig-paste—a device that met with Cora's immediate approval.

"Say, Peter, that's just fantastic! Hey, if I was a fellow, you can bet I'd be giving you the glad eye."

Her face contorted into a parody of insatiable lust. We dissolved into laughter and then into each other's arms. I was fiddling with her corset when someone knocked at our front door.

Cora covered her mouth with a bejewelled hand. "Adeline! I clean forgot that she said she might call round."

"But the time!" I wailed, as the knocking ceased. "She usually calls here much earlier in the evening."

"A publisher invited her to dinner. I said I was agog to hear if she had good news, but I guess I thought she'd be too tired to stop by."

The knocking started up again. There could be no ignoring such an imperious summons.

"You go to the door," I said. "I'll hurry upstairs and get changed."

"You'll never manage it. Remember how long it takes to get the wig-paste off properly."

"Tell her that I'm ill," I said in desperation.

"No, no, when I saw her this afternoon she asked after you and I said you were in excellent spirits."

"She cannot see me like this!" I exclaimed, beginning to struggle frantically out of my dress.

"Why not?" Cora demanded, hands on hips.

Her question paralysed me. There was no hint in her expression that she was indulging her somewhat unpredictable sense of humour. "What—what do you mean? I have a reputation, a certain standing in . . ."

"We can tell her it's just for fun," she interrupted. "You may be a doctor, but she knows you have a hankering for the theatre. She won't think you're something out of a freak show. It'll be easy. All I have to do is say I'm showing you how to dress up to play a woman's part in some sketch or other. Come on, she won't bat an eyelid. What do you say?"

The knocking was more thunderous than ever. Adeline Harrison was like Cora: She never gave up. Panic emptied my mind. I could not conceive an alternative plan less humiliating than that which Cora proposed.

"Very well," I said hoarsely.

Suffice it to say that we carried off the deception. Arthur, you told me that Adeline Harrison recalled the incident when speaking to a representative from *The Daily Express,* but even with hindsight, she saw nothing in it that struck her as tainted or otherwise untoward. She had no reason to believe that she had caught us out, or that my assumption of female costume was anything more than a frivolous fancy of the pair of us.

When she had gone, we held each other tightly and laughed until the tears ran down our cheeks. Presently, Cora seized me by the hand and led the way upstairs. When we climbed into bed, I wore no mask, and her needs were too urgent for her to have time to bind me to the posts. Yet we surrendered ourselves to a night of passion such as we had seldom known. I recall the morning that followed, my body aching sweetly from the excesses of my devotion. Soon she would forget that vainglorious interloper Bruce Miller. Our shared passion had merely been sleeping.

But Cora did not abandon Bruce Miller. He continued to call at our home. At least she made no secret of his visits, or of his affections for her. I could not help imagining her singing for him and revelling in his applause. It would be such a short step to responding to his crude overtures, surrendering to him with all the abandon that I remembered from our first night together when she was still, technically, C.C. Lincoln's mistress.

Financial privations exacerbated my distress. Eddie Marr

might have been willing to offer the benefit of his acumen, but he was preoccupied with projects of his own in New York. It was as if I was caught in a carpenter's vise, and all the life was being squeezed out of me.

One evening in the latter part of 1901, I was glancing through the pages of the newspaper when an advertisement caught my eye. It had been placed by the Drouet Institute for the Deaf of Regent's Park Road, and they were looking to appoint a consulting physician. The Institute's headquarters were in Paris, but its London premises were so famously sumptuous that even Munyon's offices in Shaftesbury Avenue faded in comparison. The late Dr. Drouet was a Frenchman who was reputed to have devised a cure for deafness. The principal product was supplemented by a catalogue full of useful remedies such as anti-catarrhal snuff. The business was conducted primarily by correspondence. My years with Munyon's had taught me that this offered many advantages, not least in establishing a barrier of distance between oneself and any dissatisfied customers.

My application was successful. Frankly, my *curriculum vitae* must have spoken for itself. Cora and I celebrated with a dressing-up charade in which we let our imaginations fly. Thank goodness Adeline Harrison was not a witness on that occasion. The remuneration offered by the Institute was hardly bounteous, but it sufficed to keep the wolf from the door. At last, I thought, as I wrote out my acceptance, my future was secure.

My misfortune has been to fall victim to a judicial machine with the imaginative sympathy of a steamroller. After the jury delivered its cruel verdict, who could have heard my declaration of innocence and not entertained a flicker of doubt? Yet the Lord Chief Justice paid no heed to my words. Why, then, was I asked if I had anything to say? The judge's cold observations thrust into me like a stiletto blade, stabbing again and again until I was almost insensible with despair.

"I only tell you that you must entertain no expectation or hope that you will escape the consequences of your crime, and I implore you to make your peace with Almighty God. I have now to pass upon you the sentence of the Court, which is that you be taken from hence to a lawful prison, and from thence to a place of execution, and that you be there hanged by the neck until you are dead, and that your body be buried in the precincts of the prison where you shall last have been confined after your conviction. And may the Lord have mercy on your soul!"

And now, Arthur, you apologise for the postponement of my appeal and tell me that the vagaries of the legal process are to blame. No matter; the delay is a pinprick. If all goes well, two extra days of incarceration are a small price to pay. What gnaws at me is the darkening of your complexion when you break the news that Mr. Justice Darling will preside.

He is not, you say, remotely sympathetic to the *crime passionel*.

But I have committed no crime. Or, at least, not the crime of which I stand convicted.

"ETHEL LE NEVE'S CHARACTER FROM HANDWRITING

'Ethel' is intelligent and rather clever. Impulsive . . . greatly influenced by those who surround her, and much interested in the opposite sex, she is easily attracted, romantic, morbidly sentimental, and allows her heart entirely to govern her head. At the same time, the handwriting shows distinct traces of selfishness. Her moods are variable, inclining to melancholy. She is ambitious and not satisfied with her lot in life . . . could keep a secret. She is careless, but sensitive, and dislikes all coarse or rough things. Her imagination is inclined to run away with her."

Joining Drouet's was at worst a tactical retreat, at best a stride forward in my career. Had I only possessed more capital, I might have made a go of Amorette—but in the mercantile world, timing is all. When circumstances were more propitious, I would seek again to carve a niche for myself as a man of business. In the meantime, the challenge was to make a success of my new role at the Institute.

Early on, I recruited the services of William Long as clerk and head of our shipping department. I had engaged Long originally at Munyon's, and he later followed me to the Sovereign Remedy Company. His loyalty was matched by a willingness to discharge even the most menial errands without complaint. He was a shy, baby-faced man whose suits reeked of mothballs. Although six feet tall, he seemed much shorter as he crept around the office, in constant terror of giving offence. He combined a thirst for hard work with a startling absence of curiosity: the ideal subordinate. Our relations were cordial, but he had a proper regard for status. Never did he indulge in excessive familiarity or seek to take improper advantage of the confidence that I reposed in him.

Soon the Institute relocated to Marble Arch. We were spending twenty thousand pounds sterling *per annum* on advertisements, and the hard-of-hearing rewarded our investment by opening their cheque books. The Drouet name was emblazoned on the sides of the London omnibuses; if one stood for an hour on any street corner, a reminder of our existence was bound to rumble by. I had worked alongside two other physicians, one Belgian, one French, but when headquarters recalled them, I assumed responsibility for the overall conduct of Drouet's activities in the United Kingdom.

Under my stewardship, business boomed. As with Munyon's, I took pains to furnish the principal rooms at Marble Arch in the best of English taste: fine specimens of Chippendale, lush carpeting, and delicate china knickknacks displayed to best advantage. Those wealthy enough to afford a private consultation must have thought they were entering a palace. My principal aim, however, was not to entice patients to our premises. I encouraged enquirers to submit postal questionnaires, on the basis of which I could evaluate their disorder. The symptoms and maladies from which they suffered could be divided into certain categories. For these, I coined technical terms with the ring of medical truth: *post otorrhea and tinnitus,* for instance, and most pleasingly, *rhinitis chronica rhino pharyngitis eustachian salpingitis.* Talking the appropriate language was half the battle. I marked the corner of each questionnaire in pencil, so that my secretary could type the appropriate standard letter for me to sign by way of diagnosis. A modern and efficient system, a world away from the cut-price charlatanry of those who peddled drugs from dingy back rooms in Camden Town or Hackney.

I could not claim sole credit for our success. Even the most assiduous manager will experience difficulties if those whom he supervises are incompetent or lazy. During my time working for the professor, I had taken pains to ensure that everyone whom I employed was reliable. The workers at Drouet's were equally industrious.

The head typist was an auburn-haired English rose by the name of Nina Neave. It required no effort of will to pass the time of day with her once I had signed the latest pile of diagnoses. With employees of any description, a kindly word, coupled now and then with an amiable inquiry as to any family or domestic matter that is occupying their attention, does wonders for morale.

Nina's sister also worked at Drouet's as a shorthand typist. Let me be honest—at first I paid little attention to Ethel Le Neve. She never spoke unless spoken to and appeared content to remain in Nina's shadow. Although younger, Nina was the longer-serving and senior in rank at the Institute, as well as much more outgoing. Ethel had a ghostly pallor and a permanent sniffle. Once I overheard a fresh young girl in the office talking to Long about Ethel and uttering the phrase: "Not very well today, thank you." Puzzling over it afterwards, I realised that this was a nickname that her colleagues had bestowed on Ethel, from her usual reply when asked how she was keeping.

Taking pity on the girl, I spoke privately to her about her health. She said she suffered from severe attacks of catarrh: a common indisposition in a damp climate, but profoundly irksome and debilitating for the person afflicted. She fretted about her condition and I concentrated first and foremost upon re-assurance rather than medication. I was all too well aware of the limitations of patent remedies. Soon she reported that her sinuses had cleared and she was breathing more easily. This improved state of health put her in better heart, and she expressed her gratitude to me in fulsome terms.

Every now and then, I invited the sisters to take tea with me in my office. Gradually, Ethel came out of herself and no longer seemed so wraith-like. She and Nina told me about their lives and their family. I had been baffled by the discrepancy in their surnames and Nina explained that Ethel's decision to abandon Neave for Le Neve was a small gesture of independence.

"You may think that butter wouldn't melt in her mouth, Doctor, but don't underestimate her. She likes to keep her thoughts to herself, but I never knew anyone with such strength of will."

The poor girl blushed to the roots of her hair. "I think Le Neve sounds more elegant," was all that she would say.

Nina giggled. "Much more romantic than plain Neave, you mean."

"Anyway, Nina," I said, with a wink at her sister, "you will not be a Neave for much longer. You have been walking out with that young Mr. Brock for quite a while now, after all. I dare say before long we will hear the church bells ringing out."

Now it was the turn of Nina's cheeks to redden, while Ethel's eyes glinted with mischief, in a way I had never seen before. She had let slip to me a few days earlier that her sister had a young man and she seemed glad I had turned the conversation to spare her further embarrassment. It was the tiniest of conspiracies, but it cemented our burgeoning friendship.

Getting to know the sisters better afforded me a deal of harmless pleasure. Naturally, I was circumspect in my behaviour toward them. When an older man, however respectable, shares the company of young women, however innocent, it is so easy for his intentions to be misunderstood. My throat still dried whenever I recalled my clumsiness during the incident with Cora's sister. But I was older now, and wiser to the ways of the world. Wiser about women, too.

Nina told me that their father was a coal canvasser and hinted that he was too fond of the drink. His daughters, however, were as refined as ladies-in-waiting. I came to look forward eagerly to our little chats at tea time, which took my mind off Cora for a little while. At least her trysts with Bruce Miller were not remotely clandestine, but at times I wished—however perversely—that they were. The automatic orchestra was taking the nation by storm, according to Cora, but Miller was not satisfied. He wanted to run his own business. She said that he could turn his hand to anything and make a success of it. The unflattering comparison was plainly implied, but I let it pass me by.

Cora's hair, her lips, her skin, all seemed so much coarser than when we first met; they might have belonged to a washerwoman. Her whole body was thickening; when I opened her *peignoir* and pulled her to me, the roll of fat around her midriff filled my hands. It is natural enough for a woman to lose the first bloom of youth, but Cora was only thirty years old. No fool, she recognised that her looks were not of the kind that last, and she sought to make an impression on others through an avalanche of joviality. Yet the vivacious manner that her friends could not resist seemed to me increasingly akin to a wearisome restlessness. She was never happy unless she was the centre of attention.

Once my chest had puffed out when my wife was at my side. Yet at Drouet's, her name scarcely passed my lips. For me, the office was a tranquil harbour where I could drop anchor each morning after a night of domestic storms. Cora began to travel farther afield in search of audiences unfamiliar with her limitations. Once, at the Dudley Empire, she was second on the bill to Dan Leno, although the local press's failure to mention her performance provoked a Niagara of tears and anger. Although I still missed her when she went away, her absences enabled me to devote my ardour to the business. At Shaftesbury Avenue, I had kept a silver-framed photograph of Cora on my desk. The picture was taken in Jersey City, not long after our marriage, when she was all smiles and tumbling curls. Now it gathered dust in a drawer at home, as forgotten as her youthful promise.

Long had met Cora at Munyon's and occasionally took messages to her at our home when work delayed my return in the evening. Although he said nothing, I deduced from his nervousness whenever she spoke to him that he found her intimidating. I did not care to mention her to Nina or Ethel.

The truth slipped out from an unexpected source. Eddie Marr, of all people, who was notorious for many things, but not candour. Marr came to visit me at Marble Arch, swaggering into my office as if he owned the whole of Oxford Street. He announced loudly that he had developed a new line in cures for obesity, which he was peddling under the name of W.S. Hamilton, and he had a joint venture in mind. The sisters were enjoying a cup of tea with me and I watched as his trademark gaze took them in. Years of sizing up customers had left him with a habit of measuring people, even as he cracked the jokes that left them weeping with delight. He could always spot how to make money out of them.

In my mind I could hear him saying, "So you've got two on the go, have you? Sisters as well. Very nice. You're a sly dog, ain't you, Doc? People who don't know you as well as me would never realise what you're capable of."

I do not count myself a boastful man, but I enjoyed making an impression upon Marr. Although his imagination was disreputable, it pleased me to think that he might envy me the pretty girls who were at my beck and call.

"Wish I had someone to make the tea for me," he said, parodying the expression of a wistful little boy.

"Do join us," I offered.

"Don't mind if I do," he said, settling his ample posterior into the remaining chair. "Say, this is cosy, isn't it?"

For twenty minutes we all chatted happily. Marr entertained the girls with a tale about how a business partner had cheated him out of a fortune. I doubt if a word was true, but somehow with Eddie, that never mattered. My attention drifted and I was dreamily admiring Ethel's flawless profile when my friend fired a question as unexpected as it was unwelcome.

"So how is Cora, then? Still living it up under the bright lights?"

I coughed and, as I struggled to contrive a reply, Nina asked innocently, "Cora?"

"Mrs. Crippen," Marr said. "The doc never told you about her?"

I feared that he was about to launch into an account of Cora's misadventures in the music hall, and so I changed the subject hastily to the purpose of his visit, the proposal that I participate in his latest escapade.

"I am afraid that my work for the Institute absorbs all my energy at present," I concluded. "Much as I would like to help . . ."

Marr shrugged and cast a speculative look in the direction of the sisters. "Well, Doc, like I said to you once before, it's your funeral. Just remember, all work and no play makes Jack a dull boy. You sure need some outlet for all that energy, you know."

This remark amused him inordinately and he was still chuckling as he left the premises. When I returned to the office, Nina's face was shining, although Ethel seemed to have shrunk back into herself.

"Your friend is such a fascinating man!" Nina said.

I did not like the thought of Marr fascinating either of the girls. Perhaps my displeasure caused me to speak more sharply than was my wont.

"We have done each other a couple of good turns in a business capacity," I said with a dismissive wave. "But it would be an exaggeration to call us friends."

"I never heard you mention a wife before, Doctor. Is it true? Are you really married?"

I felt my cheeks flushing beneath the curious scrutiny of both young women. The fancy struck me that Ethel was holding her breath as she awaited my reply. The temptation to fashion an enigmatic response was irresistible. I could not help but succumb.

"It would take the lawyers all their time to find out," I said mysteriously.

We did not speak again of Cora. The sisters must have realised that my marital status was a topic that was out of bounds. My impromptu remark was so teasing that it seemed a pity that it had no substance or meaning. If only Cora had committed bigamy, and in truth she had not been C.C. Lincoln's mistress, but his secret wife! A pleasing fantasy, and I often dwelt on it.

More than once, when Cora was away, I asked Ethel and Nina to keep me company by joining me for dinner. So it was that the three of us began to dine at Frascati's on Oxford Street, no expense spared! We favoured a table in a corner by the staircase, where we could enjoy amiable conversation and the charming melodies played by the orchestra. The horrors of Marylebone Music Hall seemed a world away.

In due course I was invited to visit the family home in Hampstead. Mrs. Charlotte Neave was an agreeable woman whose regular features and eagerness to please her daughters had

inherited. She insisted on cooking a meal in honour of my visit
and provided plain but wholesome fare. A joint of pork with
turnip and beans and lashings of thick gravy was followed by
rice pudding and a slice of sweet cake that she had baked that
very day. When I lavished praise upon her culinary skills, she
gave a pretty smile.

"It is a pleasure, Doctor Crippen!" she exclaimed. "Walter
and I have heard so much about you."

"Not too much to my discredit, I trust."

"Perish the thought!" the good lady replied. "My daughters
are always talking about you, and Ethel has told me that you
worked wonders for her catarrh. You must be very busy, Doctor,
and yet the girls say that you're never too busy to spare them a
kind word. Isn't that so, Walter?"

"I'll say, my dear."

The girls' father was a stout man with a ruddy face and a
bulbous nose. His breath stank of beer, but he treated me civilly
enough in his rough and ready fashion. I gathered that he had
worked on the railways and in his youth, he said, he had sung
solo in the choir at Norwich Cathedral. It seemed so improbable that it must be the truth. Mr. Neave made it clear that, in
the intervening years, Fate had not been kind to him. Fate, I
deduced, and too great a fondness for the four-ale bar.

The family was making preparations for Nina's marriage. I
realised that Nina was the favoured daughter and learned from
Mr. Neave that Ethel had suffered from health problems earlier
in life.

"They told us she'd be a cripple!" he declared. "Frog foot—
and the medical men wanted to operate. I was having none of
it. Thank Heaven I stuck to my guns. Take a gander at her now,
Doctor. See any sign of a limp?"

When I confessed that I did not, he nodded in satisfaction.
"As if I didn't know what was best for my own girl! Medical

men—ha! Talk through their arses, most of the time. Saving your presence, Doctor Crippen."

Nina gave a horrified laugh and contrived with skill borne, no doubt, from long experience of her father's manners, to change the subject. Ethel skulked in a corner and said nothing; her face was crimson. Later, when she told me of the pain and suffering she endured when learning to walk, I understood why she detested her father so much as to seize the chance, in adulthood, to rid herself of his name. Her iron resolve struck me as wholly admirable: she was a woman prepared to wait as long as need be in order to achieve her goals.

After the wedding, Nina intended to concentrate on hearth and home, and the question arose as to how we would manage at Marble Arch without her. One afternoon in the office, after her sister had stepped out to wash the tea cups, Nina said to me, "I wonder, Doctor, if you seek my recommendation as to a successor in the ladies' room?"

When I said yes, she continued, "Well, I believe you won't go far wrong if you consider Ethel for promotion."

"That is your considered opinion?" I enquired, taking care to disguise my reaction to her words.

"I do," Nina said. "Ethel is neater and more efficient than stenographers ten years her senior and since she started working at the Institute, I think she has come on a treat. If you are willing to give her a try, she won't let you down."

"I am sure she won't," I said warmly. "As a matter of fact, the same thought had already passed through my mind. Now that I am confident of your blessing, I shall offer the post to your sister within the next forty-eight hours."

Nina beamed and I stretched out in my chair. Another good deed done, I congratulated myself. For some months I had kept a close eye on Ethel. There were fleeting moments—a sidelong glance here, a faint and possibly accidental brush on the hand there—when I allowed myself to believe that she was doing likewise with me.

Cora occasionally called on me in the office. With Nina gone, Ethel had become my personal secretary, but I was not aware until afterwards of their first encounter. She told me that Cora had banged my door shut in a huff after a trivial disagreement and that, on questioning Long, she had learned that the angry woman was indeed my wife.

A few weeks later Cora turned up at Marble Arch in a state of temper. Her latest engagement had been cancelled, and she wanted to know why I had failed to confirm the booking. I tried to point out that I was a busy man, whereas she was seldom fully employed, but she would have none of it.

"You've made me look like a fool!" she shouted.

"Hush, dear. Please lower your voice. The walls are not so thick that the staff cannot overhear you."

She made a loud noise to signal her exasperation. "Don't worry, I'm going."

"I shall not be late this . . ."

"I won't be at home," she hissed. "I'm going round to see some of my friends. They'll just never believe this! As for you, you can get home when you like."

She flounced out, leaving the door to my private office wide open. I caught a glimpse of Ethel, peering nervously first at my wife and then at me. A sudden pain wrenched my stomach, and the agony of it caused me to slip to the ground from my chair.

Ethel put her hand to her mouth in horror. I must have made a dreadful sight. For a moment she hesitated, and then she came rushing into the room. I tried to get back to my feet, but without success. The fall had winded me. I stammered my apologies, but she was quick to hush me.

"Are you all right?" That was all the dear creature wanted to know.

"Yes," I mumbled, as she put her cool hand on my forehead and murmured words of comfort. "Thank you, thank you. You are very kind. It is nothing serious, I promise. In a few minutes I shall be as right as rain."

"Let me fetch brandy," she said.

I did not attempt to dissuade her, and when she pressed the glass to my mouth, I sipped with gratitude. The alcohol burned my tongue, but I did not care.

"Is that any better?" she asked.

She was standing close beside me, her body pressing against mine. I could feel the beating of her heart and the warmth of her chest against me. I closed my eyes and uttered up a prayer. It was as if Cora had brought the two of us together.

"Thank you so much, Ethel," I murmured. Hitherto, in the office she had always been *Miss Le Neve,* but the proprieties no longer seemed so important to me.

"Your face is stripped of colour," she whispered. "You must rest."

"It is nothing," I insisted. "A moment to compose myself, that is all I need."

"You are very brave."

My heart leapt. There was no mistaking the admiration in her tone. She did care for me!

"What cannot be cured must be endured," I murmured.

Ethel caught her breath. "Is she—unkind to you, Hawley?"

Hawley! Never before had I heard her utter my Christian name. I clutched at her small hand and gripped it tightly.

"Let us not speak of her."

She bent her face to mine and I shut my eyes, the better to absorb the bliss of having her so close to me. She smelled faintly of lavender. I needed to summon up all my reserves to fight the impulse to kiss that soft, pale cheek.

"She misuses you, doesn't she?"

My voice trembled as I answered. "Sometimes, truly, I think I can bear it no longer."

"You poor darling," she said, and for the briefest moment her lips brushed my hair.

How impossible to resist thinking of life outside my cage of stone. Last evening I became dizzy with imagined smells from London beyond the prison walls. The scent of old roses at Number 39, the succulent aroma of steak at Frascati's, even the stench from the triperies hard by the Caledonian Market.

I have lost so much, but at least my beloved remains faithful and true. Each time she visits, I urge her to have courage, to take heart from having secured funds to cover the next two years. It is a comfort to me that she is well cared for, whatever Fate may bring. When I try to cheer her with a report of the legal arguments that you and Mr. Tobin are taking to appeal, it is more than she can bear. At the mention of seeking justice, she breaks into a harsh laughter that makes my head throb with pain. And when she collapses in a flood of tears, my skin feels as though it is about to burst.

It is as if she fears betrayal. But that is absurd. What is there to betray? Besides, she is everything to me. I would without a moment's thought give my own life that she might live.

Yet it will not come to that. I still have confidence that we will once again share happy days. Our love will not come to a bitter end.

Extract from "Ethel Le Neve: her life story"
(October 1910)

"It was about this time that I learnt of Mr. Bruce Miller's affection-ate correspondence with Belle Elmore—as Mrs. Crippen was known in the theatrical world. By sheer accident I happened to see some of the letters which he had sent her. This, I need hardly say, relieved me somewhat of any misgivings I had with regard to my relations with her husband."

In the early days of our courtship, Ethel and I developed a wonderful telepathy, so that we did not need to communicate by words alone. We had been born on opposite sides of the world, but although she was twenty years my junior, and even an inch taller, the differences meant nothing, once circumstances conspired to draw us together.

At the same time, Cora and I became increasingly estranged. She insisted on placing a new photograph of Bruce Miller on the piano in our parlour and when I uttered the mildest protest, she turned an ear as deaf as that of a Drouet client.

"This is my home as well, so why shouldn't I be able to display a keepsake or two? What's the matter, are you jealous because he's such a fine-looking fellow?"

The unspoken comparison cut me to the quick, but I knew better than to provoke her temper. With Cora, the subtle approach was best. "Not at all, my dear. I was thinking rather of your own reputation. When your friends come to visit, what might they conjecture when they see that you show off in your own house the likeness of a man who is not your husband?"

"You needn't worry about them," she said. "Most of them know Bruce and they understand about him and me, that we're just good friends. Why, don't you understand, the fact that you're content for me to have his photograph standing there proves that everything is open and aboveboard."

I decided to give in with good grace. Even so, the sight of those complacent features grinning out at me would have been too much to bear had I not enjoyed the consolation of Ethel's quiet but unyielding loyalty and admiration.

For several days after the incident in my office, I tortured myself with the supposition that she might already have a *beau*. It was all too easy to believe that some youth of her own age had, however dimly, perceived her exceptional qualities and begun to pay her court. Before long, I decided that I must put myself out of the misery of ignorance. I broached the subject light-heartedly, referring to my certainty that there must be a gaggle of fellows queuing in line to take her out on weekends, but her reply was swift and emphatic.

"There is no one, I'm afraid."

She lowered her lashes and would not look at me directly. I adopted a jovial tone. "Really? What is the youth of this country coming to? Don't they realise what a lovely . . ."

She hushed me with an embarrassed laugh. "Hawley, you must not tease me so! Nina is the one around whom the boys always clustered. Not me."

I smiled and lowered my voice expectantly. "So there has been no one?"

She was too honest to assent. "Well, eighteen months ago, I did become friendly with a young man, the brother of my shorthand teacher. We used to go dancing together and he wrote me—some silly letters. My father saw the envelopes addressed to me at our home and demanded to see them. Of course, I refused and we had a terrible row. I was forbidden to go to any more dances."

"Did you have to give up the boy?"

Ethel lifted her chin and in that moment I had a glimpse of her inner strength. "I was supposed to, and to tell the truth I was already beginning to tire of his chatter. He was such a clumsy dancer. And afterwards, so persistent in asking for kisses!"

I could not find it my heart to blame the lad for his lustful attentions. "Go on."

"I said to myself that if I were to give him up, it would be my decision, not someone else's. My father has always striven to rule my life, and I've always made it my business to deny him, ever since he refused to let the doctors operate on my foot. So, when he wanted a little girl who played with dolls, I became a tomboy and learned how to climb trees and shoot with a catapult."

"I must take care not to antagonise you, Ethel."

"There is no danger of that," she assured me. "Anyway, so much for my young man. For a while I hid my dancing pumps in a locked cupboard and sneaked out with him whenever I got the chance. It sounds strange, but the intrigue appealed to me more than he did. After I started at the Institute, I became bored with him. He was so immature and inexperienced."

"So when did you throw him over?"

A slow smile. "Well, Hawley, I suppose it was not long after you arrived at Regent's Park Road."

★ ★ ★ ★ ★

Cora lay on the bed fully clothed. Her face was buried in the pillow and she had been uttering loud sobs from the moment I crossed the threshold of our home. The noise had sent me rushing to find out what could have happened, and when I threw open the door to our bedroom, I was shocked to see her whole body shuddering with emotion. I hurried over and slid my hand on to her forehead. She was not running a temperature. The fever afflicting her was of the emotions rather than the physical self.

"Cora, what in Heaven's name is the matter?"

"Go away!"

"But . . ."

"Go away!" she cried again. Less muffled, this time. "Go away, you unfeeling bastard!"

I shrank back from the bedside. Even by Cora's standards, this was uncalled for. Or was it? I swallowed hard as it occurred to me that she must know about my affection for Ethel.

"Cora, I . . . I . . ."

"Ain't you got ears? Take some of your own pills, then! I said, go away!"

I had no choice but to obey. By the time I had gained our living room, my thoughts were in better order. Cora had now met Ethel several times at Marble Arch and had behaved pretty well in her presence, without any hint of hostility or suspicion. Besides, Cora simply could not know about Ethel and me, because there was nothing to know. Our communion was of the spirit, not of the flesh.

Not for several days did I learn what had caused Cora's hysterical attack, but in the meantime I sought to elucidate the mystery in the manner of the Chevalier C. Auguste Dupin, by ratiocination. Given that she had taken even the disaster of her debut less hard, I deduced that nothing in her professional career was responsible for her despair. So the answer must lie in her personal life. There could, I decided, be only one explanation. Bruce Miller had rejected her.

The truth, when at last I teased it out of her, was less dramatic but equally satisfactory. Miller, she told me with a sniff, had decided to return to the United States. The move was to be permanent. He saw more openings for making money there in the long run, or so he said.

"So the automatic orchestra was not a success?"

"People came from all over just to watch him!" Her face was aflame. "I know just how much show business means to Bruce."

"Then perhaps his wife was missing him," I suggested.

Cora replied with an inarticulate noise of anguish. I could not help feeling sorry for her. Perhaps now she would realise that, whilst I might not be a manufacturer or a stage performer, I was not only a success in my own field but a husband—a man—upon whom she could rely.

At first, everything went according to plan, although Cora continued to display likenesses of Miller. My intention was to cleanse our home of every trace of him, but I was willing to be patient while Cora grieved for the death of her romance. Our game-playing had fallen into desuetude, but old habits die hard. Soon we took up where we had left off. The blindfold came out of the cupboard once more and so did the wig-paste when she persuaded me to resume my masquerade.

Yet things had changed. Cora's cheeks had become chubby and her jaw now had a double, but the transformation when she undressed was even more striking. Her once proud breasts had begun to sag and, when she spread herself out upon the bed, her belly was a hillock of flabby flesh. Even worse, whenever I climbed under the sheets to join her at night, there was a faraway look in her eyes.

In early summer, I received proof that the *affaire* was not dead, but merely sleeping. Cora had started rising earlier in the morning than was her custom and usually she was the first to see the post. I thought nothing of this break in her routine at first; if, following Miller's departure, she was intent upon adjusting all the details of her life, I welcomed it. On one particular Tuesday, however, it dawned on me that there was a motive for the change in her ways.

I caught her at the breakfast table devouring a letter, oblivious to the smell of burning toast that issued from the kitchen. From her guilty start as I walked into the room, I guessed at once the author of the correspondence. She tucked the paper hurriedly into her *peignoir* and greeted me with a gushing smile that struck a wholly false note.

"Someone has been writing to you, my dear?"

Baring her large teeth in a ferocious smile, she said, "Mr. Bruce Miller, of course."

As if to emphasise her triumph, she removed the letter from her gown and placed it beside the plate in front of her. Daring me to read it.

I threw the merest glance at the sheet of paper that had so transformed the balance of our relationship. It was enough to make my stomach heave. Tears misting my eyes, I left the room without another word.

The flavour of the message was clear enough from the phrase I had glimpsed above Miller's signature.

Love and kisses to Brown Eyes.

Ethel, in contrast, was fidelity itself. The time we spent together was precious, not least because it was so limited. We dined together whenever we could, and snatched occasional hours for a visit to the British Museum, followed by refreshments at the milk-shop on Museum Street. As the sombre official shepherded us along the galleries, I took no notice of the reliefs of long-forgotten pharaohs and busts of inscrutable Roman emperors. To be alone with Ethel, to take her by the arm as if we were man and wife, that was all I wished for. In her company, the onion and broccoli smells of Covent Garden became a delicate fragrance. A cup of smoky Indian tea in the milk-shop was transformed into the sweetest nectar.

If Ethel returned late from work, her father had the temerity to ask her to account for her movements. My duties compelled me to work long hours, and Cora complained if I was absent from home without a plausible explanation. This was not so much because she missed me—she found the brandy bottle a pleasant enough companion—as because she delighted in being disagreeable.

The first time she smacked me on the cheek, I was so startled that I did not say a word. When, a few months later, she blacked my eye after a petty argument, I had cause to regret my weakness. I should have put my foot down the first time she hit me. At the office, when people asked what had happened to me, I gave out that I had walked into a door. Far worse than the pain was the humiliation. I took good care, therefore, to furnish myself with a suitable excuse whenever Ethel and I stole time to be together, walking in St. James's Park or by the riverside.

One wet Sunday in July stands out in my mind. Cora had obtained a couple of bookings in the Midlands—described grandly as "a provincial tour"—and would be away for a week. I arranged to meet Ethel a couple of streets away from her home, safely out of her father's sight. Rain slammed down upon the pavements as we took a cab to Trafalgar Square. Even the bright purple and blue pansies in the flower beds were dripping and sad, but Ethel's company made me feel as though I were on a beach in a Californian heat wave.

As the downpour slowed to a drizzle, we walked together

hand in hand, a companionable silence speaking volumes. Although each of us had the knack of reading the other's thoughts, there were still occasions when she took me by surprise.

"All I wish is that she would stop hurting you," Ethel said suddenly, as we traversed the bank of the Thames. The rain was a gauze curtain, softening the outlines of the buildings. In the distance I could see Cleopatra's Needle, and I recalled strolling with Cora past the oblelisk's twin in Central Park, the day that she had promised to be mine forever. We reached a bench and I used a handkerchief to dry a place where we could sit down.

"She will never change."

"That bruise is yellow and fading," she replied, touching my brow gently, "but I cannot take my eyes off it. There is nothing, I am sure, that she would not do if she felt it served her interests. As for me—I would do anything to protect you from her. Anything at all!"

"She cannot do me harm, my love, I promise you."

"You're too gentle and kind! That's the trouble. You think everyone is as decent as you are! Remember the time when you slumped from your chair and I gave you brandy?"

"I shall never forget it."

"You were so distraught! Truly, I believed that in the depths of your despair, you had taken poison."

I stared into her lovely grey eyes and it was as if I was looking into her heart for the first time, as if until now I had merely glimpsed her through a fogged window. She possessed an imagination as wild and romantic as my own! I was thrilled to recognise how fiercely she cared.

"I was shocked by Cora's anger, that was all."

In a strained voice, she said, "I thought you could not bear it anymore and that you had decided to end it all. I was so afraid that I was not enough for you. It was in that moment that I told myself, I must make my feelings clear."

She bowed her head and began to sob. I put my arm round her and she clung to me with as much desperation as if she had been drowning and finally found a life raft. Thunder rumbled in the distance as I whispered endearments in her ear, and then started saying things that I had never said to her before. She might have been shocked, I might have ruined everything, but I could not help myself. Instead of pushing me away in revulsion, she pulled me to her.

Kisses are so special. After Charlotte, of the dry lips and heart, and Cora, with her devouring mouth, Ethel was so different. Her sweet tongue touched mine with infinite delicacy. As I buried my face in hers, I inhaled the fragrance of lavender. We remained locked in our embrace for what seemed an eternity, oblivious to the gathering storm.

Cora's remedy for the void created by Miller's absence was to devote her time to expanding her circle of friends from the music hall. Our parlour saw an endless procession of singers, jugglers, and stage magicians. I became acquainted with Fred Ginnett, the equestrian performer famed for his version of "Dick Turpin's Ride to York", and Eugene Stratton, celebrated singer of "Little Dolly Daydream." Many of our visitors had fallen on hard times, for no audiences are as unforgiving as those at the music halls. A few came, it seemed to me, expressly for the purpose of cadging a drink or meal. Most of their names meant little, but everyone knew Marie Lloyd.

Audiences loved Marie. Who, other than a Munyon or the humourless moralists of Mrs. Ormiston Chant's Purity Party, could fail to relish her saucy wit? When she accompanied ditties like *"Every little movement has a meaning of its own"* or *"She'd never had her ticket punched before"* with liberal excerpts from her repertoire of grins, hand gestures, and cheeky winks, she could reduce any audience to sobs of laughter and delight. I never encountered anyone with such a knack of shifting in an instant from innocent charm to outrageous innuendo. Her motto was simple: "People don't pay their sixpences to hear the Salvation Army." Marie understood what her public wanted and she gave it to them: that was her secret, just as it was Professor Munyon's.

In Cora, she identified a kindred spirit, someone else who had clawed her way out of the slums to carve a musical career. They were of much the same age, two tiny women with personalities big enough to fill the Royal Albert Hall. Each loved to dress with extravagant style, each knew precisely how to catch the eye of a man, each could on occasion shock by uttering a vulgarity wholly unexpected from the lips of a woman. Just as Cora had fallen under Lincoln's sway at a tender age, so Marie had found herself married at seventeen to a drunken boor. My wife had sought refuge with me and Marie had turned to Alec Hurley, a burly coster singer who often treated us to an ear-splitting rendition of "The Lambeth Walk." Again like Cora, Marie had long since abandoned the name she was born with. She once told us gaily that, before Matilda Victoria Wood finally became Marie Lloyd, she had adopted another *nom de guerre.*

"I was Bella Delamere when I first sang *'My Soldier Lassie,'* " she said with her characteristic twinkle.

"Bella Delamere?" I repeated as the penny dropped.

At least Cora had the grace to redden. Until that moment, I had been unaware that, in becoming Belle Elmore, my wife had consciously echoed the stage name her friend had discarded. Marie roared with laughter, evidently amused by the flattery of imitation. Cora would never be a Marie Lloyd.

Not all our new friends were artistes. Some, like Dr. John Burroughs and his wife Maud, were enthusiastic patrons of the music halls who loved to mix with performers. Burroughs was a general practitioner, whereas I was careful to explain my specialism in disorders of the ear, eye, and nose. He did not indulge in the fashion of heaping scorn on so-called "quackery" and, since I never discussed work with him, no room for disagreement between us ever arose.

Cora relished being in a crowd; it came from being part of a large family. With her loud Brooklyn twang, fine clothes and jewellery, and ready humour, she could never fail to be noticed. It suited me to sit on the sidelines. In company, we established a *modus vivendi* as Peter and Belle, a devoted couple. I performed little services for her whenever the opportunity arose and often gave her presents. The reward I sought was not so much the glow of her friends' approval as the prospect of her good will after they left us. There were still times when I believed I could make her forget Bruce Miller forever.

Words cannot describe Ethel's saintliness during those months and years. Her devotion was unquestioning, her patience infinite. "We must make the best of things as they are," I used to say, and with a melancholy smile she always agreed. In the early period of our courtship she was afflicted by occasional pangs of guilt. Once or twice she even said that it would be better if we were to part, since she could not bear to come between a man and his wife. I understood the tenderness of her conscience and strove to allay her fears.

Cora kept her letters from Miller in a drawer in the parlour; they were tied together with red ribbon. One morning when she was still in bed, I slipped a few sheets out of the pack and contrived to ensure that, when Ethel came into my office, she would see them lying on my desk. This stratagem succeeded beyond my dreams: Ethel told me that the *risqué* terms in which Miller had written shook her to the core. The thought that a married woman might treasure such correspondence from an admirer, and leave it about to torment her cuckolded husband, struck her as depraved. From that moment on, I sensed a new confidence in her. Yet, as time passed by, inevitably there were days when she began to lose heart.

"However cruelly she may treat you, darling, you are still a married man," she said one lunchtime as we fed the pigeons in Russell Square. "You have an important position to keep up. I simply can't see when you will ever . . ."

"Dearest," I said, squeezing her hand in the hope of forestalling tears.

Ethel rarely cried in my presence, but every now and then the cruelty of the Fate that kept us apart became too much for her. Never did I feel more inadequate than when dabbing at her cheeks with my handkerchief, murmuring desperate words of reassurance, hoping that none of the people passing by would pay attention to the middle-aged man and the young, sobbing woman.

"I cannot offer you a date to ink upon the calendar," I said. "But keep faith in me, I pray of you, and never forget that love will always find a way."

We were like the mind readers with whom my wife sometimes performed. The tacit agreement was that our love must remain chaste until I was free. Not that I found it easy to honour my side of our selfless bargain. One morning after Cora had caught an early morning train to the Midlands, I called Ethel into my office shortly after nine o'clock and made so bold as to suggest that she might accompany me back to my home. I offered to make us a snack and said that we could have our usual pleasant evening in comfort and private. She would not hear of it.

"No, Hawley," she insisted gently. "It would not be right."

How could I argue? For all Walter Neave's brutish behaviour, Ethel—like her sister—was a lady, pure of heart. In her eyes, marriage was a sacrament, and she could not contemplate giving herself wholly to me without observing the proper rituals. I found myself compelled to make do with picturing the joyous moment when circumstances finally permitted us to come together and consummate our love. In my mind, I tingled at her touch, inhaled the heady perfume of her unclothed body, tasted the sweat on her warm and tender skin. Only when it came to fathoming how I might create such a propitious state of affairs did imagination fail me.

Newspapermen had begun to subject the Institute to scrutiny as unrelenting as it was unfair. Yellon, editor of *The Albion Magazine,* a rag supposedly dedicated to serving the deaf, tricked his way into my consulting room and wrote up our discussions in a disgracefully pejorative fashion. My old friend Eddie Marr, uncannily well informed, gave me advance warning that Yellon had taken a hatchet to my good name and that of the Institute. I made sure that I obtained a copy of the magazine on the morning of its publication. Yellon's article was much worse than even I had feared. I cringed like a kicked puppy at his savage account of the way I had examined him, while his description of my person was no more, no less, than a vicious and humiliating libel.

"The jaunty butterfly tie vied in hue with the shirt. The patent leather shoes were a trifle cracked, and his face a warning to all observant beholders. The flabby gills, the shifty eyes . . ."

Calumny heaped upon calumny. Overwhelmed by a mixture of contempt and despair, I hurled the magazine into the wastepaper basket. When Ethel walked into my room to take dictation, she found me with my head buried in my hands. When I managed to explain what had brought me so low, she retrieved the journal from its resting place. As she read the offending piece, her pale face darkened with horror and hurt.

"Hawley, you must consult a solicitor at once! This man cannot be allowed to say such wicked things in print! You must seek redress."

I rocked in my chair and shook my head. "Lawyers grow fat on defamation suits. So do magazine proprietors. The cost of any fees can be set off against the benefits of increased circulation. No, Ethel, I have walked into one trap set by Mr. Evan Yellon. I have no intention of falling into another."

"What, then?" She was standing over me, her lovely eyes awash with dismay.

"Drouet's is done for. It is not simply this farrago of invention and invective. That inquest up in the Midlands has dealt us a mortal blow. This week alone, we have received less than half the customary number of completed questionnaires."

In Staffordshire, a locksmith called Johnson had died from an abscess of the brain allegedly resulting from middle ear disease. The deceased had been utilising Drouet plasters and a doctor had given evidence that our treatment was not only useless, but may even have contributed to the wretched fellow's demise. The Institute was not represented in court, and we were powerless to prevent the admission of prejudicial testimony. The coroner and his jury had no interest in the subtle ambiguities of medical treatment; nor did the reporters who condemned us with sanctimonious glee. Healing depends on the maintenance of an intimate bond of trust and confidence between doctor and patient. When that bond is shattered, the patient cannot be cured and the doctor's future is bleak.

On the day that I tendered my resignation to my masters on the Continent, Ethel also gave notice to leave. Of course, she had qualms about departing from the only firm by which she had ever been employed, but I explained that the Institute was as doomed as the House of Usher. Her loyalty was such that she would follow me anywhere.

We made a false start by joining the Aural Clinic Company in New Oxford Street, since within six months that business also failed. This left me with no choice but to swallow my pride and approach Professor Munyon. His company, so Eddie Marr reported, was going from strength to strength. Fortunately, the professor did not bear a grudge as a result of my previous departure—"You stuck to your guns, Crippen, and that's an end of the matter"—and I was offered the position of manager at the branch now located in Oxford Circus. Of course, I insisted that Ethel be appointed as my confidential secretary, explaining that she had been the rock who had supported me throughout the dark times at Drouet's.

The past few years had taught me the dangers of relying upon a single source of income and I still hankered after the days when, at the ill-fated Sovereign Remedy Company, I had been my own master. I conceived the idea of running a business of my own as a sideline. Yet I needed financial support, since Cora and I found it impossible to save money.

Eddie Marr offered me backing to set up the Aural Remedies Company, an enterprise immeasurably more modest than Drouet's, with correspondingly lighter overheads. I secured an office in Craven House, Kingsway, and Ethel helped me make ends meet by acting as both secretary and bookkeeper. Within twelve months of our departure, the English branch of Drouet's was dead and I persuaded the receiver to sell me the assets (customer lists, as well as stocks of anti-catarrhal snuff) at a knock-down price. Thus equipped, I established a business system modelled on the profitable regime at Marble Arch. The analytical forms that clients were asked to complete were accompanied by copies of a little publication I had devised. *The Otological Gazette* described in menacing terms the dire consequences for hearing and even life itself that could result from failure to remedy aural problems, while offering assurance that salvation was at hand.

Hope—that is the secret of medicine, as it is of life. Rob a patient of hope and he has nothing. It can only be a kindness to point out to people a solution to the problem blighting their lives. The Aural Remedies Company could not work miracles, but it offered hope, and that is but a short step from granting happiness.

The literature was all my own work. I flattered myself that I had a gift for translating the nuances of a general practitioner's bedside manner into the wholly distinct medium of a reassuring public advertisement.

"No matter how many disappointments . . . no matter how severe, obstinate, or chronic the form of deafness . . . this method has made it possible for patients to effect a positive and permanent cure by treating themselves in their own home."

Thus, in a few well-chosen words, I confronted the demons that tormented the sick and disabled, and shone light on a means by which those demons could be chased away. All that was required was a modest investment in "Dr. Crippen's Simple Home Treatment."

Arthur, our conversation saddens me. You accuse me of keeping secrets from you, of failing to reveal evidence that would cause the newspapers to clamour for my release. Can I help it if Mr. Horatio Bottomley pronounces himself dissatisfied with my version of events? Forgive me, but just now effecting an improvement to the circulation of *John Bull* is not at the forefront of my mind.

How many times must I repeat myself? I am *not* helping anyone to escape justice, I am *not* a piece on a chessboard, apt to be moved around by a murderous hand. You walk up and down the narrow cell, clenching your gloved fists with ill-concealed ire at my unfolding memories, but I beg you to show patience. Just as the warders who sit with me in shifts display endless calm and kindness as we while away the hours in idle conversation. It is odd: If the worst were to happen, I would have so little time left, and yet the passing minutes crawl by.

Soon, though, our waiting will be over. The appeal is no more than twenty four hours away.

Letter from H.H. Crippen to Ethel Le Neve,
21 November 1910 (extract)

". . . God, indeed, must hear our cry to Him for Divine help . . . deep down in my heart was just a glimmer of trust that God might give us yet a chance to put me right before the world and let me have the passionate longing of my soul."

Ethel never once stepped across the threshold of the apartment in Store Street. Her subtle questioning elicited that it had only a single bedroom. Although I did my utmost to persuade her that our love was not in any way tarnished by my sleeping in the same bed as Cora, she found this difficult to comprehend.

I reminded myself that Ethel was young, a virgin unfamiliar with the labyrinthine complications and essential compromises of married life. She could not be expected to imagine that a man whose wife has, in many respects, deserted him, may still entertain a residue of affection for her. Moreover, a red-blooded male in the prime of life will still have physical needs and possess an appetite for conjugal satisfaction.

To Ethel, there was no dilemma. Until the two of us could be together, Cora and I ought to move elsewhere, to a larger home where we are not compelled to share a bedroom. Time after time, with the relentlessness of her sex, she returned to this theme. For several months I temporized, but eventually I gave in. I could not risk losing her.

I raised the subject with Cora over breakfast. Her mood was bright, although she was clearly impatient for me to finish my bacon and depart to the office. The postman had delivered a letter addressed to her in a familiar hand; it bore a Chicago postmark.

"You know, dearest, we are really very cramped here. Don't you think we should consider moving to somewhere more spacious, a better address?"

"That would be swell!" Her eyes glittered. "We need a bigger place, somewhere we can entertain our friends in comfort."

"Of course, we need to consider the cost of . . ."

"We're going up in the world! Come on, no need to be a skinflint. We'll get by, you and me. Now, you'd better run along, or you'll be late and that will never do."

So began the search for a house to rent. To buy was out of the question, but after a few weeks I found an affordable semi-detached residence in a tree-lined crescent just off the Camden Road. I fancied that I would enjoy doing odd jobs inside and tending to the little garden at the back. Cora was right; the time had come for us to live in a dwelling more suited to a successful physician and his wife.

Out of superstition, Cora decreed that she would not inspect the place until she knew for certain that it was ours: she said she could not bear to fall in love with somewhere and then be denied the chance of living there. All well and good, but if she loathed my choice, I knew I should never hear an end of it. Once I had completed negotiations on a three-year lease with Mr. Lown, the landlord, Cora came with me to take a look at our new home. The omens were propitious; after a wet morning, the clouds had cleared and as I unlatched the front gate, the sun came out.

"Smell that air, Cora!" I urged, inhaling the tang from the damp laurels. "How fresh it is compared to the sooty atmosphere of the city centre!"

"So this is it," she said softly.

"You like it, my dear?"

I held my breath. Already I had become attached to the idea of planting myself in this serene and leafy environment, and I cringed inwardly at the thought that Cora might take an unreasoning dislike to the house on sight and announce that it possessed a "hoodoo." Slowly, as she surveyed the property, her eyes widened with pleasure and I uttered a silent prayer of gratitude.

"Peter, it's wonderful!"

I pounded up the flight of steps, almost breaking into a trot. At the top, I fumbled in my pocket for the front door key.

"Say, what's down below?" she demanded.

"There is a basement area, on a level with the garden. Breakfast room, kitchen, and even a cellar—look there and you may spot the coal hole."

"A cellar, huh? Mmmm. That's useful."

I beamed as I fitted the key in the lock. "Extremely useful, my dear. Welcome to your new home. Number 39, Hilldrop Crescent."

Those early months at Hilldrop Crescent were lit by a warm glow of contentment. For the first time I had a garden, and when the weather was clement I spent most of my leisure hours working outside. Pride of place in the flower beds belonged to half a dozen rose bushes, and I acquired the knack of pruning so as to foster fresh growth. Rose water had medicinal potential—by repute it soothes dermatitis and heals rashes and burns—and I beguiled spare moments with dreams of producing it commercially.

My work at Munyon's was well remunerated, and the Aural Remedies business achieved a growth in turnover, if not yet profit. Ethel's humour was much improved by my willingness to leave Store Street. Members of the fair sex derive inordinate pleasure from a man's willingness to meet their wishes.

Cora yearned for novelty in the way the drug fiend craves the needle. Throwing herself into suburban life with characteristic zest, she spoke often of practising strict economies. When shopping, she would take pains to search out the cheapest stalls in the Caledonian Market to buy a scrawny fowl for our dinner. Yet on many a trip, she would take with her a little cloth bag full to the brim with a hundred pounds' worth of her luckiest gems.

She insisted that we redecorate from top to bottom, and I did not have the heart to begrudge the expense. The occasional tables, china dogs, and lamp stands that she picked up at auctions made a strange and not inexpensive assortment. She loved placing bids and all too often became carried away. By the time she had finished, almost every room was lavishly decked out in her lucky colour. The wallpaper matched the shades of the bracket lamps. Even the paintings on our walls were adorned at the corners with pink velvet bows. As if that were not enough, Cora herself decided to undergo a transformation.

"Audiences are sick of seeing the same old faces," she announced one evening. "I need to make a change. Say, Peter, how would you like me with blond hair?"

Whenever Cora launched herself on a flight of fancy, diplomatic approval was prudent. I assured her that she looked lovely enough as she was, but for once she swatted the compliment away as if it were a troublesome fly.

"No, silly, I'm serious. I'm tired of looking like this. What do you think would suit me better, auburn hair or fair?"

Recognising that she was in earnest, I offered to bleach her hair myself. The following night, she sat down in the kitchen and I set to work. The physical act of massaging the dye into her stubborn tresses excited me. Her bosom heaved as I worked in the solution; every now and then she emitted a sigh of encouragement. I found that, long before the task was complete, my fingers were itching to stray. When I brought a mirror, she cooed at the result of my labours and within the hour she granted me ample reward.

The effect of the change was startling. She would brush her hair down and throw it over, leaving it with a puff. To glance at her, perhaps from an angle, one might be in the presence of a different, unknown woman. Sometimes I would avert my gaze from the familiar and increasingly stout figure and, looking only at the fair head, conjecture for a moment what it would be like to marry again.

A passing fantasy, nothing more. Underneath the newly golden curls, she was still the same Cora, still susceptible to fits of temper and pique. We did have separate rooms, just as I had promised Ethel. Yet upon occasion I could not help but succumb. When I crossed the landing barefoot and knocked on her door at midnight, Cora sometimes invited me in.

Shortly after we moved into the house, Cora started taking Communion at the Roman Catholic Church in Kentish Town. For years, she had neglected her religion and had given up going to early Mass altogether. On returning to fold, she was not satisfied with half measures. One evening she insisted that we go to bed early, since she must be up in good time for the service. We were sitting together in the kitchen, as was our custom. We seldom had the light on in the hall or living room unless we were receiving. The blinds of the front parlour likewise remained drawn unless we had company; otherwise, the carpet in the room would be faded by the sunlight. I had been reading a novel by Hugh Conway and I put it down with the utmost reluctance.

Consulting my turnip-watch, I said, "It's only . . ."

She caught my arm. "You can read that mouldy old book any time, Peter. Now don't pout! You could always come to church with me. Say, that's an idea! You always used to tell me about spending half your childhood in chapel in Michigan, but you never even say your prayers these days. How about it?"

Uncertainly, I said, "I'll think about it, Belle."

She smiled. All too often, I forgot and called her Cora, an error guaranteed to provoke complaint.

"Come on, you might as well make up your mind. You never know, you might find something you've been searching for."

I closed my eyes, my mind slipping back to Coldwater and the thrill of fear that made me shiver when the preacher glared with menace.

From fornication and all other deadly sin; and from all the deceits of the world, the flesh, and the devil.

My brain echoed with the young boy's faint, inadequate response.

"Good Lord deliver us."

A cool finger was travelling along my cheek. I opened my eyes to see Cora gazing at me. Fair curls falling over her brow. Pink tongue peeping out from between her lips as she focused on me.

"My church means so much to me and you scarcely seem to care about your own. We were married by Father Eakins, after all."

The logic, as ever with Cora, was faulty. To agree to a wedding service being conducted by a priest is one thing; wholly to embrace the Catholic doctrine quite another. Privately, I had long believed that, for Cora, religious observance was as much a romantic superstition as surrounding herself with the colour pink. Yet the intensity of her gaze hypnotised me.

Meekly, I said, "Very well, my dear."

In the pew beside me, Cora sat still and silent as the priest invoked our Lord. He was young and handsome and she hung on his every word. Whether this revived enthusiasm for communal worship was a sign of maturity or merely another passing fad, I could not gauge. My thoughts drifted back to the night before. Of course I had not slunk off to my own room after agreeing to accompany her to church. When she stood at the bottom of the stairs and beckoned me on, I could not help but follow. Without a word, Cora retrieved the blindfold from a cupboard and blew the dust off it. This was the first time she had invited me to wear my mask in many months.

I saw in my mind the pale face of Ethel Le Neve. Subjugated, I was free to let my thoughts roam. What if these were Ethel's breasts grazing against my cheeks, then my chest? What if these were Ethel's fingertips, probing with such zeal? What if this was Ethel's wet mouth, swallowing me? I had to choke back the words on the tip of my tongue.

Ethel, it is you I worship.

An elbow dug into my ribs. "Peter," Cora hissed, "why the silly smile?"

"Just concentrating, my dear," I whispered.

"Aren't you glad now that you agreed to come along?" she asked when we were outside the church.

A light rain having begun to fall, the act of unfurling my umbrella allowed me a moment to compose a safe reply. "You were right, my dear. He is a splendid preacher."

"There now! Didn't I tell you? So—what do you think?"

"Think?"

"About conversion, of course! Last night you as good as said you were keen."

I hesitated, wondering how I would have broken the news to grandfather Philo, had he still been alive. The very notion gave me a sick feeling in the stomach. But he was dead and I had become my own man. Besides, there was a passion about Catholicism, a sensuality, that struck a chord.

I straightened my shoulders. "Would it make you happy if I were to convert, my love?"

"We'll be able to sing God's praises together."

A broad smile spread across her face, like the smile of a tiger, admiring its lunch.

The plainest proof that life in Hilldrop Crescent suited me came when I could no longer fit into my trousers. Even on my fortieth birthday, my build had been as slight as in my youth, but now I was gaining weight. When I told Adeline and her husband that I was getting quite fat, I startled them by chuckling with glee. In my increasing girth, I discerned evidence of maturity and an unwonted happiness.

For the first time in my life, I appreciated spending time out in the fresh air and relished the damp earth on my fingers. Never before had I made things grow. I also discovered an unsuspected talent for construction. Cora asked me to build a brick wall, so as to separate our property from our neighbours', and I erected a greenhouse, together with a freshwater aquarium as a home for the fish I started to breed. We kept two lady cats, one of them a beautiful white Persian, and I made a cage to put in the garden so that they could take the air. Otherwise, the wretched creatures were forbidden to roam, since Cora shuddered at the fate that might befall our fish—or the cats themselves—if they went on a nocturnal quest for romance.

For us, the neighbourhood represented a step up after Store

Street. Hilldrop Crescent was eminently respectable—and yet we soon discovered that it fell short of being an earthly Paradise. The women's prison was not far away, but at least the inmates caused us no trouble. The Caledonian Cattle Market was a different proposition. In the small hours, when the cows were being led to the slaughter, they would make a dreadful noise. I slept soundly, but Cora's slumbers were fragile. Time after time, she complained that the bellowing of the doomed cattle kept her awake at night.

Poor dumb animals. My fellow feeling for them has never been so strong.

Cora was never one for quiet contemplation. She became so easily bored. To make matters worse, engagements were thin on the ground. The Bedford Music Hall was but a short distance from Hilldrop Crescent, and the stage superintendent, Harry Goodson, had once written a couple of songs for her. Nowadays, though, she was more likely to be in the audience than on the stage. The recollection of her first show there, dressed in full military uniform and singing "The Major," always prompted a pang of nostalgia.

For Cora, the domestic routine provided no substitute for the shivery excitement of venturing out in the glare of the theatre lights. Despite the size of the house, we employed no servant after the girl who worked for us in the first few months left for a better wage elsewhere. Yet Cora seldom deigned to pick up a feather duster.

Letters from Bruce Miller became as rare as orchids in Camden Town. This gave cause for quiet satisfaction; I had long doubted my rival's constancy. Cora mentioned him less often these days; he had, she said, become a real estate agent—evidently there was more money to be made from buying and selling land than from treading on the boards. One evening, I came home late after a *tête-à-tête* with Ethel at Frascati's, having quite forgotten the dismay I had felt earlier in the day at the arrival after a long gap of another letter from Chicago. In the kitchen I discovered Cora sitting in the dark, sullen and tear-stained. When she stomped off to bed, I heard the door bang and the key turn angrily in the lock. I assumed I had been guilty of some unintentional act of thoughtlessness and let it go, but a couple of nights later, she unburdened herself.

"Peter, his wife's had a baby."

"I see, my dear."

I deduced that this was old news; no doubt he had found it difficult to bring himself to tell my wife that he was finally out of her reach. For a few moments I even allowed myself a twinge of sympathy for the man's predicament, but it did not last. His photograph remained defiantly in place upon our piano.

That same night, she made it clear she needed comforting, and I could not find it in my heart to deny her. Taking off her chemise, she padded across the bedroom floor to her dressing table. From a drawer she produced a length of rope. I stared at it, uncomprehending.

"This is something Lincoln gave me," she said softly. "He loved it. I think you will, too."

If this was the truth, I did not believe it was the whole truth. She had left the stove manufacturer a long time ago, and the rope looked stiff and new. But what did it matter?

"What do you want me to do?" I asked, watching in bewilderment as, with the ease of practice, she used a cord to fashion the rope into the form of a noose.

"It excited him to wear it just like this—see? Now watch as I tighten it. There, Peter, feel the roughness of the hemp. Imagine it against your skin, against your neck. There's nothing more scary or arousing, I promise."

I kept still and said nothing even as she slipped the noose over my head and around my neck. She was right in one respect: it chafed against my Adam's apple. When, with a smile, she pulled the rope a little tighter, tears pricked my eyes. I was stiff with fear.

"Gee, what's the matter? You're so tense. Why don't you relax? Let me take over, you know you like it when I'm in control."

"I hate having this thing around my neck. I'm afraid you'll strangle me. Take it off, please, I beg you."

Her eyes narrowed and for reply she yanked the rope. I gasped in fear.

"I—I think I'm going to be sick."

She cast a glance at the heavens. "Oh, for God's sake! I'll take it off. Then you can go straight back to your own room."

Grudgingly, she released me and tossed the makeshift noose on to the bed. I rubbed my sore neck vigorously. "I'm sorry, but . . ."

"Don't say anything. You only make it worse when you talk. Get out of my sight, d'you hear?"

The house was large and draughty, with creaking floors. Cora complained that when she was alone, the place "gave her the willies." It would never echo with the sound of children's laughter, and in compensation she acquired first one pet, and then another. After the cats, she acquired—at no little expense—a magnificent blue and gold macaw, with a black beard and a piercing shriek. Later came a bull terrier, a jolly little chap that I enjoyed taking for walks. The place reeked of animals. Yet this menagerie did not keep her fully occupied for long. She yearned for bustle and conversation, and she found it through membership of the Music Hall Ladies' Guild.

The Guild dedicated itself to supporting the poorer women

and children of the music hall profession. Members worked assiduously to raise funds, although their labours were not wholly self-sacrificing. Certainly, the dinners they held were convivial and loud, and their balls at the Trocadero ever more glittering, with fine clothes as abundant as the flowing champagne. As for Cora, she discovered in herself a gift for persuading people to part with their money in a good cause. Or perhaps she simply began to exploit for the benefit of others a facility she had long ago honed at my expense.

Marie Lloyd was the President of the Guild. She gloried in her humble origins and liked to say that she always had sympathy for the little man. Yet Cora was her friend, not me. I thought she held me in some esteem, and it came as a blow to learn that I had become the butt of her ridicule.

"The Half-Crown King" was the nickname she bestowed upon me. Years passed before I found out. Cora told me during a quarrel that Marie used to regale her friends with accounts of how, at Guild dinners, I would offer to buy drinks for the assembled company, only to find that I had ventured out minus my wallet. So I borrowed from the others and pocketed the difference. An unkind slander, based on a single regrettable incident. I once had the misfortune to order drinks at a bar in Leicester Square before realising that I had left my wallet at home. Marie elevated this solitary error to a way of life, and so I became the Half-Crown King, not merely too mean to spend his own money but all too ready to profit from the generosity of others.

In hours of darkness, I huddle under the coarse blanket, even though it makes me itch, and recall prurient stories of the scaffold that I once devoured. *The Newgate Calendar* and all those penny dreadfuls have left a sour taste. Seldom can a prisoner in the condemned cell have been so well informed about the fate that lies ahead for him—should the appeal fail, that is. Even though I have forgotten many of the stories, details spring into my head when I would least wish to be reminded of them. The special vocabulary of the execution shed, for instance, where the rope becomes *the hempen cravat*, or, a favourite from long ago, *the anodyne necklace*. I dread nothing more than *launching into eternity.*

Like so many other decent men and women, I have hungered for information about the minutiae of the execution process, and I devoured the stories of how those convicted of capital crimes met their end. The personalities of the executioners held a special fascination for me. Each brought his own refinements to the trade.

Marwood, the cobbler, was a man of science, with his neat calculations and demand for five-ply Italian silk hemp with a three-quarter-inch diameter. It was he who fixed a brass eyelet at one end of the rope, in place of a slipknot, as well as adding a leather washer to the noose, so as to prevent untoward movement. Berry, a salesman, devised a new form of scaffold with a brick-lined pit beneath, and clips to prevent the trap door leaves injuring the prisoner during the drop.

All this I recall with dreadful clarity, as well as my mental pictures of the hangman going about his work. Pinioning the prisoner's arms and body. Baring the neck. Taking him to the drop platform and placing him beneath the beam from which was suspended the rope. Strapping the legs. Putting the white hood over his face. Putting the rope around his neck. Pulling the lever to open the trap door.

And then the prisoner would dance for him.

The ritual of the gallows used to seem so comforting, a means of purging the land of infamy. Now I writhe in my bed, tortured by the memory of the injustice I have suffered, and by fear of the consequences if wisdom does not prevail. But the first flecks of morning bring fresh light. I must have courage; I must place my trust in the judges of appeal to correct this grievous wrong.

Letter from the Aural Remedies Company to a prospective patient (undated)

Dear Sir,

As I have received no answer to my letter of a few days ago I can only conclude that your hesitation in deciding to adopt my treatment is due to previous unfortunate experiments that have very naturally caused you to harbour suspicion against all so-called cures, and a strong disinclination to spend any more money without some stronger assurance of receiving adequate return.

. . . If you will send me half the amount mentioned in my last letter, namely 10s 6d, I will at once forward the full and complete Outfit "On Trial." If, at the expiration of a sufficient time, say three weeks, you feel you have derived no benefit, you can return what is left of the Outfit and not pay me another penny . . .

Yours faithfully,
H.H. Crippen

"Paying guests?" I repeated.

"A little more money in the household wouldn't hurt," Cora said.

True. After a year at Hilldrop Crescent, our expenditure was keeping pace remorselessly with the rise in my income. Cora was back in the habit of beseeching me to add to her collection of gems. Saying no was like throwing logs on a fire. In addition came the cost of treats for Ethel and of settling my account at Frascati's.

"We have no help in the house," I pointed out. "We would need to find a housemaid."

She shook the blond curls and I noticed darkness at the roots. Lately she had taken to visiting a hairdresser rather than asking me to bleach her locks; one more bill to pay.

"No, Peter, I've thought it all out. We could do the work ourselves. We don't have to spend much on food. I can get cheap cuts at the market. What do you say?"

The prospect of sharing my home with lodgers made me shudder. Even when the Sovereign Remedy Company failed, our house had been our own. This would resemble our early married life, when we squeezed into Herr Mersinger's little home in Brooklyn.

"I'm not sure," I said, groping for an excuse to kill off her scheme.

"Besides," Cora said. "It would be company for me. At least

before we were in the midst of London. Out here it's so dull during the day."

"But you have the cats, you have Rex, you have . . ."

"Yes, but they're not *people!*" she exclaimed, as if speaking to an especially dense seven year old. "It's all very well for you. You're out at the office all day, with that little Miss Le Neve dancing attendance upon you. *Yes, Doctor Crippen, no, Doctor Crippen, three bags full, Doctor Crippen.*"

The whining mimicry was so grotesquely unfair that I did not even feel a jolt of anger on poor Ethel's behalf. But did Cora know how much Ethel meant to me? I scanned her face for clues that she might regard my secretary as a rival rather than as a source of amusement but found nothing. In wilder moments, I even wondered if Cora would care if she discovered that when I claimed to be working late, more often than not I was laughing and joking with my typist over dinner.

"You have all your friends," I pointed out. "The Ladies' Guild . . ."

"Yes, yes," she said. "But they're busy people. It's not as if we're together all day, every day. That's why it would be nice to take in one or two lodgers. See, you can interview everyone who replies. Even then, if things don't work out, I won't mind if you send them packing. Well, Peter, what do you say? Do you mind indulging little old me?"

Her face was screwed up into an expression so comically piti-ful as to melt the stoniest of hearts. Even the rowdiest audience at the Varieties in Hoxton could not have resisted it. Unable to help myself, I dropped a kiss on her powdered cheek.

"Of course, my dear. If it will make you happy . . ."

"Oh, Peter!" She was almost dancing up and down with delight. "You can compose the advertisement yourself, to make sure it suits you, how's that?"

I assented readily and when I ventured to ask her if she might be ready for an early night, she nodded, eager as a child. As we mounted the stairs, I consoled myself that her enthusiasm for taking in lodgers was a harmless whim. I doubted if it would survive the winter.

"You're worried," I said. "Don't deny it, my sweet. I can always tell."

Ethel mustered a wan smile and squeezed my hand. We were returning to the office via St. James's Park following a leisurely luncheon. Most of the leaves had fallen from the trees, yet the sun had done its best to cheer us.

"Am I so transparent, Hawley?"

"We have had a precious hour together and yet you've hardly uttered a word. What on earth can be the matter?"

She swallowed and said, "The order book is down again this week. Do you know what all this reminds me of, Hawley? Those last few months with Drouet's, before the business began to fail."

I laughed. "Is that all? Ethel, my sweet, the situation we enjoy these days bears no comparison with the Institute. Besides, I have spread the risk. Apart from the Aural Remedies, I have my connection with Munyon's. Remember, old Drouet was a scoundrel, plain and simple."

"I wish I could be so sanguine."

"You trust me, don't you?" I said it in a jocular way, certain of the answer.

"With my life!" she exclaimed. "But—that is not to say that I have equal confidence in Mr. Marr."

"Eddie?" I offered a comfortable smile of reassurance. "Well now, he's a tricky character, I agree."

"Oh, Hawley, you're too good and kind to be mixed up with someone like that! He is a double-dealer, I'm sure of it. So glib and convincing, but I don't trust him an inch."

"You can rest assured that he wouldn't have sunk his money into an enterprise like mine if he didn't think it was a sound bet."

Her lovely eyes clouded with doubt. "I suppose if you say it's all right . . ."

The rest of our conversation on the walk back to Oxford Street was confined to the exchange of endearments; nonetheless, Ethel's anxiety struck a chord. At all costs, I must not frighten her. A mishap such as the death of the locksmith that ruined Drouet's would spell the end for us.

Ethel underestimated the stakes. Financial ruin was not the worst fate that might lie in store for me. The newspapers were full of vicious attacks on so-called quacks. In darker moments, I wondered if the police might prosecute me. On the flimsiest of evidence, on any scrap of biased testimony, I could be sent to prison. Hateful, hateful, hateful. To be condemned to a cage, just like our cats—I would never be able to bear it.

Four lodgers took rooms with us. The first to present himself at our front door was a burly young fellow with a mop of fair hair and hands the size of shovels. Richard Ehrlich, from Heidelberg. Once we agreed terms, he persuaded three fellow countrymen to join him as our guests. My views on their country had in recent months been coloured by William Le Queux. *The Daily Mail* had serialised one of his romances concerning an invasion launched by the Kaiser. But Ehrlich's earnest manner disarmed melodramatic suspicions, while Cora was quick to remind me of her own family connections with Germany.

She was delighted to have a group of young and impressionable fellows in the house. "It gives me a chance to *sprechen* a little *deutsch*," she joked. "I sure was getting rusty until you came along."

The language was a closed book to me, but for a week or two

it amused me to listen to them chattering away, Cora making desperate efforts to keep up with the conversation. Ehrlich had punctilious manners and would break away from the group every now and then to try out his English on me. Since he was a good ten inches taller than I, I found that sustained conversation was impeded as much by a persistent crick in the neck as by the obstacles to translating idiom.

Every evening our guests gathered around the piano in the front parlour. Cora, liberally doused in a perfume of gardenias, would sing "She Went Never Went Further Than That." One night she stretched her arm around Ehrlich's massive shoulders and serenaded him with one of Marie Lloyd's favourites, a version of "Come Into the Garden, Maud" so freighted with innuendo as to be quite obscene. He cast me a nervous glance, and his bulky frame seemed to shrink with the embarrassment. It struck me that, to our youthful guests, their plump hostess belonged to an older generation. I stretched out comfortably in my chair and gave Ehrlich a nod of reassurance. In that moment, we were members of the same gentlemen's club, brought together by a common urge to cringe at Cora's theatrical simpering.

Taking in lodgers was hard work. At six o'clock each morning, I rose to clean the boarders' boots, shovel up the coal from the cellar, and lay the breakfast in good time so that I could be at the office by eight. My discontent was fuelled by Cora's fondness for converting the rent into gems, brooches, and assorted knickknacks. Yet to venture the mildest complaint was to risk the slap of Cora's contempt.

"You're jealous, Peter, that's what it is."

"Jealous? My dear, of whom? All I was saying . . ."

"I know perfectly well what you're saying, Peter Crippen. You begrudge me a little pleasure, that's plain enough. The boys are good fun and handsome and I enjoy being in their company, that's why you're jealous."

Her scorn took the wind out of my sails, but I muttered, "I'm working all the hours God sends."

"Well, He wouldn't know," Cora said smugly. "It's three weeks since you last came with me to church. You're too busy making eyes at that little typewriter of yours, if you ask me. That's why you're so weary, not because I ask you to help out a little when you do condescend to come home."

She was always so quick to seize the advantage. I never learned how to draw the sting of her insults. When she mentioned Ethel, I had to take care not to give the game away. So I said nothing more.

"When you studied medicine, did you learn about dentistry?" Ethel asked one evening.

We were savouring the aroma of a cup of strong coffee after our latest five-shilling dinner at Frascati's. A couple of hours had slipped away in a trice. She was so attentive to my lightest remark, sometimes she made me feel as wise as an ancient philosopher. In contrast, Cora could be relied upon to find fault with whatever I did. Worse still, she chose to vent her displeasure in front of our lodgers. Once, after taking a couple of tots of brandy, she jeered raucously at my supposed incompetence. I remember Ehrlich's face turning a shade to match the wallpaper. Small wonder that I was returning home later and later. Sometimes she would be up with the lodgers, regaling them with anecdotes of life on the halls. On other occasions she had extinguished all the lights and was locked away in her room. I no longer troubled to bark my knuckles on her door.

"Dentistry? Well, I have some familiarity with diseases of the teeth. Why do you ask?"

"It was just—I've been thinking. I was reading *The Performer* at lunchtime, while you were talking to Eddie Marr."

"Ah, yes."

Marr had sauntered into the office that morning at my request. I had found myself in some little embarrassment with the bank, and he had agreed to tide me over for a day or two.

"You're always telling me about music hall people, how they need to have such blinding smiles, and how they spend a fortune on looking after their teeth."

"Certainly, my dear."

I finished my coffee and clicked my fingers at a waiter who scurried to refresh my cup. By this time I was well known at Frascati's and I luxuriated in the little courtesies granted to a valued customer. I strove to remember the pleasure they gave me when it was time to settle the account at the end of each month.

"Well, Hawley, why don't you offer to look after their dental work for them? Already you attend several of your wife's friends. Besides, you know all there is to know about the ear, nose, and throat. Caring for teeth is a logical step."

Her suggestion took me aback. I was no more a dentist than I was a surgeon. Yet Ethel was right. Dentistry was a burgeoning field.

Reaching across the table, I patted her hand. "An excellent suggestion!"

Her face brightened at once. "Do you mean that, Hawley?"

"Of course. You're right. The Americans are making a real go of dental work. The likes of Goldberg on the Strand make a small fortune from plugging the cavities of Cora's friends."

She flinched at the mention of my wife's name. Each and every reminder that I was not free caused her distress. But that did not deter her from pursuing her theme.

"Well, as you say, the journals are full of advertisements for American Painless Dentistry. So it occurred to me: why not make the most of your nationality? With your accent and comforting personality, the patients would flock in. You could call yourself the Yale Tooth Specialist."

I clapped my hands in delight. " *'The Yale Tooth Specialist'?* Yes, it definitely has a ring about it."

"Then you'll consider it?"

"I'll do better than that, my dear. I'll start looking out for a partner."

She hesitated. "Hawley, there is just one thing. I think this is a business you should run on your own. Don't take Eddie Marr in with you, please. I just don't trust that man."

I thought for a moment. It would suit me not to be in thrall to Marr. Sovereign and Drouet's had taught me not to keep all my eggs in a single basket.

"Very well, Ethel. I shall not say a word to him about the enterprise until I open the doors for business."

Now it was her turn to give a delighted clap, leaving me to wonder how to find a colleague sufficiently expert in dentistry to turn Ethel's topical conception into reality.

A drab November morning. Walking back along Hilldrop Crescent under a charcoal sky, I reproached myself as bitterly as Cora might have done for my mistake. I had through an oversight omitted to take with me to the office a set of copies of *The Otological Gazette* that I was due to mail to customers that day. My body ached after a night starved of sleep. My throat was sore, my limbs leaden; no doubt I was sickening for a cold.

As it was not yet eleven o'clock, I nursed the hope that Cora might still be fast asleep and thus unable to chastise me for my error. In the days when she was performing more regularly, she cultivated the habit of lying in bed for as long as possible on the morning after a show. Even if she did not have the excuse of a late night to rely upon, the habit lingered.

We kept the side door on the latch and I let myself in quietly.

Sure enough, the pile of journals was on the table in the front parlour, waiting reproachfully for me. Of Cora, there was no sign.

Suddenly a whoop of delight came from upstairs. A sound that, of late, I had almost forgotten. Cora, having a fine old time.

I was about to call her name, to see what had prompted her merriment, when I had second thoughts. Instead, I crept up the stairs, moving like a tracker in one of the stories by Fenimore Cooper long ago.

A stifled cry came from Cora's room, freezing me halfway up the steps. I fancied that what I had heard was a gasp of shock. At once it had a terrible familiarity. I was reminded of an evening in New York in 1892, when I claimed Cora from her servitude with C.C. Lincoln.

In a trance of horror, I took off my shoes so as not to make the slightest noise and began to edge up toward the first landing, praying that for once the stairs would not creak under my tread. Cora had not closed her door. More sounds were coming from the room. A man, grunting. A woman, gasping words of encouragement, words I had not heard for such a long time.

Not for one moment did I contemplate retracing my steps, collecting the journals and leaving the house. As I bit into my lower lip, a voice in my head told me that I must witness what was happening. Bravery or cowardice, anger or fear, curiosity or folly, none of these moved me. I was beyond emotion. That had been drained from me in a hundred dreams about Cora and Bruce Miller.

She started crying out in ecstasy.

"Richard! Richard! *Schneller! Schneller!*"

I crossed the landing and stood in silence at the door. The pink room stank of human sweat. A scattering of undergarments spread across the carpet. A vast pair of men's pantaloons, a silk camisole that I had bought as a present for her last birthday—unworn, to my knowledge, since she had said she was saving it up for a special treat. In front of me, a pair of huge bare buttocks rose and fell like the prow of a ship in a storm-tossed sea. Two short legs locked around his trunk, moving with his rhythm. His hoarse panting failed to drown out the obscene invocations I thought she would only ever share with me.

I took a pace forward, making no sound. I could taste the sour smell of intimacy. As I watched, they shuddered to a consummation so violent that I thought the bed might break. When she screamed—I had not heard that scream of ecstasy for so long!—he bent his head forward and for a split second I glimpsed her face. Dark brown eyes met mine. For an instant they widened, and then they filled with a flame of triumph.

I closed my eyes to banish the sight of her, and turned on my heel. Stumbling down the stairs, no longer needing to conceal my presence, I half wondered if she would call out to me, but all I heard was Ehrlich's voice. Choked, urgent, perhaps a little afraid.

"What is it? What is it? Why do you wear that wicked smile?"

The courtroom bench is hard and unforgiving; it reminds me of the pew in the chapel at Coldwater. The ancient judges' faces are as grey as their wigs. Every now and then a nose wrinkles in disapproval of a point that Mr. Tobin is making; once or twice their eyelids droop as though they need a snooze. I can detect no hint that they realise that my life depends on their wisdom. When I listen to Mr. Justice Darling's scathing judgment, my stomach contracts. What of the lack of proof that the flesh belonged to Cora, the uncertainty as to whether it bore a scar that corresponded to hers? The learned judge dismisses the subtleties of the case with a clearing of the throat and an irritable flick of the hand.

"With regard to the evidence of the doctors concerning the piece of skin, we are not surprised that the jury preferred the evidence given by the medical men called for the Crown. For the doctors called for the defence, when cross-examined were obliged to abandon an opinion they had expressed in writing. We do not wish to say anything more than that."

So.

I am condemned to die, and all because of a medical bungle. How sweet an irony it would be, were my whole body not paralysed by the knowledge of what lies ahead and of how little time I have left.

Extract from letter from H.H. Crippen to Ethel Le Neve, 1 November 1910

"I quite understand what people say, and even at the trial the prosecution deliberately misrepresented our relations to each other for their own ends. But I know there are many who can understand what we are to each other, truly husband and wife, sacredly so; no more sacred relations to each other such as ours could ever exist."

My journey back to Albion House is misty in my memory. Did I hail a hansom? Was I wild-eyed? Did people stare? I recall nothing but the smarting of my eyes, the peals of thunder echoing in my brain. All I could see before me was the blotchy whiteness of the German's heaving rump as he thrust into my wife, again and again and again and again.

When I reached the office, I was panting as if I had run all the way from home. I found myself yearning for sanctuary, a place to hide. Ethel was sitting at her desk, taking a crumpled sheet of paper from her imposing new Underwood. She glanced up as I flung open the door, but my expression froze the words of greeting on her lips. If I had tried to speak, I would have choked with the humiliation of it all. Not even she could help me. Tottering past her, I locked myself in my room.

I needed a magic potion. In truth, there was only one remedy for calamity in which I had faith. Pulling open the cupboard, I fumbled for my vial of hyoscine. With shaking hands, I measured out a dose. The proportion I employed when making a tonic for the nerves was 5/480ths of a grain to a drop of water. A miscalculation might mean paralysis or even death, but I no longer cared. The misery flooding through me had washed away all emotions. I could not conceive of caring for anything again.

A timid knock. Ethel's fearful voice, breaking with distress.

"Hawley? Hawley? What is wrong?"

I swallowed the mixture and slumped down in my chair, my temples throbbing with betrayal. The drug was salt and bitter on my tongue; in my haste, I had not thought to sweeten it with sugared tea or coffee. My mouth burned. Had I misjudged the amount of medicine? Taken to excess, hyoscine ceases to act as a sedative and has the reverse effect. My heart was pumping frantically; perhaps I had made a fatal error.

"Hawley! The look on your face frightens me!"

Closing my ears, I strove feebly to prepare myself to meet my Maker. The knocking ceased, but through the door I heard a faint weeping. There was nothing I could do or say to her. I shut my eyes, blocking off my senses, and buried my head in my hands.

How many minutes passed, I do not know. The throbs subsided into a dullish ache and I began to breathe more normally. The hyoscine was taking effect and steadying my nerves. Lifting my head, I blinked hard several times. As I stared at the virgin surface of my mahogany desk, it came to me how completely I had failed in the errand that had taken me back home. I had forgotten to retrieve the missing copies of *The Otological Gazette*.

"She is cruel, cruel, cruel." Ethel's voice cracked with a desperate anger. "I hate her for what she has done to you. I hate her, I hate her!"

Fiddling with my cufflinks—Cora had chosen them for me in Savile Row—I said, "I loved her once."

The look in her grey eyes hypnotised me. "But you don't love her anymore."

"No," I promised.

A shower dampened our hair as we sat on the Embankment in gathering darkness. The rain and the smell of the leaves called to my mind the Sunday we had spent in town a couple of years before and I wondered if I could ever know such happiness again. We had not eaten, but the emptiness inside me hurt more than starvation. Although it was late in the afternoon, neither of us was in a mood to return to work. When we had left the office together, Ethel had told Long that I was indisposed and needed air; what excuse she gave for accompanying me, I never asked.

"Will you leave her?"

My head was bowed. "I cannot."

Instinct told me this was true, even though at that moment, I could not have explained why, had my life depended on it. Of course, Cora would bankrupt me if we separated. Our church did not smile upon divorce; no more did society at large. Yet that was not the whole of it. Cora and I were handcuffed together in matrimony. The invisible shackles of convention tied me as fast as those with which she used to bind me to the bed.

Ethel understood without my putting the cold realities into words. Empathy was her gift, and my good fortune. As I had recounted the events of that morning, in jerky, tearful sentences, her eyelashes lowered, her lips parting as she pictured the scene.

"In your own home?" Her voice was raw with the enormity of Cora's crime. "Beneath your own sheets?"

When I stood up, she followed me to the parapet. We gazed along the Thames, at the stone bridge with its arches, the pile of the shot-towers and, beyond, the shadowy outlines of the Abbey and St. Stephen's. A steamer hooted and the shrill cries of the newspaper boys filled the air. A barge approached, lugsail hoisted to a jury mast, freeboard almost awash with the moving tide. Hunched over the tiller, a squat helmsman guided his craft through the middle arch. It came to me that I, too, needed to make up my mind where I was going.

"I must never lose you."

She glanced quickly at me, as if taken by surprise. After a moment she said, "Hawley, you never will. You see, I adore you."

She had never before expressed herself so plainly. I pressed my face against hers and felt traces of rain on her cheeks. My lips touched her fine hair.

I murmured, "We cannot live on and not be all in all to each other. For so long we have been in harmony, even without being wedded. From now on, when the two of us are together, you and only you shall be my wife."

When I arrived back in Hilldrop Crescent, all the lights in Number 39 were out. It was not yet ten o'clock and on any other evening, I might have expected to find Cora performing at the piano, and the air reeking of tobacco and beer. Coming home, I had stiffened my resolve by saying over and over in my mind that there was no choice but to prepare for the worst. How easy it was to picture Cora and Ehrlich in the parlour, wrapped in a carnal embrace. But when I walked through the front door, I found downstairs deserted. Not a peep, not a rustle of bedclothes, issued from the bedrooms up above.

Breakfast the next morning passed in eerie silence. We might all have been mourners at a funeral, but nothing had been buried, other than my marriage. Ehrlich's face was as scarlet as the camisole that Cora had cast on to the floor the previous day. He would not meet my gaze. Having feared an exhibition of bravado, perversely, I felt my spirits lifting. Already, in a gesture of defiance, I had omitted to clean my rival's boots.

Ehrlich's companions seemed baffled by his silent embarrassment, and they conversed in monosyllables. Cora chewed her food savagely, but said nothing. I had assumed that she would lose no opportunity for gloating over her conquest, but she failed to muster a single coy remark. Something had happened in my absence that I could not comprehend.

"Jam for your bread, Ehrlich?" I enquired, emboldened by his evident discomfiture.

He shook his head violently, as if stung by a bee. A moment later, without a word, he sprang up and strode off to his room. Out of the corner of my eye, I saw Cora following him with her gaze. A beseeching look had spread across her face, but he did not flatter her with a farewell glance.

After the other lodgers had filed out, I said pleasantly to my wife, "You know, I don't believe this arrangement has been a success."

"What arrangement?" she asked, gnawing viciously at the last burnt slice of toast.

"Taking in boarders. At the time you suggested it, I was persuaded that the income would be welcome. Besides, as you so rightly said, the guests would provide company for you."

Although she had the grace to flush, she offered no reply.

"I've been thinking. Looking after these fellows is such hard work and we are not so short of money. I really believe that the time has come to give them notice to quit."

A score of times I had rehearsed the little speech in my head, foreseeing a spectrum of reactions. Anger, tears, argument, contempt. Nothing prepared me for a weary shrug of the shoulders.

"Like you say, the money is nothing. After all my hard work, all it's bought me is a handful of trinkets."

This was as rich as summer pudding, but I let it pass. "Shall I tell them, or will you?"

She placed her knife and fork down on her plate. Her small features hardened even as I watched.

"I'll do it."

She said it through gritted teeth, and yet with relish. It was as if I had offered her the chance to avenge an injury.

Ethel's diagnosis was brutal in its simplicity. "She pursued the boy and he surrendered. When you discovered his betrayal of your hospitality, he told her there must be no repetition. That is what she finds infuriating."

"So you think he has already broken with her?"

She was nestling against me in a hansom. We were on our way to dine with Nina and Horace. Ethel had been living with them for several months. I was always glad to see her sister and brother-in-law, but never more so than this night, when I was desperate for a reason not to return home too soon.

"I am sure of it."

I could only conclude that the explanation lay in Ehrlich's Teutonic code of honour. In cuckolding a man in his own house, he had behaved despicably. His shame accounted for his inability to look me in the eye. Leaving Hilldrop Crescent would surely come as a relief.

I stroked Ethel's wrist. "Let's speak no more of Cora."

She gave a calm, considered smile. "Yes. Our time together is so precious, it is folly to waste it on her."

My leg rubbed hers. "Dearest, have you thought any more about my suggestion?"

A rush of colour suffused her cheeks. In a voice barely audible above the tinkling of the horse's bell, she said, "Yes, Hawley, I have."

"And?"

I held my breath awaiting her reply. She did not let me down. "I want us to be as one."

Closing my eyes, I let out a long sigh of relief. "Darling, you don't know how much . . ."

"Hush," she implored me. "We do not want to be overheard. Have you a time and date in mind? Next week, perhaps?"

Next week. My heart almost stopped with the shock of her boldness. After waiting so long, I was within touching distance of Heaven's gates. Scarcely daring to believe my good fortune, I said, "Tuesday, perhaps, in the afternoon?"

"Yes," she said. "That is not too long to wait."

"As to where . . ." I tapped my foot on the floor of the cab. "There are several possibilities."

"Somewhere quiet," she said, "where we can celebrate our love in peace."

Eagerly, I reached forward and squeezed her knee. "Of course, my dear. I will find us an hotel where we can celebrate our wedding day."

A dusty milk-shop near King's Cross station became the setting for a solemnization of vows. I had scouted the place the previous afternoon; it was peaceful and little patronised, and we could sit for as long as we wanted without being disturbed. As soon as the lace-capped waitress left the tea tray on our table, I slipped the ring upon Ethel's finger.

"With this ring," I intoned softly, "I thee wed."

From her bag she extracted a ring fashioned in the shape of a crucifix. "And with this ring, I thee wed."

We had devised our own unique form of marriage service. It was no parody or pastiche of the established formalities, taking rather the nature of a dialogue. We pledged ourselves to each other. Over the past few days we had practised the lines. Ethel was word perfect.

"Wilt thou have this woman to thy wedded wife?" she murmured, with lowered eyelashes. "To live together in God's ordinance in the holy estate of matrimony? Wilt thou love her, comfort her, honour her, and keep her in sickness and in health; and, forsaking all other, keep thee only unto her, so long as ye both shall live?"

I clasped her hand and said, "I will."

After I had repeated my catechism, it was her turn.

"I, Ethel Clara, take thee, Hawley Harvey, to be my lawful wedded husband, to have and to hold from this day forward, for better for worse, for richer for poorer, in sickness and in health, to love, cherish, and to obey, till death us do part, according to God's holy ordinance; and thereto I give thee my troth."

The waitress returned, carrying a bowl. "Forgot the sugar."

"It's quite all right," Ethel assured her.

For a little while neither of us spoke and then I put the ring upon her finger and said, "With this ring I thee wed, with my body I thee worship . . ."

With my body I thee worship. Till death us do part.

Oh yes, Ethel, it was true from that very moment. With my body I thee worship. Till death do us part.

"We came down from Leeds earlier today," I told the cadaverous proprietor of *Bella Vista,* trusting that I had effectively disguised my American accent with a Yorkshire burr. "Apparently we were misinformed. The next train to Bristol is not until much later tonight. Aye, and my wife is weary after so much travelling, so we wondered if we might . . ."

"Room Four is free," the man said. His gaunt features were moulded in an expression of permanent disapproval, as if he were a phantom, condemned to an afterlife that left much to be desired. "Names?"

"Franckel," I said quickly. "Yes, Peter and Clara Franckel."

He indicated the register with a bony forefinger. "Put your moniker here, then."

The lighting in the hallway was so poor that I could barely see what I was writing. Yet having practised for hours, I entered the signature in the book with a flourish. *Peter and Clara Franckel.* Now we existed as a couple. I filled in the date: *6 December 1906.* A permanent record of our presence. How I wished I could rip out the page as a souvenir! At my side, Ethel beamed her approval. She was entering wholeheartedly into the spirit of our romantic fantasy. I would have said she was a born actress.

"Thank you so much," I said warmly as I handed the man the money. "It is good to find that you Londoners are so welcoming. You don't know how much we Northern folk . . ."

"Down the passageway," he interrupted. "Second door on the left. And can you keep it quiet? There's an old lady opposite taking her afternoon nap."

The corridor smelled of overcooked sprouts. As my nervous fingers tried to fit the key in the lock, Ethel said anxiously, "Do you think he suspected anything? Wouldn't it have been better for us to have brought some luggage along, if we're supposed to be travelling on?"

I fastened my arm around her waist. "You must learn to trust me, Ethel dear. As a matter of fact, I do believe we carried it off splendidly."

The grubby eiderdown and threadbare carpet were in keeping with the rate that we had been charged. A whiff of damp from a patch over the unpainted skirting board hung in the air. I sat down on the bed; it was hard and unyielding. My body was rigid with expectation. I kicked off my shoes and tried to muster a smile. Ethel stood in front of me. She was wearing a green serge costume. Green, Cora's hoodoo colour.

I must stop thinking of her. Now I belong to Ethel, and she to me.

"This is what you want?" I asked croakily, still unable to believe that we were here.

Her smile matched that of the Mona Lisa. I had expected her to be anxious and wracked by second thoughts. There was no fumbling as she unbuttoned the costume. Her calm satisfaction at once thrilled me and unnerved me. "Oh, yes, darling," she said. "This is what I want."

"Say, Peter, what do you think I should do?"

For Cora to ask my advice was almost unheard of. Since Ehrlich's departure, she had thrown herself into her work, alternately writing fresh material with Adeline and rehearsing coon songs in front of the mirror in our parlour. As a peace offering for the Holy Season, I bought her a short spangled dress that she had been ogling in a Piccadilly shop window. She needed a new outfit to mark her return to show business, and on Christmas morning she pranced around the house in the new outfit, grinning from ear to ear. I told her how much it suited her, while noticing the tightness of the waist and how it failed to flatter her stubby little legs. That night, Cora left her bedroom door open, and I hesitated for a moment before continuing. Lying back on my own bed, I stared at the ceiling and uttered thanks for my newfound strength to resist temptation. Now I was allowed to feast upon Ethel's tender, graceful frame, and she did not carry a single surplus pound.

The Ladies' Guild put a spoke in the wheel. Owners of music halls far and wide were complaining of slumping revenues. The declining spiral of artistes' income meant that charity for the indigent was no longer enough. Marie Lloyd led the shrill chorus demanding better terms and when their pleas fell on deaf ears, a strike was called. All Cora's friends—the likes of Melinda May and Lottie Albert and Lil Hawthorne—supported the withdrawal of labour. My wife would not have hesitated to fight for the cause alongside them, had the dispute not threatened to destroy her comeback. In consequence, she was torn. Part of her itched to join hands with her colleagues on the picket lines. Part of her still yearned for a standing ovation at curtain call.

"Follow your instinct," I counselled. A cautious view, designed to minimise the risk of an outpouring of vituperation at a later date.

She groaned, dissatisfied with my prevarication. "But I don't know what's for the best. Come on, Peter, they say the onlooker sees most of the game."

I shifted in my chair. "Very well. In my opinion, it is not merely a matter of honouring your contract at the Bedford. Isn't there talk of a further engagement at the Euston Palace? To give all that up would surely be too much of a sacrifice."

"You do?" The hopeful note told me that I had chosen the right answer. "I guess you're right. Marie and the others are asking a lot. But if I defy them, what will they say?"

"If they are true friends, they will understand how much this opportunity means to you. The chance to set your career alight again."

"Gee, they know how hard I've worked to raise funds for the Guild," she mused. "And they often tell me how unlucky I've been."

"Very well, then. Your decision is made for you."

Suddenly she came over to my chair, flung her arms around my shoulders, and kissed me on the cheek. "Oh, Peter, thanks! You've given me fresh heart."

I felt her bosom pressing against my chest. At once I became conscious of a familiar weakness in the knees. Suddenly her face was upon mine and her mouth had opened. I closed my eyes and our tongues met.

Presently she drew away and said, "You still like me, don't you, Peter?"

"Yes," I said in a muffled voice, not daring to look her in the eye.

"Hey, I know we've had our ups and downs." She gave me an unambiguous leer. "But they don't matter really, do they? We're still you and me. The rest don't matter much at all."

"Of course, she blamed me."

Ethel placed a cool hand on my brow. We were sitting next to each other on the bed in a little hotel in Argyle Square. It was scarcely the Ritz, but the room rate was modest and the ancient crone at the desk always greeted us with cackling good humour. For the past month we had been coming here twice a week. We resembled the cartographers of old, mapping out for ourselves astonishing new lands, of which in the past we had only dreamed.

I was in my shirt sleeves, Ethel in the lace-trimmed petticoat that displayed her lovely form to best advantage. "It wasn't your fault! You didn't force her to cross the picket lines."

Cora's return to the limelight had proved disastrous. The week at the Bedford passed without serious incident, although Millie Payne, standing on the picket line with other members of the Ladies' Guild, pleaded with her to stay out. The audience at the Euston proved less forgiving of blacklegs, and Cora's decision to revive *"The Unknown Quantity"* provoked even more hostility than her debut at the Old Marylebone. They hissed her off the stage and Cora fled to the safe haven of Hilldrop Crescent, vowing between crying fits that she would never tread the boards again.

"She has never been known to let the facts impede from making complaint. I did not stop her from making a fool of herself, *ergo* the responsibility is all mine."

"I don't believe she has any talent anyway! And no wonder she keeps insisting you buy her new dresses. The weight she's putting on, she won't be able to squeeze into anything she's had beyond the past six months!" She closed her eyes, as if willing herself to regain her customary discipline. "Our time together is so precious, darling. Let's not waste it by worrying about *her.*"

I kissed her on the lips. "Dearest, you're right. How selfish of me. Please forgive your poor old hub."

She smiled and, bending forward, began to unfasten my collar. "Of course, Hawley. A true wife should forgive her husband anything."

"Deuced good of you to invite me up here, Crippen."

"Think nothing of it, Rylance. Two Americans together in a foreign capital, both professional men, it would be a fine thing if we could not do each other a good turn. Here we have the ideal vantage point, I think you will agree. It's my pleasure to share it with you."

High summer in London. The Kaiser was visiting King Edward, and a royal procession had been arranged to celebrate the occasion and prove that talk of hostility between the two great powers was poppycock. Below us, the pavements of New Oxford Street were crammed with onlookers, all jostling for a better view. I had thrown open the window in my office. Shading my eyes against the merciless sun, I could see policemen mopping perspiration-covered brows as they tried to hold back the crowd. How much pleasanter on such a sticky afternoon to admire the pagaentry from the cool third floor, whilst sipping tea in comfortable armchairs.

"You studied dentistry in New Zealand, I hear, Mr. Rylance?" Ethel asked shyly as she handed him a cup.

"Sure did."

He scarcely glanced at her, tossing out the reply like a coin to a street beggar. I had noticed this oddity before: so few people remarked Ethel's beauty. Although she would sooner have died than give me cause for jealousy, I found it inexplicable that other men never gave her the attention she deserved.

"The world keeps getting smaller," I said amiably. "And the opportunities for men of business keep growing bigger."

Out of Rylance's line of sight, Ethel nodded encouragement. Her idea was for me to become better acquainted with the dentist who worked on the ground floor of Albion House. If I could find a "painless wonder" to take into partnership, the effective use of Munyonesque advertising techniques would, she argued, guarantee success. It struck me as a shrewd plan. My fellow countrymen had cornered this particular market. American nationality was seen as a qualification in itself by patients with maladies of the teeth and gums and money to burn.

"I guess that's right," Rylance said absently, craning his neck to see if the out-riders were yet in sight. His manner was pleasant and easygoing, but his conversation scarcely of Wildean sparkle. "Hey, was that the sound of drums in the distance?"

"I do believe it was. As a matter of interest, Rylance, what do you do in the way of attracting business?"

The young man shrugged. "Frankly, Doc, there isn't much I can do. Most of my cash goes on paying the rent and the rest of the bills. My pocket doesn't stretch to advertising. All these things require investment."

"And commercial acumen," I suggested.

"See, I never took much interest in the financial side of things. I'm a dentist, not some kind of entrepreneur. Hey, did you hear that? The band's in earshot!"

"It is so very difficult, making a go of things on one's own," I sympathised. "No wonder most of the successful business ventures involve a partnership, a sharing of specialisms for mutual benefit."

"Guess you're right. Say, was that a ripple of applause from down the street? Sounds like Kaiser Wilhelm and his uncle are on their way. I do so admire the European monarchies, don't you? Just as well they have that family link, I guess. Otherwise there might be a war."

"It is a grave situation," I said, searching for a patch of conversational common ground. "Did you read that thriller about a German attack in 1910? Quite spine-chilling!"

"I'm not much of a one for reading novels," Rylance said. Thickset and strong, he displayed the impatience with culture of a natural sportsman. His fingers, I noticed, were huge; I could not help wondering how patients with smaller mouths ever accommodated them.

"Ah."

Even my guest seemed to realise at last that good manners required more of an effort to respond to my pleasantries. "You see, Doc, I've a practical turn of mind and life's too short for fiction. Anyway, I guess your man may have a point. Somehow I don't quite trust the Germans, how about you?"

Suddenly my mind filled with a vision of a huge heaving rump: Richard Ehrlich cuckolding me. Taking a breath, I banished the image. "I don't suppose I do. Now tell me, what do you think about this notion of 'painless dentistry'?"

Shortly before you arrived, Arthur, I finished reading the first instalment of Ethel's memoir, which has appeared in *Lloyd's Weekly News*. I am lost in admiration for the able manner in which she has set forth facts that must tell with great weight in the minds of the unprejudiced.

"As time went on my friendship for Dr. Crippen grew, and he became the only person in the world to whom I could go for help or comfort. There was a real love between us."

How those words warm me! Even now she is not afraid to declare her devotion for me. She trusts me, likewise, to continue to care for her.

I have so little left. Long before my trial I wrote that letter of authorisation, at your request, so that the whole of my furniture and effects should be sold to defray my debts in relation to two quarters' rent, and gas and water rates. And yet there is this curious paradox—I am a pauper at risk of the gallows, but my spirits are lifting.

All is not lost! As you say, we may throw the dice one final time. Mr. Winston Churchill has my life in his gift. I am being tested to the limits of my endurance, yet when you describe the public petition that is being compiled to support the plea to the Home Secretary for a reprieve, a flame of optimism sparks in my heart. So hundreds of signatures are coming in by every post—and all on my behalf!

Let us not argue about the quality of my defence. I concede that it is embarrassing that the prosecution showed that the pyjama pieces discovered in the cellar belonged to myself. Yet our doctors could have saved me; without a victim, there can be no murder. Even

190

though Mr. Muir's cross-examination cruelly exposed the flaws in the doctors' assumptions, it was not until the judge's summing-up that I realised quite how calamitous their casual errors might be. It is not enough to fold your arms and ask to whom the remains in the cellar might belong, if not to Cora. In England a man is innocent until proved guilty. Never mind about the so-called scar: no navel was ever found. It is my belief that there has never been an iota of *proof* that she is dead.

Forgive me, Arthur, I know you have my interests closest to your heart, but you will not persuade me to deny the truth of the evidence I gave on oath. I decided long ago not to allow myself to be lured into the trap of exposing Ethel Le Neve to criticism or blame. Nor will I allow my memoirs to be embellished with that object. How many times need I reiterate the simple truth: Ethel Le Neve is innocent. Innocent and pure. Innocent and pure.

Extract from the closing speech for the defence by F.E. Smith in the case of R v Le Neve, at the Central Criminal Court, 25 October 1910

"You know what are the temptations to which, under normal conditions and with normal employers, a young and attractive girl is exposed going to the city as a typist. You know that the road of life is steep and dangerous enough for her under normal circumstances. What was the misfortune of this young girl, little more than a child, when it became necessary for her to earn her living? She had the extreme misfortune to come across the path, at the age of seventeen, of one of the most dangerous and remarkable men who have lived in this century; a man to whom in the whole history of the psychology of crime a high place must be given as a compelling and masterful personality. Conceive to yourselves the two people who became acquainted. Crippen, imperturbable, unscrupulous, dominating, fearing neither God nor man, and yet a man insinuating, attractive, and immoral . . . He was the doctor, and she was the typist."

"Are you sure?"

I spoke in a low voice, glancing over my shoulder to make sure that the door to my room was closed. Miss Curnow, who ran the office, had stepped out for lunch, as had William Long. However, Rylance, my new partner in the Yale Tooth Specialists, often called in between noon and one for a word about business. His surgery was two doors down the corridor from Munyon's office, and he had a deplorable habit of walking in to see me without troubling to knock. On one occasion, Ethel and I escaped by seconds from being caught in a compromising position. As the door opened, she was still smoothing down her hair and clothes. Fortunately, Rylance was a self-absorbed fellow and I was confident that he remained in ignorance of our relations.

"No, I am not certain," Ethel whispered. "But—I think it most likely. This sickness . . ."

My stomach knotted. "Your health is apt to be fragile, my darling."

Ethel's sensitivity of character was matched by her susceptibility to ailments. Yet she never lacked courage or determination. Only weeks before, her conviction that bad teeth were causing her neuralgic headaches led her to instruct Rylance to take out twenty-one at a single sitting. *Twenty-one!* He and I both thought her self-diagnosis mistaken, but once her mind was made up, persuading her to change it proved impossible.

Never had I seen a patient display such stoicism as Rylance's thick fingers prodded and probed, in preparing for the mass extraction. Although I had meant to sit and hold her hand throughout the operation, within minutes I had to make an excuse and hurry out, lest I faint at the sight of my beloved in agony. "Painless dentistry" was an excellent slogan but not a precise reality.

"Yes, but Hawley, there are further reasons why I believe that I may be . . ."

She swallowed hard, finding it impossible to complete the sentence. I said briskly, "Still, there may be other explanations. I suppose I ought to examine you."

"Are you . . ."—her face was crimson—"I mean, will you really be able to tell for certain?"

"Dearest," I said softly. "Never mind Munyon's and the Drouet Institute. Remember that I was a doctor of medicine long before I settled in London. Don't look so worried, you haven't offended me. But of course I shall be able to tell."

I conducted the examination in my room. Ethel lay motionless on the couch, tense and vulnerable. I could not disguise the tremor in my hand as I did what was necessary. Neither of us uttered a word. When it was over, I said softly, "Yes, Ethel, your female instinct did not mislead you. You are"—I scoured in my mind for words of solemnity appropriate to the awesome conclusion—"with child."

"Oh!"

Suddenly her face was a rainbow of emotions. Apprehension, yes, but also happiness and pride. Her eyes were clear, her skin had a bloom, her hair shone. This, I thought tenderly, is how she must have looked at sixteen. Untouched by the world, nervous of what it might hold, but thrilled by its infinite promise. Every young woman has an instinct for motherhood, but I sensed that she was also aware of the enormity of the change about to be wrought in her life.

"This is what you wanted?"

She nibbled at her fingernails, striving to master her emotions. As always, she was desperate not to say or do the wrong thing, lest it cause me worry or offence.

"I . . . I think so."

"We did not plan for this to happen so soon."

I was thinking aloud, struggling for balance like a sailor on deck in the midst of a gale. Knowing full well the unreliability of prophylactics, I had yet failed seriously to contemplate the possibility that my elaborate if clumsy precautions might not work. Because of Cora's inability to conceive, I never had need of artificial barriers to conception. Perhaps the very fact that I found the whole business distasteful had compromised my efficiency.

Her eyes filled with tears. "Hawley—you are not angry with me, are you?"

Seizing her hand, I said, "Darling, I swear I am not. How could your hub ever be cross with his wifie? Besides, it takes two to make a child, does it not? I bear my share of the responsibility—and claim my share of the delight."

She managed a smile, then lowered her head. "So—we are to have a baby, then."

A baby! I put my arm around her, recalling the long ago days when I cradled Otto in my arms. Little Otto, whose last letter had informed me of his engagement to be married! My second child had died along with Charlotte and, from time to time, I still felt the stab of loss. A baby, my God, a baby! Ethel and I were as man and wife, even without benefit of a priest's blessing or the knowledge and approval of the world at large. I pulled her closer to me and put my lips to her moist cheek. A child would complete our little family. It came to me in a rush of awareness that we could never contrive an unnatural end to the unborn infant's life. For both of us, it would be a mortal crime. The murder of an innocent.

"So what time do you call this?" Cora demanded as I walked into the kitchen.

She was sitting at the table, barefoot and with her hair in curlers, clad in her favourite pink pyjamas. Whether she had put them on in readiness for bed or had been wearing them since rising late, I could not tell. But I could smell cognac on her breath.

"I have been working late."

Ethel and I had spent the evening in a first-floor room overlooking rain-sodden Argyle Square. She never liked to have the light on, but I usually left the curtains a little apart so that I could admire her alabaster skin in the glow from the gas-lamps. Although she did not take off her petticoat, she kept wrapping the blanket around her, trying to hush my endearments so that we might discuss what would happen when the baby was born.

"Working late, huh?" Cora's sour grin put me in mind of a malicious troll. "With that little typewriter of yours, I bet."

I steeled myself not to dignify her cheap gibe with a reply and began to unfasten my collar. Ever since I had unwisely consented to use my influence to negotiate a room for the Ladies' Guild in Albion House on modest terms, Cora had started calling in on us each Wednesday afternoon, before and after the committee's weekly meeting. Did she wish to keep an eye on my behaviour with Ethel? I flattered myself that we had covered our tracks. We always behaved with the utmost discretion in front of others. Most likely, Cora thought me incapable of attracting a pretty young woman—far less impregnating her—and took pleasure from teasing me on the subject of my inadequate charms.

"Well, don't just stand there with that secret little grin on your mug. What've you got to say for yourself, then?"

The kitchen smelled of burnt potatoes. The heat from the stove was suffocating. Cora never permitted ventilation, for she loathed fresh air. The dresser was heaped with dirty plates and saucepans, together with a garland of false peroxide curls. On the table, a mass of hairpins were scattered over letters to the Ladies' Guild. She had recently been elected as honorary treasurer, a mark of her colleagues' forgiveness following the conclusion of the labour dispute. Seeing an envelope with an American stamp, I clenched my fist, but Cora's name and address were elegantly scripted, not in Bruce Miller's careless hand. His name had not been mentioned for quite a while. Perhaps one of her sisters had been in touch. A half-empty brandy bottle acted as a paperweight. Our fluffy white Persian was scratching frantically at the cobwebbed windowpanes. It was a lustful creature, always striving to escape from its celibate prison.

"I see you have been busy."

"Funny, funny," she snarled. "Say, Peter, you think I haven't got better things to do with my day than skivvy after you?"

Arguing with her in this mood was futile; experience had taught me to turn the other cheek. I shrugged and turned to go, but she was too quick for me. As I moved toward the door, she grabbed my wrist and pulled me round to face her. When she panted from the effort, the gust of alcohol-laden breath made me wince.

"You never fight back, do you? A bit of sarcasm is the best you can do by way of defiance. Why is that, Peter? Surely you ain't scared of what I might do to you?"

"You have taken too much drink."

"And who can blame me? Married to a shrimp like you! Yes, 'shrimp,' that's what my friends call you. Think of it. There are half a dozen men who would propose to me in an instant if I were free. And yet here I am, stuck here with a little shrimp!"

Who were these admirers? That they existed, I had no doubt, although whether they were in a position to offer marriage was a different matter. Shadowy figures, not like Miller or Ehrlich, whose devotion she flaunted in my face. My jealousy had withered, along with my curiosity.

"When you are like this, Cora, there is no reasoning with you."

"*Belle!*" she screeched, punching me on the shoulder.

"Of course," I said pleasantly. The blow had not hurt. "My apologies—Belle."

"They give me presents, you know, my admirers. Lovely presents. And that doesn't bother you?"

"That my wife earns the generosity of wealthy sponsors? Why should it?" My nails dug into my palm. This topic of conversation was one I had long avoided. "Since you gave up earning from the stage, plainly you need to supplement your income. Why not by sweet-talking philanthropists into making donations to a worthy cause?"

"What sort of a man are you?" she demanded, screwing her face up as if looking at me through a microscope.

"A man whose bones ache with sheer weariness," I was beginning to shiver. I *would not* contemplate what Cora might have done to earn her presents. "It has been a long day. Goodnight."

As I reached the door, I heard a choking sob and paused.

"Katie's pregnant!" she wailed.

Katie, her half-sister. My vague recollection was of a dimpled schoolgirl. I had no choice but to go back and stroke Cora's ersatz blond curls. Against the tips of my fingers they felt hard and dry. "She has written with the news?"

"I'm not jealous," she mumbled feverishly. "Really, I'm so happy for her and George. Katie loves children just as much as I ever did. Sweet little Katie, she was always such a darling kid.

It's only that . . ."

The rest was lost in tears. Talk of infants and families always put Cora into a maudlin mood. I did not know what to say for the best. "Perhaps," I said helplessly, "when the baby is born we can invite them over here."

After a while, she said, "That would be nice. I like this house being full to suffocation. When we don't have company, it's like a graveyard."

Marion Curnow bustled into my office. "Miss Le Neve will not be coming in today, Dr. Crippen. She is indisposed again."

I let *again* pass. Marion Curnow, plump and rosy-cheeked, enjoyed the rudest of health and made no secret of her superiority over anyone predisposed to sickness.

"What is the matter?"

"Mrs. Jackson, her landlady, spoke to me. She says Miss Le Neve is very poorly. During the night, she became unwell, it seems. The doctor has been attending to her. I asked if there was any likelihood of Miss Le Neve being fit tomorrow, but the landlady was quite sharp with me. She said it was absolutely out of the question."

I felt as if she had drenched me with ice water. "Did she explain the nature of the indisposition?"

"Not at all. But it does not sound like one of her usual little maladies."

The implication of chronic hypochondria had but the thinnest of veils. In other circumstances, my retort would have been sharp and dismissive. But all that mattered was Ethel's health. Over the past few days, her appearance had become anaemic and she kept complaining of pains in the stomach. When I entreated her to consult her doctor, she said that she preferred to trust in me. Her reliance upon me was gratifying, but sometimes it manifested itself in a dependence that placed an intolerable responsibility on my shoulders. Had I overlooked something? Might complications of pregnancy have been responsible for her symptoms?

I got rid of Miss Curnow and searched out Mrs. Jackson's telephone number. She and her husband lived on Constantine Road, and I had visited their house two or three times since Ethel first left her sister's and took lodgings with them. The older woman took a close interest in Ethel's well-being and treated her more like an honoured guest than a tenant of a tiny bedsitting room. This regard was warmly reciprocated; Ethel called her "mother" and treated her as a confidante. But she assured me that never once had she dropped even the slightest hint that our relationship was other than strictly businesslike.

No answer. I tried again a few minutes later, with the same result. I found myself pacing up and down in my room, fearful of what might have happened. In the end, I had no choice. Possibly Ethel was alone in the house, too enfeebled to answer when she heard the bell ring. Or perhaps she was merely sleeping, already stronger than the night before.

With a word to Long, I set off for Hampstead. For weeks, I had been living in a daze. Ethel's pregnancy did not seem quite real to me. It raised questions too large to be easily acknowledged, let alone answered. I was hoping against hope for a miracle, praying that divine intervention would set everything right.

I arrived at Number 80 on the stroke of one, my arrival coinciding with that of a cab coming in the opposite direction. Mrs. Jackson descended from it and I hurried over to her. Her cheeks were drawn and eyes downcast. When I called her name, she started.

"Doctor Crippen!"

"I gather that Miss Le Neve is unwell," I said, disguising my agitation with a sickly smile. "I wondered if there is anything I can do."

"Well, that is very kind of you, Doctor. I'm sure Ethel will appreciate it when I next see her."

"When you next see her? Is she not upstairs in her room?"

"Oh, no, I'm afraid she really is very bad, Doctor. She has gone to stay with her aunt in Hove. I've just come back from taking her to the station. I'm afraid it will be some time before she is fit enough to resume her duties with you."

"Never mind her work," I said. "Miss Le Neve's health is my sole concern."

"Well, she's always singing your praises, Doctor. I hope I'm not speaking out of turn when I say that she obviously loves her work with you. I often . . ."

"What is the matter with her?" I was almost wailing. "I should say, I am sorry to interrupt, but . . ."

Mrs. Jackson gave a quick glance to left and right, bent her head toward me, and gave an anguished hiss. "Well, you're a medical man, as well as her employer, so I suppose I'm not speaking out of turn."

"Please accept my word of honour my only interest is that Miss Le Neve should receive every assistance to restore her health at the earliest opportunity."

"Very well, then, Doctor. I'm afraid that Ethel has been carrying a baby. And now she has lost it, poor soul."

Memories bob like flotsam to the surface of my mind. I recall Marie Lloyd's ribald snort of laughter as she described how she once appeared on the same bill as James Berry, the hangman. After resigning as principal executioner, he took up a fresh career in the music hall, touring with magic lantern slides that depicted the gallows rites. His party piece was to recite the poems he had written for "melancholy occasions" at the scaffold. In addition, he boasted an expertise in phrenology, the science of determining criminality by way of physical measurements. This prompted Marie into a coarse joke that had Cora weeping with laughter and Paul Martinetti sniggering behind his hands. Berry told Marie that he no longer favoured capital punishment, and described himself as an "evangelist." For all that, she claimed, he eyed her neck with an interest that made her spine prickle.

I know little of the new man, Ellis, save that he is a dour Lancastrian. According to the press, he takes a close interest in all his clients. I wonder if he has already studied my case and whether he understands the flawed nature of the prosecution. If so, will that carry any weight with him? Or is it simply a matter of a fair morning's work for a fair morning's pay? Twelve pounds per drop, plus expenses, is said to be the going rate.

For all my curiosity, I have not cared to question the governor about the fellow. Poor Major Mytton-Davies—sometimes I think that he is more distressed about the Court of Appeal's cavalier dismissal of my case than I myself. When he and I talk, we tour around every subject under the sun, from the wonders of Paris to the future of the omnibus. Anything other than the unfortunate events that have brought us together.

The warders feed me tidbits of information that the governor might think it impolitic to mention. The latest news (not public knowledge as yet, I understand) is that Chief Inspector Dew has tendered his resignation to his superiors at Scotland Yard. They speculate that he can afford to live off the damages from those newspapers that so cruelly libelled him over his handling of my case. He is as much a victim as myself, save that he can now look forward to a long and prosperous retirement, growing roses at his cottage in the country. During our conversations on the voyage back to England, he confided that he was a keen gardener. He mentioned that he'd noticed the vigour of the roses at Number 39 and we exchanged ideas on how to cultivate the most luxuriant blooms.

As for my own future, that remains taboo, even with the most loquacious warder. From portraits in the press, I gather that Ellis is balding, with sad eyes set deep and a huge soup-strainer moustache. Alas, he and I now have an appointment on the 23rd, which I am bound to keep in the absence of intervention from God or Mr. Winston Churchill.

R v. Crippen, first day, 18 October 1910, evidence for the prosecution

Edgar Brett, assistant bank manager: *"We got a notice of withdrawal of the whole amount, dated 15 December 1909, and signed by Belle Elmore only. We accepted that, notwithstanding that part of the account was in the two names."*

Mr. Muir K.C.: *"If the notice had expired would you have paid it over without the signature of Dr. Crippen?"*

"Yes, I think so."

"Belle, I need to beg a favour of you," I said one evening.

After dinner we had adjourned to the parlour and Cora was picking out a melody on the piano. I chose my moment with care, having taken pains to arrive home promptly from work so that she could not accuse me of spending private time in Ethel's company. From the stench of tobacco in the hall, I deduced that she had been entertaining an admirer. No matter; if she had been left receptive to persuasion, so much the better. Besides, she was still flushed with excitement following the Ladies' Guild's annual banquet the previous week. A special presentation had been made to her of a silver slave bracelet, in recognition of her tireless fundraising. The inscription blended irony with awe: *"To the Hustler."*

She kept her gaze on the sheet music, but her voice was freighted with suspicion. "You can always ask."

I squatted at her feet like a native worshipping a graven image. "Rylance and I are enjoying a deal of success. Only this afternoon, a couple of new patients called to arrange appointments. The only fly in the ointment is this. Not all of them are quick to pay their bills."

With an exasperated groan, she turned to face me. I smelled alcohol and cursed the fact that drink might have put her in an uncertain temper. But it was too late to abandon my strategy.

"I just knew this was going to happen! Remember when I asked, what kind of work is it, to spend all day peering at other people's choppers?"

"It is just a question of tiding us over a sticky few weeks."

"You should've listened to me, instead of that little typewriter of yours. This was her idea, wasn't it? You were never a dentist."

"You do Miss Le Neve a disservice," I said stiffly. "As well as forgetting that I practised dentistry for a while back in Detroit."

"You were never even qualified!"

Unkind, but undeniable. My flirtation with dental work had been an exigency, at a time when it was difficult to make homeopathy pay. I pride myself on an ability to adapt to changing circumstances, on being a chameleon of medicine. Healing has fashions, just like clothes. Specialism is necessary in the modern era, but the doctor who allows it to become a straitjacket gambles with his prosperity. Dentistry was Rylance's province. He could utilise stumps and shells as the bases of crowns that were perfect for masticating. Nonetheless, I flattered myself that I could find my way around a set of teeth as well as the next man. I helped Rylance out when he was busy, but my forte remained the business side. My money set the Yale Tooth Specialists afloat, and my name preceded my partner's on the door of the surgery. All I needed was the chance to buy time. And luck.

"Think of it as an investment. I cannot make use of the funds we have at the Charing Cross Bank . . ."

"You need my signature to make any withdrawal," she said with a sly grin.

"Not only that. By virtue of the beneficial interest rate I negotiated, we are obliged to give a year's notice and our business needs funds in the much shorter term. But I am aware that you are also a customer of the Birkbeck Bank and so I wondered . . ."

Her face turned the same shade of purple as the curtains at the Empire. "I never said a word about Birkbeck! You've been reading my mail!"

"If you wished to keep it a secret, you might have been wise not to leave correspondence from the Birkbeck lying on the kitchen table. But I have not pried, and I swear I do not know how much you keep in that account."

"It's not much. Not enough for what you're asking."

Even a Lestrade could have inferred that she was lying. The tint in her cheeks and the hastiness of her manner gave her away. In any event, I had happened to catch a glimpse of the statement she had been sent only the previous week. The account was in credit in the sum of over two hundred pounds. The Hustler's gentlemen friends were remarkably generous; I never speculated whether they received value for their money.

"Suppose you sold a couple of trinkets. Not one of your special treasures, of course. That marquise diamond ring, perhaps, and the tiara brooch. You would scarcely miss them, you have so many."

She gave an incredulous snort. "Are you kidding me? Don't you know how much I adore my jewellery?"

"Pawn them, then." Desperation was choking me. "You could

easily raise a couple of hundred pounds. I would gladly redeem everything as soon as . . ."

"You must think I was born yesterday."

She chuckled like a witch in a story by the Brothers Grimm. A fat witch with a taste for glittering diadems and ostrich feathers, but a witch nonetheless.

I stroked her neck, striving for calm. "Belle, dearest, I have not asked you for much these past few years. Will you not help me to make sure that the business does not fail? After all we have been through together, I thought you might be willing . . ."

She swung back to the music propped up on the piano and pounded the opening bars of the Funeral March with brutal relish.

"Over my dead body."

"Is it very bad?" Ethel asked.

"We'll pull through," I said, unbuttoning my white smock and hanging it up behind the door. Rylance had already left for the evening, with a grumble about a woman who had failed to keep an appointment. Ethel had spent the last half hour frowning over the business ledgers, and I needed to muster the confident humour that is second nature to general practitioners attending bedsides of the terminally sick. "The fundamentals of the business are sound."

For once my optimism failed to smooth the furrows on her brow. "But even when we were at the Institute, you said that . . ."

"That was different," I said. "Now, listen to me, Ethel. This is a little crisis, but we will survive it, as we always do. We have shared a great deal together, you and I. Happiness and also pain. Even if our little one had lived . . ."

As the words left my lips, her face crumpled and I cursed my ineptitude. Eight months after the tragedy, our scars still had to heal.

"Don't talk about the baby," she implored. "Oh God, Hawley, if you love me, do not talk about the baby."

The death of an unborn child has a strangely paradoxical effect: one is diminished by the loss of what one has never possessed. For me, lightning had struck twice, but the second shock struck me harder than the first. To have had a child by the woman I adored—ah, the very thought thrilled me. Yet my sense of desolation was nothing compared to Ethel's.

I dared not tell her that Otto and his new bride were expecting a child. Instead of becoming a father once again, I was soon to be a grandpapa. I could not help but feel a jolt of pride. Even though I had not seen my son for so long, he was a conscientious correspondent and seemed to be doing well in his job with the Pacific Telephone and Telegraph Company. Alas, that would be no consolation to the woman I loved. Of course, I did not mention that I was still sending an allowance to America. Part was meant for Otto, part for my father. Reading between the lines of Otto's letters, I could tell that the old man was down on his luck and short of cash.

Once, at her lowest ebb, Ethel said she had been left with nothing. There was no reasoning with her. She was young and I adored her; there would be opportunities aplenty, and yet her dreams were in eclipse. Throughout March and April I feared as much for her state of mind as for her physical well-being. Of course I swore that soon we would be together permanently. She needed to believe that, in order to regain her strength. Nor was I lying; but I did not know how to achieve the ambition that the two of us held so dear.

"I am sorry," I said humbly. "I did not mean to hurt you. I could have bitten off my tongue as soon as I uttered . . . oh, I am such a fool. Please forgive me, Ethel."

"Of course I forgive you. It's simply that we agreed . . ."

"Yes, and I am a silly idiot, upsetting the woman who means

everything to me. This trouble with funds is no more than a passing phase."

"Hawley, the month's receipts are only three-quarters of what is required."

"Dearest, you forget that we are in the middle of December," I said in a kindly tone. "Hardly a typical month in the lifetime of any budding enterprise."

"Yes, but already a large portion of the investment you made has been eaten away. There is Long to pay, and Miss Curnow, as well as the materials that Gilbert Rylance requires. And now that the professor has ended your salaried position with Munyon's, your income has been halved at a stroke."

"But I retain my connection by way of the Imperial Press Agency. Don't you see, dearest, that I can place advertisements for Munyon's remedies in newspapers and magazines at a handsome discount that represents pure profit?"

Ethel lifted her jaw, a sign that she was not to be comforted. "The discount is modest, and Munyon's sales are not what they were. Why else would the professor dispense with a manager and keep him merely as an agent? The last time he did this, your earnings dwindled to nothing. You said only last week that it was not worth the candle."

"This is a difficult time of year for those of us who do not keep shops. People look forward to Christmas, not going to the dentist. All businesses go through testing phases."

"Yes, and many of them fail to survive." She gnawed at her lip. "Hawley, I've been thinking. It is time for me to swallow my pride. Ask Eddie Marr if he will increase his investment in the Aural Remedies Company. That will help to see you through the festive season and then perhaps in the new year, if people have money left in their pockets, things will look up again."

"I thought you wanted me out of Marr's clutches?"

"Needs must," she murmured.

"I will gladly consider it, but do not worry so. The decline in our revenues is a temporary phenomenon."

She seized my hand. "Promise?"

I shifted uncomfortably, but she left me no choice. "Promise."

"Then I'll sleep a little easier, darling. But I could not bear a repeat of the calamity when Drouet's failed."

I squeezed her fingers. "This is a very different enterprise."

I judged it impolitic to confess that following Cora's rebuff, I had asked Eddie Marr if he would make a short-term interest-free loan. His response was unexpectedly sharp. He complained that already he was seeing little enough from his investment. Worse, he accused me of diverting the profits from sales of Ohrsorb, the ear salve that was my most commercially successful remedy, into the Yale Tooth Specialists. He said that he had half a mind to instruct a specialist auditor to examine the books. Referring to our long friendship and the need for trust and confidence between colleagues, I contrived to set his mind at rest. Unfortunately, he had hit the nail on the head. I had found myself obliged to transfer funds from the Kingsway venture to that in Albion House in order to keep the latter alive. Robbing Peter to pay Paul is seldom a desirable course, but on occasion Fate presents no viable alternative.

Each year the Ladies' Guild organised a Christmas party for its ever-expanding constituency of impoverished widows and orphans. Belle stayed on afterwards, distributing plum puddings to the women and wooden toys to their children with her customary zeal. Not until after ten did she return home. I was waiting for her in the kitchen, a letter from our bank in my hand, when she tottered through the door.

"I suppose you left this out for me to find?"

She yawned and said carelessly, "Oh, that? Not tonight, Peter, for Heaven's sake. I've been on my feet for hours. Now all I want is a bath and a good night's sleep."

Ignoring her, I read from the letter. " '*Dear Madam, I beg to acknowledge receipt of your notification of intention to close the above accounts and withdraw the whole sums therein. As we explained to you in person, the terms of the deposit require that you give us a full year's notice of closure and therefore I confirm that the funds then standing to the credit of the above accounts will be transferred to you on 15 December next. Yours etc.*' I might have hoped that you would be courteous enough to consult me before seeking to render me destitute."

Cora collapsed onto a chair. "Say, a lot can happen in the space of twelve months. I was taking precautions, that's all."

"Precautions? Against what?"

With a sweep of her hand, she indicated the unwashed breakfast things on the table, the splashes of coffee on the kitchener, and the patch of rust on our gas stove. "In case I get tired of all of this and say yes to a friend who's asked me to go away with him."

"I see. Is that what you intend to do?"

"Who knows? Maybe I will, maybe I won't. Maybe you'll get rid of that little typewriter of yours and maybe you won't. Nothing's certain in this life. All we can do is trust in the Lord."

"You're drunk, Cora."

"*Belle!* My name's Belle!" She hiccoughed violently. "And don't—don't be such a strait-laced little pipsqueak. It's Christmas, have you forgotten? My God, to think of the men who have courted me, how did I finish up here with you? Who could blame me if I did leave you in the lurch?"

"Go to bed," I said wearily. "There is no talking to you in this state."

She tottered to her feet. "All right, but not because you give me permission, Peter. I'll go to bed because I've been working like a dog. But remember this. I'm a dog with more money than you. Oh yes, I hold the purse strings and don't you forget it."

After she had stumbled upstairs, I remained in the kitchen. I was in no mood to sleep, and so I washed the dirty crockery and busied myself in an attempt to restore a semblance of order to the room. A piercing cry roused me and I sat bolt upright. Cora in terror? I hurried up the stairs and hammered on her door.

"What is the matter?"

"Help me! Help me!"

I rushed inside and knelt by her bed. She was clutching at her throat. "Water! I cannot breathe, I cannot breathe!"

A jug and tumbler stood on her table, but I made no immediate movement toward them. A tide of conflicting emotions washed through me. Might she have suffered, like Charlotte, a fatal seizure? Could history repeat itself in such a shocking form? What paralysed me was not the sight of her plump features, distorted by pain and dread of the unknown. It was the numbing guilt of seeing an answer to my incoherent prayers.

Cora's pyjama jacket was open. Her breasts rose and fell as she wheezed with the effort of sucking air into her lungs.

"Peter! Fetch a priest—I think I'm dying."

With a shudder, I forced myself to check her pulse. Her flesh was hot. When I laid my hand on the padding of fat around her abdomen, she yelped in pain. I lifted the jug and filled the tumbler. When I put it to her lips, she gave me the smallest nod by way of thanks. As she sipped noisily, I put my fingers against her forehead and concluded my diagnosis.

"Is that better?"

"A little," she said in a croak.

"Drink up the water."

She obeyed without demur, a sure indication of her fear. I took the glass from her and dabbed her lips dry with my handkerchief.

"What is it, Peter? What do you think?"

"I think," I said with an asperity borne from the dull thud of anti-climax as much as from a desire to reprimand, "that you are suffering from overindulgence in plum pudding and brandy."

When I recounted the drama to Ethel over lunch in a Lyons teashop the next day, she put down her knife and fork and fell silent.

"What is wrong, dearest?" I asked.

"It's . . . oh, nothing."

"Please. Tell me."

Her voice muffled, she said, "My thoughts frighten me and I could not bear it if, once I confessed them, you were to turn away from me."

In a low voice, I swore that her anxieties—whatever they might be—were groundless. My devotion to her could never be shaken. We must never keep things from each other, for we were man and wife, even if no one else in the world knew of our union. Ours was no ordinary bond. The secrecy of our ceremony served to sanctify it. All this I said, and much more. As she listened, she reached across the table and squeezed my hand.

"Very well, Hawley. You promised not to think ill of me, so I shall say what went through my mind. If the worst had happened last night, then we would be free for each other." I was about to speak, but she hushed me with a look. "But there is more, darling. You must not be disgusted with me. I cannot keep on pretending. It is wicked, I know, but every night, I get down on my knees and pray for her to die, so that you become mine irrevocably."

Midnight on New Year's Eve. Cora and I standing with our guests at the top of the flight of steps leading down from our front door to the street. Sirens hooting, trays hammering, and church bells ringing out the old year, ringing in the new.

Each of us held an American cocktail, made to a special recipe Cora had brought from Brooklyn. Even I was included, my usual light ale or stout seeming inappropriate to the occasion. Lifting our glasses, we toasted each other. John Nash leered at Lil, his wife. Melinda May, tiny as a sparrow, fluttered her eyelashes and I thought to myself that, twenty five years before, she must have been an attractive woman. Well, thirty years before, perhaps. Cora savoured the drink.

"Happy new year, Peter."

"Happy new year, Belle."

My thoughts were elsewhere. The surgery had closed until the first week in January; the appointment book was empty, and there was no sense in paying staff for days when they would have nothing to do. Ethel was spending the New Year with Nina and Horace; a pound to a penny, by now they would all be asleep in their beds. I liked Horace, but he lacked *joie de vivre*. Cora would have made mincemeat of him.

Cora had regaled the assembly with a lurid account of her indisposition following the Guild's Christmas party. She embellished the story, so that I became the baffled medical man, hunting wildly through a stock of patent cures for outlandish maladies, while she suffered bravely from common indigestion. Everyone, including myself, laughed heartily.

The Nashes' chauffeur was standing down below in the street, deep in affable conversation with a police constable. Cora asked them to join us in a small libation to celebrate the coming of a new year. They accepted with alacrity, the constable remarking that this was not exactly a criminal neighbourhood. He said jovially that he believed he would be failing in his duty if he did not accept the hospitality of householders who contributed to the peaceful atmosphere of Hilldrop Crescent.

Again, we lifted our glasses. *To all of us. Good luck.* 1910: what would it hold for us?

My wife turned to Melinda May. She was a fusspot who had initially demurred at our invitation on the improbable ground that she was "untidy." Cora believed that Miss May had been a prime mover in the decision to award her the silver bracelet and was keen to show her appreciation. At Cora's prompting, therefore, I had satisfied Miss May's anxieties by telephoning Lil Hawthorne and asking if she and her husband would collect their colleague on their way to join our little party.

"I'm so glad you're here, Miss May," Cora said to her. "I do hope we shall be together again this time next year."

Miss May twittered a platitude and Lil Hawthorne beamed sleepily. Despite everything, I found myself putting on a smile and nodding my assent.

"At last we can celebrate," I said.

Ethel mustered a little smile. "Happy new year, Hawley."

"Happy new year, darling."

We indulged in a long kiss. Our favourite room in the shabby hostelry was taken and we had to be content with accommodation in a single person's chamber, with a view over a yard and a washing line. We had marked the new year with an exchange of presents: a new velvet dress over which she exclaimed with delight, and a shiny turquoise tie-pin fitting my taste to perfection. A cloud of sadness descended upon her, however, as soon as we were shown up to this cubbyhole.

"I have made a new year's resolution," I announced in my cheeriest tone.

"What is it, Hawley?"

"I shall make a standing order for our usual room. Yes! We won't be treated like casual passersby any longer. We won't have to put up with whatever happens to be available at the time. This bed! It's barely enough for one slender person, let alone a couple. Our own special room, that's what we need. Darling, it is the very least you deserve."

She uttered a low sigh and bent her head.

"Ethel, what is it?"

I slid my arm around her, but she gave a little cry and wriggled away. Evidently she was under the weather. I had seldom known her to dismiss my attentions, however bleak her mood. Naturally, during the weeks following her miscarriage, I had been the very model of restraint. But time had passed. One cannot mourn forever.

"Sweetheart, are you feeling unwell?"

"Last night I talked at length with Mrs. Jackson. She urged me to be frank with you."

"Naturally," I said, although this sounded ominous. "Given a love such as ours, there is no room for mistrust or lack of candour."

"Yes, but Hawley, I fear that you will not welcome what I have to say."

"Speak," I urged her. My face was set in an expression of encouragement, but my mind was whirling. So many times in my life I had been wounded. "I need you to tell me what is on your mind."

"Oh, it is just that when your wife looks in after her committee meeting, and you take her arm and go off home with her, I realise what my position is."

She said it in a rush, the words tumbling into one another, and then she put her head against my chest, as if she had committed some dreadful crime. I breathed in, thrilled by her constancy.

"Is that all?"

She looked up sharply and, again, I became aware that I had chosen the wrong words. Hastily, I added, "I mean, is it simply that we are not together all the time that upsets you so?"

Breathing hard, she said, "Mrs. Jackson says that it is most unfair that you ask so very much of me."

This was like receiving a kick from a favourite nag. I had regarded Ethel's landlady as an ally, almost a friend. But women are so very close with each other. How could I guess what disappointments the older lady had suffered at the hands of men? In the company of her young and impressionable tenant, Mrs. Jackson was bound to be partisan. She might not be a suffragette, but the principle was all too familiar: men were the enemy and women should combine to resist their supposed influence and power.

"Dearest, I concede that this hotel is not ideal for a rendezvous."

"It reeks," she said hoarsely. "Not just these sheets. Everywhere."

I had scarcely noticed, such was my delight in sharing private time with her in this grubby place, but she was right. "I want you in my own house," I said impulsively. "Undisturbed by the scuttle of mice and by raucous shuntings in the goods yard. You must come home with me, Ethel. Home to Hilldrop Crescent. For so long I have dreamed of the night when finally we share a bed in comfort. Soon, I swear to you, I will make that dream come true. Soon."

Never had I seen her eyes so wide. "Soon?"

"Soon," I promised. "Soon, soon, soon."

"How much do you need?" Cora asked.

I started. For the past half hour, I had believed her to be asleep. I was sitting at the table in the kitchen, examining the books of the Aural Remedies Company. And now she had read my mind, for all the world like Mr. Sherlock Holmes, startling Watson with his perspicacity.

"Why do you ask?"

"I thought you wanted me to help."

My heart beat faster but I told myself to take care. With Cora, there was always a price to be paid. "And I thought that you were unwilling."

She shrugged. "I never said that. What I did say was that it all depended on you. Specially on what you did with that little typewriter of yours."

I stiffened. "Miss Le Neve? Why do you mention her in this regard? She is a paid employee, just like Long and Miss Curnow and . . ."

"I wasn't born yesterday, Peter," she said, with not a trace of ill temper in her voice, merely weariness. "Don't embarrass yourself, huh? I know full well what's been going on between you. Surely you didn't think it was a secret? Oh God, I can tell from your face that you did! Peter, you never cease to amaze me. What kind of fool do you think I am?"

"Miss Le Neve is an excellent worker," I said doggedly. "She is efficient and wholly trustworthy. Her reputation . . ."

"She always looks like an invalid to me," Cora interrupted, "but I guess she's tougher than she seems. How long did it take you to talk her out of her drawers? Five years, six?"

"Cora! I won't have this!"

Her chubby face hardened. "Don't try and lay down the law with me, Peter, or it'll be the worse for you. Remember, I can walk out of here at any time. Any time, d'you hear? There's more than one man would love to take me in."

"I rather think that several men have taken you in," I said coldly. "I see no sign of anyone wishing to make the arrangement permanent."

Never in the whole of our married life had I spoken to her in such a manner. The slap of my contempt made her flinch, yet in a second she recovered her composure.

"So," she said quietly, "you're finally standing up for yourself.

That's just fine. I like a man with spirit. The good Lord knows, it's taken long enough to rouse you. So what are we talking about? Do you really want a divorce?"

Her bluntness knocked me off my stride. I stammered something vague and incoherent and a slow smile spread across her face.

"Not made your mind up, then? Well, we both know the church won't recognise it anyway. So I guess we might just be stuck with each other, you and me. What do you say?"

Struggling to regain my dignity, as well as the initiative, I said, "I am conscious of my obligations."

"That's good, Peter. Maybe we can find a way of working something out. See, you need money and I have it. So why don't we strike a deal? I bale out the company and you get rid of the little typewriter."

"Dismiss her?" I was aghast.

"Clear her out completely. Out of your office, out of your bed."

"A word in your ear, Crippen."

With a quick look over his shoulder, Rylance sidled into my room and shut the door. I glanced up from the post book in surprise. My partner seldom spoke in anything less than a boom and never sneaked around in a surreptitious manner.

"Sorry to interrupt, old fellow," he said, pulling off his white coat. "I know the accountants are pressing for the figures and you have the devil's own job trying to make them look a little better, so I won't take up much of your time. But there's something I thought you should know. It's about Miss Le Neve."

I swallowed hard. "Miss Le Neve?"

"Yes." Rylance fiddled with his pocket watch. "This is a rather ticklish thing, Crippen. Of course, you have the highest regard for her, and I know she's worked as your confidential secretary

219

for years. But I wondered how well you knew—the sort of person she is."

My mind raced, trying to fathom what was on his mind. "The sort of person she is?"

"I'll come straight to the point. A few minutes ago I went out to visit the cloakroom. On my way back, I passed the committee room of the Ladies' Guild. The door was open and I couldn't help overhearing two of the old biddies—not your wife, my dear fellow, please don't misunderstand me!—talking about Miss Le Neve."

"What on earth would they know about her?" I demanded.

Rylance lowered his voice. "If they are to be believed, old man, they may know rather more than you and me. Listen, I won't beat about the bush. I heard them mention your name and in the next breath one of them said it was a shame that you didn't know the truth about the girl who typed for you. When she was expecting a baby last year, she didn't even know which of her beaus was the father."

As I gaped at him, he shifted uncomfortably. "After that, I carried on back to the surgery. I didn't want to be caught eavesdropping. Besides, I thought they were talking nonsense. Miss Le Neve! She wouldn't say boo to a goose, in my opinion, and the very notion that she leads such a fast life struck me as incredible."

"Quite," I said, fighting to control my horror.

"Frankly, I wouldn't have thought her constitution would permit it. But she did have a long period of sickness last spring. I recall noticing how much thinner she seemed when she did come back to work. So I wondered . . ."

"It's an outrage!"

At last I had found my voice and it brimmed with fury.

"Well, I'm not so sure we can . . ."

"An outrage, I say! Rylance, I am surprised at you. It is sufficiently intolerable that these women have nothing better to do with their time than waste it in purveying malicious slanders about a girl who has done nothing to harm them. But for you, a man whose discretion and judgment I respected, to give credence to their vile tittle-tattle, I find shocking beyond belief."

Rylance blinked. My unaccustomed vehemence had taken the wind out of his sails. As he wavered, I followed up my initial onslaught.

"Let me say this. I have been acquainted with Miss Le Neve and her family for the past ten years. In all that time I have never known her to behave with anything other than the utmost integrity. I am appalled that, without a scintilla of evidence, you are ready to convict her of immorality and deceit."

"Well, Crippen, when you put it like that, I suppose I am bound to accept what you say. Can't say I have as high a regard for the woman as you do, but she's never let me down. Perhaps there has been some dreadful misunderstanding . . ."

"There has been no misunderstanding," I said grimly. "Mark what I say. This—this foul lie is worse than idle gossip. It is the product of a wicked mind, warped by envy of someone pure and gentle."

Rylance frowned. "But Crippen, old fellow, why on earth would anyone want to discredit Miss Le Neve? Half the time, I don't even notice her when she's in the same room. Why should women with whom she has barely even a nodding acquaintance take against her so? Sounds to me like a sordid rumour that has grown on the basis of no smoke without fire."

I shrugged and let the matter pass. Rylance was persuaded, and I did not wish him to suspect that Ethel and I were more than master and servant. But I knew my accusation made perfect sense.

During my childhood in Coldwater, I suffered from a recurring nightmare, in which a group of rough boys seized me and threw me into the lake for their fun. My limbs became tangled up in the clinging weeds beneath the surface and I flapped helplessly, unable to save myself. The dream always ended the same way, with the water closing in over my head, filling my mouth and nose and lungs, while I closed my eyes and prayed for rescue. Each time I was at the point of drowning when I awoke in my little bed, coated in sweat and shivering. Only by learning a few crude strokes that might suffice to get me to the bank if ever I fell into a stream did I manage at last to banish the nightmare.

I spent those weeks after Christmas slowly drowning. Cora was pushing my head below the surface and, as I sank deeper and deeper into the chilly depths, I had no hope that Ethel could rescue me. Once again, salvation lay in my own hands. I must do *something*.

At last an idea came to me: a scheme so original and audacious that I hardly dared believe that even I could execute it. Only a man as desperate as he was determined could make it work. I told myself that I could achieve the impossible and keep my promise to Ethel whilst obtaining the money that would keep the business alive. It could work, it *would* work; a short period of grace was all I needed. With time bought and the business saved, I could build a future for Ethel and myself.

Poisons, poisons, poisons. So adaptable, so full of guile. Aconite, belladonna, cocaine, morphia, mercury, gelsemium, and rhus-.tox. For years these had been my close companions, my stock-in-trade. I often purchased them from Messrs. Lewis & Burrows, pharmacists, who had premises on New Oxford Street. On 17 January, I leaned on the polished plum mahogany counter and asked Mr. Hetherington, the pharmacist, if he could supply me with so much as five grains of hydrobromide of hyoscine. The request seemed to take him aback, but in response to his enquiry, I explained that I wished to make up homeopathic preparations. I had conceived a new tonic, which I called Blood and Nerve.

This was the first time I had asked him for hyoscine, and he explained that they did not keep it on the premises in its pure form, since there was such a limited demand. He offered to supply me a quantity mixed with sugar of milk, but that was no good. I cursed inwardly and reflected that I should have called on Ashton's, the other drug store that supplied me. But Mr. Hetherington assured me that the order could be fulfilled by their wholesale house within forty-eight hours and, although I did not wish to waste any time, that was soon enough.

Two days later I called in to collect the hyoscine. An assistant, an earnest young fellow called Kirby, served me and asked if I would sign the Poisons Register. Notwithstanding the statutory requirements, I had found the people at Lewis & Burrows not only amiable but also rather slack—much more so than at Ashton's. They knew me well, and trusted me; thus, as a rule, they did not insist that I sign the poisons book when making my purchases. Of course, when Kirby produced the book and a pen, I completed the entry—on behalf of Munyon's—without objection. There was nothing to be gained by making a fuss.

When I reached home, I put the hyoscine in a drawer in my room, which I always kept locked, and murmured to myself a parody of De Quincey.

"Thou hast the keys of Paradise, O just, subtle, and mighty hyoscine."

A gallant old soldier has, the warders tell me, offered to take my place in the condemned cell. Apparently he strode into a Cambridge courthouse and urged the magistrate to exchange his life for mine, since the skills and humanity of a medical man should not be tossed away lightly. Inevitably, this improbable martyr was sent away, although the magistrate amused himself by opining that I would not object to the substitution.

Is there still a chance? One minute, I persuade myself that I can yet escape the gallows—there are now fifteen thousand signatures to the petition demanding that my life be spared. The next, I plunge into a chasm of misery. Every fragment of good news is counterbalanced by a heart-stopping reminder of my plight. The warders mutter that my likeness is already installed in the Chamber of Horrors at Madame Tussaud's. I am cheek by jowl with the likes of Burke and Hare and Charlie Peace.

Dear Lord, Charlie Peace. I read about his hanging in a yellowback. He had the gall to complain that the noose was too tight, but Marwood the executioner had the last word: *"He passed away like a summer's eve."* Such a calm and gentle phrase. I might almost be seduced into imagining that the end will steal upon me so quietly that I shall scarcely be aware of life slipping out of reach forever..

Extract from trial transcript, R v Crippen, 3rd day, evidence of the accused

"I have for years been familiar with the drug hyoscine. I first learned of it when I came over to England in 1885; I learned the use of it in the Royal Bethlem Hospital for the Insane. . . . I purchased it for treating nervous diseases, nerve cases. It was sold to me in the form of crystals. I then dissolved it in alcohol, and then I dissolved 5 grains in an ounce of water, that is, in 480 drops, giving to one drop 5/480ths . . . of a grain. . . . I used four drops of this . . . in conjunction with another mixture consisting of gelsemium, asafoetida, and some other homeopathic preparation. This, with a drachm of the other mixture, I used for medicating 300 small discs to make one bottle of a preparation sent to each patient; that would be about 150 doses. . . . The bottles would be labelled with the dose, and packed in a heavy little pasteboard case. The dose would be in the form of small sugared discs. . . . I think I dispensed about two-thirds of the hyoscine that I purchased on 19 January. I might mention that, besides using it for nerve cases, I also found it useful for spasmodic coughs and spasmodic asthma."

I admit to a certain pride regarding that last, throwaway sentence. As with any artistic success, its effortless appearance was the product of much labour. Necessity is the mother of invention. I spent hour after hour planning my evidence in chief, taking such pains over those small yet crucial details that are the hallmark of authenticity. I rehearsed in my cell until I was word perfect. So many times I had dozed in my armchair as Cora learned her lines; now I was performing for my life. Arthur, please do not frown. You know as well as anyone that the court is a theatre, and all the actors have to play their part. None more so than the man accused of a capital crime.

Of course I needed to construct an explanation for my conduct, the more plausible the better. Faced with a Leviathan in the case for the Crown, surely I can be forgiven for reminding the jury of my professional status? The mystique of the medical man is as daunting and impenetrable as are the technicalities of his lexicon. With so few cards in my hand, I determined to play them to best advantage. Rolling each fraction on my tongue with exaggerated care, savouring each infinitely small measurement as if it were a slice of Turkish Delight, I permitted myself a quick glance at the stolid jurors. Their eyes flickered with bafflement as I took them through the delicate process of distilling the drug. How could they fail to be impressed?

Daring, ingenious, resourceful. Such was my mood as I collected the package of hyoscine from Messrs. Lewis & Burrows. Blood and Nerve! Nick Carter's example inspired me. I have never lost my youthful taste for dime novels, so relaxing to dip into after a long, fatiguing day spent tending to the maladies of worried patients. Even after I moved to London, I found a plentiful supply of penny dreadfuls packed with stories about the likes of Carter, King Brady, and Cap Collier. Carter, though, stood head and shoulders above his rivals. His exploits were fantastic but enthralling, he was a master of disguise. He could turn himself into a chef or a cabbie merely by turning his coat and pockets inside out. When the need arose, he could always lay his hands on handcuffs, rope, or a gun. Well, I had my own revolver, and forty-five ball cartridges to go with it. Yet weapon and ammunition remained tucked away in bedroom drawers. I never fired a shot in anger.

Even Carter would have been exercised by the problem that confronted me. It shimmered and mystified; it had as many facets as an exquisite diamond. Only when we are tested to the limit do we have the chance to show our mettle. For all her saintliness, Ethel was losing patience and I dared risk anything but the forfeiture of her love.

How much simpler everything would have been if Cora had carried out her threat to elope with one of her gentleman friends. For a time I had thought they might answer all my prayers. By giving the bank notice of intention to withdraw funds, Cora had paved the way for her departure. But would she ever go?

When, in wintry mood, I pictured her in the company of another man, his face was always the same. The face that stared from the photograph in our parlour. Bruce Miller. No, not young Ehrlich, but my original nemesis. *Miller.* At Christmas he had sent her a card, which inevitably took pride of place on our mantelpiece. The day before I ordered the hysocine, an envelope bearing his florid script slithered though our letterbox and landed on our carpet. The flame of their liaison had not guttered. In seventeen and a half years of marriage, I had learned more about Cora than perhaps she knew herself. To my mind, there was no doubt that Miller was *the* man for her. He might be married and an ocean away, but when she wrapped around a man and shut her eyes, it was Miller's hands she imagined around her, Miller's sweaty flesh hard against hers, Miller's name that she murmured under her breath.

If she was not about to desert me, what then? Cora's fondness for fun at bedtime had scarcely diminished, but presumably the Admirers satisfied her demands. When she stayed in, the brandy bottle was companion enough. I had finally achieved that marital celibacy that I had promised Ethel on moving to Number 39.

As for divorce, our faith blocked the way. For a union between man and wife to fray was one thing; for it to snap, quite another. Our priest in Kentish Town would much rather turn a blind eye to irregularities of behaviour than accept a divorcee in his church. I could have reconciled divorce with my own conscience, but Cora's Catholicism was as much a part of her as lungs and liver. She saw no contradiction between her craving for physical ecstasy and the passions of her creed. Living with a man out of wedlock could be reconciled with God's teachings. Divorce could not.

Thus Cora and I remained bound together, as securely as ever she had tied me to the bedstead. Money had become her weapon; throughout the twelve months' notice period required by the bank, a Sword of Damocles would hang over me. I was powerless to defy her, or to rush to the defence of my beloved when she blackened her name and spread lies about abortions and *affaires*.

But I had survived the Drouet scandal, and a string of business failures. Adaptability was my middle name. The agency for Munyon's was paying buttons by way of commission, and I gave notice to terminate the arrangement; my last day would be 31 January. I must become the master of my destiny. I had a weapon far more powerful than any at Cora's disposal. *Hyoscine*. Ever since my Bedlam days, it had been a talisman. At times of hardship it had come to my aid and never let me down. Now I would exploit its properties again. No tranquilliser was, to my knowledge, more powerful. Hyoscine could do much more than depress the sexual appetite; in slightly larger quantities, it had a profound sedative effect.

The dilemma was plain. Ethel wanted us to spend nights together, but Cora would not yield her place at Number 39. The solution was to ensure that Cora did not object when Ethel shared my bed, and the means for achieving that was an adequate dosage of hysocine. Never did I doubt that Ethel could be persuaded to fall in with my suggestion. Although her manners were refined, in our most private moments she exhibited a lusty willingness to shed the inhibitions of polite society, coupled with a streak of devil-may-care. These traits I found all the more intoxicating because no one else—not even Nina— suspected their existence. For all her pale cheeks and meek demeanour, there beat within her breast the most passionate heart.

She would risk anything for love. For me.

When I first broached my plan over dessert at Frascati's, she almost choked on her strawberry ice cream.

"While she sleeps next door . . . ? Oh, Hawley!"

"Hear me out," I urged. "She takes a sleeping draught. I worry, of course, because of the amount of brandy that she drinks, but she never listens to anything I say about her health. No matter. She will leave me soon, I am sure of it. In the meantime, why should we not start to live as man and wife? We have been as one for so long that it is a crime—yes, a crime!—that we still have not spent one single night together."

"Not one night," she echoed, a dreamy look coming into her eyes.

"Your lodgings are no more than a quarter of an hour's walk from my home, and Mrs. Jackson lets you have a key. She is a sound sleeper, you told me, so you can come and go as you please."

"But . . ."

"Listen, dearest. You can arrive at Number 39 late in the evening, returning at dawn. No one will ever know—and all the while, we shall be together, in preparation for the day when Cora is gone and we have each other all in all, forever."

"Hawley, it does not—it does not seem right."

True, but you pray each night for her death. "My conscience is clear," I said firmly, "after Miller, and Ehrlich, and all the rest."

"Yes, yes, I understand. But somehow—beneath the same roof . . ."

"Is it so much worse, my darling," I enquired gently, "than spending afternoons together in the claustrophobic rooms of dingy, flyblown hotels?"

After a pause, she said, "I suppose not. And yet—somehow it scarcely seems decent."

"You are concerned about Cora's finer feelings?"

Time to play my strongest card. I recounted Rylance's description of the way in which Cora had branded my love a scarlet woman. By the time I had finished the story, her face had assumed a dreadful pallor.

Quietly, she said, "Are there no depths of depravity to which she will not sink?"

"Do you agree to my proposal?"

She scrutinised me minutely. "Hyoscine—it is a poison, is it not?"

"Dearest, you must trust me. I am familiar with its properties."

"Of course I trust you," she said softly. "I trust you to bring the two of us together. Forever."

On Saturday, 22 January, I administered hyoscine to Cora for the first time. I asked if she fancied a little drink before bed; the predictable answer prompted me to pour a generous tot of brandy with soda and add a minute quantity of the drug to it. There could be no better disguise for the pronounced bitter taste; I usually took hyoscine with sweetened tea, but the alcohol's strong flavour was more suitable. She swallowed the drink greedily, without a word of thanks. Within twenty minutes, she was slumped in an armchair in the parlour, emitting snores loud enough to make her beloved white Persian jump.

Buoyed by this success, I struggled up the stairs with her dead weight. By the time we gained the landing, I was exhausted. I found myself dragging her to the bedroom much as I would lug a sack of coal into the cellar. I was panting hard as I unlaced her corset, but from exhaustion rather than desire. For a few alarming moments Cora's eyelids moved, and she muttered something, breathing stale alcohol into my face before relapsing into her stupor.

As I unfolded her nightdress, I surveyed her flabby white

frame. She had underestimated my resolve. My power over her was absolute. I passed a hand lightly over the sagging breasts, the white ridge of the abdomen scar. Her skin was as cold as snow. Her womanhood was exposed to my gaze, but I felt neither lust nor contempt. For so many years her little cruelties had caused me to develop a carapace in order to survive. Now I found it scarcely possible to credit that I had ever felt for her anything other than indifference. It must have been in a different life that I adored her body and longed for nothing but the chance to lose myself in its mysteries.

The task accomplished, I retreated to my room. As I lay in bed, I imagined Ethel enfolding me, with Cora next door, oblivious to our intimacy. My spine tingled with excitement at the knowledge that soon it would become reality. Nick Carter himself would surely have admired my guile.

Cora slept until noon on Sunday. On regaining consciousness, she displayed the bleariness and irritable temper familiar from countless nights spent consoling herself with the brandy bottle. I detected no hint of abnormal behaviour or other ill effects, and she made no mention of my putting her to bed the previous evening. Hyoscine has a reputation for unpredictability, but once again it had proved a trusty servant.

As soon as Ethel and I had a moment alone in my little office at Albion House, I started to describe the success of my experiment with the hyoscine. To my surprise, she put a slender finger to her lip and hushed me.

"Let us not talk about it, dearest."

"I simply wanted you to know that . . ."

"All I wish to know," she said, quiet yet resolute, "is that you will keep your promise and that soon we shall be united forever. Now, I need your assistance with this query over an invoice for rhus.tox. from Messrs. Lewis & Burrows."

Dinner with the Martinettis on Monday the 31st was Cora's idea. Paul Martinetti had earned renown as "the prince of mimes." A small man with rubbery features, even in retirement he preferred a lifting of the eyebrow, a quirk of the lips, or a gesture with the hands to orthodox conversation. A martyr to hypochondria, he sought my advice often about his latest phantom ache or pain. Clara Martinetti was a large, opinionated woman of equine aspect. Although she was twenty years Paul's junior, it was hard to imagine her ever displaying the bloom of youth. Her teeth were gapped, and I had hoped that she might consent to a course of treatment from Rylance, but so far she had proved impervious to my overtures, claiming to have a phobia about dentists. Cora liked her from the outset and induced her to lend support to the Ladies' Guild. From then on, we entertained each other regularly.

Paul and Clara lived in King Edward's Mansions on Shaftesbury Avenue. At Cora's insistence, I called on Clara late on Monday afternoon and asked them round to Number 39 that evening. She told me that Paul was at the doctor's—no doubt he had his own personal seat reserved in the waiting room—and asked me to come back later to see if they were able to join us. When I returned at six, Clara told me that they would be happy to do so, and two hours later they arrived at our home.

Cora had cooked a joint of beef and Clara assisted her in preparing it for the table. As they chattered in the steamy kitchen, the aroma of the meat wafted through into the breakfast room, where Paul and I enjoyed a companionable silence, punctuated only by his enquiry about the treatment of haemorrhoids.

After a filling repast, the four of us moved to the parlour for a few hands of whist. I played badly; my mind was not on the cards. I had spent long hours pondering my next experiment with hyoscine. I dared take nothing for granted. I must conduct a further trial before I invited Ethel to stay the night. I could not risk Cora waking, perhaps starting to prowl about the house, when Ethel was in my room. A fractionally increased dose was called for. Poison is not to be trifled with, and I could not discount the chance that Cora would react adversely. Dizziness and nausea are recognised side effects. If she experienced any discomfort or sickness, I intended to pass it off as another episode of indigestion, brought on by excess. The richness of the meal would support this explanation.

As if to lend background colour to my tale, Paul declared himself indisposed shortly after taking his final mouthful. He had occasion to make several trips to the bathroom during the course of our game. Toward the end of the night, he developed a cough that Cora pronounced was my fault, because (not believing him to be a helpless cripple) I failed to accompany him upstairs and, moreover, left a window open upstairs. She scolded me so severely that Paul became wretched with embarrassment and protested, with improbable heroism, that he was quite all right.

Outside, the wind raged like a termagant in the foulest mood and Clara diagnosed that Paul had caught a chill. Cora instructed me to find them a cab and so, wrapping up warmly against the gale, I walked as far as Camden Road in search of a driver who would take them home. My thoughts were devoted to Ethel and the endless pleasures that lay within our reach. One incident stands out in my recollection. As Clara kissed my wife at the top of the steps, she whinnied her insistence that Cora should hasten back inside, lest she "catch her death."

At last the door closed on the Martinettis. I glanced at the clock: half past one. "Would you like a nightcap, my dear?"

She yawned and I took that for assent. Excellent! I barely

234

suppressed the urge to rub my hands with delight. I was learning fast, however. On this occasion, I had no wish to drag her up all those steps again.

"Why don't you go up to your room?" I suggested. "You must be tired after such a long evening. I shall pour the brandy and soda while you are doing your hair and I'll bring it up in a couple of minutes."

"You'll never be a card player if you live to be a hundred," she scoffed. When I gave a sheepish smile, Cora turned in disgust and lumbered up the stairs.

I had secreted a quantity of hyoscine in a high cabinet in the kitchen. My heart was jumping like a jack-in-the-box as I brought it out. No longer was I Cora's slave. Within a short time she would be at my mercy. What doctor can say that he has not been thrilled by the prospect of controlling his patient's fate? Who would not be tempted to play God?

My hands shook as I poured the drug into the spirit glass. Perhaps it was nervous excitement, perhaps the effect of a glass of stout of which I had partaken earlier. A single thought kept coursing through my brain. *Before Saturday dawns, Ethel will have stayed with me here—and Cora will not have the slightest idea.*

When I entered her room, she was sitting at her dressing table, examining her hair in the mirror, one of the Hinde curlers in her hand.

"Here you are, my dear," I said, handing her the drink. "Pleasant dreams."

At five to two, I was getting ready for bed. Even with the increased dosage, a little while might elapse before the hyoscine began to take effect. After a prudent interval, I would look in on Cora and check that all was well. I began to undress, imagining the touch of Ethel's fingernails as they glided across my chest and loins.

A scream paralysed me. And then came another scream, even more terrible than the last, ripping through the night.

A burglar! That was my first cogent thought. Cora had looked through the window and espied someone breaking in. I was unclothed, defenceless and suddenly afraid. With no time to lose, I ran to the chest of drawers and grabbed my revolver.

Cora shrieked again. An incoherent plea for mercy.

I swallowed hard. At once I realised there was no burglar. I was hearing the sounds of delirium. I must quiet her, at any cost. What if the neighbours were to be woken by her cries?

"Cora!" I cried as I ran from my room. "Don't worry, I am here!"

She was lying on the bed, wearing only her combinations and clutching her throat. Her eyes were wild, her bleached hair a tangled mess. When she saw me, she screamed in horror. I realised that I was a fearsome sight. A naked man, with a gun in his hand. As I advanced toward her, I tossed the revolver on to the carpet, to show that I meant her no harm. But my gesture was to no avail.

"Murder!" she wailed. "Murder!"

"Cora," I hissed. "For pity's sake, be quiet!"

Her face was red and bloated. She heaved herself up from her supine position, her whole body trembling. "Peter, I'm dying!"

I reached for her and she buried her head on my chest, sobbing violently all the while. "It's going to be all right," I said.

"No," she gasped, "not all right, not all right. Going to be sick."

Staggering to her feet, a hand still at her throat, she moved unsteadily toward the door. I rose to help her, but she pushed me back with surprising force. Within a couple of moments she had gained the bathroom. I watched as she gurgled and sobbed and vomited over the bowl. I could not help but feel pity for her wretched state. Pity, coupled with a sickening despair. Had I miscalculated in my haste after a long, fatiguing day? Had I administered too severe a dose? It was all too possible.

Silently, I cursed myself. How could I have been so careless? Years of making up homeopathic remedies that could never, due to their anodyne ingredients, do anyone more than minimal harm, must have blunted my appreciation of the fine measurement requisite in the dosage. Not once had I experienced more than a slight giddiness after taking hyoscine, but each patient is distinct, and Cora might be more susceptible.

She was screeching in between the gusts of nausea. I tried to reassure her by putting an arm around her shoulder, but she threw it off.

"Cora, please! I beg you, calm yourself."

Quite beyond reason, she smacked me on the cheek. My eyes smarted at the blow, but for all my frantic state of mind, I fought to keep my nerve.

"Cora, I need to examine you. Remember, I am a doctor."

"No!"

With an agony of effort, she rose. She could barely do more than assume a crouching posture. The revolver was in her line of vision. Fearing what she might do while in the grip of a fleeting insanity, I snatched the gun up from the floor.

"Cora, please! Everything will be all right, I swear it! You have simply had a nasty turn."

Never have a doctor's words of comfort been uttered in such desperation. Over the years I had found her a difficult patient. Always wilful, she failed to hide her impatience with my bedside manner. *In extremis,* I found myself powerless to calm her.

"I'm . . . I'm dying."

I could barely make out the words. Surely it was not true: I could not have miscalculated to such an extent.

"No, Cora, no!"

She was staring at the gun in my hand. I could tell from her pupils that she was finding it difficult to focus, but the gun seemed to have a hypnotic effect upon her. Suddenly she made as if to lunge for it, but overbalanced and fell heavily. On her way down, she cracked her head on the edge of the enamel bath with a noise that sounded like a clap of thunder.

"Cora!"

My heart bumping against the inside of my chest, I gazed at her prostrate form in horror. She was lying face down and blood was leaking from the gash in her temple, darkening the peroxide curls. For an instant, the shock froze me, but then I bent down and checked for a pulse, moaning in dismay as I prayed that she might survive.

"Cora, for the love of God, please don't die!"

The pulse was barely discernible. I began to weep at this sickening jest of Fate. Was it the hyoscine, or had her heart given way? Even as I sobbed in distress, the pulse faded altogether.

A hideous shriek sliced through the air, as though a dead soul meant to put a curse on me. I knelt by the corpse, covered my face with my free hand, as if to ward off evil spirits, before I realised that the cry came from Cora's blue and gold macaw, locked in the room across the landing.

Time slipped by. The gale rattled in the chimney, the faint stink of urine hung in the air. I kept her wrist in the tightest grip. It was all that I could cling to as the implications of her death seeped into my fevered brain.

The clock was striking three as I huddled in a chair in the parlour, an empty glass of brandy at my feet. I had not bothered with soda. Long ago I had forsworn spirits—they were inimical to my digestion—but nothing else could carry me through the night. Stomach cramps were a small price to pay for the strength to survive until morning.

In a daze, I had filled the scuttle with slack from the cellar and stoked the fire. The gun was back in its drawer. Outside, the wind lashed the laburnum trees and even though I had put on my pyjamas, I could not stop shivering. It was as if I had been stranded in the maze at Hampton Court. Yet there *must* be a path to safety. Cora had died by accident—but how to explain the screams? Perhaps by luck no insomniac neighbour had heard. Even then, a sudden death would demand a post mortem. Would traces of hyoscine be detected? What plausible explanation could I devise for Cora's death? My mind, naturally so fertile, remained an obstinate blank. Like so many innocents, I had a mortal dread of the law's long arm. Fear of imprisonment was numbing my imagination. How bitterly I regretted that a career combining business management with homeopathy had resulted in an utter lack of knowledge regarding forensic jurisprudence.

I had only wished for Cora to disappear. If she had vanished, Ethel and I could have shared our lives openly. Now there would be police enquiries and bank clerks wearing worried frowns. Eddie Marr could not save me by writing out a cheque. Freedom had been snatched from our grasp by the callous vagaries of unlucky chance.

If only Cora *had* disappeared. After all, she talked of leaving more times than I could recall. If only she had made good her threat. A thought vaulted into my mind. Suppose everyone believed that she had done exactly that? Then I would not have to call the police. Instead, Ethel could stay here as my wife, the mistress of Number 39. Even the diamonds would be hers.

It *could* happen, if I made it happen. All I need do was to focus all my energies on the task at hand. Never am I more successful than when I have a settled aim. All I need is to see light at the end of the tunnel. I am a true Crippen. Whatever my shortcomings, no one ever dismissed me as an idle shirker.

That light kept shining, tempting me on. A single obstacle lay in my path—or, rather, lay upstairs on the bathroom floor. I finished the brandy with a slurp, as if in ironic homage to Cora's coarse manner of imbibing. Suddenly I recognised the nature of my task. Even so, I needed Dutch courage before undertaking it. Then I banged the glass down and searched out my overcoat. I needed to wear something over my pyjamas if I were to brave the elements in dead of night and venture out to the little shed at the bottom of the garden. That was the place where I chopped up wood and kept an axe and saw.

Arthur, do you remember the witnesses for the Crown telling the world what they really thought about me? After the hysteria whipped up by the press, I might have expected the lash of their tongues—but nothing of the sort.

"He always appeared exceedingly kind-hearted and courteous toward his wife": Doctor John Burroughs.

Mr. Tobin: "Did he seem a good-tempered man always?" Mrs. Clara Martinetti (a trifle grudging, but nevertheless): "He seemed so."

"Would you agree that Dr. Crippen seemed always a good-tempered, kind-hearted man?" Mrs. Smythson (rather more willingly than I had feared): "Yes, he always seemed so."

"I think you said at the Police Court that you thought he was one of the nicest men you ever met?" Mrs. Jackson, Ethel's former landlady: "I did."

And so the testimonials continued. Had circumstances differed, I might have preened. No dispassionate onlooker could fail to have been impressed by the consistency of the evidence. Where everything went so terribly wrong was in the evidence for the defence. Yet what could I do? It was impossible to tell the whole truth. In particular, Arthur, you will understand that I dared say nothing about my plan with regard to the hyoscine.

R v Crippen, second day, evidence in chief of Dr. Augustus Joseph Pepper

"Having examined the manner in which the viscera have been extracted from that body, are you able to say whether it was done by a skilled person or not?"

"Yes, it must have been."

. . . (The Lord Chief Justice): *"That is dissection, I suppose?"*

"Dissection. . . . There is no cut or tear in any part except where it is necessary for the removal. . . . All the organs I have described were connected together and the diaphragm or the septum between the chest and abdomen had been cut round."

I shall say little more about the events of that night. Drink anaesthetised me against the horrors of my task. Fear and love were the stimuli that kept me labouring beyond all previous limits of my endurance as well as past the break of dawn. I take no pride in what I did. As I swore in evidence, when a young man I went through a *theoretical* course of surgery. I have never in my life conducted an autopsy.

Did I despise her? Was it hatred that gave me the strength to separate the head from its neck and sever the stumpy legs from the torso? Did an electric charge of pleasure ripple through me when I sliced the soft organs beneath the skin?

No, no, no, no, no! Dismemberment was a necessary evil. I had to debone the corpse and render it unrecognisable. Otherwise, if her body were discovered, in whatever location I used as a hiding place, it would lead the police straight to my door. Ever since consummating my union with her, I had cared little for Cora. It was just as well. Had my sensibilities become engaged in the small hours of 1 February, I could never have achieved what I set out to do.

Numb with dread, I conducted the operation in the bathroom. The air was rank with soap and death. Cora's body, white and inert, lay in the enamel tub, where all the blood could drain away. A voice in my head begged me not to have pity, to treat this dreadful exercise as one more job to be done. Yet I could not help thinking—*poor Cora.* Not only had she ceased to be a woman, she had become a heap of meat, not unlike the joint we had tucked into earlier that evening.

Averting my gaze from her lifeless eyes, I took a deep breath and set about my business. I intended to cut and chop the body into transportable segments, separating the bones from the flesh. Once the remains were beyond identification, I could decide upon their final resting place. Perhaps they should be buried underground; perhaps I would hurl them in the Thames. All that mattered for the moment was to obliterate all clues that might connect me with the corpse.

For all my precautions, drops of blood kept squirting here and there. I had put on my oldest pair of pyjamas—one of a set that Cora had purchased for me in a winter sale the year before—to try and keep warm. Splashes landed on my chest, a few hit my cheeks and eyes. All I could do was blink and wipe myself clean. I sawed with a steady rhythm, heedless of the dull ache of my arms and shoulders. My wife had strong bones, and they did not fracture easily. Every now and then I resorted to the axe.

By six o'clock, it was done. I ripped off the pyjamas stained with her life-blood and threw them on the bathroom floor. The bathtub was crammed to overflowing. Exhausted as I was, my work for the day had only just begun. One thing was clear: the truth must remain hidden. Everyone must believe that Cora had carried out her threat and left me. The instant I gave Rylance or anyone else cause for suspicion, I was lost.

My first priority was to stay awake enough not to let my guard slip, even for a second. This was no time to experiment with stimulants; caffeine would have to suffice. Downstairs, I dosed myself with countless cups of the strongest coffee and pondered how to cope with the day ahead. My grandfather had so often preached the importance of self-discipline. Over the next few hours I must live up to his exacting standards.

I summoned the courage to crawl back to Cora's bedroom. In the top drawer of her dressing table, she kept ready cash that would tide me over for the next few days. After all, had I not paid for most of the clothes and knickknacks that were strewn around? She had surrounded herself with tokens of her extravagance; there were enough feathers to have covered her from head to toe. I scooped up the notes and coins and filled my pockets until they overflowed.

I took pains to arrive for work at my usual hour, travelling in by omnibus, practising casual pleasantries to utter, so that nobody might guess that anything in the slightest untoward had occurred. Even with Ethel, I dared yield no clue about the change that the night's events had wrought in our lives. Time was what I needed, time to decide what to do with the bloody remains piled high in the bathtub.

"So!" Ethel greeted me as I stepped through the door. "You're free at last!"

I recoiled as if she had put a red-hot poker to my cheek. "What?"

Her expression was as innocent as a nun's. "Don't look so alarmed, dearest! Surely you haven't forgotten? Finally, today, you are rid of the yoke of Munyon's Remedies."

Of course! The agency agreement had expired at midnight, although perhaps I could be pardoned for having let it slip my mind. Recovering my poise, I gave an airy wave.

"Oh, them! I have already forgotten about the professor and his works. The future lies with painless dentistry rather than mail-order cures!" An idea jumped in my mind. "I suppose I ought to speak to Miss Curnow and wish her well."

Ethel gazed at me fondly. "That is what I so admire in you, Hawley. You are always thinking of others."

I pecked her on the cheek; there would be time enough to kiss properly in the future. "Now, if you'll excuse me. I'll look in on her whilst I remember and then I'll have a word with Rylance about today's patients."

"Only a handful," she said quietly. "There isn't enough business to keep him fully occupied, let alone yourself, and the creditors are beginning to press. Only this morning . . ."

"Cheer up!" I commanded. "You are worrying needlessly, darling. We are experiencing a temporary embarrassment, that is all. Have no fear, we shall pull through."

Her lower lip quivered, so prettily I thought. "Oh, Hawley, are you sure?"

"Trust me, Ethel dearest. Have I ever let you down?"

Her timid smile was all the answer I required. Strolling down the corridor, I looked in on Marion Curnow. She had been appointed as manageress of Munyon's, following the termination of my agency. I reasoned that she would have cause to remember the date if questioned afterwards, and I wanted her to recall my air of unconcern.

"I'm sure you will make a success of the position," I assured her. "After all, haven't you had the best possible mentor these past twelve years?"

She tittered at my jest. "I'm so grateful for all your help and guidance over the years, Doctor, really I am. Without you, I would never have been offered this opportunity."

I departed, satisfied with the impression I had made. After a brief exchange with William Long, I spoke to Rylance. As a rule he left financial matters to me, but he had become so troubled by the state of our accounts that he asked if the time had come to cut our fees in order to attract more custom. I counselled against such a drastic step.

"It would smack of panic, and the first rule of commerce is never to panic."

"I suppose you're right," he said doubtfully.

"Depend on it, my dear fellow. The second rule, by the by, is that a profit margin, once eroded, can never be reestablished. I may be able to make a modest financial injection into the practice. We shall weather this storm by keeping calm. There is no other way."

Reassured, he retreated into his consulting room for a read and a smoke. As the door closed behind him, I sank into my chair and asked myself what further steps I could take to paint a picture of normality, so that no one who met me would believe that I had spent the night chopping my wife's body into pieces.

The moment the idea of visiting the Martinettis occurred to me, I realised it was the right thing to do. Criminals do not display solicitude, I said to myself. Moreover, I was *not* a criminal. Cora's death had been a tragic accident, and my actions had been designed solely to obviate unpleasantness and misunderstanding: a case of *force majeure*.

When I called at King Edward's Mansions and enquired

after her husband's health, Clara told me that Paul was tucked up in bed. We agreed solemnly that it was the best place for him.

"And how is Belle?" she asked.

A horrid vision of the bathtub's contents swam into my mind. My gorge rising, I stammered, "She is . . . all right."

"Do give her my love."

"Of course."

Having dealt with a momentary awkwardness, I departed with her brays of goodwill echoing in my ears.

On the short walk back from Shaftesbury Avenue to the office, it began to pour down, but although I had forgotten my umbrella, I did not care. Rain would wash the dirty city, leaving it fresh and clean. I stopped off at the bank to pay in the money I had taken from Cora's dressing table: a sum slightly in excess of seventeen pounds. As the clerk signed the receipt, I allowed myself to believe that my boldness might be rewarded.

All afternoon I kept one eye on the clock. Fortunately, Rylance was so absorbed in his pipe and the perusal of *Titbits* that he left me alone while I wrestled with a single problem: what to do with the remains. Even when Ethel sought to engage me in conversation, I replied in monosyllables. We could do our talking later. It was with a profound relief that I wished her goodnight that evening and watched her set off for Hampstead. Before I started on my own homeward journey, I needed to equip myself for the dreadful business that lay ahead. Calling in on a shop on New Oxford Street, I purchased two large bags, wrapping paper and string.

With every hour that passed, the consequences of Cora's death, and its concealment, were coming home to me. Now divorce was impossible, but did it matter? Ethel and I had no need of a formal ceremony. As for Cora's friends, I would have to lay a false trail.

Number 39 stood in darkness when I returned. The rain had ceased, but the laurels outside were dripping wet, their shadows as menacing as ruffians in the glow cast by the street lamp. The moment I unlocked the front door, the sour smell of decay came wafting down the stairs. Dear God, I thought, before the night is over, I must be rid of the body. I could keep going only by promising myself that, this time tomorrow, Ethel would accompany me back here and we would embark on a new life in a paradise of our own creation.

The gas jets in the parlour hissed like nervous cats. I needed to fortify myself with a drop of brandy. As I sipped, my eyes fell on the photograph of Miller, beaming at me from its place of honour on the piano. I stared at the complacent face while I finished my drink. At last I was the master in my own house. Setting my glass down, I strode across the room. I smashed the frame and ripped the photograph into a hundred pieces. For years it had taunted me; in seconds I had destroyed it.

My next stop was the cellar. I selected a dozen of the heaviest lumps of coal, which I put in the bags I had bought. Carrying the bags, together with scissors and the brown paper and string, up to my room—soon it would be *our* room—I took off all my clothes. Closing my eyes, I called upon the Lord to have mercy on Cora's soul, and on mine. At least she had not suffered long and nothing that I did now could hurt her. I must save the living, not scruple about the dead.

According to my calculations, I would need to make five journeys that night. A few minutes' walk away behind Camden Park Road lay a reservoir, notoriously deep, that I had designated in my mind as Cora's final resting place. There would be no headstone, no physical memorial at all, but she believed that God's followers would be granted eternal life. For all her failings, I could not begrudge her that.

★ ★ ★ ★ ★

Three times I trudged through drizzle to the reservoir, lugging my bags full of parcels weighted down by coal. My shoulders ached and my feet hurt. My shoes pinched at the toes, but for economy's sake, I had not bought a new pair. Yet I dared not pause to catch my breath, nor wait for the ripples to disappear after each package sank into the water with a splash. If I allowed myself to reflect on what I was doing, I might find myself incapable of taking another step.

As I plodded down Hilldrop Crescent for the fourth time, the rain was falling harder. In the distance, cattle in the Caledonian Market were roaring. I pictured them, wedged together like so many figs in a drum, thick steam rising from their fat bodies as the drover goaded them to their doom. Soon they would be carcasses on hooks.

The bag in my right hand contained the head. Somehow I had managed to avert my gaze as I wrapped it up, but as I walked along the street, I endured a waking nightmare. This was the heaviest load so far. What if the burden became too much and the parcel slipped from my grasp? I imagined the package coming apart and its contents rolling into the gutter for any passerby to see.

At least the dismal weather was keeping everyone in who did not have a very good reason to be abroad. But as I turned out of the Crescent, I found myself staring at an approaching figure dressed in a cape and wearing a helmet. A police constable, patrolling the suburb in quest of malefactors.

"Good evening, sir," the man said as he drew nearer.

"Good evening, officer," I said. If I squeaked the words, that was surely forgivable. It was a wonder that I did not burst into hysterical laughter.

"Filthy night."

He scrutinised me, and I could see his mind working: *scrawny gent, out later than you'd expect, but seems respectable enough; maybe he couldn't find a cab.* His eyes travelled to the bags that I was carrying and I prayed that the reputation of the London peeler for a lack of imagination was well earned.

"Filthy." I swallowed. "The sooner I get back home, the happier I shall be."

He nodded in sympathy, possibly because it was so plain that I was speaking the truth. "Well, goodnight, sir."

"Goodnight, officer."

He strode on and by a miracle I resisted the urge to sink to the ground and wail with relief. Rather, I quickened my pace, swearing to myself that if I regained Number 39 without further incident, I would find another way of ridding myself of the last few lumps of flesh.

After gulping down another tot of brandy, I sat in the parlour and pondered. I could no more make a fifth visit to the reservoir than fly to Mars. The last spark of my energy was guttering, but to spend another night in close proximity to the bits and pieces that had once been my wife was more than I could bear.

Suddenly, the door of the parlour creaked open. My throat dried and I had a hysterical vision of Cora's severed and bloody remains, come crawling back to torment me, as in a story of revenge by Poe. A small head and two glassy eyes appeared around the door. Cora's white Persian was taking a nocturnal prowl. I moistened my lips; at least I was not losing my senses, not yet awhile. Gently, I gathered the fat, warm creature in my arms and carried it back to the breakfast room, the door of which I had forgotten to lock.

Forcing myself to rational thought, I pondered burying what was left of Cora in the garden. Even digging a shallow grave was likely to prove beyond the last vestiges of my physical powers. Worse, the garden was overlooked by neighbouring houses, and those in Brecknock Road backed directly onto it. What if someone heard me working outside and took a look out of his window? It would be akin to hailing a constable. By carving up Cora's body, I had raised the stakes. In the numbing aftermath of her death it had seemed impossible to explain away traces of hyoscine in her tissue, but how much more challenging would I find it to devise a plausible reason for interring the last few lumps of her flesh? If only I had not acted so impulsively the previous night! Within moments, I banished self-recrimination. I must cling to a single truth: the prize was within reach, if only I held my nerve.

As I massaged my sore feet, the answer came to me. The cellar! For months I had meant to level up its floor. The bricks were uneven as well as loose; beneath them was nothing but earth. It should not be impossible to inter the last mass of flesh there.

Heart pounding, I lit a candle and hurried downstairs. The cellar was at the bottom of a short, gloomy passage running from the kitchen to the back door. It measured about nine feet by six. Apart from coal, we kept a few odds and ends there: branches cut from the trees in the garden that could be used for kindling, a badly chipped chandelier, a rusting shovel, and a broken brush. In the glow of the candle, I caught a glimpse of a small pile of lime left over from a bag I had used in the garden the previous summer. Was the hand of Providence on my shoulder? I now had the means to destroy the tell-tale flesh.

Kneeling down on the bricks, I scrabbled at the floor. I kept scuffing my fingers and making them bleed, but the discomfort meant nothing. The condition of the mortar was worse than I had surmised and within minutes I had lifted up a pile of bricks, uncovering a patch of clay soil perhaps three feet square. I picked up the shovel and, with much puffing and grunting, dug up a mound of earth so as to create a sizeable cavity.

Returning to the bathroom, I gathered together everything that I wished to conceal. The pieces of flesh, Cora's combinations and oddments such as three or four Hinde curlers that had also been flecked with blood. My ruined pyjama jacket became a makeshift hold-all. No need for brown paper or string; a few sprinklings of lime should do the trick. Never had I imagined that experience gained in constructing a garden wall would prove so valuable. In comparison, replacing the brick floor, so as to give the impression that it had never been disturbed since the house was built, was child's play.

By five o'clock, the deed was done. I dragged my aching bones back up the stairs to my room. Fatigue enveloped me like a pea-soup fog, misting my thoughts. And yet I experienced a strange elation as I undertook the final preparation for the morrow. The worst was over, and soon Ethel would be mistress of Number 39. This would be the very last night when I would not feel the warmth of her cheeks against mine.

Bright and early, I arrived at Albion House and left a note for Ethel enclosing a packet and two letters. I feared that if I broke the news of Cora's disappearance to her directly, the emotion of the moment might tempt me into an indiscretion. Better to keep my distance for a few hours, while she accustomed herself to the departure of her rival and I laid the foundations for our new life. In composing the note, I opted for simplicity, directness, and the promise of better times to come.

"*B.E. has gone to America. Will you kindly favour me by handing the enclosed packet and letters to Miss May as soon as she arrives at her office, with my compliments? Shall be in later, when we can arrange for a pleasant little evening.*"

B.E. has gone to America! I had crafted a dozen more elaborate explanations before settling on a plain form of words. No need for embellishment. Cora had gone forever.

The packet contained a cheque book, paying-in book, and other items relating to the Ladies' Guild that I had found in Cora's room. The timing was convenient, for this was the day when the committee met in their room along the corridor. I hoped to take advantage of the coincidence by letting the ladies know that Cora would no longer be amongst them. The letter to Melinda May, in my hand, began and ended as follows:

"Dear Miss May,
Illness of a near relative has called me to America on only a few hours' notice, so I must ask you to bring my resignation as treasurer before the meeting today . . . I wish you everything nice till I return to London again. Now, goodbye, with love hastily.

Yours, Belle Elmore, pp H.H.C."

The other letter was addressed to the committee of the Ladies' Guild and made it clear that her absence would last for several months. I had written it as from Belle, and although the text was written in my undisguised hand, I contrived a facsimile of her signature as a gesture toward verisimilitude.

Hurrying to Kingsway, I wondered if I had made a mistake. In seeking to contrive an impression of panic on Cora's part, arguably I had succumbed to the vices I sought to mimic. But I had not been sure that her friends would accept my word alone if the messages did not purport to come from her. Ethel would accept whatever I said without question, but the Guild members were a different kettle of fish. No matter; it was too late for regrets. I must pray that the messages failed to arouse curiosity and that Cora's fellow committee members had better things to do with their time than to dwell on the unexpected disappearance of their mercurial colleague.

After lunch, I called back at Number 39. In my haste to remove the spare money Cora kept in her room the previous day, I had neglected to consider what should be done with the jewellery. I saw an overwhelming logic in converting a number of superfluous items into ready cash. First, though, I wanted to select a few pieces for Ethel. Her discreet beauty would be complemented by some of the less vulgar gems. I loaded my pockets with as much as I could safely carry and returned to Albion House. Ethel greeted me in high excitement.

"Is it true? Has Belle Elmore really—*gone away?*"

Her cheeks were flushed and her tone breathless. Even her voice was pitched a little higher than usual. I could not resist reaching out to stroke her silky hair. "Yes. She has left me."

A strange light came into her eyes. "Did you see her go?"

"No. I found her gone when I came home last night."

She moistened her lips, her gaze fastened upon me. "Do you—do you think she will come back?"

I shook my head. "No, I don't."

"Did she take any luggage with her?"

All these questions! Thank the Lord that I had prepared my story thoroughly. "I don't know what luggage she had, because I did not see her go. I dare say she took what she wanted. She always said the things I gave her were not good enough, so I suppose she thinks she can get better elsewhere."

Ethel gave a satisfied nod, as if we were teacher and pupil, and I had passed a test. As if to emphasise my answers, I thrust my hand into a pocket and took out an assortment of jewels.

"Look here, you had better have these. At all events, I wish you would please me by taking one or two. I should like to know you had some good jewellery. They will be useful when we are dining out."

She was almost lost for words as she gazed at the gemstones. They dazzled fit to match her smile as she absorbed what I had told her. "Well, darling . . . if you really wish it."

"I do."

"Very well," she breathed. "Pick out which you like. You know my tastes."

You know my tastes. That last phrase sent a thrill of delight down my spine. The casual assumption of intimacy combined with implicit trust. I chose a couple of solitaire rings, a ring set with four diamonds and a ruby, and a small diamond brooch in the shape of a rising sun. She caressed them as a new mother might fondle a longed-for baby. There remained a large brooch set with stones in the shape of a tiara, with rows of diamonds arranged in a crescent, a pair of diamond earrings, and half a dozen other fine rings.

"What will you do with them?"

"The business needs money," I said. "By a welcome co-incidence I have regained possession of the presents I made to her. I shall either sell or pawn them."

She gave a contented smile. "If you pawn them, then as soon as things look up, you will be able to redeem them."

I smiled. "Good idea. I shall take your advice."

Three quarters of an hour later, I was walking out of Attenboroughs on Oxford Street with eighty pounds in my pocket book; the manager had advanced that sum for the marquise diamond ring and the earrings alone. Now I could pay off my personal debts as well as a couple of the creditors of the Yale Tooth Specialists. I would pledge the remaining items at my leisure and use the funds to provide a few little luxuries for Ethel and myself. Perhaps I might take her over to France for a treat. After all we had endured, we surely deserved to enjoy ourselves together.

I said as much to her over dinner that evening. I had booked a table at Frascati's—where else? Ethel was wearing the rising sun brooch as well as the ring with diamonds and ruby. Her skin shone, her lips were lavishly rouged. Never had I seen her looking so radiant.

"Easter is less than a couple of months away," I pointed out. "We might make a little trip to Dieppe, say?"

She clapped her hands in delight. "Hawley, how wonderful! You know very well that I have seldom had the chance to venture abroad."

"Then it is just as well that your hub is a seasoned traveller," I said lightly. "Perhaps one day we shall sail the seas together. I should like you to see the land where I was born. Canada, too, is a fine country. If I had not made my home here, I would gladly have settled in Toronto or Montreal."

At half past ten, a cab dropped us off outside Number 39. For the first time, it was Ethel who accompanied me up the steps to the front door, Ethel whose fragrance I inhaled as we hurried up the stairs to my room.

Later, as we lay in bed side by side, she whispered, "Hawley, I must ask you a question."

"Anything, my sweet."

"Promise me that she isn't coming back."

I thought of the brick floor in the cellar; I had taken such pains to conceal any signs of disturbance. Yet in the deepest recesses of my sinuses, the smell from downstairs lingered. Wet earth and lime-eaten flesh.

"She never will come back," I said, more harshly than I intended.

Ethel was as persistent as any member of her sex. "When I took the letters to the Guild meeting, they told me that she spoke of returning in a few months' time."

I sat up in bed. "You must accept my word on this, Ethel, and swear not to press me for corroboration."

As I paused, she said, "I swear."

"Listen to me, darling." I hissed in her ear: "No one will ever see Cora again. She has gone forever, never to return."

She made no sound, merely shifting her position a little so that I saw her face in the narrow shaft of moonlight that slid through the curtains. Her hot breath on my cheek, I glimpsed the sharp white dentures Rylance had fashioned for her. Shining in exultation.

The wonder is that I have not lost my appetite, just as I did not starve myself after disposing of the bloody remains. I drink a glass of stout each night and tuck into a beef steak or Irish stew. The Pentonville cuisine is an unexpected blessing: hardly matching Frascati's, but plain and wholesome. Yet there are times, I admit, when I spare a thought for the cattle of Caledonian Market, to whose plaintive cries I used to pay no heed. Wretched creatures, destined for abattoirs, bone-boiling houses, and gut-scraperies, for tallow-melting, gut-spinning, paunch-cooking. Should we remember their innocence as we tuck into the scrags, the saddles, the sirloins that grace our dinner tables?

Perhaps. But even now, when presented with a plate of chops, I feast upon it ravenously.

Letter from H.H. Crippen to his wife's half-sister Louise and her husband, 7 April 1910

"Dear Louise and Robert,

"I hardly know how to write to you of my dreadful loss. . . . A few weeks ago we had news that an old relative of mine in California was dying, and to secure important property for ourselves, it was necessary for one of us to go and put the matter into a lawyer's hands at once . . . the next I heard by cable was that she was dangerously ill, and two days later . . . I had the dreadful news that she had passed away. . . . She is being sent back to me and I shall soon have what is left of her here. Of course, I am giving up the house; in fact, it drives me mad to be in it alone. . . . I do not know what I shall do, but probably find some business to take me travelling for a few months until I can recover . . ."

Never have I experienced such heavenly bliss as in those weeks following the events of 1 February. I needed to quell the urge to preen so as to play the part of the deserted husband to good effect. My fondness for the theatrical stood me in good stead. Everyone in my circle must become accustomed to Cora's absence as well as to my altered circumstances. Out of sight would become out of mind.

I cancelled Belle's subscriptions to *The Stage* and *Era,* an economy that I found liberating. By my estimate, the unpledged jewels were worth upwards of one hundred and thirty pounds; within a week, I paid Attenboroughs a second visit and pawned them for just fifteen pounds less than that sum. In addition, I had gained unfettered access to the account at the Charing Cross Bank. As Ethel gleefully pointed out, before long I would have no further need of Eddie Marr's backing. Thus comfortably placed, I approached Rylance with a view to agreeing to revised terms of partnership.

"I have a little money put by for investment," I confided, "and the business is a welcome distraction for me at the present time."

"Oh, yes?" Rylance was the most remarkably incurious of men. At least for once he refrained from yawning.

"You may have noticed that I seem a little lonely just now."

"Well," he said, colouring as if I had made an indecent remark. "I had not actually spotted that, Doctor."

"It is my wife," I said, suppressing my irritation with difficulty. "She is halfway across to America. On legal business, you know."

"Ah." Rylance coughed, perhaps uncertain as to whether to voice regret, and then a fresh thought rescued him. "Very well, I'll contact my solicitor without delay and ask him to draw up a fresh partnership deed."

When next I called on the Martinettis, Paul was up and about again. When he and Clara ushered me in to their living room, it was plain that they had heard from Melinda May of Cora's departure.

"Well, you're a nice one!" Clara neighed. "Belle gone to America and you don't let us know anything about it. Why did you not send us a wire? I would have liked to go to the station and bring some flowers."

This was far from the pleasant greeting for which I had hoped, but I replied with good grace, explaining that time had been short. We had received a cable to say that one of us must set off for America and that, as she wanted to go, I let her. I had needed to look out for some papers, and the rest of the night we did the packing.

"Packing and crying, I suppose?"

Irked, I said, "Oh, we have got past that."

"Did she take all her clothes with her?"

Racking my brains, I said hastily, "One basket."

Clara's eyebrows shot up. "That would not be enough—one basket to go all that way!"

This inquisition was becoming wholly unwelcome. Determined not to sound too testy, I said casually, "She can buy something more over there. There is a possibility that this whole business might lead to a title, you know."

"Really?" Paul was nonplussed.

"It is not certain, though, not certain at all." I gabbled. Perhaps I had taken a step too far. "The trouble is that the whole business is likely to be protracted. I do not expect to see her again for at least six months."

"Six months!" Clara exclaimed.

"I might think about selling some of our furniture and moving elsewhere," I said. "The house is uncomfortably large for one person, even with all the animals."

Clara's lips were wobbling and I could tell that she was close to tears. It was hard to understand. It was not as if she *knew*. "Well, she is sure to send me a postcard from the ship."

I gave a vague nod, but under my breath I muttered, *I think it most unlikely.*

This conversation troubled me and my anxiety grew when,

without warning, Paul called the following day and said that he had been thinking. That thinking is a dangerous pursuit, not lightly to be undertaken by the unqualified, was quickly demonstrated. He said that it was not right for a couple to be separated for as long we appeared to expect. Thus he advised me to follow Cora and take the first steamer to America.

Taken aback, I stammered, "She—she is unwell."

"I will assist you in packing and with selling the furniture, if that is delaying you."

It then struck me that he and Clara might have been talking about Bruce Miller and speculating that she meant to join him in Chicago. Splendid! Perhaps before long everyone would be putting two and two together. I began to relax. All I must do is to continue to show calm in the face of adversity. Paul's further enquiries proved easy enough to deflect, but I remained anxious about Clara. Women are such ferocious talkers. If only I could set her mind at rest. Three or four days later, I decided to call on the Martinettis again on my way home from work.

"Belle hasn't sent me a postcard!" Clara complained. "I suppose she will write when she gets to New York."

This time I was quick to respond. "Oh, she does not get to New York. She goes straight on to California."

As I had hoped, this kept her quiet. It was not until later that night that I realised I had committed a *gaffe*. Most members of Cora's family lived in New York. I must have been thinking of my father and son, both of whom lived in California. But all being well, this tiny slip would escape Clara's notice.

A couple of evenings later, I heard a knock on the front door at Number 39 and found Clara outside on the top step.

"I was passing by," she said, "so I thought I would look in on you for a minute."

"That's good of you," I said warmly. "Do come in."

Would I have welcomed her in such fulsome manner had Ethel been present? Perhaps in those early days I might have cringed with embarrassment when my visitor realised that my secretary was keeping me company. But Ethel was back at Mrs. Jackson's. She was not yet staying with me every night, although she did call in after lunch each day to help with the housework and look after the pets. All of them took straight away to their new mistress. Not even the white Persian, most highly strung member of our little menagerie, seemed to pine for her departed owner.

I led Clara into the parlour and proposed a cup of tea. She said no with as much alacrity as if offered a glass of hemlock.

"I wondered if you had heard from Belle?"

I shook my head. "So far, no."

Clara seemed put out, but thankfully did not press the point. "There was something else. The Benevolent Fund Ball is at the Criterion on the 20th of February. I wondered if you wanted to go?"

"I don't think so," I said sombrely. "Without Belle it would not be quite the same."

"Of course, but it is such a pity. The Fund does marvellous work, as you well know. If by any chance you would like to come, Paul can get you the tickets, they are half a guinea each."

I was about to decline when it struck me that it might be rather delightful to take Ethel along. Cora had fussed for so long about the wretched Music Hall Ladies' Guild that it would be a pleasing irony to take my beloved to one of the principal events in its crowded calendar. Let those grizzled old harpies see a real lady!

"It's a worthy cause," I said, mustering a courageous smile. "I'll take two."

"Doctor Crippen!"

I was walking up the corridor in Albion House when a familiar voice hailed me. I fixed on a gently mournful expression and turned to greet Melinda May.

"Good afternoon, Miss May, it is nice to see you."

"I was wanting to speak to you, Doctor." As usual, she was pink and fluttering. "It is about the matter of your wife's subscription to the Guild. The annual payment of one guinea falls due tomorrow."

"Ah." I was disinclined to write a cheque, but an outright refusal would have appeared unneighbourly.

"Perhaps I could write to Belle and remind her," Melinda May twittered. "I wonder if you could let me have her address."

"Well," I said, "she is away in the hills of California. Right up there in the mountains, as it happens. If you let me have your letter, I shall make sure it is forwarded to her. No doubt she will authorise me to make payment on her behalf."

That did the trick. She gave two or three vigorous nods of her little head and, once back inside my room, I could not resist hugging myself at the ingenuity of my improvisation.

If it is trite to say that time heals, it is nonetheless true. In all my years as a doctor, I have discovered no better medicine: if only one could package it and supply it through the mail! Soon the worst memories began to fade. The inhuman glassiness of my wife's dead eyes, and the stench from the parcels that I carried under my arms.

Life must go on. I had agreed with Ethel that she should move in with me after a decent interval. The following month, perhaps. It seemed excessive to wait longer. She made no secret of her dislike for Number 39. The bedrooms held endless reminders of Cora. Everywhere were lengths of silks for making up into frocks, together with feathers and furs: more than enough to stock a milliner's shop. Ethel kept the doors locked, as if to banish the past. The house was large and difficult to keep tidy. Cora's solution to the dilemma of housework was to allow the place to overflow with knickknacks and dust, but Ethel preferred to impose order upon her surroundings.

We went to the theatre together regularly. How refreshing it was to have a companion who did not indulge in *schadenfreude* when actors missed their cues, and who did not insist on telling me at every opportunity how, with a little more luck, she might have become as celebrated in her own line as Miss Ellen Terry.

I told Ethel what I had said to the Martinettis and to Melinda May. She nodded with satisfaction, and I could almost hear her repeating the story in her head, so that she would not become confused and contradict what I had said. When I first broached the possibility of our attending the ball together, her response lacked enthusiasm. She said that she had not danced for years, and besides, she did not have anything suitable to wear. As so often, however, I sensed that she had left the door ajar; my task was to push it open. I pointed out that it would be a shame to waste the tickets I had paid for. Besides, the lovely silk dress she had bought at Swan and Edgar's the previous autumn would be ideal for the occasion, perhaps complemented by Cora's fox furs with matching muff.

"But all her friends will be there."

"So much the better." I beamed as she slipped a slender, proprietorial arm around my midriff. "For too long we have lived in the shadows, dodging around shabby hotels, afraid to be seen together in public. By escorting you to the ball, I convey a message to everyone whose mind Cora tried to poison against you. We are together—and that nothing can divide us."

Her smile was impish. "I shall love to see their faces."

"For me, the greatest pleasure is that you will be by my side."

"It is where I belong," she said softly, and within a few moments we had found a better way of expressing our love for each other.

We looked forward to the ball with mounting excitement. Our game was bold, but Clara Martinetti was aware from the start that my second ticket could not be intended for her friend. What more natural than to take my confidential secretary?

The Criterion! As we searched for our table that evening, Ethel gasped at the vastness of the gilded hall. The ceilings seemed to reach up to the heavens.

"It's like a Turkish palace!" she whispered to me in awed delight.

My chest swelled as we settled in our places at the Martinettis' table. Ethel had never looked more elegant. Surrounded by stars of yesteryear, she shone far more brightly. I sat between Clara and Ethel, with Paul on Ethel's right and the Nashes opposite. Having acclimatised to our game, Ethel was participating with all her heart. She had wrapped herself up in Cora's sealskin coat and fox furs and, as a *piece de resistance,* adorned her lily white bosom with the rising sun brooch.

Introductions were brief and stilted. This did not dismay me; a degree of reserve on all sides was only to be expected. The disapproving faces around me were a painful reminder that Cora had done her utmost to turn her friends against Ethel. Recalling Rylance's story made me clench my fists under the table. This evening, I hoped that the members of the Ladies' Guild would have the grace to renounce their prejudices. Once they realised that Ethel was innocent and refined, they would perforce revise their opinion of their old friend. Eventually, I had no doubt, all but the stupidest of them would see that Cora had been twisted by jealousy: ironic indeed in one who had spent so long finding men with whom to deceive me.

The menu made my mouth water. I succumbed to the lure of

cantaloupe glace followed by a piping hot *poularde Strasbourgeoise,* and Ethel followed suit. As we tucked into the sumptuous fare, one by one, our companions noticed the brooch. I saw their eyes drawn to it, like slivers of metal to a magnet. Clara pursed fat lips; Lil raised bushy eyebrows. Paul Martinetti gave a nervous cough. Ethel was at first unconscious of their scrutiny, but toward the end of the main course, conversation became spasmodic and finally died. The poor girl became visibly uncomfortable; pink spots appeared in her cheeks, and during the dessert course she developed a nervous cough. Grimly, I wiped the traces of my dessert from my chin, determined to say nothing that might encourage a comment or, worse, a question about Cora.

No one attempted to draw Ethel out. Indeed, Clara did not say a word to her all evening; on a couple of occasions she and Lil whispered to each other while keeping their eyes fixed on my friend. My heart sank at this lack of goodwill—and at an event in aid of charity!—toward a girl who had done nothing to provoke antipathy. Were other women envious of the freshness of a young English rose? The smoothness of her skin made such a contrast with their leathery, powdered cheeks.

The orchestra struck up with selections from Strauss and I did my duty in securing dancing partners for Ethel. Clara and Lil remained more absorbed in disapproving scrutiny of her than in the usual chat about the way music hall had changed for the worse. Finally it occurred to me that they might have recognised the rising sun brooch as having belonged to Cora. This was a possibility that had not hitherto crossed my mind. Despite having dined with Paul Martinetti a score of times, I could no more describe his taste in tie-pins and cuff links than recite by heart the works of Alfred, Lord Tennyson. But a woman observes the same scene in a different way from men. To ask a man and a woman to describe a person is akin to commissioning a portrait from painters of different schools.

When Ethel and I essayed a cautious waltz together, her cheeks were cold and her body trembled against mine. This was not what I had anticipated. In my imagination, I had conjured up a picture of the two of us whirling around the floor, lost in each other, Ethel's eyes closed in a happy dream. The waltz has always seemed to me so much more intimate than the minuet, polonaise, or quadrille that I have long regretted possessing two left feet. I murmured endearments in her ear, but to no avail. The instant that the music stopped, she said that her calves were aching and she wanted to sit down.

When we approached our table, the women were engaged in animated conversation, but as soon as they caught sight of us, they clamped their mouths shut. As soon as decency permitted, I yawned and said that perhaps we should be on our way. Ethel's relief was palpable. Again our fellow diners barely deigned to acknowledge her goodbyes, and I found myself burning with anger at their barely concealed indifference. How dare they shun her!

To make matters worse, Louise Smythson waddled over and accosted me as we left the ballroom. Chins wobbling furiously, she demanded to know whether I had heard from Cora lately. I said I had, but that was not enough for her. She insisted upon having an address so that she could write.

"She's right up in the wilds of the mountains of California," I said, fearing to contradict what I had told Clara. For all that I knew, these infernal women were exchanging notes.

"When you get to hear of her, you will be sure to let us know?"

"Certainly," I replied, my civility disguising my scorn. "When she has a settled address."

In her quiet way, Ethel has always been strong-willed. Once she makes up her mind about something, nothing can shift her.

After her shabby treatment by Cora's friends, she became all the more determined to put her own stamp on Number 39. She insisted that, before she moved in permanently, I should dispose of some of the furniture as well as Cora's music hall attire. She was happy to keep the furs.

"After all, she will have no further use for them where she is, will she? I mean—*California* is very hot, isn't it?"

At this, I looked her in the eye. Her face remained straight for a moment, and then it dissolved into laughter of pure mischief. For reply, I kissed her passionately. This was a woman with hidden depths; how thankful I was to be the man granted the honour of exploring them.

The unwanted costumes having been sold to a firm on Shaftesbury Avenue, I had the remaining effects transported to Albion House for storage. Fond as we were of Rex the bull terrier and the other animals, we decided to find good homes for them so as to make a further break with the past. Nina took the dog and her mother the cats, while to Adeline Harrison I made a present of the blue and gold macaw. At a stroke, the house became quieter and less cluttered, and by the simple expedient of living mainly in the kitchen and the bedroom, we created the illusion that Number 39 was a compact and cosy dwelling-place.

Our trip to Dieppe we regarded as an overdue honeymoon. Ethel was settling in to her new way of life. Of course, we never talked about Cora's fate. Whenever my wife was mentioned—less and less often as the days passed—she was named, simply, as "her." I understood how fiercely Ethel hated what my wife had said about her to the Ladies' Guild. For my part, I coped with the ghastly events following dinner with the Martinettis by dint of a technique I had developed in childhood.

For as long as I can remember, I have had a dread of forked lightning, and to this day, the sight of a lightning flash chills my flesh. In my infancy, whenever a storm raged in Coldwater, I had a terror that I would be struck dead by an electric shock. To guard against this, I would run up to my room and bury myself under the bedclothes until the danger had passed. In a small, breathless voice, I would recite stories to myself, anything that might distract my mind from the possibility that lightning would destroy me. The method worked; I survived each storm. Thus I learned how one can defeat horror, by the simple expedient of closing one's mind to it.

Before we left the country, I wished to quiet any fluttering in the dovecotes of the Ladies' Guild. The prospect of continued interrogation was both daunting and tedious. The strain of trying to remember what I had said to whom would become intolerable. If my wife had vanished, surely it was no one else's business but my own.

Despite the setback of the ball at the Criterion, I still hoped to win the sympathy of Paul Martinetti. Such an amiable man might surely be persuaded to take my part. Accordingly, two or three days after Ethel came to stay with me, I went to visit the Martinettis at King Edward's Mansions. My idea was to pave the way for bad news about Cora by revealing that my relations in California had written to say that she was very ill. To add a touch of verisimilitude, I added that Cora herself had written, saying that she was perfectly all right: showing her pluck, in other words. To my dismay, Paul seemed unimpressed. When I proposed dinner with Ethel and me, he declined with an excuse that was (I am not so easily deceived) a transparent fiction. I found this all the more distressing because we had been good friends.

Undeterred, I wrote later in the same week to Paul and Clara, saying that I had received a message by cable that Cora was dangerously ill with double pleuro-pneumonia. I told them I was considering travelling over to America to be by her side. A couple of days after that, I bumped into Clara and Annie Stratton by the big door at the entrance to Albion House. They said that at a Guild committee meeting half an hour earlier, it had been resolved that "a letter should be sent to Belle Elmore enquiring as to her health and wishing her a speedy recovery." Barely able to contain my impatience, I reiterated that attempts to contact my wife were pointless. I was expecting the worst news at any moment.

"She is as poorly as that?" Annie Stratton's face was the colour of ash.

"I am afraid it is very bad." I had the presence of mind to brush a tear from my eye and blow my nose. "If anything happens to her, I suppose I shall go to France for a week for a change of air."

Neat, even though I say it myself.

Before we sailed for France, I took one more step, hoping to end a story that had run its course. I placed an obituary notice in *Era,* and from Victoria Station, I wired Clara Martinetti: *"Belle died yesterday at six o'clock. Please phone to Annie. Shall be away a week."*

Ethel was by my side as I sent the message and gladly helped with its composition. My first thought had been to express my sorrow, but she shook her head and told me to keep the cable short.

"No one would expect a bereaved husband to open his heart in such a wire. It's best to say as little as possible. If they have an ounce of compassion, they will understand."

This insight exemplified her knowledge of human character. Although there were twenty years between us, I leaned on her judgement. I had worried that she might suffer from sea-sickness when we travelled to France, but she proved a robust sailor, despite a tempestuous crossing. We travelled with a single valise and spent four nights at a small hotel in the rue de la Mariniere, registering as husband and wife. Dieppe was so different from Argyle Square; no sour looks from the proprietor and no need to keep one eye on the clock. We giggled at the rude cries of the stallholders in the market, ran up to the old castle, and collapsed breathlessly into each other's arms as we reached the top.

From the pencilled postcards she sent to family and friends, I gleaned that Ethel had told them that we had married at a registry office a few days earlier. Her inventions brought a smile to my lips. Like me, she found it easier to convey the larger truths than small and trivial facts.

We made a friend of the concierge and spent rather more time in our little room than wandering along the narrow streets of the town. Although the holiday passed all too quickly, it did us both the world of good and we sailed back to England happy and refreshed. After a tumultuous few weeks, both of us had been exhausted. No matter: I was many times blessed. Now I had capital, and the constant support of the woman I worshipped. A glittering future beckoned.

Any hope that I had dampened the interest of the Ladies' Guild in Cora's fate was quickly disappointed. On the Wednesday following Easter, Clara and Louise Smythson came to see me at Albion House. Fortunately, I was dressed in mourning. Ethel had sewn a black armband onto my sleeve. The task seemed to give her pleasure, perhaps because it emphasised the permanency of our relations. After offering their condolences, my visitors asked how Cora had been taken ill.

"It was on the boat. She never could take full care of herself."

"Then you will have to go to America to transact the business?"

"Oh, no. She managed that before she died."

"And where did she die?" Clara demanded.

"In Los Angeles, with my relations," I said in a hushed voice.

"Can you give us the address? Naturally, the Guild wishes to send a letter of sympathy and an everlasting wreath."

"It is quite unnecessary," I said bluntly. "My relations are not familiar with the Guild and the part that it played in poor Cora's life."

"But we would so like to send a little token," Clara said. "Where is she to be buried?"

"My family thought they would have her cremated," I improvised. "They promised to send the ashes over here. Perhaps we could have a little ceremony in London, as well."

"Cremated?" I had hoped that my answer would cheer them. Instead, both women appeared to be thunderstruck. I plainly saw Mrs. Smythson mouth to Clara a single phrase: *"But she was a Catholic."*

"Yes," I said firmly. "Cremation is becoming commonplace in America, regardless of creed. It is the modern way, you know."

Mrs. Smythson's chins trembled. "But will you not give us the address in California?"

I had no wish to appear to be evasive. Racking my brains, I came up with a means of sidetracking their enquiries. "I shall give you Otto's address."

"Was your son with her when Cora died?"

"Yes," I said, bowing my head as if to choke back the tears.

Never mind about Cora, Otto's last letter had brought more than enough of his own bad news. He reported that Father was ailing—the old man was in his eighties now—but far worse, his child was dead. The little boy had passed away when he was only two days old. So I was not to be a grandfather just yet. I confided the sad story to Ethel and she was kindness itself, scolding me for having failed to tell her that the child was on the way.

"Perhaps one day we will be blessed with a little one," she said.

I clasped her hands in mine. Weeks had passed since she had made even fleeting reference to the tragedy of her miscarriage. A woman's emotions are ever unpredictable, but I was elated that she was back on an even keel.

"Nothing would give me greater happiness, my darling."

Although I prayed that the members of the Guild were tiring of their pursuit, early one evening in early April, a knock came at the door of Number 39. I was greeted by a young man who introduced himself as Mrs. Eugene Stratton's nephew and said that his aunt and her friend had something to ask me. Waiting at the kerb was a taxicab, and I saw Clara and Annie looking out at me from the back seat. I followed the young fellow down the path and Clara put her head out of the window.

"What was the name of the boat Belle sailed by?"

"Why, it was *La Touraine*," I said, with the easy confidence of one who, leaving nothing to chance, has undertaken precautionary research. This was the name of the liner that travelled the route from Le Havre to New York.

"Thank you."

"Is that all?"

Can the face of a horse be furtive? Clara murmured, "Yes, thank you very much, it is everything."

"May I invite you in for tea? Miss Le Neve has baked a rather delicious-looking cake and . . ."

"No, thank you, Peter. We just happened to be passing by and we thought you wouldn't mind if we stopped to ask about the boat."

"Very well. It was nice to see you again. Perhaps you and Paul might like to come round for a hand of whist some time?"

She coloured and made no reply. As the taxi pulled away, I waved farewell. Frankly, I did not believe that the three of them had just happened to pass by Hilldrop Crescent, but I had gained the better of the exchange. What on earth did they have in mind—poring through passenger lists? The fuss the Ladies' Guild had made simply proved how much time was on their hands since their—or their spouses'—careers had waned. Mercifully, it was inconceivable that they would devote much more energy to worrying about Cora's tragic demise.

I wrote Otto to say that Cora had died in San Francisco, but I felt it unnecessary to go into details. As soon as I had stocked up on black-edged paper, I sent a note to Dr. Burroughs, whose wife was one of the more agreeable Guild members. I also wrote to Cora's half-sister Louise with the sad tidings, asking her to tell all other members of the family. The very act of tying up the loose ends gave me a gratifying sense of completion. I felt like an author putting the finishing touches to his manuscript.

Just before Whitsuntide, Ethel and I were on Tottenham Court Road, shopping for table linen (any colour but pink, Ethel quipped), when she nudged my arm. Turning, I caught sight of Mrs. Smythson, puffing and grunting her way through the shop door.

"I think I should be getting back to the house," Ethel whispered.

"I'll see you later," I replied under my breath.

It was as if we were playing hide and seek with members of the Ladies' Guild. As Ethel slipped away, Louise Smythson caught sight of me and came over. I greeted her in cordial fashion, but all she could do was ask about Cora's funeral. I said it was all over and that I had the ashes at home. For a moment I thought she might demand to accompany me home and inspect the contents of the urn. But she simply turned on her heel and waddled out of the shop.

Ethel and I enjoyed another trip across the Channel for the Whitsun weekend. This time we travelled to Boulogne, making the most of the clement weather. Both of us liked everything about France, with the conspicuous exception of the Drouet Institute, and on the first night we discussed moving to Paris to supply the demand for patent medicines. My own French was serviceable, but Ethel remained nervous when speaking in a foreign tongue. I hit upon the idea of killing two birds with one stone. If we employed a French maid, Ethel would have help in the house and with the language. She readily agreed, and we engaged the services of a young maid by the name of Valentine whose father worked in our hotel.

The pattern of life at Number 39 had changed beyond recognition, and the constant mewing, squawking, and growling had given way to a restful silence. Until Cora's death, her friends had been mine. Now the house had a new mistress, our guests were no longer faded stars of the music hall, but rather Ethel's family and friends. Her young brother Sidney often came to play in the garden with his sister and Valentine, Nina and Horace called from time to time, and Ethel's aunt stayed for a couple of nights after we returned from Boulogne. Another regular visitor was Lydia Rose. Ethel and she were close friends at Brock's School and had kept in touch ever since.

Ethel's romantic streak revealed itself in the different tales she told to different people. To Lydia, she said that a relative of mine who had been living at Number 39 had been called to America. Nina was told that Cora was dead. Ethel was determined that those close to her would regard our relations as entirely proper and respectable. She took pains to wear both the wedding ring I had given her four years earlier and an engagement ring purchased early in February. The story was that we had married without fuss at a registry office early in March. Whilst this account might not have been pedantically true, it reflected our mutual commitment with a fierce honesty.

Both of us were looking forward to the day when we could quit London. Ethel had spent her early years in the countryside, and there was so much that I was ready to escape: the Ladies' Guild, Eddie Marr, and the secret of the cellar at Number 39.

My spine tingled whenever I passed the entrance to the coal cellar. In any other part of the house, I could lock away images from my married life as if they were items of discarded underwear, but the cellar was different. The mere thought of reentering alone and in the dark made my knees buckle.

Number 39 was mostly lit by gas fires, but one cold evening in May, Ethel asked me to fetch up some coal. I tried to make an excuse, but found myself stammering near-gibberish.

"Dearest, is something wrong?"

"Please—please come with me," I said. "You can lean against the door and hold a lighted candle whilst we talk."

She followed me to the cellar and watched curiously as I shovelled up the fuel. I tried to avert my gaze from the brick floor and the remnants it concealed.

"Hawley—are you sure you are all right?"

"This place . . ."

As the sentence trailed away, I saw a light dawn in Ethel's eyes. Was it understanding, sympathy, perhaps even pleasure? At least I can swear that without the strength she gave me, the moment I crossed the threshold of that burial chamber, I would have had a screaming fit.

Just when I allowed myself to hope that I had heard the last of Cora from members of the Guild, John Nash and Lil Hawthorne came to see me at Albion House. It was a bright day toward the end of June, and our first encounter since the ball at the Criterion. In the interim, they had spent two months in New York. Having heard of Cora's death, they wished to convey their condolences in person. Dabbing at my eyes with a handkerchief, I allowed myself to believe that their visit had no ulterior motive. Perhaps an invitation to a show would be well received? Once again, my optimism was misplaced. John Nash proved to be a veritable Torquemada, determined to discover the name of the town where poor Cora had met her end. For a quarter of an hour, he persecuted me on the point, hurling questions as if they were grenades. Every detail he sought revealed an extensive knowledge of Californian geography (almost as if he had been reading up on it during his trip to the States) that I found as disconcerting as it was unwelcome.

"No," I said with a touch of desperation, "she did not die in any of those towns. If you will allow me a few moments to compose myself, I shall do my best to remember."

"Really, Peter," he said, blowing the smoke from his Havana right into my eyes. "First you say Los Angeles, then you say San Francisco, then it's somewhere on the outskirts of San Francisco, you think a place with a Spanish name, but you can't remember it. You must understand, it seems most extraordinary to any friend of Belle's that her husband is so vague on the very place where his wife spent her last days."

What note to strike—asperity or pathos? An easy choice; I had no wish to start an argument. "I think you may underestimate the shock I have suffered as a result of the suddenness of her passing," I said quietly. "You are obviously familiar with the area . . ."

"I spent two and a half years there," he said, as smugly as if we were playing poker and had laid down a royal flush.

Dear God! My ill-luck in the matter of Cora's disappearance was uncanny.

"Perhaps you could mention a few of the places in the vicinity," I suggested feebly. "If my memory is nudged, the name may come to me."

"Well, how about Alameda?"

I scratched my chin. "Perhaps. Yes, I think that was the town."

"Are you sure?"

I was too astute to stroll into a baited trap. "No, John, I am not."

"For Heaven's sake! So you really don't recall where Belle died?"

I glanced at his wife, hoping for a hint of sympathy in the face of this brutal interrogation, but I found no encouragement in her porcine features.

"It has been a difficult time for me," I ventured.

He chewed at his cigar. "I hear you have received her ashes."

"Yes, I have them in the safe."

"What was the name of the crematorium?"

His single-mindedness was suffocating. I found myself fighting for breath, as surely as if he were pressing a pillow over my face.

"I . . . I can't recall the precise name. You know, there are about four crematoria around there. I think it will be one of those."

"Surely you have received a death certificate?"

I moistened my lips. "I believe I have it somewhere."

By a miracle, they departed before I fell down in a dead faint— but it was a close run thing. For an hour I crouched over the desk in my private sanctum, trying to get straight in my mind what I should do if this campaign persisted. It seemed that all Cora's friends were plotting against me. I found it shocking that, after all the gay times we had shared together, they refused to take me at my word.

How I wished that I had devoted more thought to the story

of the trip to America, rather than making it up as I went along. With hindsight, the legal business that I had chosen as the motive for her trip seemed implausible. This was spilt milk, however. Suspicions had been aroused. The task now was to make sure that Ethel and I remained safe.

If the challenges persisted, I would admit my lies and say that Cora had left me following a bitter quarrel. I had made up a story simply to avoid the embarrassment of a scandal. I could say that I suspected that she had gone to join Bruce Miller at last, but that she had sworn I had heard the last of her. This would explain why she had left her clothes and jewels. Given her desertion of a loyal husband for a married man living in her home country, her friends could hardly be surprised at her failure to keep in touch with them. Yes, the more I thought about it, embarrassed candour had much to commend it.

And so to Friday, 8 July. As was my custom, I left the house at a quarter past eight. Ethel rose at the same time as myself: unlike Cora, she had worked all her life and did not have a lazy bone in her body. She used to busy herself with making the bed and other housework. We embraced at the door and she promised that, in the evening, she would make my favourite meal, a shepherd's pie.

At around eleven o'clock I was with Rylance in the surgery, working at some gold plate, when the door was flung open and someone came in and touched my arm. I glanced up in surprise to see Ethel bending over me. In her eyes I saw both tenderness and fear. When I asked what had brought her into town, she urged me to come out so that we could speak together.

I followed her out of the room and she said, "There are two men from Scotland Yard. They want to see you on important business. For heaven's sake, come and talk to them. They have been worrying me for about two hours."

A dagger thrust between my ribs would have caused less pain, but I suppressed the urge to scream. To panic was to forfeit everything.

"From Scotland Yard? That's very odd. What do they want?"

"They are asking about *her*," she said hoarsely. "One of them is a Chief Inspector!"

"Of course, I shall speak to them." I squeezed her wrist. "Don't worry, darling. You have nothing to worry about."

Her lower lip trembled. "But what about you?"

"I shall explain everything in my own way," I said airily.

"I don't know how much they know," she whispered.

"Rest assured," I said, "the police have no evidence of any misdeed."

"Are you sure—there is no trace?"

It was time to summon up all the confidence with which, when confronted by sceptical questioners, I used to extol the restorative powers of Munyon's Paw-Paw Pills, and their Special Liquid Blood Cure.

"I am sure," I said with a masterful smile.

Today is the darkest of all. The Governor tells me that word has arrived from America that my father is dead. He was eighty-three years old and we had not set eyes on each other for a decade—yet as Major Mytton-Davies lays his heavy hand upon my shoulder, mute with dismay at bearing such bleak tidings, I cannot help but weep. Long racking sobs that make me sound like a wounded animal rather than a man.

Oh, how I blame myself for the misery of the old man's last weeks on earth. To fall so far from proud chapel-going at Coldwater. He was profligate with money in his later years, but it was my notoriety that left him in the gutter. Dependent upon me for his allowance, he had to rely on charity following my arrest. He was reduced to haunting the newsstands, desperate for word of my fate. The shame I caused him leaves a bitter taste in my mouth. I cannot help wondering if, all too soon, the two of us will be reunited.

Now I wait for dear Ethel to arrive. God help us to be brave.

MURDER

AND MUTILATION

Portraits, Description and Specimen of Handwriting of HAW-LEY HARVEY CRIPPEN, alias Peter Crippen, alias Franckel; and ETHEL CLARA LE NEVE, alias Mrs. Crippen and Neave

. . . Description of Le Neve alias Neave—a shorthand writer and typist, age 27, height 5 ft. 5, complexion pale, hair light brown (may dye same), large grey or blue eyes, good teeth, nice looking, rather long straight nose (good shape), medium build, pleasant, lady-like appearance. Quiet, subdued manner, talks quietly, looks intently when in conversation. A native of London.

Chief Inspector Dew of Scotland Yard. Tall and erect, he trimmed his moustache with a precision that I could never emulate. His ruddy cheeks had been scrubbed so hard that they shone. Taking in a breath, I caught the sharp tang of carbolic soap. Mr. Dew might have stepped straight from a parade ground, yet as he sized me up, his frown was thoughtful rather than condemnatory. His whole demeanour inspired confidence rather than alarm. As he introduced himself and his sergeant on the stairs of Albion House, my intuition told me that this was an Englishman of the very best kind. A man brave and true, upon whose integrity one could always depend. He called me *sir* and his voice, like Ethel's, had a faint rural burr that was pleasant on the ear.

"Some of your wife's friends have been to us, sir, concerning the stories you have told us about her death. They aren't satisfied with what you have told them."

A strange calm settled upon me, soothing as a warm blanket. "I suppose I had better tell the truth."

Out of the corner of my eye, I saw Ethel's hand dart to her mouth. Her lovely features had become gaunt in anticipation of my response. For a shocking instant I had a glimpse of her as she might be forty years hence, if time did not treat her with the kindness she deserved.

Dew gave a brisk nod. "That would be as well, sir."

I looked up into his eyes—he towered a good eight inches

above me—and said quietly, "The stories I have told about her death are untrue. As far as I know, she is still alive."

Ethel recoiled as though a harmless bumble bee had inflicted a painful sting. Thankfully, the Scotland Yard men were watching for my reactions rather than hers. Chief Inspector Dew did not so much as raise an eyebrow. I sensed again an inbred respect; he saw me as a professional man, rather than a foreigner with something to hide. At no time has he judged me, ventured a reproach or betrayed a hint of scorn.

"Any explanation you desire to make shall be written down in your own words. Perhaps it would be more convenient if you told me all about yourself."

"Certainly, Mr. Dew. I shall tell you all I know with the greatest of pleasure. You had better come into my office."

I led them up to the third floor and turned to Ethel, trying not to notice the trembling of her tiny hands. How I longed to kiss her and murmur soft words of reassurance. "Thank you, Ethel," I said. "There is no need for you to remain. I shall tell these gentlemen what they need to know."

Not daring to meet my gaze, she scurried out of the room like a rabbit that has caught sight of a mastiff. Mr. Dew closed the door behind her and then we faced each other across the little table, as coolly as if we were about to play a hand of cards. To his side, the sergeant sat, with pencil poised. I swallowed hard. This was my chance to disown the tales I had told to the ladies of the Guild, the lies that had handcuffed me for the past five months. It was as if a huge, clanking iron gate were being unlocked, and I was being freed at last from prison.

For hour after hour, the words poured from me in a floodtide of disclosure. I concealed nothing about my relations with Ethel, nor did I pretend that, in private, all had been sweetness between myself and Cora. She had left, I explained, following a quarrel late at night after the visit of the Martinettis. I said that she had warned me that I would never see or hear of her again. How easily events might have taken precisely the turn that I described in such detail. I had thought often about telling the tale exactly in this way and had almost persuaded myself that was what had happened. It seemed so much more rational than the bizarre reality.

We started at noon and by lunchtime I had done little more than sketch my origins and how I came to marry Cora. When the Chief Inspector decided that it was time to eat, he suggested that I might like to join him and his colleague. I was delighted to assent; this was a fellow in whose company I already felt at home. Besides, what senior police officer would wish to dine with a man whom he believes to have murdered his wife? The invitation was as good as a testimonial to my innocence.

In good heart, I accompanied the detectives to a small Italian restaurant a couple of doors away, where I tucked into a rich beef steak with vegetables cooked to perfection. Our conversation ranged widely, as I discovered that Mr. Dew and I had much in common. We reminisced affectionately about the late King and found that we had both been disappointed by Halley's Comet.

"A bit of a damp squib, after all that fuss," was the Chief Inspector's verdict, as he dabbed a speck of gravy from his chin.

Although not one of us touched a drop of alcohol, the atmosphere was convivial. The sergeant had the least to say; *he* might have been the outsider under suspicion. I finished the meal with a cup of Kenyan coffee, which I took without milk. My natural optimism was asserting itself. Already, the battle was half won.

Back in the office, I resumed my statement. The policemen were only doing their job and I bore no grudge for that. Besides, it was not a painful task; that afternoon, I came in an odd way to enjoy myself. It was a unique opportunity to indulge in the storyteller's art. Never in any of my discourses on miracle cures had my neck depended on the plausibility of the tale I told. Perhaps if young Otto had stayed with me, or if Ethel had been spared her miscarriage, I would have found fulfilment in spinning yarns to entertain the infant at bedtime. As it was, I relished holding my audience in thrall. This was not like extolling the virtues of electro-massage for rheumatism. Those listening did not shuffle their feet or surreptitiously check the time. The eyes of Mr. Dew and his sergeant never left me. Was this, I wondered, what Cora had hankered after for so long, yet never found? The sensual, stroking pleasure of having intelligent people hang on one's every word?

We did not finish until six o'clock. Mr. Dew handed me the statement that his assistant had transcribed and I read every word with scrupulous care. He asked me if, once I was satisfied that the account was true and fair, I would initial every page, as well as adding my full signature at the very end. I did so with a flourish. True and fair? In a metaphorical sense, absolutely! I was describing to the police what *should* have happened, had not ill luck intervened.

After he had done with me, Mr. Dew sent for Ethel. Her eyes were red and she looked tired and hungry. We had quite forgotten to ask her to join us for luncheon. When asked if she would care to tell him all she knew, she cast me a furtive glance and I gave a warm smile of encouragement. We needed the police to see us as lovers rather than conspirators. For a moment she closed her eyes, and I knew that she was summoning up her reserves of courage. She would have to overcome natural modesty and confess to strangers about our liaison. I crossed my fingers that she would remember to emphasise that Cora treated her as a friend. Ethel and I had spoken about this once or twice and it was a phrase she liked to use. If not exactly accurate, at least it conveyed a good-natured impression.

While the detectives interviewed her in my office, I went about my usual business. Seldom had I been so glad that neither Rylance nor Long were nosey parkers or gossips. For myself I felt no anxiety. But how would my beloved cope with the questioning from officers of the law without me there to lean upon?

After an hour or so, the three of them emerged. Ethel's shoulders were drooping, but when she mustered a brave smile, I relaxed. She had held firm. Once she had signed her statement, Mr. Dew said that he would like to take a closer look at Number 39. Of course I agreed to his request. To decline would have looked suspicious, and I did not wish him to think that I had a guilty secret. Besides, it was inconceivable that he would start excavating the cellar floor. With hindsight, I recognised that an inquiry by the authorities was nigh on inevitable. I had been deluding myself to believe that I could stave off all questions with my hastily improvised romances about Cora's sudden and mysterious departure from home.

The four of us travelled back in a "growler" to Hilldrop Crescent. Ethel sat by my side and I took her chilly hand in mine. Her body stiffened in alarm and embarrassment, but I gave her fingers a friendly squeeze and slowly she began to thaw. We had nothing to gain by dissembling in front of the police officers: how much better to display an honest pride in our relationship. As we clattered along the city streets, I half-turned in my seat and kissed her soft, fragrant hair.

My gamble in allowing the detectives free access to every nook and cranny of the house paid off. Escorted by Ethel and myself, Mr. Dew and his sergeant inspected each of the eight rooms in turn, examining wardrobes, dressing tables, and cupboards with quiet persistence. The only emotion that either of our visitors betrayed was when they entered Cora's room and wrinkled their noses at the musty smell. Confronted by the mass of her clothing, festooned by feathers of every colour in the rainbow, Mr. Dew's eyebrows lifted, as if in sympathy for what another man had had to put up with. He said nothing, however. This man was the very soul of discretion; I would trust him with my life.

The urge to confide in him seized me. He was a man of the world; surely he would understand that I had not meant Cora to die? Standing at the bottom of the stairs, waiting for the police officers to descend, I cleared my throat. And then I caught sight of Ethel. Her face was drained of blood, her unblinking gaze upon me. No words could have implored me to keep my counsel with the eloquence of her distress. I could not speak.

"So the coal cellar lies beneath the steps to your front door?" Mr. Dew enquired.

I nodded, as casually as could be.

"We'll have a look there too, if you don't mind."

Without a word, Ethel and I followed the two men down the passage. We stood side by side in the doorway as Mr. Dew kept striking matches that flickered and then died, while we strained to accustom our eyes to the darkness. He kicked at some of the lumps of coal and pieces of wood, and when he sounded the floor with his feet, I held my breath, as Ethel must have held hers.

Presently he turned to me and said, "Very well, Dr. Crippen. Thank you for your assistance."

"I am glad to be of service." The temptation to gabble with relief was well nigh irresistible.

"Of course, I shall have to find Mrs. Crippen to clear this matter up."

Dismay knifed me. Had I not spent the whole day trying my utmost to satisfy the most curious enquirer? I had thought we had developed a *rapport,* puzzling together over a baffling mystery.

After a moment's thought, I said, "I will do everything I can. Can you suggest anything? Would an advertisement be any good?"

He stroked his chin. "An excellent idea."

"Perhaps you would be kind enough to assist me with suitable wording?" I coughed discreetly. "You will appreciate I have no experience of matters of this kind."

"Naturally."

Not for the first time, an ability to think on my feet had served me well. Ethel excused herself and I sat at the kitchen table with the two detectives, composing a notice to be inserted in the American newspapers. Our mood was companionable as we debated the *nuances* of the announcement. Mr. Dew was so very different from the friends and acquaintances I had made since coming to England: faded vaudevillians and their admirers, dusty denizens of the medical world, and sly businessmen who lived by their wits. Mr. Dew would do his duty without fear or favour, but instinctively I sensed that he believed in fair play. Although I have never understood the rules of cricket, I could imagine that it was his game. I was a foreigner, a man from an altogether different, more exotic way of life. Yet he betrayed no hint of prejudice.

Finally, we settled upon the text.

"Mackamotz. Will Belle Elmore communicate with H.H.C.—or authorities at once. Serious trouble through your absence. Twenty-five dollars reward to anyone communicating her whereabouts."

"There," I said, admiring the phrasing as an artist might approve skilled brushwork. "I think that strikes the right note, don't you?"

"I should say so, Doctor."

We shook hands, although his grip was so ferocious that I

could not help wincing.

"I'll leave that advertisement with you, then, Doctor."

"Very well, Chief Inspector. I am grateful to you and Sergeant Mitchell for your courtesy. I realise that you have no alternative but to follow official routines and undertake all the proper enquiries."

He nodded and I saw a tint of pink in his cheeks. My ready acknowledgment of the intimate nature of my relations with Ethel, coupled with the confession that I had lied to Cora's friends, had taken him aback. It was easy for him to see that I was a civilised fellow and that, if the Ladies' Guild had painted my character in lurid colours, the portrait was a fake. To this day I would take an oath on the Holy Book that Mr. Dew wanted nothing more that evening than to satisfy himself that I was wholly innocent of any crime.

"Dearest, please, calm yourself, calm yourself. Don't you see? We have come through our darkest day."

The moment I had returned to the kitchen after shutting the door on the policemen, Ethel had flung herself upon me, buried her head against my shoulder, and begun to wail hideously, like a creature of the wild bemoaning the death of its young. From Mr. Dew's arrival here in the morning, she had got by on nervous energy. Now she was in a state of emotional collapse. The refined young woman had become consumed by terror, all because of the unspoken secret we shared. Caressing her hair, trying in vain to dry her cheeks with my pocket handkerchief, I murmured words of reassurance, but to no avail. Her body convulsed against mine. For once the scent of lavender was sickly suffocating. Exhaustion and distress were understandable, but the extent of her despair exceeded the bounds of reason.

I tried to explain this and, when her tragic whoops redoubled in intensity, I made the profound mistake of reminding her that

I, too, had endured a difficult few hours and that it was surely time to pull herself together. She moved in my arms and her soaked face gazed up at me. For an instant, I was horrified to see the features of a stranger, wrinkled and ugly and afraid.

"We will hang!" she screamed. "Don't you see? We will hang!"

Of course, this was madness. No one could have been more civil than Mr. Dew, and he had left the house none the wiser about Cora's fate. I let her weep in silence for a while before squeezing her arm and saying, "Darling, I am so sorry that I snapped at you. Please say you will forgive me. I am not myself. Neither of us could expect to be unmoved by what has happened. But trust me. Things are not so bad as they may seem. The police . . ."

". . . will never let us go! We are marked forever! Doomed!"

"They have no evidence, my dear. Nothing but tittle-tattle from jealous crones with time on their hands."

But evidence is for lawyers, not for frightened lovers. She shook her head and said, "Don't you see? For God's sake, this is just the start! They will do their best to hold you. Any excuse will do. You heard that man! He will not rest until he knows where he may find your wife."

"I heard him," I said after a pause.

"Well? How do you think he will find her? Safe and sound in California, perhaps? Happy to answer your little advertisement and set everyone's mind at rest?"

Sarcasm was a weapon that Ethel seldom deployed, and never before had she chosen me as her target. I could have had no clearer sign of how the day's events had shattered her equilibrium.

"She will never be found," I said firmly.

Involuntarily, Ethel glanced through the open door, toward the cellar. I straightened my shoulders. What was interred below the ground save a few slices of flesh? No bones, not the slightest indication of sex, let alone identity. Even if the remnants had not been obliterated by the lime, they would prove nothing. Ethel wriggled around so that she could sit properly on my lap, as she had done so often in happier times.

"Are you sure, Hawley?"

"I swear to you, Ethel. She has gone forever, *leaving no trace.*"

"But—that means that the detectives will never close their enquiries."

She was right. The mere fact that they did not know the precise nature of Cora's fate did not mean that they would not trouble us again. Ethel must have noticed a flickering uncertainty in my expression, for she began to chivvy me. "So how can we ever be safe? We will never be rid of them, don't you see?"

I swallowed hard. Her fear let loose the man of action inside me. Faced with a crisis, one must be bold. "Then we should rid ourselves of them."

She stared. "What do you mean?"

"We will leave here."

"Well," she murmured, "you know I have never liked this place. Besides, there are—too many sad memories for you."

"Not just this house." I marvelled at my own daring. "We must leave England."

"You want us to flee the country?" Her voice throbbed with astonishment.

"Emigrate." A plan was forming in my mind even as I spoke. "My dear, we must not think and talk as if we were in the wrong. There are plenty of openings for a hard-working couple on the other side of the Atlantic."

My decisiveness knocked the breath out of her. "So far?" she gasped.

"I say nothing to our having a little vacation on the Continent first," I said, rather gaily now that I had wrested the initiative.

"After all, the two of us have rather become old hands at crossing the Channel."

Next morning the sun slid through the curtains early and Ethel woke not long after six. Having hardly slept, I was ready in case she had second thoughts. I need not have worried; the shock of the police investigation had begun to fade, and once again, Ethel was ready to do my bidding.

"You are sure it is wise, darling?" she asked. "What will people think if we run away?"

"I have never cared for what people think," I whispered. "As long as I am with my dearest, nothing else matters."

"You say the loveliest things," she said dreamily. "But this is a matter of life and death."

"Oh, the scandal will be terrible, but what choice do we have? All Cora's friends will be abuzz with the news of an investigation by Scotland Yard. The police have attended at Albion House, and not everyone is as discreet as Long. Already the word will be out."

"And people are such fearful gossips!"

"Exactly. For myself, I care nothing, but I would not wish you to run the gauntlet of idle mischief-makers with slack tongues. Everyone will want to pry into our affairs. Far better that we escape until the whole sorry business has blown over."

"We must leave no clues," she said slowly. "And yet . . ."

"My darling, all night I have thought of nothing but how we might contrive to get away from all the fuss. It will not be easy. The police will be looking for a professional man accompanied by a charming young lady."

She closed her eyes. "It is dreadful, dreadful."

I pulled her toward me. "Do you trust me?" I demanded.

"With my life," she said fervently.

"Well, the answer is simple." I paused for dramatic effect.

"You shall wear a disguise."

It was as if the ghost of Nick Carter had his hand on my shoulder and was muttering words of encouragement into my ear. Blood skipped in my veins. Never before had I contemplated life as a fugitive from the law, but now my old hero's exploits provided inspiration. Events had forced me to pit my wits against those of Scotland Yard. Without false modesty, I believed it was a contest to which I was equal.

She blinked. "What do you have in mind?"

"You would do very well as a boy," I announced, smiling as her lips parted in bewilderment. "Haven't you often told me how you used to play the hoyden in your early years? Climbing trees with your uncle, shooting a catapult?"

"But I was only a child," she protested.

"Even so," I insisted. "During the small hours, I worked out all the details. You may leave the arrangements to me."

"I could not dress as a lad," Ethel said. "Besides, where would I find . . . ?"

"Enough," I commanded. "I readily picture you in a young fellow's get-up! There could be no neater way of our avoiding notice. We can pass as father and son and no one will be any the wiser."

"If you're sure," she said, sounding rather like a dubious client of the Drouet Institute.

"I am sure. As I say, I shall obtain the clothes and organise the luggage. We shall have to travel light, in any event. If we are to slip away unnoticed, we ought to take as few things as possible."

A thought struck her. "But Sidney! I agreed that he could call on me here later this morning!"

"Leave a note with Valentine, asking her to let your brother have a message. You have been compelled to go away. There is no need to gild the lily. Most unfortunate, but it cannot be helped."

"And Nina? I could not abandon her without a word."

"Certainly, it would not be right to have her worrying when there is no need. We will go in the ordinary way to the office. From there you can take a taxi to her house and explain that you will be away for a little while. Don't stay talking too long, mind. Time is of the essence."

Even to my own ears, my words sounded uncommonly masterful. Ethel was too sensible and well disciplined to argue. When she nodded and said she would do as I proposed, I jumped out of bed and clapped my hands.

"That is settled, then! All we need now is a hearty breakfast and we shall be ready to start upon our great adventure!"

On Saturdays, it was not my custom to arrive at Albion House before ten, and when Long walked through the door shortly after nine, he jumped on seeing that I was already there.

"Is there any trouble, Doctor?"

"Only a little scandal," I said, in a matter-of-fact tone. "Now, Long, I have a commission for you. Here is a list of items of clothing. There is a young chap whom I wish to help. Would you be good enough to take this money to Baker's and purchase the clothes on my behalf?"

He undertook the errand with his habitual efficiency. As usual, he asked no questions. Within three-quarters of an hour he returned with an impressive haul: a brown suit, felt hat, two shirts and collars, a tie, and a pair of boots. All these I asked him to leave in room 91, which was kept shut on the weekends. In the meantime I had been experimenting with a change of clothes that I had brought from home: a sombre jacket and trousers in coarse fabric, rough to the touch, that might have been made for a street preacher or a lay cleric. The success or otherwise of Ethel's disguise would, I knew, be crucial to my scheme.

By eleven o'clock, she was by my side again and I locked us both in room 91 to ensure that we would not be disturbed. I kissed her, and as she pressed her body against mine I felt the rush of her excitement. Her nervous temper of the previous evening was no more than a horrid memory. We were embarking on a course fraught with danger, heading for a destination unknown, and yet the experience was peculiarly exhilarating. We were like small boats on a river in spate, swept along and no longer in charge of our destinies.

As I showed her the new outfit, we both burst out laughing. "You will look a perfect boy in this," I assured her. "Especially when you cut off your hair."

Her face was a picture: hilarity battling with consternation. "Must I?"

"Why, of course. It is absolutely necessary. But first, your new garb."

She wriggled out of her blue serge costume and soon her clothes formed a pile in the middle of the room. I raised a hand before she could slip on the boy's outfit and nibbled at her bare shoulders, tasting her sweet skin. Time was short, but I could not resist. Acting out the scheme was more intoxicating than any alcohol. We shared a few intimate moments, and then she started dressing as a boy.

"Oh, the suit is splitting at the back already!" She giggled.

"It cannot be helped! There, the fit is not so bad. Now I must complete the transformation."

I felt a pang at the prospect of shearing off those lovely tresses, but I steeled myself to the task. Sentiment must not impede our plan. I picked up the large pair of office scissors I had brought into the room. A picture flashed into my mind of the bathroom at Number 39 after Cora's death, as I hacked the limbs from the trunk. I banished the awful vision and inhaled deeply. With a few snips, Ethel was transformed.

She strutted up and down, scrutinising herself in a mirror I had taken from the surgery. In manner, as well as in appearance, she had become a different person. Confident, determined, free.

"I shall never be able to face the world in these things!" she said, with a merry glint in her eye.

"You will do famously. No one will recognise you, looking like that. The perfect boy!"

"I keep wanting to tug my skirt," she said. "It's a habit, I suppose. Oh, Hawley, I don't think I shall get on in the streets. I haven't the pluck to go out."

But I knew her well enough to realise that, for all her protestations, she longed to carry off the masquerade. When Cora dressed me as a woman, I had experienced a similar *frisson*. The closest I had ever come to flaunting a change of gender in the outside world was when Adeline Harrison called on us unexpectedly. Ethel would need to play the part all day, every day.

"Here, I have a cigarette. Put it in your mouth at a jaunty angle, that's right. Here's a Vesta. You can light it outside. Don't splutter, you'll draw attention to yourself! Now for your first opportunity to venture abroad as Master Robinson. Are you ready? Very well, I shall see you outside the station at the top of Chancery Lane in forty minutes."

We would leave Albion House separately. For all I knew, Mr. Dew had placed a guard to keep us under surveillance. Thus we would both have to leave by way of the winding staircase that led to a door at the back of the building.

I gave the strange boy a last passionate embrace and then unlocked the door. As soon as she had gone, I settled down with a couple of sheets of Rylance's headed paper. The two of us had exchanged banal pleasantries earlier in the morning; as usual, he showed no more than perfunctory interest in my activities. I wrote that, in order to escape trouble, I should be obliged to absent myself for a time and made a few suggestions as to financial matters, including the payment of the remainder of the advance of rent due to our landlords.

In the message to Long, I asked if he would wind up, as best he could, my household affairs. Again there was rent due, and I said that in lieu of the moneys outstanding, the landlord could seize the contents of Number 39. As for Valentine, I pointed out that she should have saved enough from her wages to be able to afford the journey back to France. Finally, I wished my faithful servant every success and happiness. How much pleasanter it would have been to make farewells in person, but we needed a start if we were to elude the long arm of Chief Inspector Dew.

I changed my clothes and shaved off my moustache, a tragic but essential sacrifice. My upper lip, bare for the first time in many years, felt peculiarly smooth. Now the moment had arrived for me to quit Albion House. Abandoning what I had laboured so long to build was a wrench, but more than once in my business career I had started afresh and prospered. I could do it again.

I took the stairs down to the ground two at a time. No policeman was prowling outside the back door. Yet as I pushed my way through the crowds to our rendezvous at the Tube station, fear crept up from behind and took me captive. The crash of horses' hooves was deafening, and the harsh July sun blinded me. My pulse began to race and my stride faltered. So many times, happiness had been ripped from my grasp. Would Ethel be waiting, or might she have fled in terror on her own?

Of course I was wrong to doubt her. Never in my worst nightmares—and I had endured a few since Cora's death—has she been anything other than steadfast and true. When I caught sight of her across the road, I ran over and flung myself at her. It was all I could do not to weep with joy and relief.

"Do—do you recognise me?"

"I would know you anywhere," she said with an answering smile.

Her answer almost made my heart stop, before I realised that she was not disparaging my disguise, but rather expressing the scale of her love. I seized her hand and we ran into the dark station.

At Liverpool Street, we found that we had just missed a train to Harwich, from where I planned that we should cross to the Hook of Holland. The next was not due to depart for another three hours. Ethel's face fell; no doubt she was wondering how long it would take the police to find that we had evaded their net.

"I know!" I said in a bright tone to cheer her up. "Let's go for a ride in an open-top bus."

Such a simple and yet splendid idea. We cared nothing about the route the bus took; we were doing no more than killing time. Ethel whispered as she moved her hand along my leg that one place was as good as any other, provided we were together. I recall our jolting along the shabby streets of Hackney, blinking the dust out of our eyes. Every now and then, the bus hit a pothole and she was thrown hard against me. Each time, I kissed her and she responded with fervour. Mr. Dew no longer looked over our shoulders. It seemed then, and seems to me now, the most perfect afternoon we ever spent in each other's company. Our hair blew in the breeze as we luxuriated in freedom.

"I went straight past the front door of Albion House!" Ethel laughed. "After all those years, nobody noticed me! Not a soul suspected I was a girl."

"I knew you could do it."

She laid her head against mine and we exchanged endearments. A gentler creature never walked the earth, and yet she had such courage. Abandoning family and friends, embracing an unknown future in a foreign land—and all for the love of me.

Within twenty-four hours, we were drinking in the sights and sounds of Rotterdam, holding our noses as we passed dank canals, watching gnarled Dutchmen saunter along in baggy trousers and big wooden shoes. In the zoological gardens, we giggled at the monkeys and marvelled at the lazy hauteur of the lions. Finding a shady corner, we indulged in a cuddle, only to spring apart when a fearful screeching broke out. Our intimacies had been observed by a parrot that was all too easily embarrassed.

London and Mr. Dew already seemed so far away. The trip across the Channel was plain sailing. No one paid us any heed; our anonymity was a blessed relief after the ceaseless inquisitions. Soon, I said to myself, Mr. Dew would forget all about us. Scotland Yard surely had much bigger fish to fry.

I would never have made a barber. Ethel's locks were ragged after my efforts with office scissors, and I proposed that we go to a professional to complete her transformation. So far, the disguise had been wholly effective, but I did not wish to leave anything to chance. As soon as we saw a suitable shop, we went inside. The hair grease smelled so strong that I could almost taste the stuff, but I settled into a seat at the back while Ethel, who had begun to master the jaunty stride of an adolescent lad, swaggered up to the man in charge. He selected the clippers and set to work. I caught Ethel's alarmed expression in the mirror as he gave her a poll as closely cropped as Jack Sheppard's. She had always been proud of her hair, but her loss was all in a good cause. I did not pick up the slightest hint that the man doubted that she was a boy, and by the time he was finished with her, I was almost deceived myself.

My plan was to follow a circuitous route with a view to ensuring that the trail from London would soon grow cold. Amid the holiday crowds, it was easy to be inconspicuous, but I meant to take nothing for granted. That evening, we travelled to Brussels, where we engaged a room at the Hotel des Ardennes in the Rue de Brabant, at the back of the Gare du Nord. It was a grey three-story building, with a smoke-filled café and restaurant on the ground floor. I signed the register as Mr. John Robinson—a suitably nondescript alias—and conversed in my best French with the amply bosomed landlady.

"I am a merchant from Quebec," I explained. "My son and I have been touring through Europe."

"Have you had a nice time?" the woman asked Ethel, who was hovering behind me in the hope that she would not attract attention.

I interceded quickly. "He is stone deaf, the poor young chap. Shy, too, and rather under the weather at the moment. You won't hear him speak, I'm afraid."

Ethel assumed a downcast expression. She was still wearing the straw hat and her hands, I was pleased to see, were kept firmly in her pockets. This crafty ruse we had settled upon before leaving London. So beautifully manicured were her hands that nobody seeing them would believe that they belonged to a boy. The best course was to conceal them until we could begin our lives afresh in the New World.

The landlady gave her a pitying smile and clicked her fingers by way of summons to her husband. He was a sallow man in crumpled brown serge, coiled like a lizard in a chair by the café door. When he came over to shake hands, I caught a whiff of stale beer on his breath. To my surprise, the couple indulged me in conversation, testing my French to its limits. How different it had been with the surly hoteliers of Argyle Square—and how long ago all that seemed.

Monsieur Delisse showed us upstairs, grumbling about a pain in his back. At least we had only brought a single bag. The chamber was tiny, with dull yellow wallpaper and a cracked looking glass. The bed—a double, I noted happily, rather than two singles—itself took up nearly all the space. But we did not mind the confined environment. Each other's company was all we needed.

The next day, I did not shave at all. Parting company with my moustache was not enough; I wanted to make sure of avoiding identification by growing a full beard. Our first stop was a printer's, where I ordered a set of business cards bearing the legend *E. Robinson & Co., Detroit, Mich., presented by Mr. John Robinson.* Attention to detail was the key to succeeding with our bold subterfuge. Thereafter we called at an office of the Red Star Line. I had thought we might return to England via Hull, travel over to Liverpool, and make a fast crossing to Canada from there, but this scheme was overelaborate. If we were unsafe anywhere, it was in England. Far better to set off from a Continental port and enjoy a leisurely voyage. Explaining that due to my son's ill health, we desired a two-berth cabin for our exclusive use, I booked our passage to Montreal.

Contentedly, we explored the shops and sights of the capital. We feasted on chocolate and toured the International Exhibition and the old Flemish fair. When the sun was bright we strolled along the cobbled streets, and haunted picture galleries and museums on a couple of rainy days. Often we picnicked on the lawns, listening to birds singing and selections from Lehar performed by the band. We never spoke of Chief Inspector Dew or the Music Hall Ladies' Guild. As Ethel said dreamily one afternoon while we squeezed each other's hands under a shady elm, we were at peace and on the brink of a new beginning.

For all that, I seldom relaxed my guard. The café at the hotel was plentifully supplied with newspapers, but to my relief, the only publications in English were yellowing editions of *The Illustrated London News.* We sat together in the evening on a bumpy wood and leather bench, Ethel dozing as I scanned the front pages for any hint of trouble.

Ethel's French remained timid. In consequence, we took pains to keep together at all times. When the café filled with customers, we fled to our room. The regulars kept long-stemmed clay pipes by the bar, and within minutes of their congregating together, the air became so thick that my beloved's eyes began to water and I feared she would choke.

Madame Delisse took a continuing interest in us. On one occasion, she had the temerity to enquire if my wife would be joining us, but I scotched that by explaining that the poor woman had died just two months earlier. Undaunted, she would ask our plans for the day each morning as we ate our croissants. I told her that at the end of July we were due to set off back for Canada. The sea air would do my boy's chest good, I said, at which Madame Delisse nodded vigorously. She beamed at Ethel and studied her chest with a curiosity that caused me no little alarm. The suit did not perfectly conceal my darling's contours. Could the woman guess that the ailing, silent youth was really a girl?

Maintaining a sustained pretence is always a challenge, and on occasions we made a mistake. One evening, I was whispering to Ethel in a corner of the café where we could not be overheard. Her face was in shadow; we had agreed that this was a sensible precaution, for the smooth cut of her features gave another clue to her sex. I became aware of Madame Delisse standing in the doorway. When I turned to look at her, she chortled in greeting, then moved away. But with a sinking heart,

I was able to read her thoughts: *if the boy is deaf, why is the father whispering to him?*

Nothing came of it. When we came down the next morning, Madame Delisse was her usual jolly self. It was as if, whatever her suspicions, she'd taken a fancy to us. Heartened, I joked with the maid who served us and announced cheerily that I intended to persuade Ethel to indulge in a change of headgear. The straw hat did not give her pale skin enough protection from the sun's burning rays, I said, but this was hardly the whole truth. I had decided that a felt hat with a rim that could be turned down over the eyes would be far more effective in protecting her identity.

After breakfast, we took a bus to a charming village a few miles outside the city. During the morning, we stopped off at a small café and, as had become my habit, I reached for a rolled-up copy of *L'Independence Belge* in a rack on the wall. The sight of the headline struck me like a kick in the solar plexus.

"Hawley, are you all right?" Ethel asked.

I had lost the power of speech. With a dismissive nod, I buried my head back in the paper, hoping that she would put my shocked expression down to a bout of dyspepsia. At all costs, I had to avoid frightening her, but the first task was to quell the terror that made my bowels churn. Even before I had read the reporter's excited prose, the harsh words in leaded type told me that my confidence had been misplaced. The cellar had yielded its secret.

I kept staring at that headline, trying to change the words into a more innocuous pattern by sheer power of will. But the headline remained the same and the words thundered in my brain

ACTRICE ASSASSINÉE.
ACTRICE ASSASSINÉE.
ACTRICE ASSASSINÉE.

305

My darling, let me dry your tears with the hem of my sleeve. Even though the warders will not permit us the warmth of an embrace, I beg you to stop shivering. There is so much wickedness in the world. The cruel headlines that you describe on the billboards of *John Bull* testify to that. How shameful to be hounded, in our last moments, so sacred to us, by newspaper men publishing lie upon lie. They say that I have confessed, but of course it is not true. I have confessed to nothing, nor would I. Dearest, you know that I would sooner die than expose you to the slightest danger.

What I cannot fathom is why *John Bull*, Mr. Horatio Bottomley's very own journal, should point an accusing finger. After all the money he has invested in my defence, there is no rhyme or reason to it. There must be some mistake. An excess of zeal on the part of an incompetent subordinate?

Your suggestion that all the time Mr. Bottomley was simply chasing "good copy" shows how even the sweetest nature can be rendered cynical by the vicissitudes of fate. Do not forget that the case of conspiracy made out against Mr. Bottomley two years ago collapsed in ruins. It cannot be said that there is a stain on his character. He is a man of distinction—a Member of Parliament.

As for your suspicions about Arthur Newton, I swear on my life that they are utterly groundless. Arthur would never betray me. Do not be deceived by the way he caresses those dove-grey kid gloves. Mannerisms mean nothing; they are not clues to deceit. The reason he instructed Mr. Tobin rather than Marshall Hall, the Great Defender, the man who saved the accused Wood in the Camden Town case, is

306

that Hall was temporarily unavailable. In his absence, Hall's clerk to chambers proved importunate in his demands for a brief fee.

Arthur would never allow others to exploit my unwelcome fame for his or their own ends. Only with the best of intentions did he engage Doctors Turnbull and Wall to supply expert evidence about the flesh that Mr. Dew found in the cellar of Number 39. He could not have foreseen their flimsiness under pressure. Expert evidence! They tipped the scales—but against me. One minute Turnbull testified that the mark on the flesh was a fold, not a scar. The next he was bending under cross-examination like a sapling in a gale. What a fool!

Beside his monstrous incompetence, my own error in believing that a sprinkling of lime would destroy all trace of the body was neither here nor there. It never crossed my mind that the lime might absorb moisture from the clay and thus act as not as means of obliteration, but rather as a preservative.

That those engaged to support my defence hastened the calamitous verdict is for me a source of the profoundest unhappiness. But does it prove that the man who engaged them was bent on my destruction? Nonsense! We are not merely solicitor and client. We have become fast friends.

Alas! Time is running out for Arthur to save my neck.

I pray, Ethel, do not go pale and shake your head. The petition may have failed to move Mr. Churchill, but Arthur would not lightly give up a cause in which he believes. Who knows? He may yet snatch triumph from the jaws of catastrophe.

Note found on a business card belonging to H.H. Crippen.

I cannot stand the horror I go through every night any longer, and as I see nothing bright ahead and money has come to an end, I have made up my mind to jump overboard tonight. I know I have spoiled your life, but I hope some day you can learn to forgive me. With last words of love, your H.

My cheeks were on fire. As I read the report again, my gorge rose and I hardly dared look up for fear that all eyes in the café might be upon us. Despair swamped me. Mr. Dew was pursuing us. The suddenness of our departure had prompted him to explore Number 39 yet more thoroughly than on his first visit. All would have been well had not some stroke of detective genius, some extraordinary intuition, caused him to go back to the cellar and start to dig.

Wanted for murder and mutilation! Stumbling over to the rack, I returned the newspaper. None of the other patrons bothered to glance in my direction, and their indifference was a soothing balm. Hope flickered. Nobody, surely, could identify those few lumps of lime-eaten flesh. Policemen and paid scribblers might speculate that the bits belonged to Cora. Only I knew the truth. But what does logic matter to a mob? With such a hue and cry, how could Ethel and I ever be safe?

Conflicting thoughts warred in my head, but I strove to maintain a composed facade. I dared not contemplate the effect upon Ethel's delicate temperament were she to realise that the whole world was watching out for us and that our flight to freedom might end in imprisonment—or worse. She must suspect nothing.

Faced with a crisis threatening life itself, one has a choice: to surrender or to fight for survival. I resolved that I would not give in—I *could* not, if only for Ethel's sake. Within minutes of reading the dreadful news, I started planning ahead with a mathematician's iciness of reasoning. Even as I exchanged pleasantries with her about the Belgian countryside, I was mapping out our next move.

To Ethel, I said nothing about the need for haste. Rather, I suggested that our holiday had already so refreshed us that, it would be nice to sail for Canada even earlier than planned.

"How lovely!" she exclaimed.

Not so many weeks before, a trip to Dieppe had seemed to her like a voyage to another world, but in my company she was becoming a seasoned traveller. The prospect of our living and working together in Montreal excited her. Why delay a moment longer than necessary?

On arriving back in Brussels, we hurried to the shipping office, where I discovered that the *S.S. Montrose,* of the Canadian Pacific Line, would depart from Antwerp to Quebec on the following Wednesday. Our luck was turning again: a second-class cabin for two was available for reservation. I did not hesitate to change our booking; although the steamer was hardly the quickest of ocean-going vessels, we would be leaving Europe eleven days earlier than planned and, given the international alert, the sooner we were on the high seas, the better.

I made sure that we kept busy throughout Saturday, so that I had little time to fret, but every now and then I managed to sneak a glance at a newspaper. To my horror, several sheets carried blood-red headlines above photographs of Ethel and myself. It was all I could do to control the shaking of my hands as I fumbled through the pages. Yet because she could not read French, she never once looked over my shoulder and thus never realised that anything was amiss. I uttered thanks to God that the lessons from Valentine had not proved more successful.

In the small hours, while Ethel slept trustingly by my side, I scowled at the cracks in the looking-glass. The splintered reflection made me resemble the monster the newspapers described. A price was on my head; Scotland Yard men were chasing me like the rustler-hunting sheriffs whose exploits entranced me as a boy in Coldwater. The reports were riddled with inaccuracies, starting with the proposition that Cora had been murdered. According to one rag, I carried a gun and would not be afraid to use it. Half of Europe, it seemed, was being enjoined to assist with the hunt for a smooth-talking rogue who was armed and dangerous.

How galling that the possibility of my innocence seemed not to have occurred to a single soul! Nowhere could I find any acknowledgment that Cora might have died by an unlucky chance. I had been tried and found guilty in my absence, with Fleet Street acting as judge and jury. Such a travesty of justice! Had no one bothered to mention what I was really like? There was no hint of the innumerable little services I had rendered to my wife, or the way I had supported her foundering career on the stage, far less of the loyalty inspired in servants like Long and Marion Curnow. The reports took my wickedness as much for granted as my supposed determination to use firearms to resist arrest.

At least in the absence of sleep, I escaped the torment of nightmares. When day finally broke, I dragged my weary body out of bed and, in between extravagant yawns, peered at the tiny writing on the tickets for our passage aboard the *Montrose*. It was a crude device to lift my spirits, but it worked. At the thought of reaching our destination a thousand miles away, I became infused with a fresh energy. The game was not yet up. There was still everything to play for.

Sunday passed quietly. The weather was so glorious that we would have attracted unwelcome attention had we remained in the hotel, and we spent hours listening to the music in the city gardens. Ethel was restless and complained that she had exhausted the possibilities of Brussels. For a different reason, I found myself unable to relax. Every passerby who cast a glance in our direction caused my heart to flutter.

A reward of £250, no less, was being offered by Scotland Yard for information leading to my arrest. This I found a bitter pill. Such a sum of money would have tided me over at the start of the year. I would never have needed to plead with Cora for financial help; perhaps I might have been tempted to make the break from Number 39 and set up home with Ethel. Two hundred and fifty pounds! A splendid nest egg for any nosey parker who chose to betray us.

At breakfast, Madame Delisse had chatted to us with a smothering amiability, while her husband lurked in the background, a coy smirk on his saurian visage.

"And what might my two favourite guests be up to today, Monsieur Robinson?" she enquired with, I swear, a salacious wink.

I murmured something about exploring the sights and hurried Ethel out through the door. In my heightened state of anxiety, I could not help wondering whether the landlady's unwonted curiosity in us had a sinister connotation. The more I thought about it, the more I fretted. She had enunciated my name with a genial mockery, as if she made sure it was an alias. Had she penetrated our disguise? Was she plotting to claim the reward? Late in the afternoon, I said to Ethel that it was time for us to return to the hotel. Would we find representatives of the police waiting for us there? I had no choice but to take the risk; I dared not frighten Ethel by raising the prospect of imminent arrest. Besides, all our worldly goods were packed in the small valise under the bed in our room.

I sneaked a glance through the window and saw Madame Delisse sitting in her usual chair. I took a deep breath and led Ethel in. The landlady greeted us with her customary gust of bonhomie. No posse of detectives was crouching behind the bar, ready to handcuff us and arrange for our removal back to London. As we chatted, Madame Delisse's gaze lingered on Ethel. The curve of her smile was vulpine. For a wild instant I wondered if she wanted to help us, if perhaps she had some festering grudge against the authorities and wished to help two underdogs hide from discovery. Yet that did not explain her roguish humour. Even if she knew that Ethel was a girl, she gave no hint that she believed us to be desperate murderers.

"I am sorry," I said. "We have to change our plans. We will be leaving tomorrow."

I watched her closely to see if this news caused any alarm. Would she be afraid that the chance of the money might slip through her fingers? It was in my mind that, if she telephoned the police, Ethel and I would hurry out through the back door and hope against hope that we could dodge the spreading net.

Madame Delisse gave a throaty laugh and said that it had been a delight to accommodate us. At once an explanation for her odd behaviour came to me. She must have decided that I had spirited Ethel away from her home so as to conduct a clandestine *affaire* and, in the Continental fashion, found the whole business delightfully amusing.

Such was my relief that I invited her and her husband to have a drink at my expense. A grand gesture, given that our money was running short. As we conversed, Madame Delisse's unsubtle innuendoes confirmed my deduction. Thank goodness for the overheated imagination of the Frenchwoman! Ethel, mystified, remained mute and as soon as we decently could, the two of us fled back to our squalid cubbyhole.

"I'm glad you've cheered up," she said once I had locked the door. "Earlier on, you seemed rather miserable. But why not stay here tomorrow night before we travel to Antwerp? I can't understand a word of what those people are saying, but they seem decent sorts."

"A change is as good as a rest!" I said heartily. "Monsieur and Madame Delisse mean well, but it's no fun for you, not being able to join in. Let's find another place on the other side of town where the *patron* minds his own business and we can make the most of each other's company."

"Oh, Hawley," she said in the sweet manner that always warmed my heart, "you are so thoughtful."

The deck of the *Montrose* was sleek with rain, but it offered sanctuary. As I stepped gingerly on board, with Ethel at my side, I could not help emitting a long, low sigh, as if I had been holding my breath ever since learning that the police had dug up the cellar. At every opportunity, I had scoured the press for the latest news whilst shielding the reports from Ethel's gaze, in case she spotted our photographs. Thankfully, it was clear that Scotland Yard had no clue as to our whereabouts.

To my fury, some reports suggested that the police had been at fault in allowing the two of us to elude their grasp. Mr. Dew deserved better; I took the criticism as a personal slight. Why not give me credit for daring and ingenuity? A question had even been asked in Parliament, with a foolish Member demanding to know who was responsible for keeping an insufficiently close watch upon us. As if a police officer could arrest an upstanding professional man on the basis of idle gossip!

Most outrageous of all was an interview with Ethel's father. Mr. Neave claimed he was issuing an "appeal" to her to give herself up to the police authorities. I pictured him holding forth, a foaming pint glass in his hand, revelling in the limelight. To make matters worse, he speculated that, because of our fondness for Continental holidays, we might have sought refuge in either France or Belgium. Such perception was as uncharacteristic as it was unwelcome. I cursed the oaf under my breath, not least for his gratuitous suggestion that I might be masquerading as a woman, given what he described rudely as my "gait and effeminate mannerisms."

The *Montrose* was a Babel. We were surrounded by three hundred souls, all of whom seemed to be gabbling at the same time and in strange tongues. Nine-tenths of those who embarked with us were foreign. From their poor clothes and hopeful olive-skinned faces, I guessed that they were emigrants off, like us, to make a fresh start in the New World. The man in the shipping office had told me that the ship used to carry troops to the Boer War. In peacetime, it transported people to futures full of promise.

We were a pale and slender pair: a small man in a grey frockcoat and soft white hat, and a lad with trousers held together by safety pins. No one could be more ordinary. I prayed that nobody else would give us a second glance. Besides, I dared wager that the name of Crippen meant nothing to those on board the *Montrose*. People sailing steerage to a new life had more to think about than a make-believe murder in a city they had never seen.

As we shuffled through the crowd, tension seeped out of me like sweat. Never mind about safe harbours; where could we be more remote from detection than on the open seas? Before long we would be on the other side of the Atlantic. Stopping next to a lifeboat, we watched the roofs of Antwerp recede in the distance. Ethel squeezed my hand and echoed my thoughts.

"We're on our way."

Our cabin represented an improvement on the claustrophobic accommodation at the Hotel des Ardennes. Even if it was no bigger, the beds were not as lumpy, and after a pleasurable private hour, we went back onto the deck and took our ease under cloudless skies as the ship steamed out of the Scheldt.

Shortly before noon, I was sucking in deep draughts of the salty air when I became aware of a buzz of excitement around us. We had been staring out over the grey waves and, on turning, I almost bumped into a lean, beaky-nosed man in uniform. He thrust out his hand and I realised with a start that the captain of our ship was taking the trouble to introduce himself.

"Kendall. Welcome on board the *Montrose*."

We shook. At least his grip was not as ferocious as Chief Inspector Dew's. I said, "John Philo Robinson, merchant of Quebec, at your service." *Philo* was a nod to my grandfather. "It is good to meet you, sir."

"And this young fellow?" Tipping his cap back on his head, he beamed down at Ethel.

"My boy, young John," I said carelessly. "We've been travelling in Europe, but I'm taking him back for the sake of his health."

Ethel coughed and sniffled to cue. Few could have mastered that doleful look with a comparable facility. Years of practice at the Drouet Institute, when she suffered so wretchedly from catarrh, were now paying unexpected dividends. I felt my own chest swelling with pride as the captain considered her delicate form.

"Good to meet you, Mister Robinson. Perhaps you and your

son would do me the honour of taking lunch at my table?"

I caught my breath. "This is a signal honour, Captain Kendall! Of course, we shall be delighted to accept your invitation."

"Capital! I shall look forward to seeing you later."

With that he strode away so rapidly that for a moment I had the absurd notion that he wished to escape before we had the chance to change our minds.

At first we were baffled by the personal interest that the captain took in us. Ethel whispered to me that she found his intense scrutiny unsettling. I was quick to reassure her; it was unthinkable that the captain of such a vessel would behave otherwise than as a perfect gentleman. Skippering a ship largely populated by travellers with scarcely a word of English, Captain Kendall was bound to value the company of passengers travelling second class who talked the same language. Relieved, she said with a giggle that he was remarkably handsome, having such light, curly hair and sun-tanned features. Her teasing did not trouble me. I never had a moment's cause to doubt my love's fidelity.

Lunch on the *Montrose* (chops and abundant crisp vegetables) was a marked improvement upon the fare provided by Madame Delisse. Captain Kendall excused himself halfway through the meal to undertake some urgent business, but before and after his brief absence, he took pains to draw us out. It did not take him long to establish that both Ethel and I were great readers.

"We have plenty of novels and magazines in the library," he told her. "Do you care for detective stories?"

"I like Rouletabille and Arsene Lupin," Ethel volunteered, in the reedy adolescent voice she had cultivated for the benefit of the ship's company. "Father lent me his copy of *The Mystery of the Yellow Room*."

"A splendid puzzle! You can borrow a couple of my own

favourites from the ship's library." He gave a genial smile. "What do you say, Mister Robinson? Keen on murder and mayhem, are you? Read *The Hound of the Baskervilles,* by any chance?"

And so we fell to discussing the works of Conan Doyle and his peers. I ventured a few words in praise of my childhood hero, Poe, and the captain nodded a vigorous assent.

"Rattling good yarns! *The Murders in the Rue Morgue* sends a shiver down any spine!"

It is so rare to find a kindred spirit in any walk of life that I was quite overcome. This was the first of many conversations between us, and I relished every single one. Of course, I was conscious of the irony of our circumstances. Here we were, in full flight from the Metropolitan Police, drawing closer and closer to our destiny, and yet chatting on the friendliest terms with a respected naval officer about topics ranging from vaudeville (as to which he was surprisingly well informed) to the literature of sensation.

Everything Captain Kendall said and did was infused with a rare energy and zest for life. He spoke briskly, and whenever I saw him bustling along the deck, I fancied that at any moment he might break into a run. Perhaps a dozen years my junior, he had risen rapidly to high rank, and his anecdotes about life at sea enthralled us. He recounted how he had caught out the cardsharps plaguing the *Empress of India,* where he had been chief officer, and had us on the edge of our seats with his tale of a terrible storm that nearly sank the *Milwaukee* during the first week of his command.

For all his achievements, he was no egotist. I admired the unselfish way he showed as much interest in our doings as we did in his. I often asked him to tell us about the remote corners of the world he had seen—Tierra del Fuego, the Cape of Good Hope, and the Tasman Sea—but he preferred to hear about my own travels. Canada and the United States were two countries

317

of which he was especially fond and he asked if I was familiar with such places as Toronto, Detroit, and California. When I expressed my sorrow about the terrible fire that had wrecked San Francisco, he shook his head gravely and we agreed that God moved in mysterious ways.

An odd thing happened after that initial lunch on the *Montrose*. When Ethel and I returned to our cabin, I gained the distinct impression that our belongings had been disturbed. Nothing had been taken—indeed, we were travelling so light that a thief would have had scant pickings. Yet I was certain that neither our hats nor our washing things were placed where we had left them. To Ethel, I said nothing, for I had no wish to cause her concern—or have her believe that my imagination was running away with me. For who would wish to ransack the luggage of a father and son with so little in the world between them?

My apprehensions were soon eased away by the pleasures of life at sea. Seldom have I encountered such courtesies as those that the captain and his officers granted to Ethel and me. Nothing was too much trouble for them, and Ethel's delight in her first ocean trip did much to improve my morale.

We took care, however, not to invite undue attention from our fellow passengers. Suppose one of them did know the names of Crippen and Le Neve? The reward for betraying us would be a king's ransom to those benighted souls. From time to time, nonetheless, we conversed with the handful who spoke English and Ethel became chummy with a cross-eyed youth who was an enthusiast for association football. The game was all Greek to me, but Ethel startled me with her knowledge.

"What's your team, then?" her newfound friend demanded one morning.

I cringed inwardly, fearing that her ignorance would be exposed, but if Ethel paused, it was only for a moment.

"The Spurs," she replied with confidence.

Was this a sensible answer? My heart missed a beat as I awaited the lad's response. He frowned and said that his team was the Arsenal. Even so, it seemed that she had passed some kind of test. I had to suppress the temptation to applaud. Ethel was no adolescent youth, but a woman in her late twenties— and yet she was pulling off the impersonation with *élan!* I recalled that young Sidney was a football fanatic, and I guessed that she had picked up from her brother enough to pass muster as an enthusiast for the game.

That same evening, Captain Kendall invited us to attend a shipboard concert. Ethel was keen and so, against my better judgment, I agreed. Few of the passengers boasted a talent for singing, yet everyone compensated for the lack of skill with sheer gusto. Someone had persuaded me to take a glass of beer, and it relaxed me so much that when one member of our company launched into a hearty rendition of *We all walked into the shop*, I stepped forward for a duet with him.

> *Inside a big confectioner's*
> *We saw a big display*
> *Of pastry there, and a ticket said,*
> *"Our tarts are cheap to-day."*
>
> *So we all walked into the shop*
> *To shelter from the rain.*
> *We ordered some tarts with jam inside,*
> *Then we all walked out again.*

As each chorus rang out louder than the last, the other passengers roared with delight. One old fellow clapped me on the back, and a fat Italian woman in an immodest dress gave me a saucy smile. Despite all that had happened, I could not resist the thought: *perhaps Cora would have been proud of me.*

Ethel did not sing, but the lustiness of my voice caught her by surprise and her eyes shone with delight. On board the *Montrose,* people accepted us for what we were—or, at least, for what we wanted them to think we were. We could wish for no more.

We strove to remain in character, as father and son, until we could escape to the privacy of our cabin. Yet playing a part twenty-four hours a day would test a Garrick or a Mrs. Siddons. Occasionally, our concentration lapsed. Up on deck one morning, I heard the captain calling, and it was not until Ethel dug me in the side with her elbow that I realised that he was addressing me by my chosen pseudonym.

"Mister Robinson!"

Belatedly, I turned, desperate to cover my embarrassment. "Ah, Captain Kendall, please forgive me. I—I was woolgathering. I'm so sorry. This cold wind, you know, it affects the hearing dreadfully."

"Of course it does. Please do not apologise." His smile glittered, as if he had won a secret wager with himself. "I wondered, Mister Robinson, whether you would like to indulge in a little blood-and-thunder?"

"I beg your pardon?"

"I have just finished. *The Four Just Men,* by a fellow called Edgar Wallace. First class, I recommend it."

"You are too kind." I coughed. "Young John and I are quite flattered by your attentiveness to our every need."

"Think nothing of it," he insisted. "We pride ourselves on looking after our passengers."

Our days were spent wrapped up in steamer rugs on the deck, engrossing ourselves in our books. On one occasion the captain invited us to take a look at his immaculate private quarters, all shining brass and soft leather. On another, we were given the opportunity to enter a little square cabin on the upper deck where we saw a young man wearing telephone headgear, with receivers over his ears, sending messages to places beyond the far horizon.

"I was second officer on the *Lake Champlain*," Captain Kendall said with pride. "The first British ship to be fitted with this apparatus. Marconi himself sent the master good luck wishes by wireless telegraphy."

As we watched, the operator began to signal. A vivid electric spark threw a bluish light over him and his machinery. He took up a pencil so as to transcribe the message, a cue for the skipper to show us out into the fresh air.

"Like a magician's cave in there, don't you think?" he said with his customary affability.

I could not disguise how deeply I was impressed by the march of science. "What an invention that is!"

The captain laughed and clamped my shoulder with his hand. "How right you are, Mister Robinson, it is utterly marvellous!"

The wind out on deck became too harsh for Ethel. Without an overcoat, her suit provided scant protection from the climate, and increasingly she passed time in our cabin or curled up in a corner of the lounge, devouring the latest romance by Mrs. Sheldon. I stayed up aloft, staring out at the black emptiness of the ocean.

I have never been susceptible to melancholia, yet with nothing apart from the Edgar Wallace to occupy me until bedtime, my thoughts kept turning to the intractability of our plight. With every day that passed I saw the truth more clearly, as if a veil was lifting from my eyes. The discovery of Cora's remains changed everything. Had Mr. Dew not disturbed her last resting place, all would have been well. As a result of his detective work, the names of Crippen and Le Neve were inextricably associated with a crime of unimaginable horror.

All I had done was to seek to avoid unpleasantness. How could I have explained to the police the suddenness of her death and the presence of hyoscine in her remains? In disposing of the evidence, I had sought to save everyone a great deal of trouble. Myself included, that I readily admit. But now I had contrived an outcome a thousand times worse than that which I had laboured so hard to avoid.

I noticed the ship's surgeon, an elderly and overweight Scot called Stewart who perspired freely even on the coldest days, strolling toward me and I contrived a smile of greeting.

"Fancy a game of whist later on, Mister Robinson?" he wheezed. "Mister Husmer wondered if you and your boy might like to play?"

"Thank you, but no," I said quietly. "The lad is under the weather at present. Neuralgia, you know."

"Sorry to hear it," he said. "Can I help at all? I'd be glad to give him a check-up."

"No, no," I said hastily, almost making the fatal error of saying that I was a doctor myself. "All he needs is rest and quiet. He'll be right as rain in a day or two, just you see."

Edgar Wallace? My dearest, I can scarcely believe my ears. You say that Edgar Wallace is implicated in this—this *conspiracy* against me?

Ethel, you do not know what you are saying. The man is a novelist of rare talent. For all my mental torment, I became absorbed in his thriller as we crossed the ocean. The mere fact that Wallace supplements his income by writing for that scandalous rag *The Evening Times* should not be held against him.

Forgive me, but I am a man of the world, while you are innocent, naïve. Far too trusting. Who are these friends in the newspaper trade who have, you say, tipped you off about this supposed grubby plot to make a fortune at my expense? A man like Arthur Newton deals in dark deeds; that is his profession as a criminal lawyer. He shows no fear; no doubt he has made powerful enemies. It is absurd to despise him for the mistake he made so long ago over the Cleveland Street Scandal. Poor Arthur's conviction for conspiring to defeat the ends of justice was nothing more than the establishment's revenge. My belief is that his real crime was to defend an aristocrat accused of betraying his class by patronising a brothel populated by boys. Arthur's speciality lies in defending those who are seen by polite society as beyond the pale.

People like me.

The claim that Arthur benefits if I hang is monstrous. My acquittal would be the crowning triumph of his career. Far from abandoning me, he takes the closest interest in my fate. Yes, following the appeal he has urged me to embellish my tale about Cora's disappearance, but his heart is in the right place. A lurid story would command a high price, and he is right to point out that meeting legal fees is burdensome.

If Arthur has a fault, it lies in his yearning for melodrama. I refuse absolutely to believe that he would have any part in fraud, let alone at the expense of his most celebrated client. The notion that *my solicitor* has drafted a supposed confession under my name to appear in *The Evening Times* on the day of my execution, and that *Edgar Wallace* is to improve upon it by adding "human colour" belongs in one of Mr. Wallace's fictions, not in real life. The allegation of conspiracy is surely actionable. Have a care, Ethel, and do not repeat it outside this tiny cell.

Arthur's resourceful brain is no doubt employed, even as we speak, in conjuring up some way of rescuing me from the gallows at the eleventh hour. Professor Munyon was right. We all need hope.

But what if all does *not* go as I hope?

Of course, I must face up to that possibility.

Well, when I see the Governor for the last time, I shall present him with my brown bead rosary and crucifix ring: small tokens of my esteem. All the rest is for you. My will is written, my last wishes formulated in my mind. I shall ask that your letters and dear photograph, my greatest treasures, be buried with me—should it come to that.

But still I hope against hope. Miracles do happen, Ethel, and it is for a miracle that I shall pray tonight.

Lies, lies, lies. Nothing lay ahead of us but an endless ocean of untruths, in which one day we were bound to be shipwrecked. I checked our position on the ship's track chart as often as I could without arousing suspicion. We were drawing closer to Quebec, but that was cold comfort. The need to maintain a false identity and a relentless good humour had drained me of energy. I wanted to lean over the railings and scream.

Even my new beard was growing more slowly than I had hoped. Once or twice, the captain congratulated me in jovial fashion on its distinguished appearance—"You look quite like a naval officer, Mister Robinson!" Yet the taut-skinned, bulgy-eyed face that stared at me from the mirror in the cabin remained all too recognisably that in the photographs of "the London cellar murderer."

Worse yet, I had become afflicted by a personal indisposition as humiliating as it was unfamiliar. In short, I found myself incapable of performing my duties as a husband—albeit a husband unacknowledged by the church. On the first occasion, Ethel made a cheerful joke and said no more about it. She was kindness itself, entirely content to enjoy a platonic embrace with the man she loved. Initially I dismissed the incident as an aberration, but when the failure recurred, despondency enveloped me like a shroud. Ethel's persistent, tickling caresses were to no avail. I could not understand it. Until now, coping with all life's vicissitudes had come naturally to me. I was practised in contending with the Fates, but nothing had prepared me for a loss of manliness. I dreaded the prospect of never again surrendering myself utterly to overpowering passion. Without love, I was nothing.

Standing on the spray-spattered deck, I gazed at the waves. A fresh gale drove the rain into my face. As I squinted through the murk, it felt as though pins were sticking into my eyes. We were in the middle of nowhere, but it was the only safe place to be. Friday evening, forty-eight hours from dry land, but I foresaw no let-up. Our new lives would be spent scanning people's faces for the dread light of recognition. In my pocket was tucked the prescription for *Sans Peine*. That remedy was meant to form the cornerstone of my New World enterprise, but now I saw that it was an illusion. For our malady, I could concoct no cure.

How easy to slide over the ship's railing under cover of darkness. A splash, the smack of cold water, an unavailing struggle for air—then nothingness. Tears dribbling down my cheeks, I pulled out from my pocket one of the cards that had been printed for me in Brussels. On the reverse side, I scribbled in pencil a note for Ethel. My apology for deserting her was short but heartfelt. My befuddled brain could not find the words to do justice to my adoration of her.

Blundering down the steps, I headed to our cabin, where I passed to Ethel all the money that she had in the world. At the time of our departure from London, she had given me a total of fifteen pounds sterling, which I had changed into notes.

"My dear, I think you had better take charge of these."

"Why?" she exclaimed. "I have nowhere to put them except in these pockets. You can keep them, can't you, until we get to Quebec?"

"Well," I said thickly, "I may have to leave you."

"Leave me?"

The horror of her expression stabbed my heart. I searched

frantically for soothing words, conquering my own distress as I strove to allay hers. "Listen, dear. When you get to Quebec, you had better go on to Toronto. It is a nice place and I know it fairly well. You have not forgotten your typewriting, have you?"

"Ah." Her brow began to clear. "You will be looking around in the meantime so that we can settle in some out-of-the-way spot?"

I hesitated, lost for a reply.

"But how about these clothes?" she asked, pouting prettily.

"You are tired of being a boy?" Despite myself, I could not help smiling.

"Well, I used to think I'd made a good boy, but now I long to get into girls' clothes as quickly as I can."

"You can buy them when you land."

"But it would be absurd for me to go into a shop dressed as a boy to buy women's garments. You will have to get them."

"Ah, I hadn't thought about that," I admitted. "Very well. Immediately on landing we must go to a hotel. I will get some clothes for you, and you will have to do a quick change. Then you will leave and I will follow you out."

"That's settled, then." She smiled. "Are you ready to come to bed, Hawley?"

My face must have given too much away, for she added quickly, "I just want to hold hands, that's all."

Sunday morning. The last day of the voyage, after another night without sleep. When we looked outside, we could see the faint lines of the shore; already we were steaming down the St Lawrence. Mist hung over the water like a shroud. In answer to the deep ship's whistle came the mournful boom of a foghorn. Despite all the odds, we had reached Canada. Was it possible that we still had a chance?

I hardly touched my breakfast, but when Ethel asked if

anything was wrong, I denied it. Twelve hours from Quebec! Nor was I the only one whose nerves were frayed. Even Captain Kendall kept pacing up and down, hands clasped tightly behind his back. Despite a life spent sailing the seven seas, he seemed apprehensive now that our destination was within reach. He cast a couple of glances toward us before halting at our table.

"Morning, Mister Robinson! How are you, Master John? We're just coming up to Father Point."

"Will we be stopping?" Ethel squeaked, with a creditable attempt at boyish enthusiasm.

"We pause to take the pilot on board. He's come to guide us on the up-river journey. Oh, and we'll need to pick up a few other men. Customs officials, you know."

He cleared his throat noisily and shifted from foot to foot, as if expecting me to lodge a complaint. The least that I could do was to set his mind at rest. I put down my knife and fork and nodded pleasantly.

"A short delay is neither here nor there. A pity that Canada is greeting us with such miserable weather!"

"My apologies on behalf of the Line," Captain Kendall said, regaining the twinkle in his eye.

When breakfast was over, I asked Ethel if she would join me up on deck, but she declined, citing the wretchedness of the cold and damp atmosphere.

"I hope Canada isn't all like this! I think I'll stay down here till it brightens up. Besides, I want to finish this book before lunch."

I wanted her by my side, but an argument was unthinkable, so I wrapped up against the chill and took my usual place on deck in solitude. The brief flurry of optimism inspired by the sight of land had deserted me. For a few minutes I watched the waves and then took another look at *The Four Just Men*. I had been so restless that I had made scant progress. Finally, I had reached the chapter where Sir Philip Ramon receives another missive from the Four threatening his life. "I am tired of all this," he said to a policeman assigned to protect him, "detectives and disguises . . ." Precisely.

The mist began to clear and I could make out Father Point. A bleak spot, comprising a handful of wooden shacks, a wireless station, and a lighthouse. Ahead of us in mid-stream was a small boat, and we slowed as it drew alongside. A ladder was hurled over the side and a couple of burly uniformed pilots climbed up it. Unable to settle to my book, I got up to stretch my legs, watching as the newcomers strode to the bridge and wrung Captain Kendall's hand. A few moments later, the skipper and one of the pilots came down again, heading in my direction.

I glanced at the pilot's face. The clipped moustache seemed bizarrely familiar, but I supposed my imagination was playing tricks. Yet when the man spoke, there was no room for doubt.

"Good morning, Doctor Crippen."

I swear there was pity in his eyes. My throat dried, yet I did not go to pieces, or rant or rave. In a manner of speaking, we were equals, very different men, yet cut from the same cloth. He had always behaved with decency toward me. I must not let myself down before him.

"Good morning, Mr. Dew."

We must have faith. Mortality is all too brief, but I am bolstered by my creed. I do not need the chaplain to tell me that, from the moment of our birth, we are under sentence of death. What does it matter, if we trust in God's infinite mercy? There is a life beyond the travails that we know on Earth.

But Ethel, I am frightened.

My whole body trembles.

Listen closely, my darling, while I whisper to you. My ingenious turn of mind may yet save me from the gallows. I have devised a plan to cheat Mr. Ellis of his stipend. Do not attempt to dissuade me. Thank Heaven for my medical expertise. A small consolation is that at least my knowledge may enable me to choose a more peaceful end. If I snap off the steel part of my glasses and puncture an artery, then I may bleed to death slowly during my sleep.

It is a far, far better thing . . .

Tears well in my eyes as I contemplate the alternative. Masked by the hood, facing infinite darkness. The rough grip of the rope on my windpipe.

If it should come to it, if it should come to it, I would pray only for the deed to be done in an instant.

In an instant, dear Lord, oh please—in an instant.

I pray, I pray, I pray, that I am not compelled to dance for the hangman.

Not even for a minute.

No, for even a minute of torment, a mere sixty seconds of thrashing and twitching on the end of that rope . . .

Oh God, those sixty seconds would be an eternity.

An eternity of unspeakable pain.

Extracts from the diary of Major Mytton-Davies, governor of Pentonville Prison, relating to H.H. Crippen

Nov. 21 Broke off rim of glass while retiring to lavatory with the presumed idea of attempting self-injury.

Nov 23 Execution 9 A.M.

Notes made by Major Mytton-Davies on an index card headed "CRIPPEN H.H."

Wt. on reception, remand	136 lb.
On admission, guilty	142 lb.
Ht.	5'4"
Drop	7'9"
No stretching of rope.	

Fracture of vertebral column high up around third cervical vertebrae

Fell dead—60 seconds.

Headlines in *The Evening Times*, 23 November 1910

CRIPPEN HANGED TO-DAY AT PENTONVILLE
HOW HE MURDERED BELLE ELMORE AND MADE AWAY WITH THE BODY

HIS FULL CONFESSION
THE POISON WAS ADMINISTERED IN INDIGESTION TABLETS

Extract from *John Bull*, 26 November 1910

CRIPPEN'S REPLY TO OUR LETTER
HE DECLINES TO IMPLICATE OTHERS . . . BUT HINTS AT POSSIBLE REVELATIONS

To the Editor of John Bull
DEAR SIR,—I am extremely grateful for the interest you have taken in me, and I am much touched by some of the passages in your letter . . .

Mr. Newton has not only been my solicitor, but, especially during these past few dreadful weeks, has been a sincere friend to me in my trouble. He has my fullest confidence, and I am leaving all my affairs in his hands.

If when it is all over, he cares to tell you more than I can say to-day, I am sure you will treat the matter in the same broad and sympathetic spirit in which you have written me . . .

Again thanking you for your kindly expressions,
H.H. CRIPPEN

★ ★ ★ ★ ★

Extract from letter from Ethel Le Neve's solicitors to the editor of *The Daily Chronicle* and to other publications

SIR, *we have information that the letter printed in* John Bull, *of the 26th inst., purporting to have been signed by Dr. Crippen . . . was not written or signed by him.*

No such letter was sent out of the prison.

We shall also be obliged if you will permit us to state most emphatically that Dr. Crippen made no confession.

Your obedient servants,

HORWOOD AND SONS

Extract from letter from Messrs. Arthur Newton and Co. to *John Bull*

". . . *With reference to the answer from Doctor Crippen to the 'Open Letter' . . . we beg to say that the same was forwarded through us, after our Mr. Arthur Newton had read the 'Open Letter' to Doctor Crippen."*

Extract from *John Bull*, 3 December 1910

THE CRIPPEN CASE

THE TRUTH AT LAST—WHO WAS THE CONFEDERATE?

. . . To sum up, Crippen was party to the murder of his wife. He had a confederate . . .

Crippen died in loyalty to that somebody—whoever he or she was. *But something more may yet come to light.* Murder will out.

Findings of the Law Society, 1911

That Arthur Newton "had on November 21, 1910, in the capacity of legal adviser to one Crippen, been permitted to visit him . . . and, in abuse of the privilege . . . aided and abetted one Horatio Bottomley, the editor of *John Bull*, to disseminate in that publication false information in the form of a letter purporting to have been written by Crippen from prison, although as the respondent well knew, no such letter in fact existed, and had further published . . . other false statements relating to the same matter, well knowing them to be false, whereby the public might be deceived."

Note by Home Department Archivist

On 12 July 1911, the King's Bench Division of the High Court ordered that, on account of his misconduct, "Arthur John Newton, of 23 Great Marlborough Street, solicitor, be suspended for 12 months from 25 July 1911, and that he pay the costs of the inquiry and of the hearing."

In July 1913, Newton was sentenced to three years imprisonment for a fraud involving Canadian timberlands, and was struck from the Solicitors' Roll. Horatio Bottomley remained at liberty until receiving a seven-year sentence for fraud in 1922.

After leaving Parkhurst Prison, Newton practised as a private inquiry agent until his death in Chelsea in 1930.

EPILOGUE

Note from Director of Media Relations to Government Chief Archivist, marked "Leo—strictly confidential," 8 May 2008

So Arthur Newton hid those papers until his dying day? Unable to risk negotiating a sale, of course. No wonder our people kept quiet. The abolitionists would have had a field day if they knew an innocent man went to the scaffold, while the man who killed him lived to a ripe old age.

Of course, I agree—Newton murdered Crippen, sure as if he'd laced his porridge with henbane. He took his client's guilt for granted and defended him so as to ensure a guilty verdict. If he'd had his way, Ethel would have swung too. She was saved from death by the simple expedient of changing lawyers.

When Newton found the manuscript too dangerous, he provided Horatio Bottomley with a phoney letter that he wrote in Crippen's name for publication in John Bull, *then sold a fake confession to* The Evening Times, *which Edgar Wallace sexed up with as much* brio *as any of our own spin doctors could command.*

Extraordinary. A murder committed by a solicitor of the Supreme Court, aided and abetted by a Member of Parliament and a legendary novelist.

Of course, Crippen made it easy for Newton by protecting Ethel. Interesting that Newton wasn't banned from practising law until he cheated another client of a fortune. So when he came out of prison, he took up a career as a private investigator? He was probably a better sleuth than dear old Dew. More insight into the criminal mind.

My advice? Honour the little doctor's last request. This administration is committed to rehabilitating offenders. I'll draft a press release. Let's publish and be damned to Arthur Newton—and his perfect crime.

NOTES FOR THE CURIOUS

Captain Kendall lived on into the age of Beatlemania, dying in 1965 at the ripe old age of 91. Walter Dew enjoyed a peaceful retirement up to his death in 1947, when he was 84. Even that old hypochondriac Paul Martinetti survived until 1924 before meeting his end in the unlikely setting of the Hotel Mustapha in Algiers. Eight years later, Edgar Wallace died, at the height of his fame, but deeply in debt; his contribution to the faking of Crippen's confession had helped to ruin *The Evening Times.* Ethel Le Neve spent time abroad before returning to England and marrying Stanley Smith, a co-worker in a furniture store. Their fate was to settle in East Croydon. Stanley never learned of his wife's true identity; neither, until after her death, did their two children. Ethel died of cardiac failure at the age of 84. The war in Vietnam was in full flower and the newspapers were full of the murder of Joe Orton by his lover. Ethel's passing was not even noticed.

As for Crippen, everyone knows his name, but how many people know exactly what he did, and why? His tale has been told countless times by writers of "true crime," and has sourced upwards of a dozen plays and novels, plus an ill-fated musical whose composer is better known for "The James Bond Theme." Maybe the fascination of the detective work, notably Walter Dew's cellar-digging and his pursuit of the *Montrose,* has obscured other aspects of the case. There are many significant gaps in the story of Crippen's life, as well as in the published attempts to understand his nature and actions. Those attempts have been hampered by the bizarre contradictions that abound in the case and that have helped to shape the Crippen legend. Crippen was not the only witness who said different things at different times. After close on a century, endless questions about the man and the fate of his wife remain unanswered. One thing is certain. With friends like Arthur Newton and Horatio Bottomley, he had no need of enemies.

The paradoxes of Crippen have puzzled lawyers, criminologists, and commentators. Raymond Chandler said of Crippen: "You can't help liking this guy somehow." I did not want to be a slave to factual detail, but equally I had no wish to play fast and loose with those parts of the evidence that are—or seem to be—trustworthy. Recent suggestions that the flesh found in the cellar did not belong to Cora raise many more questions than they answer. There is no evidence to support the theory that the flesh belonged to the victim of an abortion botched by Crippen. Another claim, said to be supported by DNA testing, is that the flesh had nothing to do with Crippen, who was the victim of police corruption. Such speculations fail to explain what happened to Cora, and much else besides.

Who knows how close this fiction is to whatever did happen? Where I made up incidents in the story, I sought to do so in a manner respectful of the evidence in the case, so far as it was established. All the named characters in this book, without exception, featured in the real-life events, and none of the trial extracts or quotations from contemporary publications are invented. Nothing in this novel (as far as I know) is irreconcilable with the proved facts.

One immediate problem in shining a torchlight into the secret places of 39 Hilldrop Crescent is, however, that many of the key facts themselves are in dispute. The books about the case themselves, as well as published statements by some of those involved in the story, contain much conflicting information. "Untrue crime" would better describe some of the accounts. The text on which I have drawn most heavily is Tom Cullen's enjoyable *Crippen: The Mild Murderer,* and I gratefully acknowledge my huge debt to his researches. Yet even his information-packed account is bedevilled by strange errors and omissions. Despite including a formidable array of footnotes, the book provides scant attribution for several of its key assertions. I was hoping to track Cullen down, but less than a week after drawing a blank with his last known address, I found myself reading his obituary in the newspaper. David James Smith's recent *Supper with the Crippens* offers an interesting assessment of the case, although it omits some of the material—such as the role of Edgar Wallace—covered by Cullen.

The Trial of Hawley Harvey Crippen, edited with notes by Filson Young, was an invaluable source. I also benefited from information supplied by two distinguished present-day criminologists. Richard Whittington Egan, now the owner of Crippen's rosary and crucifix ring, gave me valuable insights into the case. The late Jonathan Goodman compiled *The Crippen File,* which contains many extracts from contemporary reports, on which I have drawn extensively. Goodman also wrote a little-known but fascinating and instructive article in *The New Law Journal* about a letter from Cora's sister Tessie, which accused Crippen of molesting Cora's sisters and of taking drugs. Tessie was biased against Crippen, but the *allegation* of sexual impropriety at least chimes in with the atmosphere of sexual obsession that pervades Crippen's story. In the post-Shipman age, the claim that Crippen was a drug user may explain much that has long mystified those who have studied this tantalising case of was-it-murder.

Martin Edwards

ABOUT THE AUTHOR

Martin Edwards won the Crime Writers' Association Dagger for best short story in 2008 and he has been short-listed twice previously for CWA Daggers. The first of his three Lake District Mysteries, *The Coffin Trail,* was short-listed for the Theakston's prize for best British crime novel of 2006, and *The Arsenic Labyrinth* was short-listed for Lakeland book of the year in 2008. The latest of his eight novels about Liverpool lawyer Harry Devlin is *Waterloo Sunset* (2008). In 2008, he was elected to the prestigious Detection Club. He has edited 16 anthologies and published eight nonfiction books. His website is www.martin edwardsbooks.com and his blog is www.doyouwriteunder yourownname.blogspot.com.